I0723668

The Ungovernable series:

Zero Day Threat

Jailbreak

Time Bomb

Insider Threat

Firewall

Trojan Horse

Security Incident

Threat Agent

Attack Path

SECURITY INCIDENT

R.M. OLSON

ISBN-13: 978-1-990142-04-8

To Amalia and Bjorn, upon whom Olya and Misko
are based.

SECURITY INCIDENT:

An event wherein an organization's systems or data have been compromised; often includes unauthorized access to, disclosure of, or modification of sensitive information.

1

Jez, day 1

It was so early in the morning it could hardly be called morning. The dim Prasvishoni streets were cold, and mist rose from the river, obscuring the damp cobblestones at Jez's feet. Dim streetlamps flickered and guttered outside of the alley, creating foggy orange globes in the haze.

Jez tucked her hands into the pockets of her pilot's jacket, shivering slightly in the chill air. It had been a while since she'd been in Prasvishoni. Even after all this time, though, it was almost as familiar to her as breathing—the cold, the damp, the chill mist, the pungent smell of dirt and garbage, the footsteps following behind her, almost certainly belonging to someone who wanted to inflict some sort of bodily injury—

She gave a small sigh of satisfaction, flexing her fingers in her pockets to get the blood flowing. Easier not to break your knuckles if you had some feeling in your hands when you threw a punch.

Whoever was following her was being a lot quieter than the person she was following.

She grinned to herself.

Of course, that wasn't saying much.

Behind her, the footsteps sped up. She knew that purposeful sound, the sort of determination to the steps. It meant whoever was making them believed that what was coming next would hurt, and probably not the owner of the footsteps.

Easy mistake to make, really.

Up ahead, she heard a grunt of pain, cut off abruptly, in a voice she recognized. She swore, and sprinted forwards.

Behind her, the following footsteps also broke into a sprint.

She rounded the corner of the dingy alley at a dead run. As she turned out on to the larger street, she saw, in the dim, flickering lights of the decrepit streetlamps, three dark figures struggling in a desperate huddle.

The one in the centre staggered backwards.

She swore again. "Genius! Get down!"

To his credit, Lev didn't hesitate. He dropped to the ground as she pulled out her heat gun and fired. One of his attackers gave a strangled grunt of pain and collapsed, writhing in agony.

"Jez?" There was a slight note of incredulous irritation mixed with the relief in Lev's tone.

"Hey now, thought you'd be happy to see me."

He rolled over and yanked out his own heat pistol as the remaining attacker turned from him to face the new threat.

"I find it slightly offensive that none of you believe I can go out for a walk without an escort," he grumbled, squeezing off a careful shot. The figure, who'd been raising their heat gun to point at Jez, dived out of the way as the heat from the gun Ysbel had modded blistered the air above their head.

Jez grinned. "I wasn't exactly wrong."

"I do actually know how to protect myself. I have a gun."

"Yeah? Well, from what I saw, you were protecting yourself by letting them punch your damn face in."

He sighed, then his expression turned to one of alarm. "Jez!"

She spun around as five more figures burst out of the alley. One of them grabbed her by the arm and planted a fist in her solar plexus. She gasped, doubling over, and her attacker kicked her legs from under her, sending her to the ground. Someone aimed another kick at her head, but she ducked out of the way so the boot only grazed her temple.

She swore breathlessly, and rolled out of the way of another boot. "What, you plaguers never learn how to do anything but kick?"

"You never learn to do anything but get hit?" said the man, an ugly grin on his face.

"Guess we'll find out." She kicked out as she spun, knocking the legs out from the man who'd spoken. He went down hard, and there was a satisfying crunch as the back of his head hit the cobblestones.

She scrambled to her feet, just in time to catch a fist in the ribs. She staggered sideways, grabbing her attacker's arm, and yanked her around.

"See how you like it, you bastard," she muttered, and planted an elbow in the woman's face.

From the muffled profanity, the woman didn't like it very much.

Jez grabbed another of the figures by the front of the shirt and swung him around between her and a third man. The blow that had been aimed between her shoulder blades hit her reluctant shield in the throat, and he went down, gasping.

In the confusion, a woman had stepped back and was raising a pistol, pointing it at Lev.

Jez yanked her gun arm free and snapped off a shot just as someone else slammed into her from behind. She yelped and rolled as she hit the cobblestones for the second time, but from the gasped curse words behind her, no one was lining up a shot on Lev anymore.

Damn. She was going to be sore tomorrow.

She scrambled to her feet and glanced around quickly.

If they made it to tomorrow.

The small intersection was made up of the wider street and the two small, dirty alleys beside it, was distinctly more crowded than when they'd arrived. And there was no mistaking the colours on their outfits.

Blood Riots.

And hell, not like she hadn't fought with Blood Riots in prison. And also on the pleasure planet. And also probably a hundred other times she couldn't remember—never knew who you were fighting sometimes, and she'd been in plenty of fights.

But that was before she and the rest of the crew had taken down the gang's boss, and also possibly thrown the entire damn system into complete chaos.

Anyway, point was, this was probably going to get messy.

Lev was also looking around, with that speculative look he always got when faced with a seemingly insurmountable problem. He tapped his com inconspicuously. "Jez," he said quietly in her earpiece. "The woman in the corner closest to me. With the red scarf. She's the leader. If you take her out, I imagine it will improve our odds significantly."

Adrenalin pumped through Jez like a drug. She was going to have a whole damn collection of bruises at this rate, but she couldn't stop grinning.

She lunged at the woman. The woman had barely begun to turn when Jez hit her, and they both went down.

The rest of the gang members weren't waiting for a command

anymore. Every damn heat gun in the place was pointing towards her now, but hell, weren't going to shoot if they might hit their boss. Probably wouldn't do much for their job prospects.

The gang leader went for her face, and Jez caught the woman's wrist and twisted it backwards, just as the woman drove her knee into Jez's stomach. Jez grunted, holding on for dear life.

"Got to try a little harder than that," she said through her teeth.

The woman's expression said she planned to oblige.

Then someone grabbed Jez by the shoulders and jerked her backwards, and she released her grip on the woman in red.

Damn.

"Hey! Ysbel! You figure you're just going to sit up there all night?" she called, struggling ineffectually to land a punch on her most recent attacker.

Lev, who'd been half-running towards her, heat gun raised, got a slightly incredulous look on his face. "How many of you followed me?"

Whoever it was holding Jez by the shoulders released her abruptly, and she turned.

She could only tell where Tanya was because of the quiet collapse of the gang members nearest the mouth of the alley. Ysbel, on the other hand, wasn't at all inconspicuous. Difficult to be inconspicuous when everything in your near vicinity was blowing up loudly.

Jez sighed happily and tapped her com. "Ysbel. I ever tell you how hot you are?"

Tanya paused from whatever it was she was doing. "Jez."

"I know, I know, piss off. I'm right though."

"You are right. But she's married. To me."

"Details," Jez drawled.

Ysbel glanced up from the rubble that had once been a section of street, and tossed a small device in Jez's direction. Jez snatched it out of the air. In front of her, the gang leader was scrambling to her feet, brushing the dirt off of her clothing.

"Hey, you bastard," said Jez, grinning.

The woman barely had time to look alarmed before Jez pointed carefully and hit the button on Ysbel's device.

The woman collapsed.

Jez turned on the other three behind her, whose expressions said they knew they ought to start forward into the fight, but were suddenly having second thoughts on the wisdom of this course. She hit the button again.

The three of them collapsed beside their leader.

"What in the name of everything holy or unholy—" Lev's voice was strained.

Which was understandable, since apparently five of the gang members had decided that having a hostage was probably their best bet for survival in this situation. And after looking at Jez, Ysbel, and, of course, slender, wistful-looking Tanya, who could probably have taken them all out with one hand tied behind her back and both eyes closed, they'd decided the scholarly-looking young man, with his ruffled hair, thoughtful eyes, and slightly disreputable shabby jacket, was their best bet.

She might have thought that once upon a time herself. Before she actually got to know him.

She grinned. "Hey! Genius!" She tossed Ysbel's device towards him.

"Jez!" he said through gritted teeth. "If that works how I think it does, it'll ruin my damn information chips."

"Yeah? Well, figure your head's about to be ruined if you don't use it," she shot back.

He sighed, wrestled his other hand free from one of his attackers, and pulled something from his pocket. "Catch."

She snatched it out of the air, and he raised his other hand, the one holding Ysbel's device, and pressed the button.

His attackers collapsed.

Jez glanced around her.

The square, though certainly not empty, was no longer filled with people who wanted to kill them. Now, it seemed mostly filled with people who were trying desperately to get away.

Considering the look on Tanya's face, she figured they had about the right idea.

It was only moments before the four of them were alone under the flickering streetlamps.

Well, if you didn't count the sprawled-out bodies, some of them groaning faintly.

Lev looked around him, sighed, and ran his hand through his hair. "Well," he said, "I suppose I should thank you. I do, however, wish that you all didn't have such a low opinion of my ability to take care of myself." He paused a moment. "Ysbel. What was that thing? I'm ... impressed. I've never seen something like it."

Ysbel shrugged. "It's something I've been working on. It disrupts the electrical pulses in your brain. Knocks you out." She glanced at one of the prone bodies. "I don't think that it causes permanent damage, but I haven't really had time to test it."

"So you decided to test it on the Blood Riots."

"They were trying to kill you."

Lev gave a wry smile and looked around at the fallen gang members. "Point taken. Alright, now that we've rescued me, shall we go back to the others?"

"You got what you came for?" asked Jez.

Lev sighed. "Yes, I did." He paused. "I assumed you'd know that, since apparently you've been following me all morning."

Jez shrugged easily. "Figured you wanted your privacy. So I stayed back. Just close enough to keep those plaguers from beating the hell out of you."

Lev looked at her, his face softening. "Um. Thanks. I hadn't expected things to be so bad yet." He gave a rueful shake of his head. "It's been, what, less than twenty-four hours since we left the pleasure planet? I thought we'd have at least two days before rumours reached Prasvishoni."

"I don't like it," said Ysbel grimly. "If it's this bad already, I don't know how we're going to keep things under control."

"Guess we better go back and find out," said Jez cheerily. She turned to survey the fallen gang members in the darkened streets. In the background, the dim grey light of early morning was slowly creeping across the city, making the dull streetlights look even dimmer than usual, and casting everything in grey and black shadows. "How long will they be out?"

Ysbel shrugged. "Like I said, this is the first time I've tested this. Possibly permanently."

Jez grinned. "Well, if not, hopefully they'll at least have a decent headache to remember us by. Come on." She turned, and the four of them headed back towards Masha's abandoned hangar bay.

2

Lev, day 1

Lev ducked through the door into the dark interior of the hangar bay. There were bar lights, high up on the ceiling, but they flickered and guttered and hardly illuminated any of the space except what was directly underneath them. Off in one corner, he could make out the dark bulk that was the *Ungovernable*, the shape of her somehow comforting.

"Lev." A figure stepped forward into the light, resolving into a woman of medium height and medium build. She had an average face, black hair pulled back into a rat's tail, a long, battered pilots coat, and an expression of calm competence. Her voice was as bland as always, but Lev could feel his muscles stiffening at the sound of it.

"Masha."

She smiled at him. "I assume you got what you went for?"

"Yes," he said, keeping his voice purposely mild. "As I told you I would." He pulled a small, hard container out of his pocket. "The list of government codes on these should be fairly accurate, if slightly dated. I hid them outside my family's former apartment just before I was arrested."

She studied him, that sharp, piercing glint of intelligence

gleaming from her eyes as she took the box of information chips. He forced himself to meet her gaze.

Masha was dangerous.

She'd always been dangerous. He'd know that since he met her. But somehow, in the course of their crazy schemes, their rescues, their near-death experiences, he'd allowed himself to believe that she was only dangerous to the people they were working against. Not to them.

And he'd been wrong.

They'd almost paid for that with their lives.

And even though they'd survived, she'd managed to trap them again. Managed to force them to follow along with her agenda. Whatever that was.

He still wasn't sure.

"So." Masha looked around at the four of them. "I assume, Jez, from the state of your clothing, the streets were not as calm as we might have wished?"

"Speak for yourself, you bastard," said Jez, with an easy grin. "Far as I'm concerned, calm streets are pretty damn boring."

"Yes," said Ysbel grimly. "There are Blood Riot members lying on the pavement right now who either won't wake up, or if they do, might wish they hadn't, but there were over a dozen of them that tried to jump Lev."

"I wasn't in their territory," said Lev quietly. "I made very sure of that. I do actually have a sense of self-preservation, despite what some members of this crew may think." He shot a meaningful glance at Jez, who winked at him. He sighed. "There's no reason they should have been spreading out like that, unless—"

He didn't finish. From the look on Masha's face, she understood the implications of this as well as he did.

"Well," she said, after a moment. "I suppose this means that we'll have to move quickly." She looked around. "Is everyone here? No one seriously injured?"

"Depends on if you count those bastards that tried to jump Lev," Jez drawled.

Masha suppressed an expression that could possibly have been a smile. "No, Jez, I'm not interested in the well-being of the Blood Riot gang members at the moment." She paused. "Although it is certainly possible that we'll all have a vested interest in the well-being, or lack thereof, of the gang members of every gang in this city in a very short period of time, unless we can accomplish what I hope we can."

"Speaking of that," said Lev, "you still haven't explained your plan. I assume, although I am no longer comfortable assuming almost anything about you, that you do, in fact, have a plan, and didn't just tell us that to get us to come with you?"

Masha gave a brief smile, but he could see the strain in her face, and the smile didn't reach her eyes.

The last few weeks had worn on her, more than he'd realized.

He couldn't help the small spark of satisfaction, mingled with another small spark of something that could have been sympathy, or could have been shame.

Somehow, he wanted to believe that betraying them had not been as easy for Masha as she'd made it seem.

She glanced around the room again. "Tae left shortly after you did. He took Ivan with him. I understand he went to check on his friends, and to try to discover if there's a way to get them out safely. But I can at least explain that portion of the plan that will concern those of us who are present." She turned, and made her way up the *Ungovernable's* loading ramp, and the four of them followed.

He could tell the moment Jez set foot on the ship's ramp, even though he wasn't looking at her, by her soft, blissful sigh. He smiled to himself, even though something twisted in his chest.

Things between him and Jez were … good. Better than they had any right to be, probably. They were friends, and their friendship had become something comfortable and familiar. But —

But still, sometimes, when he wasn't thinking about it, that ache would return, the ache he'd thought might actually kill him that night, weeks ago, on Grigory's ship, where Jez had looked at him, face haunted, and told him that she loved him, and then turned away, and he'd thought his heart might actually crack in two.

He shook his head, smiling ruefully at himself.

Despite everything, he was coming to believe that Jez had had the right idea after all. He needed her in his life. He wasn't honestly sure he could function without her anymore. A relationship meant things could go sideways, and that was no longer a risk he was willing to take.

So, friends it was. And honestly, it was good. Even if there were days he wasn't sure he'd survive it.

They took their seats around the long table in the conference room of the *Ungovernable*, and once they'd settled themselves, Masha looked around at them.

"As you know," she said, "since our last … endeavour, the situation in Prasvishoni has become somewhat delicate."

Lev cocked an eyebrow at her.

Delicate was an understatement.

Of course, any time two of the biggest crime organizations in the system were taken out simultaneously, crime organizations that were indelibly interwoven with the government itself, he assumed that would cause certain problems related to transfer of power. He should have foreseen this when they'd agreed to Masha's plan to take down Grigory Korzhakov. Which they'd agreed to because the alternative, that Masha had personally arranged, was certain death. However, he'd been fairly occupied at the time trying to keep them all from being brutally murdered. And then they'd pulled their elaborate con on the mafia, and by some miracle survived it, and it wasn't until then that he had time to step back and breathe, and realize the inevitable consequences of their actions.

"Considering Lev's experience this morning, the situation may be even more delicate than I'd foreseen. So." She glanced around the table again. "Our first move will have to be to delay the inevitable. We will need somehow to convince the city of Prasvishoni, and the government officials, that Grigory and Olyessa are still forces to be reckoned with."

"So that's your plan," said Lev, giving her a wry look. "Try to pretend like this didn't happen?"

"No, Lev," said Masha patiently. "My plan is to delay the moment when word gets out for long enough that we can put make preparations for when the word inevitably does get out." She paused. "I'm going to send Tae out with the street kids. I'm hoping he'll be able to connect with his street contacts, and put some sort of infrastructure in place to keep the streets from devolving into chaos when word of Grigory and Olyessa's misfortune arrives. And in the meantime, there is a government official who was supposed to have arrived in town today. She's from another part of the system, and she was just promoted to a high-up minister position. However, she stopped by a financial symposium on the way, to pay a visit to her friend Grigory."

"And you killed her." Lev's voice was flat. "Or rather, we killed her."

"That is correct," Masha said calmly. "However, the relevant government officials were unaware she was planning on making an appearance at the symposium, and so word of her death has not yet reached them. And I have taken steps to ensure that it will not. She has, it appears, a lover on this planet. A paramour. And you, Lev, are positioned perfectly to play him."

He took a deep breath.

Back into government. Of course.

He tried to force the unease from his expression, and raised an eyebrow. "I see. So I'm to be the lover. And who will be playing the government official?"

"Not me," said Tanya dryly, a hint of humour in her voice. She turned to Lev. "No offence. But I'm not playing your lover. I'm not that good of an actor."

Lev gave her a flat look.

"I'm certainly not doing it," grunted Ysbel.

Jez snickered. He glared at her.

"I suppose, Jez," said Masha calmly, "that leaves you."

Jez's snicker cut off abruptly, her expression going suddenly panicked.

"Nope. Not happening. I'm not—"

"Sorry Masha, that's a no," said Lev at the same time. "We're not going to—"

"Do you have a better suggestion?" asked Masha. "I could use Tanya and Ysbel with me, and it will certainly be the easiest on the children. I believe that Jez is in the best position to go with you. I didn't want to suggest it directly, considering ..." She let her sentence trail off delicately. "However, I do think it's the most logical option."

Jez turned to face her, expression still panicked. "Hold on just a minute, you bastard. I'm not about to—"

Masha held up a hand. "Jez. I would not ask you to do this if it weren't vitally important. However—"

"However nothing! I can't—I'm not going to—"

Lev dropped his head in his hands and groaned quietly, his stomach tight with something like dread.

They'd just, finally, figured things out. He'd just, finally, figured out how not to lose her.

And now this. Pretending to be lovers.

He raised his head. Jez was looking at him, desperation in her eyes, and he held her gaze, trying to insert a confidence he didn't feel into his voice. "Jez. It'll be fine. We'll be fine. It's just an act, we can do that. Masha's right, this makes the most sense."

She took a deep breath, visibly tamping down her panic. "Fine. Fine, I'll do it." She turned to glower at Masha. "This had damn well better be worth it, you bastard."

"I sincerely hope it is," murmured Masha.

Lev watched Masha.

She was worried.

That should probably worry him, as well. This plan of hers wasn't as solid as she was pretending it was.

Then again, had any of her plans been? Every single thing Masha had gotten them into, they'd escaped by the slightest of chances.

Masha's voice resumed its typical pleasant tone. "Jez, Lev will be providing you with backup over the com, so you don't need to worry about memorizing any information except the basics for your cover, which I'll give you shortly. Once inside, you'll need to do two things: first, you'll need to push the government towards restructuring such that Grigory's and Olyessa's biggest players are neutralized before word of their demise gets out. The most straightforward way for you to do that is to get the ear of Goran Mihov. Our biggest dangers are the Minister of Defence, and the Minister of Internal Security. The Minister of Defence is owned by Grigory, and the Minister of Internal Security was recently bought by Olyessa. If we can neutralize them, it will help a great deal, but there are very few people in position to do that. Goran is the most accessible. In order to do that, you may have to pass him some sensitive information, but I believe I have something you can use that won't hurt us. Your second task is to obtain information, which you will pass along to Ysbel, Tanya, and myself. There's a person in the government with a code name Myrni. I need to know who this person is and how to get to them, as they appear to have gained a great deal of power in recent months. And further, I will need the most up-to-date information on government structure. While I have access to a listing of the government positions from when I was last there, I suspect things have changed substantially since we left for Vitali's compound. I will need the newest and most up-to-date information if we are to pull this off."

Lev looked over at her. "And why will you need to know—"

Masha smiled at him. "We'll need to know who to contact, as we'll be impersonating Grigory and Olyessa. Using a secured device, and through various secure channels, of course, but if we can send messages that look genuine, we should be able to sow enough confusion to give us time. No one will dare act if they're not certain Grigory and Olyessa are gone. And hopefully, that will give you, Jez, and Tae enough time to do what you need to."

There was a moment of silence as they all digested Masha's words.

"I don't like this," said Ysbel at last. "I'm not going to pretend I like anything about this. But considering you have put us into a position where we have no other option—"

"Of course you have another option," said Masha archly. "You could let the natural consequences of our actions play out, and watch the students at the University of Prasvishoni, and Tae's street kid friends, die in the inevitable bloodbath."

"As I said," said Ysbel, "you've put us into a position where we have no other options. At least, not tenable options." Lev noticed that she glanced at Tanya before she spoke again. "But I am warning you. I don't trust you, and I will be watching for anything hint of something wrong."

"That is perfectly acceptable," said Masha calmly. "If we can work together for long enough to get this done, your personal feelings towards me have very little relevance. So." She looked around the small group at the table. "Is there anything else we need to discuss? Jez's ship—or Layla's ship, I should say—is scheduled to arrive in—" She glanced at her com. "Four standard hours and twenty-three minutes. In the meantime, I'll change all the records to reflect Jez's face and background. There's no one in government who's met her in person, and Layla has a reputation for … eccentricity. I'll send you with government uniforms, but there's no need to change into them yet—they'll be expecting her in traveling clothes. Although Lev should probably wear something nice. Jez will need to be at the dock when the ship lands, and you, Lev, should be there waiting for her. Apparently it's been some time since you've seen each other, and I would expect you've missed each other a great deal."

Lev groaned inwardly, and glanced over at Jez. The panicked look was back on her face. He caught her eye and tried to give her a reassuring smile.

He wasn't entirely certain it was a success.

He was inclined to agree with Ysbel. There was nothing about this he liked.

He'd be going back into the government, the place where he'd all but sold his soul. Where he'd become a person who could plan a mission to kidnap an innocent woman and send her wife and children to prison for years, and not even have the decency to wonder who he'd done it to.

He wasn't going to be that person again. That, he'd decided on Grigory's ship, when he'd seen where that road led. But he still hadn't finished working through the practical implications of that decision. And going back to the government was not going to help.

And then, of course, there was Jez.

He glanced over at her again. She was biting the inside of her lip, her foot tapping restlessly against the leg of her chair, her fingers drumming on her thigh.

He shook his head grimly.

They'd make this work somehow. He wasn't going to lose Jez, and he wasn't going to lose his first tentative beginnings of a moral code. Although at the moment, he wasn't entirely sure that either of those things was still possible.

3

Tae, day 1

"Down!" Tae hissed, pushing himself back against the tall prefab-block fence. Ivan crouched beside him, face shadowed in the dark of the early Prasvishoni morning.

Footsteps echoed off the cement, approaching their hiding place. Tae tightened his grip on his heat pistol.

If he used it, they'd have to leave in a hurry. But better that than being captured.

Neither he nor Ivan moved a muscle as the heavy tread of the guard moved slowly past along the fence line.

Tae sank back against the wall in relief as the footsteps faded, and hit his com.

"Caz," he whispered. "Are you there?"

"Tae? Is that you?" There was a moment's pause, then Caz's voice again, slightly more awake now, and worried. "Is something wrong?"

"Shhhhh," Tae whispered. "Listen Caz, that blocker I sent through to your com—is it on?"

"Yeah," said Caz tersely.

"Alright. Listen to me. We need to get you out. There's—look, something went wrong. You're in danger, all of you. I'm figuring out a way to get you out, but when I do, we'll have to run for it. Can you be ready?"

"I'll have them ready." Caz's voice was tight with a familiar strain. There was a moment's pause. "Tae, can you tell me anything at all? If you can't—"

Tae gritted his teeth. "I'm sorry."

"It's fine," said Caz. "Just—stay safe, alright? We'll see you soon."

"Yeah," Tae said.

He hit his com off, and tried not to think about the sheer impossibility of this whole stupid thing.

When he turned, Ivan was watching him, sympathy mixed with the strain on his face.

Tae still wasn't certain why Ivan had agreed to come, put himself in mortal danger yet again for kids he'd never even met, but … well, but the truth was, he was sickeningly grateful, despite the guilt the thought brought.

"Alright," Tae said. "Meet back here in ten standard minutes. We're looking for anything that might interfere with a signal. They have a shield around the place, but if there's a place that it's weaker —"

Ivan nodded, and gave him a quick smile. "Good luck." He pushed himself off the wall and made his way in a low crouch in the direction the guard had disappeared.

Tae waited a moment longer, then headed off in the opposite direction.

He walked quietly, keeping low and as close to the fence as he could. From inside the compound, he could hear voices—guards, people waking up, coming out of their apartments and going about their day. It was early, but in Prasvishoni, that didn't mean a thing. He strained his ears for sounds on his side of the fence, sounds that could mean someone was coming.

This apartment complex should have been the safest in the city. It catered to family members of government officials, and it was guarded by people who were on the payroll of Olyessa, untouchable by Grigory's people. That's why they'd put Caz and Peti and the others in there in the first place.

That, of course, that was before they'd gotten on Olyessa's bad side as well.

Honestly, sometimes he wondered if there was a murderous would-be dictator in the system who they weren't currently on the bad side of.

He shivered slightly, the cold damp creeping down his collar, up his sleeves, through his boots. The feeling was as familiar, almost, as the smell of the dirty streets. Before he'd joined the *Ungovernable*, he wasn't sure he'd ever been warm a day in his life.

There. Ahead. There was a place where the ground dipped away, and the fence went straight over it. Not much, but it was something. Possibly enough to disrupt a forcefield signal. And the resulting gap under the fence was possibly enough that a child could fit through, if the child were small and used to wriggling through tight spaces.

He glanced quickly around, and sprinted for the shadows of the small opening. He crouched into the dip, pulled out his com, and hit the scanner.

The green light blinked as the scanner set to work.

He wasn't actually expecting there to be a hole in the force field. That would be far too lucky. But as long as there was a weakness, a small disruption in the signal, he was pretty sure he could get through.

He was a street kid. He was used to working with slim odds and crap equipment.

He rubbed his hands together and blew on them, trying to get the feeling back into his fingers as the scanner worked.

It had been less than forty-eight hours since Masha had taken both Grigory and Olyessa down, ruined them, and demolished their entire organized crime infrastructure. But she hadn't rendered them toothless. There would still be people on the streets loyal to them, even if they had no way of getting paid. The more dangerous situation, though, was the people who weren't loyal. There'd be plenty of bloodthirsty, hungry young boyevik soldiers who'd see this as a perfect opportunity to murder their way to the top. And considering the part Tae had played in all this, a group of defenceless street kids who everyone now knew were his personal pressure point would be a valuable asset.

Or, a valuable opportunity for revenge.

The scanner beeped softly, and he glanced down at his com.

Just like he'd suspected. There was a small irregularity in the signal, just the slightest blip created by the dip in the ground.

That, he could work with.

He tapped his com. "Caz. Listen. Back behind the apartment building, on the northeast corner, there's a gap under the fence. Do you know the place I'm talking about?"

"Yes." Caz's voice was tense. "I try to keep the kids away from that. That's the one place I thought maybe someone could get in."

"You're right. But I think we can use that to get you out. It's going to take me a couple of hours to write a program that will disrupt the force field, but I think it's doable. Get the kids up, get them dressed, pack everything you can't leave behind. Blankets, coats, whatever you need to keep warm. I don't know where we're going to go, but for a while, at least, we'll be on the streets." He paused a moment. "How's Mila doing? Is she——"

"She's not sick, at the moment. I think the food and the rest have been doing her good. She still gets fevers sometimes, but she's alright now."

Tae swallowed down the sick tension in his stomach.

He'd just gotten them somewhere safe. He'd just thought he'd actually, maybe, succeeded in protecting them, like he'd promised.

Instead, he'd put them in danger. Again.

"Alright. I'll meet you back here in a few hours. I'll try to give you some warning, but we'll have to move fast." He paused a moment. "If you don't hear from me—" He broke off the thought.

There wasn't another option, honestly.

"If you don't hear from me by the end of the day, you're just going to have to get them out somehow," he finished finally. "You're not safe there. And when you're out—run. Don't stop running. They know you know me. They have files on you. They're not going to stop coming after you." His voice choked.

"OK. I'll … see you soon." Caz's voice was grim.

It wasn't until Tae tapped his com off that he heard it.

Footsteps. Coming closer.

He swore quietly, and pushed himself back into the shadows as far as he could.

The footsteps were approaching quickly, and with them, a beam of light.

Damn. Damn, damn, damn.

The guard was only a few metres away, just out of sight around a turn in the fence.

Holding his breath, Tae crept forward. If he could just get out of the way—

More footsteps, from the other side.

Damn it to hell.

He glanced around quickly, then tapped his com and hissed, "Ivan. Get out of here. Don't wait for me."

"Tae! What—"

"Just get out!"

He looked around quickly. Ahead of him, the tall walls of the building next to the apartment complex. And the guard's footsteps, coming from each side down the alley towards him.

Ivan would find a way to get word to the kids somehow. Somehow, Lev, or Jez, or Ivan, or Ysbel would find a way to get them out, he had to believe that.

The guard stepped around the corner, and the flickering glow of her torch momentarily blinded Tae.

"What the hell—" she began.

The other guard stepped in to view as well, and paused.

"What is this, a street kid?"

"Not skinny enough to be a street kid." The first guard's voice was grim. She snatched her heat pistol out of its holster, and Tae dived to the ground as the heat blast scored the wall of the building behind him. The other guard had already pulled out his gun and was aiming for Tae. Tae scrambled to his feet, but both exits were blocked, and there was nowhere to go. He grabbed for his own gun, but even as he did so, he knew there was no way out of this. The guards had heat armour and visors. And maybe it wouldn't be enough to stop one of Ysbel's mods, but it would certainly be enough to keep him from killing with one shot.

Then the second guard grunted, stumbled, and went to his knees on the pavement.

Ivan stood behind him, face grim. "Tae! Come on," he hissed.

Tae scarcely had time to feel the rush of relief. He sprinted towards Ivan, and Ivan grabbed him by the sleeve, shoving him forward as another heat blast scorched the air of the alley. Then they ran for their lives, the hiss and sizzle of heat blasts cutting through the cold chill of the early morning air behind them.

As they came up to the hangar door, panting and breathless, Tae glanced quickly at his com, checking for heat signatures.

None.

They were alone.

He leaned up against the hangar bay wall, gasping for breath, shaky with relief.

Ivan leaned up beside him. His face was strained, but he was wearing a small grin.

"Well. That was a little more exciting than I'd expected."

Tae looked at him, shaking his head. "What did you do to that guard?"

Ivan laughed softly. "I told you, I used to organize protests against the government. We all learned how to take out a police officer quickly and quietly." He gave a small, wry grin. "Perhaps not well enough, considering I was arrested and thrown in jail. But still—"

Tae chuckled despite himself. "Alright," he said. "Come on. We should probably get in there. At least we know Caz and the others are alive."

The hangar bay was empty, but he could see lights spilling down the loading ramp to the *Ungovernable*. They followed the light down the corridor and into the conference room, and Tae hesitated a moment before he stepped inside.

He wasn't completely sure if he was ready to face Masha yet.

"Tae?" asked Ivan softly.

Tae managed a small smile, then stepped inside.

Masha looked over at them with that bland smile as they took their seats at the table.

"Masha." He tried to keep his voice civil, but he was pretty sure his words had come out much more harshly than they normally would. "What's the plan? You told us you had a plan."

"Yes," she said. Her expression was calm, but there was an unfamiliar strain in her voice, and he could see the tension in the corners of her mouth and eyes. "We've been discussing that. Since you're more familiar with the streets than any of us, I'll need you to somehow ensure that the gang wars that will inevitably break out won't spread through the city. How you do that is up to you— whether through organizing, through threats, or through violence. I'm sure Ysbel can give you all the explosives you need to make an impression, if that's what you'd like to do."

"No Masha." He was speaking through his teeth. "I'm not you. I'm not going to threaten my friends, I'm not going to threaten the street kids, and I'm not going to kill people just because it would make things easier."

Masha raised an eyebrow. "As I said, I leave the method to you. But we'll have to move quickly."

"First, I'm getting my friends out," said Tae grimly. "Once they're out, I'll do what you ask, because if I don't, people I love will be killed. I'm not doing this for you."

"I know," she said quietly.

He had to turn his head away quickly.

There was a tight, hard knot of tension in his stomach.

He'd be on the streets again. On the run again. The only one standing between his street kid friends and certain death.

Flying with this team, on the *Ungovernable*, working with people who were a thousand times smarter than him, and a thousand times better at getting out of bad situations—it had made him soft. The weight of responsibility he'd been carrying basically his whole damn life, that he'd grown so used to that he'd hardly noticed it anymore except in the constant tension in his muscles, the way his eyes snapped open at the slightest sound, no matter how deep he was in sleep, the constant headache from a clenched jaw—well, once he'd put it down, the thought of picking it back up again was almost unbearable.

But he'd do it.

Because he had to.

"Ivan," continued Masha, "it would be very helpful if you could be with me and Ysbel and Tanya. We could use your expertise in—"

"No." Ivan's face was set. "I promised Tae I'd do what I could to help his friends. That's what I intend to do."

Masha raised an eyebrow. At last she said, "You're not one of my crew, so I suppose I can't tell you what to do. But I would urge you to reconsider—"

"I've considered everything I need to," said Ivan quietly.

Tae looked at him for a moment, a mixture of relief and guilt flooding through him. Ivan turned and caught his eye, and for a moment, his familiar face, dark hair disheveled from their run, curls plastered to his forehead from the sweat and the mist, concern in those dark eyes, strain in his expression, and still, even then, the hint of that familiar good humour—made Tae's breath catch.

It was stupid. Masha was right, they could use Ivan here, and it was selfish of him to—

"I know what you're thinking Tae," whispered Ivan, affection and amusement in his voice. "You're thinking of a way to tell me I should stay here." He shook his head, a small grin on his face. "You may as well save your breath. I'm coming with you. I told you, back on the pleasure planet, that if there's anything I can do to help you, I will. And I meant it."

Tae looked at him for a long moment, the relief and the guilt churning in his stomach.

That was what he should have said. But he wouldn't have. He knew that now, just looking at Ivan. No matter how selfish, or stupid, or ridiculous—he wouldn't have asked Ivan to stay.

He wouldn't have been able to bring himself to.

4

Ysbel, day 1

"Mama?" Olya looked up at Ysbel with big, frightened eyes. "What's wrong?"

"What makes you think anything is wrong, my love?" asked Ysbel, trying to smile.

"Mama. I'm not stupid," said Olya, a hint of her usual superiority creeping into her tone. "You and Mamochka are worried. And Uncle Lev saw me and he only said hi and didn't stop to talk to me, so I know he's worried too."

Ysbel sat down on the bed, resting her hands on her knees, and considered her daughter for a moment. "Olya," she said at last. "You remember Grigory, yes?"

Olya nodded wordlessly.

"Well, he wants to kill us, and the people who worked for him want to kill us too. Your mamochka and I will keep you safe, but it will take a lot of work, I'm afraid."

"And you're worried, Mama."

"Yes, my love," said Ysbel quietly. "I'm worried." She stood, giving Olya a small smile. "Have you cleaned your room?"

"Are we staying here on the ship?"

"For now. And you still to have to clean your room."

Olya gave a long-suffering sigh, and turned to the door, pulling it open and shouting, "Misko! You have to come clean our room! Mama said so."

Ysbel smiled to herself as she watched her daughter leave.

A moment later, the door from the hallway opened, and Tanya stepped inside. There were lines of strain on her face—but then, after the last few weeks they'd had, it would have been surprising if there hadn't been.

"Ysi," she said quietly. "Is everything alright?"

Ysbel shook her head. "I don't like this. I don't like working with Masha. She's up to something, she's always up to something. And I'm tired of working for someone who will only be loyal as long as we are useful."

"I know, my heart," said Tanya, sitting down beside her. "I don't like it either. But—" she shrugged. "I don't know that we have a better option at this point." She rested her hand on Ysbel's knee. "We'll figure out a way to protect the others, and keep the children safe. That's all that counts."

"Let's hope we can," said Ysbel quietly.

"The others are heading out," said Tanya. "I think they wanted to speak with you before they left."

"Yes," said Ysbel. "I promised Tae some explosives. And I'd be more comfortable if Lev had some as well."

Tanya raised an eyebrow. "You remember that Lev will be going with Jez. Are you going to send explosives with her?"

"The only thing that makes me more nervous than Jez without explosives is Jez with explosives," Ysbel grumbled, pushing herself to her feet.

Tanya chuckled, and pulled open the door.

Tae, Ivan, Lev, and Jez were gathered in a small group by the hangar bay entrance. They looked up as Ysbel and Tanya came down the loading dock.

"Tae," she said, reaching into her jacket pocket and extracting a small, padded bag. "I have some things in here for you." She held it out to him.

Tae almost stepped back, a look of mild panic on his face, but at last, reluctantly, he took the bag from her.

"Be careful with these," she said. "If you accidentally set one off, there won't be enough left of you to scrape off the concrete."

"Believe me, Ysbel," he muttered. "I've seen what your explosives do. You have no idea how careful I'm going to be."

She cracked a small smile. "Good. Because I would actually feel bad if you blew yourself up, at this point."

Tae smiled back reluctantly. "I'm glad our friendship means so much to you."

"I have some for you, too, Lev," Ysbel said, pulling another small bag from her jacket pocket and handing it to him.

He tucked it, gingerly, into his own jacket pocket. "And let me guess. If I make a mistake with these, there won't be enough left of me to scrape off the concrete."

"Yes, well, that's one way of putting it," said Ysbel.

Lev sighed. "I suppose that's reassuring, in a gruesome sort of way." He turned to Tae. "Tae. You've given Tanya—"

"Yes," said Tae. "I gave Tanya everything she needs for your apartment. I've set the bugs she's going to plant so they'll garble the signal through the government bugs, but you should come through clear to the rest of us." He paused. "I've set everyone's coms into a private loop, except for mine and Ivan's. I've put us on the closed loop I used with the street kids, before. We'll be on the streets, and the police will be after us, and if they notice a private loop connected to the rest of you, it will be a problem. So don't contact me unless it's an emergency. You won't have a secure channel, and every time you do, there's a chance it could be compromised."

Lev drew in a long breath. "Well." He looked around. "I suppose we should get going." He glanced at his com. "Jez, your ship comes in about half a standard hour, so you'll have to be ready to mingle with the crowd coming off. I'll be waiting for you at the dock."

Jez looked uncharacteristically somber. Ysbel raised an eyebrow. She wasn't entirely sure if it was because of the danger they were all in, or the fact that the crazy pilot girl would be pretending to be Lev's lover.

She didn't know all the details of what had happened between the two of them on Grigory ship, and to be quite frank, she didn't want to. But whatever it was, it had knocked both Lev and Jez swamp-footed.

She didn't blame the pilot girl for not wanting to do that again. Honestly, she didn't think any of them wanted to do that again.

Somehow, though, Jez managed a snarky grin. "See you there, genius," she said.

"I'll set Tae's bugs into your apartment," said Tanya. "Then I'll find you at the docks. Don't expect to see me, though. I'm certain that there will be at least three government agents following you, so it won't hurt to have a friendly pair of eyes. And," she added, almost as an afterthought, "I assume you'd prefer not to be assassinated. I don't anticipate that, but—you never know. This is Prasvishoni, after all."

"Yes," said Lev dryly. "I am aware. I appreciate the reassurance." He turned to Jez, and she gave him a wink.

"See you on the other side," she said. Then she sauntered out the hangar bay door.

Lev watched her for a moment, concern clear in his face, then he sighed. "I suppose I should go as well. I assume they'll expect me to be waiting early." He straightened his jacket, took a deep breath, and stepped out the door after Jez.

Tae turned to Ivan. The former street kid's face was tight with strain, and Ysbel couldn't honestly blame him. His friends would almost certainly die if he didn't get them out in time, and she'd spent enough time in Prasvishoni to know that living on the streets was an uncertain prospect at best.

"Ivan? You ready?" Tae asked.

Ivan gave him a small smile. "Ready as I'll ever be, I suppose."

Tae nodded, and the two of them stepped out the hangar bay doors as well.

At last, it was just Ysbel, Tanya, and Masha, alone in the empty, echoing space.

For a long time, Ysbel watched Masha.

She had no idea if this was the job, at last, in which their lives would become dispensable. She didn't know Masha's long-term goal, or how she planned to accomplish it.

But Masha was right about this, at least—for now, their best chance of survival was to work with her.

And never, for one moment, to let down their guard.

At last, Masha turned towards the back, where Tae had rigged together a communication box with Lev's codes.

"So," said Ysbel, once she and Tanya had joined Masha. "What is it you want to do?"

Masha pulled up the holoscreen on her com. "We can't direct any messages to specific people until we have some information from Jez and Lev. So I propose that we broadcast a message on the general channel that can be easily intercepted. Something that will be enough to calm tensions until we have time to engage in a more direct strategy."

"And what will this message be?"

"Do you have a suggestion?" asked Masha.

Ysbel paused for a moment. Then she gave a small smile. "Yes. We broadcast a message from Grigory. A list, with the names of all the people killed on his ship. That's all."

Masha looked at Ysbel thoughtfully. "I believe that would be sufficient," she said at last.

Ysbel heard the words she didn't say.

Sufficient to paint Grigory as a threat, yes. But also sufficient, if they were found out, or if anything went wrong, to paint a target on all of their backs big enough that every boyeviki and gang member and government official in the system would be able to take aim.

5

Lev, day 1

Lev stepped out of the hangar bay and onto the dirty Prasvishoni streets.

His hands, he realized, were sweating.

He gave a wry smile.

This was actually ridiculous. They'd just brought down the two most powerful mafia krestnaye in the system, they were in the process of a desperate, frankly ridiculous attempt to halt what would likely be full on civil war, and the lives of thousands, or hundreds of thousands, of people hung in the balance.

And he was worried about pretending to be the lover of a crazy, ridiculous pilot, with whom he happened to be good friends. And he was finally learning how to do friends.

A crazy, ridiculous pilot, who also happened to be the woman he loved more than he'd ever dreamed he could love anyone.

He closed his eyes grimly, and took a deep breath.

It would be fine. He would be fine. He and Jez were adults, and they were both fully capable of focusing on the task at hand.

He opened his eyes, straightened his jacket one last time, and started off down the streets.

A small crowd was gathered outside the docking bay, as there often was when the big long-haul ships came in, and he worked his way into it, trying not to think about that spot between his shoulder blades that always seem to itch when he had his back turned to almost certain danger.

Yes, it was highly likely that he was being watched, but if he were being logical, it was unlikely someone would try to kill him now, in a crowded area, without at least waiting for Jez to show up. There would be much more profit in killing him when they could kill the government minister who was, apparently, his lover—or at least, the woman who would be impersonating the government minister who was his lover.

Somehow, the thought wasn't making him feel any better.

When the ship finally arrived, he found himself peering at the stream of people walking past, eyes going from one to another, searching out a familiar shape, a familiar form in the crowd. A familiar smile.

Then he caught sight of her, her lanky form, her disheveled black hair, the grin on her face that meant she was as aware of the danger as he was and was utterly delighted by it.

He pushed his way through the crowd towards her. "Layla!" he called. "Layla, over here."

She looked around, trying to pinpoint the source of the voice.

"Layla!"

She caught sight of him, and her grin widened into a genuine smile. "Hey, you bastard!" she called cheerfully, shoving her way through to him. "Been looking for you." She was grinning mischievously, her eyes twinkling with that mixture of excitement and devilry that was her trademark, and before he could react, she grabbed him in an embrace.

He stiffened, almost unable to breathe.

The smell of her, ship's grease and burnt ozone and the musky-sweet smell of the *Ungovernable's* wood-panelled interior, the feel of her pressed up against him, sent a familiar ache through his whole body. His arms had come up around her as well, and he pulled her to him, his face buried in her short hair, eyes closed against the twisting in his stomach.

He felt like a damn addict, finally getting a shot of his favourite drug after weeks of shaky, agonizing withdrawals. And just like an addict, he knew this would only delay the inevitable, would only make the withdrawal worse, but he couldn't seem to help himself.

No.

No. He was not going to do this. He was an adult, and he could control his own damn actions, even when they involved Jez, and her arms around his neck, and his hands on her back, pressing her to him …

He took a deep breath and forced his arms to loosen.

"You know," he whispered, trying to keep the shakiness from his voice, "most people wouldn't call their lovers 'bastard.'"

She pulled back slightly, grinning. "Yeah? Well, Masha said this Layla plaguer was eccentric."

He smiled despite himself. She smiled back, and for a moment, the ache in his chest sharpened.

"Anyway," she said cheerily, "probably called most of my lovers 'bastard' at some point." She paused a moment, reflecting. "Of course, most of them also wanted to shoot me at some point, so …"

This time, he did chuckle.

She grinned at him again, then turned to look over the crowd. "Guess we better get going. Tanya here yet?"

"I have no idea," said Lev. "However, since it's Tanya we're talking about, I'm fairly certain we wouldn't know unless she actually killed us."

Jez grinned. "Just saying, Ysbel's a lucky woman."

The crowd around them was thinning, the chatter and noise and excitement of hundreds upon hundreds of arrivals, departures, family members or friends or lovers reuniting or bidding each other farewell, slowly fading. He and Jez made their way out through the crowded, open docking bay and back into the streets.

"So," said Jez, once they were outside. "We going to the apartment, I guess? Been in that part of town plenty of times, so figure I can get us there."

He turned to her and raised an eyebrow. "You were listening? To Masha? You—didn't look like you were listening."

She grinned. "Yeah, well, maybe that was just to annoy her. I do actually listen sometimes."

He chuckled again, despite himself. "You know, people would want to strangle you a lot less if you didn't go out of your way to irritate the hell out of them."

She smirked. "What would be the fun in that? Besides, if Masha'd wanted to strangle me that bad, she'd have done it months ago. Come on, genius."

They strolled along casually. The streets here were bare cement, without even the half-hearted attempt at class that cobblestones brought, dirty, as always, and crowded for this time of day. Lev glanced around surreptitiously, trying to gauge threats that may or may not exist.

They'd only been walking for a few minutes when a voice in his earpiece made him jump.

"The two of you are supposed to be lovers," came Tanya's voice, faintly amused. "You don't look very much like lovers."

Jez glanced over at him, and he sighed, tapping his com against his thigh. "Thank you, Tanya," he muttered into it.

"All I'm saying is, there are at least three government spies following you right now. It might be a good idea to give them a show." Her voice still sounded amused.

"Yes, well I was under the impression that even in Prasvishoni there were certain activities lovers only did indoors." He was speaking through his teeth.

Jez gave a snort of amusement.

"I'm not asking you to have sex in the street," said Tanya, sounding even more amused. "But you could at least hold hands. Pretend like you've met before."

Lev rolled his eyes to the sky, then turned to Jez, a slightly grim smile on his face. She raised an eyebrow at him, and, with a deep breath, he took her hand in his.

"I'm sorry, you'll have to do a little better than that." Tanya sounded like she was trying very hard to bite back a laugh.

Jez gave him a wry look, and twined her fingers with his, moving closer so their shoulders were touching.

He closed his eyes for a moment and blew out a breath.

This would be fine. This would be completely fine.

He glanced over at Jez from the corner of his eye. She was looking fixedly straight ahead, and there was a slight stiffness to her posture, and he could feel her hand tightening on his.

He forced himself to breathe normally. It was more difficult than it should have been.

"Well, at least now you look like you know each other," said Tanya, still sounding amused. "Just so you know, someone from the government is on his way to meet you now. You'll see him in the next couple of blocks." She paused a moment. "I understand he's coming to offer his greetings to Jez in person, before she attends the meeting today. I assume that both of you know the details of your roles?"

Lev glanced at Jez.

She gave him a wink.

He tapped his com. "Yes, Tanya," he said. "And anything we don't know, I'm confident Jez will be able to improvise."

He glanced back at her, and was surprised at the spark of gratitude in her eyes.

Apparently, he really hadn't been very good at this friend thing before.

He saw the man as soon as they rounded the corner onto the next street. He was wearing a standard government uniform and a self-important expression, and when he saw them, he came towards them at once.

Lev smiled wryly to himself. The man wasn't even pretending the government didn't have eyes on them. According to Masha, there was no way anyone here should recognize either of them.

He stopped in front of them, and held out a hand in greeting. "You must be Layla," he said, looking at Jez.

She raised an eyebrow at him. "What makes you think that?"

The man looked at them closer, slight uncertainty in his face.

She grinned. "Yes, I'm Layla."

The man frowned, his expression shifting to one of annoyance. "Yes. Ah. It's good to meet you, Layla. I was sent to make sure that you got to your quarters safely. We have a very nice apartment we've arranged for you here." He turned to Lev, then glanced back at Jez. "And this is—"

Jez's eyes flicked toward Lev for a moment, eyebrows quirked, then she turned back to the government official and grinned suggestively. "This is my sweet kotya."

The government official looked slightly embarrassed. "Your …
kitten?"

She winked.

Lev wasn't entirely sure whether he wanted the sigh or laugh. She
clearly didn't remember, and she was clearly just going to brazen it
out, although in her defence, she'd never pretended to be good at
remembering names.

He stepped forward, holding out a hand in greeting. "I'm
Ruslan."

The official hesitated, then took Lev's outstretched hand, shaking
it gingerly. "Very good to meet you, Ruslan." He turned back to Jez,
his expression flickering between disapproval and faint annoyance. "I
hear things were a bit exciting on Boloto when you left?"

She grinned. "Well, guess if you think diving out of the way of
flying shrapnel is exciting. Firebomb in my office and whatever. But
hell, no one was killed, so I figure—" She shrugged.

Tanya's voice came through Lev's earpiece. "She was actually
listening to Masha? She didn't look like she was listening."

Lev hid a small smile.

The official stared at Jez. "I—see," he said at last. He gave a
nervous chuckle. "I suppose, then, there's no need to warn you about
the situation here. We haven't had any firebombs in the recent past."

"Guess we'd better see if we can change that, eh?" said Jez
cheerfully. "I always figure you can't be doing a very good job if
someone doesn't want to kill you."

"You—get frequent threats on your life?" the man probed
gingerly.

Jez shrugged. "Depends on the week."

"I—see." He glanced around, apparently trying to find a safer
topic of conversation. His eyes lit on Lev, and Lev groaned inwardly.

He knew what was coming next.

"I understand you were quite excited to be assigned to Prasvishoni. Considering your, ah—" he gestured at Lev, and let the sentence trail off delicately.

In his earpiece, he heard Tanya cleared her throat meaningfully.

He took a deep breath, put his arm around Jez's waist, and pulled her in.

Her eyes widened momentarily, but then she slipped her arm around him as well, and bumped him playfully with her shoulder.

Damn. Damn, damn, damn. How the hell was he supposed to do this job when every damn time his body came into contact with Jez's, his damn brain seemed to shut off? There was something about the way the hard angles of her fit perfectly against him, the way she softened under his touch, the way—

He tried to paste a pleasant smile on his face.

"Yep." Jez's voice sounded slightly breathless, but that could have been just his imagination. She hooked her fingers into the belt loop on his trousers, and his stomach tightened, his pulse quickening.

Damn it, this was just an act. They were just friends.

"Been a while since I spent any time around my kotya." She raised an eyebrow suggestively at the official and grinned. "Hope you're not expecting me to come into work early in the morning. Figure me and him'll be pretty busy."

The official cleared his throat uncomfortably. "Ah. Shall we— head to the apartment?"

Jez was still grinning. "Sounds good to me. About time me and him caught up, if you know what I mean." She gave the horrified official a meaningful wink, and he turned away quickly, clearing his throat again.

"Yes, well, I'm sure you have plenty of things to talk about—"

Jez snorted with laughter. "Doubt we'll be doing much talking."

The man seemed to give up the conversation as a bad job, and started hurriedly off down the street.

Jez turned to Lev and winked, and despite the fact that his heart was beating ridiculously fast, despite the fact that his stomach was twisted into an almost painful knot, he couldn't help but smile back.

With the government official walking ahead of them, he didn't dare take his arm off from around Jez's waist.

If he was being honest, he didn't want to. But at least with the official ahead of them, he didn't have to admit that to himself.

By now, the sun had worked its reluctant way up into the sky. Its lethargic warmth cut the chill of the early winter morning slightly, turning the air cool and clammy, rather than bitter. The people of Prasvishoni hurried past them, hoods and scarfs raised against the cold, heads down, eyes fixed on the cement beneath their feet. The identical white prefab buildings of the business sector rose around them, walls grimy with dirt and yellowed with mildew, crumbling around the edges from years of frost and weather, and the sharp, unmistakable smell the Prasvishoni street lingered in his nostrils— unwashed bodies, a whiff of day-old food from the street vendors, the pungent tang of discarded rubbish in the mouths of alleys, the chill mist that lingered even at midday.

He'd grown up with that smell, breathed it in for so much of his life that it had become a simple background fact. It was only now, coming back here after so much time away, that he noticed it at all, the familiar, dreary scent of his childhood.

Even here in the business district, if he looked around, he could see signs of a faint unease. People peered over their shoulders, walking more quickly than usual, huddled together in small groups.

Something had happened. No one knew what yet, but they knew

that something was wrong. And if he and Jez and the rest of them couldn't do their job, it wouldn't be more than another day.

They passed out of the business district and into the residential area. The apartment buildings were hardly different than the industrial buildings, except the windows were smaller, placed closer together. When he'd worked in government, he'd known people who'd hide cot pads under their desks, because not only did it save them from the cold of walking home in the middle of a bitter Prasvishoni winter, their office was frankly larger and more comfortable than anything they'd find in an apartment.

He held back, allowing the government official to lead the way. When the man finally stopped in front of one of the complexes, identical to every other complex on the block aside from the large number above the doorway, he gestured Lev and Jez forward.

"Here you are." He fished in his pocket and pulled out a key chip, handing it to Jez. "Your apartment is on the second floor. Over in the corner, number 271."

Lev hid a frown.

Second floor, in the corner. The perfect place for an observer, standing across the street against the grimy artificial streetlamp, to be able to see in through the window.

It wasn't any more than he'd expected. Still, the thought of being watched by people who would almost certainly kill both him and Jez if they knew the truth was never a comfortable prospect.

"Well," Jez was saying, still wearing a lascivious grin. "Got some things I've been waiting a long time to do."

The government official, looking, if possible, even more uncomfortable than before, cleared his throat again. "I have been … instructed to wait here, and escort you to meet the rest of the ministers. As I'm certain you are aware, you're expected in half an hour."

Jez winked at him. "Well, guess we'd better get busy, hadn't we?" She shoved Lev playfully with her shoulder, and he staggered slightly. "Come on," she said with a grin.

He forced himself to grin back, and squeezed her tighter for just a moment, planting a quick kiss on her cheek. "I suppose we'd better," he murmured.

She turned to him, and for a moment, the teasing look had disappeared from her eyes. Then she squeezed him back, and pulled him after her through the door into the apartment building.

The inside of the complex was grungy and dimly lit, flickering orange bar-lights providing the only illumination in the narrow, dirty hallways, and up the ragged stairwell. Their apartment was up a flight of disreputable stairs, and down a long, dingy corridor on the second floor. As he'd expected, the window faced out to the street.

The government would keep close tabs on this new arrival until they knew who she was.

He'd read up on the file of the woman Jez would be impersonating, and he felt he knew who she was very well. She was … unpredictable. A rising star in the government ministry, apparently called in to deal with the latest unrest stemming from the *Ungovernable* crew's stop at the university a few months previous. She was smart, savvy, and politically astute—or she had been, before he and Jez had blown her into space dust.

And despite everything, he couldn't help a twist of guilt when he thought about this woman he'd never met, this woman whose life he and Jez had co-opted.

What had happened to the real Ruslan? He was certain that Masha had considered this detail—he'd have to ask her tonight, make sure there was nothing he was missing—but still—still, there was a man on this planet, in this city, who was waiting for a woman who would never come. A woman who, perhaps, he loved as much as Lev loved Jez.

Jez shoved the door open to their apartment, and gestured him inside.

"Go on, genius," she said. "If we have to be in the government meeting in half an hour, we'd better get moving."

He nodded, and stepped inside, and Jez followed him, closing the door after them.

He hit the artificial lights, and after a few reluctant seconds, they flickered dimly on.

The apartment itself was exactly what he'd expected—almost indistinguishable from the apartment he'd lived in back when he was working in the government himself. Before he'd been thrown in jail, of course. There was a small living room and a small kitchen, with barely enough cupboard space for week's rations for two people, a heating plate that looked like an illustration for a fire hazard warning, and a small cooling box, in case either of them should feel ambitious enough to get something that wasn't ration packs. A bathroom, off to one side, and the bedroom tucked in beside it, made up the remainder of the apartment. There was an old couch, a table big enough for two, and some shelves up against the wall with built-in space for information chips.

He looked around, a lump rising in his throat.

He didn't miss this. He didn't miss the government. But this small apartment brought back more memories than he was really prepared to deal with right now.

Jez glanced around, eyebrows raised. "Not too bad," she said. "I mean, it's not my sweet, beautiful angel, but it's a damn sight nicer than anything I've ever lived in on Prasvishoni."

He glanced over at her curiously. He'd seen her old basement apartment, of course—the entire crew of the *Ungovernable* had lived there for a week and a half before it had been blown up, which was something that tended to happen to apartments that Jez lived in, he was coming to learn—but honestly, he realized he didn't know all that much about her—her past life, where she'd lived, her family.

He swallowed down the bitter taste in his throat, regret and guilt mingled.

Jez was looking around more slowly now, surveying their new lodgings. At last, she turned back to him and grinned. "Well, genius, guess it's not all bad being in government, eh? I mean, hell, living in a place like this? Honestly—"

Her words faltered, and he realized they were standing closer than he'd thought.

The grin on her face faded slowly, replaced by a look he'd seen there far too often, the one he'd spent the last few weeks trying desperately to forget. She hadn't dropped her hand from his waist, and he hadn't dropped his, and he was suddenly ridiculously aware of her, the rough fabric of her jacket under his hand, the way it dipped in against her back, the pressure of her hand on his waist. His heartbeat pounded in his ears, and everything in the room that wasn't Jez seemed to have faded slightly.

She swallowed hard, still watching him, and swallowed again, then at last, with a visible effort, wrenched her eyes away from his, dropping her hand from his waist like it had burned her.

He dropped his hand as well, trying to remember how to breathe.

Damn it to hell, there was no way he was going to survive this.

Jez cleared her throat. "Um. I guess, um—" she trailed off, as if unsure where the sentence was leading.

Lev swallowed as well, since his throat was so dry he wasn't sure he'd be able to form words. "We'd better get ready." He looked around quickly for the suitcase Jez had brought with her. It should contain everything Masha had procured for them, as far as IDs and clothing. "I believe they asked you to bring me to this first social event. They like to know the partners of the higher up officials, for surveillance purposes, and to see if they pose a security risk."

Jez, who seemed to have regained some of her composure, smirked at him. "Pretty sure you're the damn definition of a security risk, genius."

He smiled at her reluctantly.

"Anyway," she continued, "guess I'd better get changed into my government uniform crap. Since that bastard downstairs is just going to wait until we come down." She paused a moment, then grinned at Lev. "Hey, bet if we open the windows, and that couch is squeaky enough, we could make him think—"

"No," said Lev firmly. "I don't think we have time for that."

Honestly, he didn't think he'd be able to handle that right now without actually exploding.

She gave him a disappointed look, then shrugged philosophically and began stripping out of the loose smuggler gear that was her usual form of dress.

He averted his eyes hastily, and she snickered.

"Hey now, thought Tae was the innocent."

He clenched his jaw, and didn't answer.

The very last thing in the entire system he needed right now was the picture in his head of Jez unlacing the front of her shirt.

"I'm—just going to look around the apartment," he said.

Tanya had already performed a scan, he was fairly certain, but 'fairly certain' was the sort of thing that tended to get you killed. He pulled up the scanner Tae had set on his com, and did a quick sweep of the apartment, then a slower sweep around the two windows facing the street.

Nothing. At least, nothing he hadn't expected. There were several bugs set up, but they appeared to be standard government issue—nothing planted by some unknown third party, which was what he'd been concerned about.

By the time he finished his scans, checked all the specs on the various bugs and listening devices, and, facing out the window, counted very slowly to sixty, he took the chance of turning around.

Jez was dressed again, this time in the uniform of a government minister. She looked, somehow, absurdly out of place in the drab, straight-cut, greyish brown of a standard issue government uniform —the glint in her eyes, her dangerous grin, her short, tousled black hair, all stood out in strict incongruence to the stern conformity of the government colours.

She winked at him, and, like always, his heart stuttered for a moment before he remembered himself.

"Well, genius, how do I look?"

"As—close to a government minister as I expect you could."

"Is that supposed to be an insult?" asked Jez.

He smiled slightly. "Jez. If you remember, I worked with government ministers for years. Believe me, it's not an insult."

She smiled back at him, then quickly averted her eyes and cleared her throat. "Anyway, that bastard downstairs is waiting for us. Probably better go."

"Yes," Lev murmured. "I believe you're right."

Jez shoved the door open, and held it for him as he walked out, then closed it behind them.

There was an awkward moment, where neither of them looked at each other, and then, finally, Jez mumbled, "Suppose we'd better," and slipped her hand into his. Again, something like an electric shock ran up his arm, but he gritted his teeth and ignored it.

Jez, too, seemed not nearly as comfortable with this as she'd been in the street. She conscientiously avoided his eyes as they started down the stairway to where the government official waited.

The man didn't react when he saw them, except the polite raise of his eyebrows. "I assume, then, you're ready, Minister?" he said.

Jez grinned. "Ready as I'll ever be."

There was something in her voice, though, that belied her words.

6

Tae, day 1

Tae glanced at Ivan, walking beside him. Ivan's posture was tense, and there was a grim set to his jaw.

In the foggy light of day, the dank alley behind the fence around the apartment complex looked like any other alley—refuse choking the corners, dirty huddles of blankets where street kids had spent the night trying to stay warm. He shivered slightly. It had been a long time since he'd slept on the streets, and he'd grown accustomed to sleeping warm. To not waking up at night to check whether any of the others were on the verge of freezing to death.

He pulled up his com and did a quick scan as they approach the mouth of the alley.

No heat signals. One good thing, at least. He turned to Ivan. "I think it's clear. For the moment."

Ivan nodded tersely. "I'll keep watch." He held out a hand. "Give me one of Ysbel's flash-bangs."

A tendril of worry twisted in Tae's stomach, but he reached gingerly into the small pouch where he'd tucked the explosives. He handed the flash-bang to Ivan, who gave him a small grin.

"Tae. Distracting guards was part of my job description, before I got arrested. Worry about yourself and the kids."

Tae nodded mutely.

Ivan was right. Still, he couldn't help the tightness in the back of his throat.

Back on the pleasure planet, Ivan had faced a woman with a knife. And he'd stood there, passively, and let her carve a line across his throat and down his chest. The scar was still there, an angry, raised line.

And the whole time, he'd had a heat gun in his pocket. The whole time, he could have killed the woman and her two companions, and they wouldn't even have had time to fight back. But he hadn't, because he'd known if he did, Tae's friends would die.

He'd been willing to let his throat get cut to keep a bunch of kids he'd never met safe. And Tae had no reason to suspect he'd do otherwise now.

"Just—" Tae shook his head. "Just be careful. Please." The words seemed to catch in his throat.

Ivan's smile softened. "Tae. It'll be fine. Now—" he put a hand on Tae's shoulder, and gave him a slight push towards the alley. "Go on. I'll let you know if anything happens."

Tae nodded, swallowed down his panic, and slipped into the alley.

Once he was out of sight of the road, he leaned back against the wall and tapped quickly on his com. "Caz. Are you there?"

Caz's voice answered almost immediately. "Yes. We're ready. I hadn't heard from you, and I was starting to worry—"

"I'm fine. Let's worry about getting you out. Can you meet me down by the fence?"

"We can be there in two standard minutes." Caz's voice was tense. "We'll have to be quick. There are guards patrolling inside the compound. They started last night."

Tae cursed silently. Lev had warned him that things were going sideways on the streets, but hadn't realized it had gone this far. If the guards were already patrolling inside the compound, that meant they knew, at least something.

He glanced around one more time, then strode quickly towards the dip in the fence.

When he reached it, he crouched and hit the blocker he'd set into his com. He flipped up the scanner, checking the green crosshatch that represented the security system.

Where he crouched, there was a slight distortion in the field. And …

Yes. It was hardly noticeable, but the green lines crosshatched by the fence had opened slightly, distorted by his blocker tech. It wasn't much, but hopefully enough to let, for example, a child slip through.

He barely had time to tap the scanner off when he heard Caz's voice from across the fence.

"Tae. We're here."

Tae glanced through the narrow opening. He could just make out someone's legs. Someone small, with worn, battered boots.

"Blocker's set," he said. "Come on."

Mila's head appeared in the opening, and Tae reached down and helped her through. Her brother Luca followed next, and one by one, the rest of the children. The gap under the fence was small, barely big enough to fit them, but then, even after a few weeks of food and rest, they were still all so skinny it almost hurt to look at them. Peti wriggled through, second to last, her hips catching for a moment against the prefab blocks of the fence. Tae grabbed her hands and pulled, gritting his teeth as she hissed in pain.

It didn't matter. They didn't have another option.

Just Caz left.

"Come on!" Tae whispered.

Caz knelt, peering through the crack. "I won't make it. Peti barely fit, and she's a lot smaller than I am. Take the others, go."

Tae swore. "Why didn't you bloody tell me that this morning?"

"Because you'd have tried to think of another way, and from what you said, we don't have time for that."

Tae swore again, and turned to the others. "Peti, take the kids. My friend's waiting at the entrance. He'll get you out if I—if me and Caz—"

Peti looked at him for a moment, her eyes wide and frightened. "You won't leave Caz?"

Tae shook his head shortly. "I promise."

She hesitated, then, face set, herded the younger children ahead of her down the alley.

"What are you doing?" Caz hissed at him.

"You know damn well what I'm doing. You'd do the same for me."

"The guards are here!" Caz's voice was tight with strain. "Go!"

From the other side of the fence, voices raised in anger or surprise.

"Stand back," Tae said through his teeth. "As far as you can." He yanked one of the smallest explosives out of the pouch Ysbel had given him and tossed it into the dip under the fence, stumbling backwards as he hit the controller. There was a loud pop, a flash that almost blinded him, and a choking cloud of smoke and debris.

Through the bright afterimages crowding his vision, he could make out Caz's skinny form, thrown backwards by the explosion, on the ground across from where the fence had been, the larger figures of guards running towards them, heat guns drawn.

He snatched out his own heat pistol. He aimed at the nearest guard's face where her visor was tipped up, and pulled the trigger.

She collapsed with a choked-off scream. Tae lunged forward, grabbed Caz by the arm, hauled him to his feet, and dragged him down the alley.

He hit his com as they ran. "Ivan. Get the kids out. Caz and I are on our way, but the guards are after us."

"Got it," came Ivan's voice. "I'm sending them down Ledya Street."

As Caz and Tae reached the mouth of the alley, heat blasts crackled over their heads and scored the walls of the buildings on either side of them. Tae glanced around frantically as they burst out into the street.

Ivan stood against the wall to one side, posture tense. When he saw them, he jerked his chin in the direction the children had gone. Tae hesitated for the briefest moment, then, still pulling Caz after him, ran after the others. He saw, out of the corner of his eye, Ivan step forward as the guards emerged, something clutched in his hand.

There was a sound like a body hitting pavement. Tae almost turned back, panic spiking through him, but now it was Caz who pushed him forward.

Ivan's voice rang out, shouting loudly to the police for help, and Tae drew a quick gasp of relief.

At least he was still alive.

He turned on the street after the children. Peti, who was in the lead, glanced behind her, the relief visible in her face when she saw them. Tae let go of Caz and scooped up Mila as he came up to them, settling the six-year-old on his hip like he'd done so many times before, her arms clasped tightly around his neck.

"Peti," he hissed. "Where are we going?"

"First alley off Rybachka Street, right after the river," she said over her shoulder, her voice strained. "There's a place back there the police haven't checked lately. And there's an exit onto the river, so at least they can't surround us."

Behind them came the distant wail of police sirens, rapidly growing louder. Tae swore quietly.

"Listen, Caz, Peti. If they find us, take the younger kids and go. I'll try to distract them."

Caz looked as if he was about to protest, then his gaze fell to Mila. He took a quick breath and nodded. He came up, matching Tae's pace, and Tae detached the girl's arms from his neck and passed her over. Mila's expression was terrified, silent tears running down her cheeks.

From behind them there was a loud bang, a flash of light, angry swearing from the police officers.

Tae glanced over his shoulder involuntarily. What the hell was Ivan doing?

They pelted down another street, and Tae tapped his com, pushing their location through the closed loop. Hoping against hope Ivan was still alive to use it.

And then, as they turned onto the street that led to the alley behind the river, there were footsteps behind them. Tae spun, jerking his heat pistol out, and then felt his legs go weak in relief.

Ivan sprinted up behind them. There was a cut on his forehead, and what looked to be shaping into an impressive black eye, but other than that he seemed unhurt.

He caught up with them quickly, his long legs covering the ground at a rapid pace. "Is everyone alright?" he asked, his voice tense.

Tae nodded, too breathless to speak.

Peti turned down into the alley, and they followed her, Tae and Ivan bring up the rear. At last, they collapsed into a small opening between two buildings, panting and gasping.

When he caught his breath, Tae turned to Ivan. "How did you—" he began.

"I told you," said Ivan, grinning slightly. "I've distracted police plenty of times before." He looked around the narrow space, barely big enough for all of them. Off to one side, out of sight, the river flowed sluggishly through its constricted banks. "Although," he added, "I'll admit, I've never done anything quite like this."

Tae glanced around as well.

Yes, he'd lived on the streets for his whole life, and he'd had police after him more times than he could count.

But what they were doing now was something more than that, and all of them knew it.

"I don't know that any of us have," he said at last.

7

Jez, day 1

Jez looked at the group of government officials, standing in small clusters in the long, low room around a large, semicircular table. The table was covered with spartan-looking alcoholic beverages that she knew damn well were strong enough to peel non-reactive paint, and a depressing array of wilted food. Which, she guessed, must constitute a social event here in the government.

After Grigory's ship, she wasn't impressed.

The government officials, all of whom had turned at her entrance, stared back at her. None of them seemed particularly impressed either, although she figured it was probably for slightly different reasons.

"Well, Layla," said one of the officials, stepping forward to greet them. She was a stern woman, maybe mid-sixties, with a hard face, and a look about her of someone whose sense of humour had been surgically removed years ago. "It's good to have you here, finally. We've been waiting for you for some time."

"Well, you know what they say—some things are worth waiting for," said Jez, with a wide grin. "At least, that's what some people think." She turned to Lev and gave him a broad wink.

"I see," said the woman, with no noticeable thawing of her expression. "I hope that will prove to be the case." She paused a moment, gesturing around at the others. "I assume you know who everyone is."

Jez glanced around the room again.

The officials didn't look any more cheerful than the room itself. They each could have been born into the grey-brown uniform they wore, for all she could tell—it sat on their frames like a baggy, ill-fitting exoskeleton, as if they were insects waiting to moult. There were probably around twenty of them in total, including the bastard who'd spoken, and although there were a couple who might be closer to her age, most of them didn't look much younger than fifty.

She didn't know much about government, honestly, but judging from what Lev had told her, the fact they'd survived it this long probably meant they were both powerful and important. And no, she didn't know any of the names, but being introduced again sure as hell wouldn't help that.

She shrugged. "Figure I know enough."

The woman sighed, with an expression of mildest distaste. "Very good. I'm Branka. And this must be—"

"Ruslan," said Lev smoothly, stepping forward.

Jez smirked. She wasn't sure how much of it was his desire to save her from embarrassment, and how much was his desire not to be called "kitten" again. But hell, she'd honestly tried to remember the damn name.

"I'll let you get to socializing in a moment," said Branka. "I'm sure, though, you have no objection to a standard security check?"

Jez cast a quick glance at Lev.

He was looking ahead, expression one of polite interest, and she didn't notice any tensing of his posture at the woman's words. Which meant, probably, that Masha had figured this in and prepared for it already.

Or, that Lev was just resigned to the certainty of death. Honestly, that was an option too, after the last couple months they'd had.

She turned back to the woman and grinned easily. "Course not. Check away."

The security checks consisted of a small wand being waved across them, and one of the security guards in the back doing a quick electronic scan.

Jez looked around the room as whoever-the-hell-that-was went through whatever the hell data he'd gathered.

If they were going to be caught, probably too late to do anything about it anyway, although thanks to Ysbel, they'd make a hell of a splash on the way out. So in the meantime, may as well see what she was in for. Even though socializing with these bastards was about the last thing in the entire system she wanted to do.

Branka is a good person to get to know, came the quick taps through the earpiece of her com. She glanced at Lev, but he was looking innocently up at the ceiling. *You'll want to be careful of that man in the back, though. And the younger man, across the room with his back to you. He'll be a good one to have on your side, if you can get him. I'll fill you in on all the details when we have a little more time.*

She didn't look at Lev again, but she was surprised at the strength of the relief that flooded through her, and how the small, cold knot of worry that had been sitting in her chest since they'd showed up at the damn government office buildings, that looked a hell of a lot like a prison complex, loosened just a little.

Thing was, she was crap at acting like some fancy government minister bastard. Which, hell, maybe wouldn't be a big deal, except for the fact the lives of every damn person on the crew were riding on her ability to pull this off.

But … well, but with Lev on the other end of her com—maybe she'd survive this after all. Somehow.

"So, Layla," Branka was saying. "I expect you're up to speed on the political situation here?"

Jez turned to her. "Think I know enough," she drawled.

Considering that she and the rest of the crew had been the ones that had basically engineered the 'political situation' in first place, she was actually pretty up to speed on that, honestly.

"Good. As you know, we asked you here for a very specific reason …"

Jez gave her a wink, the restless nervousness that had been gathering in her since that morning, when she'd reluctantly agreed to this stupid plan, pumping through her like blood. "Yep. Heard that you couldn't handle your own damn crap, so you needed to get someone in who was actually smart."

The older woman's face took on a distinctly cool veneer. "As you are well aware, Layla, that is not precisely—"

Jez shrugged. "Kinda sounded like it to me," she said. "Although, I mean, I know I'm hot and all, so can't blame you for wanting me here."

OK, maybe this wasn't exactly what Lev had meant when he talked about getting to know Branka. But hell, she and that bastard in front of her had about as much of a chance of becoming friends as Ysbel had of taking up a philosophy of non-violence.

Lev's arm tightened slightly around her waist, but he didn't say anything, and she figured he was going to let her handle this the way she thought best.

Which wasn't, honestly, all that much of a comfort.

The woman's gaze grew even colder, but before she could

respond, the guard who'd done the security check glanced up from the back of the room and caught Branka's eye, giving a quick nod.

Branka's expression lost none of its grimness, but she gave Jez the parody of a smile. "It appears your credentials check out. As do those of your lover."

She paused a moment. "As you are no doubt aware," she continued, her words coming slowly, "we are … dealing with the crisis at the moment. Between our ruptured relationships with Vitali Dobrev and Grigory Korzhakov, and Olyessa's rise to power, the situation had been volatile for some time. I don't know how in-depth your briefing went, but suffice it to say, the Viernest Protocol, which we had been counting on to deal with the unrest, has been disrupted, and we are uncertain when we will be able to resume it. We will have to make do without it for the time being."

She paused again, seeming almost unwilling to continue. At last, though, she sighed. "I had hoped not to have to give you this news. However, as we have received no intelligence to dispute the rumours thus far, it is probably wise for you to know. I sent Undersecretary Boris to escort you to your apartment, and then here to the meeting, because rumours have reached us that something may have happened to Grigory Korzhakov. The Rims and the Blood Riots are already starting trouble in the streets, and as you know, they work hand in hand with both branches of the mafia. There's nothing we can do to stop them short of calling in the army, and we can't do that without risk of offending Olyessa, and Grigory as well, should the rumours prove false." Her expression was grim. "I'm sure I don't need to explain this to you, but the entire situation is an explosive waiting for someone to hit the controller."

Jez glanced over at Lev, and was startled to see his face was almost as grim as the government official's.

"We are monitoring the situation closely," the woman continued, "and the moment we have some news one way or the other—"

An older man, with grey streaks beginning in his beard, stepped forward quickly, and placed a hand on Branka's arm. He barely managed a polite nod in Jez's direction, then turned back to Branka, his voice low and urgent. "Pardon my interruption, but I need to speak with you in private."

The woman frowned. "Now?"

"Yes."

There was something in the tone of his voice that seemed to convince her, because she turned to Jez. "Pardon me," she murmured, and walked quickly over to the man.

Jez glanced over at Lev, but he only gave a small shrug.

Another woman stepped forward. She was shorter than Branka, body softer and rounder, and there was a sharp intelligence in her gaze. "Layla," she said, her voice oozing solicitation. "I do hope your trip here was without incident. We're delighted to have you as part of the ministry."

Jasna, Lev tapped through his com. *She's over Interior Finance, so she likely thinks she can use you. You're an unknown quantity at the moment, and there will be plenty of people feeling you out to see what they can get from you.*

Jez grinned at the woman. "Not a bad place to be, I've heard." She lowered her voice. "Although, I'll be honest with you, heard Goran was the man to know in these parts. Figure I'd be pretty grateful to anyone who could get me through to him, if you know what I mean."

The woman's eyebrows raised slightly, calculation in her expression. "Well," she began.

Then Branka's voice cut through the quiet chatter. "Ministers. Please. While this has been delightful, I'm afraid we have to reconvene in the board room, immediately."

Jez frowned, but the woman in front of her looked as confused as she did.

Branka came over quickly, and gave Jez a smile that didn't reach her eyes. "Layla. I hope you're ready to begin your work. You've come at an interesting time. Ruslan, it was very nice to meet you. I assume you can find your own way back to the apartment?"

Lev nodded, and when Jez glanced over at him, she could see the interest gleaming from his eyes, even though his face was impressively impassive.

She sighed to herself, then leaned in and kissed him on the cheek for the benefit of the rest of the room, whispering in his ear, "I'll have my com on. You can listen in."

She could have kissed him a little more thoroughly, but from the look of the shrivelled-up bastards around the room, a kiss on the cheek would be sufficiently scandalous. And hell—well, she'd felt how Lev had tensed up when she'd hugged him at the docking bay. And it was probably a good thing, considering she was pretty sure neither of them had any desire to revisit the mess that was her and him in a sort-of relationship.

Anyways, it made it easier for her to ignore how natural hugging him felt, holding his hand, leaning into his arm around her waist …

She cleared her throat and drew back, steadfastly avoiding Lev's eyes as he bade everyone a polite farewell. Once he'd left, she followed the other officials out into the wide hallway and a few doors down.

The room they entered was large and drab, and looked something like the boardroom on the *Ungovernable*, if the boardroom on the *Ungovernable* had been stripped of every scrap of anything that lent it charm or personality, and expanded by about three times. Branka beckoned everyone to take their seats. She, however, remained standing.

"What is it?" asked a man from the end of the table, once they were seated.

Branka took a long breath. "We intercepted a message from Grigory," she said at last.

There was a sharp intake of breath from more than one of the officials, and Jez raised her eyebrows. Masha worked fast.

"And?" the man demanded.

Again, Branka paused. Her face was noticeably more grim than it had been when Jez had first arrived.

"It was a list," she said finally. "The names of various government officials who were at the symposium. Just under fifty of them."

Jez glanced around the table.

She saw realization dawning on the government officials' faces, and a dawning horror.

"The ones we haven't heard back from yet," the man said, voice stricken. His words were a statement, not a question.

Branka nodded.

It was a long moment of silence.

To be honest, Jez felt a little sick herself.

She'd been the one who killed them. She and Lev. Neither of them had known what they were doing, of course, but that hardly made a difference to the people who'd died, or to their families. Or to the people in this room.

"Who was the message addressed to?" snapped a woman whose name Jez had already forgotten.

"It was sent through the general lines," Branka said quietly. "I expect it was intended for us."

There was another moment of silence. At last, Branka dropped into her chair and looked over at Jez, her face a ghastly attempt at a smile. "Well, Layla, I suppose your time here will be more exciting than we had imagined. It appears that Grigory Korzhakov has declared war on the government."

"You don't know anything about the symposium," Lev whispered into her earpiece.

She somehow managed to keep from rolling her eyes. "OK, so what's this all about?" she asked out loud.

The man who'd first spoken turned to her. "There was a financial conference a few weeks back. Grigory was involved. There was some disruption to the proceedings, and we heard reports that around fifty government officials were taken onto his ship by force. We haven't heard from them since."

"And I suppose, now, we must assume they're dead," Branka finished quietly.

Jez raised an eyebrow. "Guess you won't have to ask me about what having your office firebombed is like pretty soon here."

Branka's look of shock was now overlaid with irritation. "Thank you, Layla." She turned back to the others. "If this is true, we'll have to transition the government out of Grigory's hands. We won't have a choice. Thankfully, we've moved in that direction since the rift with Vitali, but we'll have to move more quickly now, before he can seize control of anything vital."

There were grim nods around the table.

Branka shook her head. "The people in this room were selected specifically to transition the government structure. Now, it appears, the parameters of our task have changed, but the urgency—and the mandate that no one outside our committee knows the details of what we're doing—have not. I'll put a list of which government officials are owned by Grigory on a chip for your coms. We'll have to move quickly, but without paralyzing the government in the meantime." She turned to the man in the corner. "Aliko? I assume you've taken every possible step to remove the broadcast from the air?"

He nodded.

"Very good. Hopefully, that will buy us some time. I'll give you the rest of the day to go through the information. It's highly classified, and will auto destruct if anyone other than you tries to access it, so please be sure you've set the retinal scanners onto your coms. When we reconvene tomorrow morning, we'll create a plan of action."

The others in the room stood slowly, muttering quietly among themselves.

Branka turned back to Jez. "Layla. I understand you'll be sharing an apartment with Ruslan. I assume you can vouch for his discretion?"

She grinned. "'Course. Wouldn't have brought him along if I didn't think he could keep his damn mouth shut."

"Good," said the woman. "Because I'm certain I don't need to tell you, but if word of any of this gets out, the results could be disastrous." She paused. "And I will do anything necessary to prevent that."

There was something in her voice that made Jez shiver.

They were right in the damn middle of this now. And there'd be no going back.

They pulled this off, or they died.

8

Tae, day 2

Tae blinked awake in a disoriented panic, jerking upright. He looked around quickly, then sagged in relief.

Each huddle of blankets rose and fell softly with the breath of the child underneath it.

He'd been back on the streets for one night, but already his brain had gone back to the automatic rituals he'd grown up with—a quick count to make sure that everyone was here, and then a second, more slowly, to make sure everyone was breathing. He could still remember that morning five years ago, breathing a sigh of relief after the first count, and then realizing that Kira's back, under the blankets, was no longer rising and falling. And every morning since then, he'd had that moment of sick, stomach-twisting panic, that momentary reluctance to even look.

But everyone seemed to have survived the night.

He shifted painfully, pushing himself to his feet. Every part of him was sore, and every part of him was cold, and the creeping chill of the night had worked its way into what felt like the marrow of his bones.

He glanced back once more at the sleeping children, then,

shivering slightly, stepped out into the alley. He looked up and down quickly from habit, then pulled up his com and did a quick scan.

Heat signals from the pile of bodies behind him, but nothing besides that.

He breathed a short sigh of relief and slumped back against the alley wall.

There was a movement behind him, and he turned quickly.

Ivan leaned against the wall, his coat pulled around his shoulders, watching Tae. His face was set, and a little sad.

"You alright?" Tae asked softly, voice cracking with sleep.

Ivan gave him a small smile that didn't reach his eyes. "I'm fine."

This was probably his first night sleeping on the streets, at least in cold like this.

Guilt twisted in Tae's gut, cut with frustration.

He hadn't asked Ivan to come. But … he hadn't asked him not to, either.

"Sorry," Tae muttered. "I know it's not—"

Ivan pushed himself off the wall and came over to stand beside Tae. His smile was slightly more genuine this time. "Tae. I've slept on the ground before." He paused. "But this —" He made a short, frustrated gesture behind him at the sleeping children, huddled together under their blankets. "No one should have to live like this. No one should have to damn well wonder whether their friends will be alive in the morning, or whether they've frozen to death overnight." He gave a sharp shake of his head. "That's what we were bloody well protesting when I got thrown in jail. And nothing's bloody changed."

Tae stared at him for a moment. He'd never actually heard Ivan talk about what had landed him in prison, besides that he'd been leading protests. "You —"

Ivan gave a humourless laugh. "Yes. See? That's the worst part of it. You're shocked that anyone gave a damn about street kids, because you never knew. That's how this government works. There were lots of us. Even more who felt the same way, but didn't dare say anything." He shrugged, and tried to smile. "That's what the government counts on, people being too afraid to do anything. People thinking that they're the only ones that care, so there's really no point trying to change it."

Tae watched him, unable to take his eyes off his friend's face.

Ivan was quiet for a while, staring out at the alley wall ahead of them. His voice, when he next spoke, was soft. "They care, Tae. But they're afraid. And I can't blame them. I ... watched the police kill my best friend. In front of me. They beat him to the ground with shock sticks and they ... didn't stop. There was blood coming out of his mouth by the end, out of his ears—" he paused, a muscle working in the corner of his jaw, and Tae wasn't sure if he'd continue.

He didn't know if he wanted him to. He felt sick, unsure what to say or do.

"He was one of the bravest people I knew," Ivan said finally. "But in the end, he was crying. Begging for them to stop. And they made us watch the whole thing." He was quiet for a moment, lost in his own thoughts, and Tae wasn't sure if he remembered anyone else was there.

Finally, Tae reached up and put a hand on Ivan's shoulder.

Ivan looked up, startled out of his reverie, then gave a faint, strained smile. "I'm sorry."

Tae shook his head. "No," he said. "No, don't apologize. I—"

What did you say to something like that?

There was a tightness in his chest, and he wasn't sure if it was sympathy, or horror, or a kind of sick, guilty gratitude.

Ivan and his friends had been out protesting while he was living on the streets. Wondering every night if he'd wake up the next morning, if the kids he was desperate to protect would wake up. Knowing that no one, anywhere, gave a damn.

But someone had.

"I—wish I'd known," he said softly, at last.

Ivan turned to look at him, and this time his smile was that kind, familiar one that always loosened the knot in Tae's chest.

"I wish you'd known too," he said. "Because there were a hell of a lot of people out there that cared. That still care."

Tae nodded, wordlessly. Ivan's smile broadened a little, crinkling the corners of his eyes, and making Tae's chest ache, in a small, unfamiliar way.

"Anyways," said Ivan, shaking his head briskly. "That's in the past. The important thing is what we're going to do now." He looked up and down the alley. "They haven't found us yet, I take it, but I assume that won't last forever."

Tae shook his head, the worry that had been momentarily dissipated by the sight of Ivan's smile creeping back. "No. We won't be able to stay anywhere for more than a day, if that. The police are going to be looking for us, and with the streets like they are, there will be a lot more of them. And it's not just surviving. I hate to say it, but Masha's right. If we don't do something, every damn street in Prasvishoni will be a battleground, and the kids will be the first to die."

He sighed, leaning back against the wall again. "Once Caz and Peti are up, we'll work on a plan."

Hopefully. He still wasn't sure if what Masha had asked was even possible.

Ivan nodded, and they stood there for a while, leaned against the wall of the alley, close enough that their shoulders almost touched. Neither spoke, but somehow, the silence wasn't uncomfortable.

When at last there was a soft noise behind them, Tae spun on instinct, his hand going to his heat gun.

Peti rolled over in her blankets, blinking, then set up quickly in panic. When she saw Tae, her shoulders dropped in relief. "It's been a while since I've woken up to see you there," she said, her voice raspy with sleep.

Tae smiled at her, despite himself. "I missed you, you know," he said.

Caz woke up a few minutes later, and soon the four of them were crouched on the cold cement of the alley floor around Tae's holoscreen, open to a map of the streets.

Tae took a long breath, and blew it out again. "I told you last night what happened while I was away. If we want to stop things going to hell when word of Grigory and Olyessa gets out, we need to figure out where the fighting's likely to start. I know how the streets looked a year ago, but—"

Peti studied the map for a few moments, her eyes narrowed in thought. Finally, she glanced up.

"Tae. Remember when I was on Grigory's ship?"

He gave a tight nod. That wasn't something he was likely to forget, ever.

"Well, I managed to learn some things while I was there." She pointed to a tangle of streets in the northwest corner. "This is the headquarters for Grigory's boyeviki. I've been keeping track of their movements since we got back, just in case—in case something happened. The other kids tell me what they see when they're in the streets, and I've been marking it down. So ... between that and what

I learned on the ship, I think I have a pretty good idea of the layout."

She bit her lip, then traced a quick shape on one side of the map, and tapped it, shading it orange. "This is Grigory's territory." She drew another slightly larger shape overlaying the first, and tapped again, shading it yellow. "And this is the Blood Riots'. They normally work with Grigory, so it makes sense their territories overlap. But here," she tapped a section of the overlapping shapes, "there've been power struggles. The Blood Riots don't want to give the boyeviki access to their more profitable areas. The boyeviki complain to Grigory about it regularly, but he hasn't intervened yet. I think everyone assumes he will at some point, and so each of them is trying to get themselves entrenched, so when he finally does pay attention, the matter will look already settled. There's no outright war, because they're both afraid of Grigory. But if they hear he's gone ..."

Tae was staring at her. "You—just figured all this out?" he asked at last.

There was a grim set to Peti's expression. "They had me on that ship for two and a half weeks," she said at last. "Believe me, I know more about those bastards than they probably want me to."

She turned back to the map and drew another shape, shaded blue. "These are the Rims, and these are Olyessa's boyeviki." She shaded another overlapping shape purple. "Right now, they're expanding their territory, so there's not much to fight over, but I don't know what will happen if Olyessa's gone." She studied the map again for a few moments, frowning. "If there's going to be fighting, it's probably going to start here. Up north of the university. There's been gang fights there in the past few weeks. It's not a wealthy enough area that the police care much about it, and there's enough alleys and back ways that it's easy to set an ambush. There's something going on a few blocks south of there—communications are locked down, and whatever it is involves the police. But the police have never ventured up here, even though it's just a few blocks away."

Tae nodded slowly. "Alright. So, if we want to stop the violence, we start there." He paused a moment, frowning at the shapes Peti had drawn on the map. "You said it's easy to set an ambush in these streets?"

Peti nodded.

"But if the alleyways weren't empty—that would make it a lot harder, right?"

Caz frowned at him questioningly.

"Street kids," said Tae shortly. "The gangs will kill us if they find us alone, sure, but they don't usually mess with groups of us. If we could get enough street kids moved into the streets there, it might make it inconvenient enough for the gangs that they find somewhere else to fight." He glanced back at his holoscreen. "We're not going to be able to stop the fighting, I know that. But if we can get it out of the residential areas, down in the warehouse sectors maybe, and if they can't take over the best streets because they're already taken—it might keep the killing mostly limited to the gangs and the boyeviki. That's probably the best we can hope for at this point."

"How the hell are we going to convince the street kids to work with us?" asked Caz, his voice grim. "Things are bad out there right now. I've seen kids kill each other over a warm place to sleep."

Tae nodded. "I know. But we figure it out, or they're all going to be killed."

It had been a long time since Tae had walked the streets of Prasvishoni as a street kid. Funny how quickly it came back to you—

the constant vigilance, the way every sound made you spin around, ready to fight or flee.

He kept his eyes on the concrete as he walked, his head down, his shoulders hunched. The less threatening he could look, the easier it would be for people to ignore him. But somehow, it didn't feel as natural to him as it had before, sliding under the radar, shoulders slouched in sullen despair and hopeless impotence.

He'd done too much. He'd started to think that he was someone that could change things.

Here, on the streets, that was dangerous.

The air was cold, a small, bitter breeze biting at his face, and the streets grew narrower and dirtier as he walked.

This was gang territory. Even the street kids tried to avoid it, when they could.

They often couldn't, though. When the police were after them, they went wherever the police didn't dare go. And this, here, was somewhere the police didn't dare go.

Already, from the corner of his eyes, he could see shadows following him down the street, slipping from alley to alley.

They were watching him. They'd noticed him, and they were watching to see if he was someone who could kill them, or someone they could kill.

He hunched down farther into his worn jacket. He'd grabbed the most ragged clothes he could find from the *Ungovernable*—some of the old things he'd brought with him, and some things Masha had scrounged up—but still, they were warmer and nicer than most of the clothing the street kids wore.

He wasn't invisible anymore.

Perhaps he'd forgotten how to be invisible.

Every sense was on edge as he walked. The dirty, grimy, mildew-y industrial buildings loomed over him, some of them abandoned, some of them broken open, perhaps serving to shelter street kids, but more often a brisk drug trade, or weapons trade, or some other activity sanctioned by Grigory Korzhakov.

The running footsteps in the alley ahead were so quiet they were almost inaudible, but Tae was already ducking out of the way when a figure materialized from the alleyway, grabbing for his jacket. He jumped back, jerking his arm up to block a blow that should have doubled him over.

He'd spent way too much time around Jez not to know how to get out of the way of someone's fist.

The figure lunged at him, bringing an elbow around at head height. Tae dived to the side, just in time, and caught his foot around his attacker's ankle as the figure stumbled forward, knocked off balance. Whoever it was went down hard, and Tae spun, ready to end the fight with a kick to his attacker's temple. Then he saw, and pulled up short.

It was a kid, maybe a year younger than Caz. He was skinny, his eyes startlingly big in his pale face, his hair a dirty straw colour, his expression one of sheer hatred.

The boy scrambled to his feet and crouched, looking ready to attack again.

Tae held up his hands. "Easy," he said, heart pounding from the adrenalin of the fight. "Easy. I'm not here to hurt you."

He had damn well changed. A year ago, he might not have hesitated. But he'd grown used to having options, not just kill or be killed.

"Get the hell out of my streets then," the boy hissed. "Get the hell away from here. What do you think you're doing? You're no Blood Riot. You're a street kid, aren't you? You think you can just come in here, with your fancy boots and your fancy coat, and take this? Do you know how hard I fought for this? I've killed plenty of people before, don't care if I kill you."

"I'm not here to take your street," said Tae, still breathing heavily. "I've got my place. I'm not looking for another one."

"What the hell you doing here then?" said the boy, his eyes narrowed. "Group of us here, you know. All of us are killers. Killed for Grigory, killed for the Blood Riots, whatever. Not worried about doing in one more."

From the corner of his eye, Tae could see the shadowy figures that had been following him move closer. He resisted the urge to slip his hand into his pocket and rest it on his heat gun. That wouldn't do him any good here. Not surrounded like this. He'd met plenty of street kids who'd turned killers, and they'd fight until the last spark of life left their body.

He could get the boy in front of him, perhaps, if he could bring himself to shoot a kid. But a gang of them? There was no chance.

His heart pounded, but somehow he managed to steady his breathing.

The moment they thought he was afraid, he was as good as dead.

"Look," he said, trying to catch the kid's eye. "I've got my own kids. We're not looking for anything more than what we have, just trying to stay out of the way of the police."

"Not here you don't," the kid snarled, moving closer.

Behind Tae, the shadows had taken shape—four or five of them, he couldn't get a firm count. All of them skinny, all of them ragged, all of them deadly.

He held up his hands again, palms out. "I'm not trying to take anything. I'm just looking to talk."

"What the hell you want to talk with us about?"

Tae shook his head, trying not to let the trembling in his muscles show. "There's trouble coming. We'll have to work together if we want to live through it."

"We'll have to work together?" The kid's voice was mocking. "You, with your damn fancy boots, and your damn jacket, looking like you haven't gone hungry in your whole damn life."

Tae didn't even see the blow coming, but some instinct warned him, and he ducked as a metal rod whizzed past his head. He spun, and came up facing the girl who'd dealt the blow. Her face was as hard as the face of the boy who'd attacked him, and there was a look in her eyes he'd seen far too often on the streets, someone who'd killed before, and would do it again.

He grabbed her wrist, and she kicked out at him hard, her knee connecting with his thigh. He grunted in pain, twisting her arm up, and hooked the back of her knee with the heel of one boot. She stumbled, losing her balance, and landed on the cement, and Tae snatched the metal bar from her hand and turned quickly, swinging it in a tight arc and catching the wrist of the third kid, another girl, who'd taken advantage of his distraction to try to grab him by the throat. She hissed in pain and lurched back, cradling her wrist, but at the same time, a boy stepped in, catching the edge of Tae's jacket and yanking him forward. Tae stumbled, caught off balance, and the girl he'd knocked to the ground scrambled to her feet and shoved him hard.

He fell, and she dropped onto his back before he could roll away, her knee landing on his spine and knocking the breath from him. She grabbed his arm and twisted it up behind him, and planted her elbow at the base of his neck, shoving his face against the hard, filthy surface.

"Give me the damn pole," she snapped at one of the other kids.

"Gonna kill the bastard."

"Wait," Tae panted, through the blood filling his mouth. "There's trouble coming. You don't listen to me, it'll kill you. None of us are going to stand a damn chance."

The boy who'd first attacked him knelt, bending so he was looking straight into Tae's face. His expression was half suspicious, half mocking.

"Trying to save your life, yeah? You want to keep your pretty face from getting scraped across the concrete, that's the kind of trouble you're worried about, isn't it?"

"Look, I lived on the street my whole damn life," grunted Tae. "Think I'd come into your territory if I didn't have a reason to be here?"

"Grew up here?" The boy's voice was thick with suspicion. "Where did you stay, then? Before the cops started killing us all."

"Rybachka street."

The boy frowned slightly. "What gang?"

The girl holding Tae down dug her knee harder into his spine and shoved his face harder into the pavement.

"Used to be Kira's," he muttered. Blood trickled from his nose, and the iron tang of blood was sharp in his mouth, and she was resting her whole weight on him, making breathing difficult.

The boy was still watching him suspiciously. "Who's gang now?"

"Caz and Peti's. Mine before that."

The boy watched him for a moment longer, eyes narrowed in suspicion. Finally, he pushed himself to his feet, and gestured with a quick jerk of his head to the girl holding Tae. The pressure on Tae's spine increased briefly, and he sucked in a shallow breath as his face was shoved harder into the concrete. Then the pressure released, and the girl let go her grip on his wrist.

He waited for a moment, but when she didn't slam the iron bar into his head, which he'd been pretty sure was going to be her next move, he rolled over painfully and pushed himself to his feet.

The five of them were surrounding him in a loose half-circle. The girl had retrieved her metal bar, and she held it threateningly, and the boy who seemed to be the leader glared at him, eyes narrowed.

"You that tech kid?" he asked at last, voice brusque. "The one that got thrown in jail?"

Tae looked at him warily. Pain throbbed in icy jags down his spine, and his face burned where it had been pushed into the concrete. His muscles were still shaky, but he'd been almost killed plenty of times before, and he knew damn well what his body could do. If it came to it, he could still probably get away.

He might have to kill one of them first. Even back when he'd lived on the streets, he'd never been a killer. But if he was willing to kill them, he could still probably get away.

"Yeah." He leaned back against the wall. No point in letting them get around behind him.

The boy was still watching him. "Heard about you," he said at last. "Heard Vadim Dulik tried to con you. Heard you took him down."

"Yeah," said Tae shortly. "Stupid damn choice. Almost got my gang killed."

"Yeah?" the boy asked. "How come it didn't, then?"

Tae shrugged, then winced as the movement shot another jolt of pain down his spine. "Turned myself in."

"You could have let them take the fall, picked another gang, run with them."

Tae glared at him. "Is that what you would have done? Sold out your friends? Let them burn, just so you could stay safe?"

The boy was still watching him. Finally, though, he shook his head. "No," he said. "No, figure I wouldn't. At least—at least I hope I wouldn't." He paused a moment. "Heard about you, Tae," he said at last. "Didn't believe it, though. Figured if there was a kid on the streets who was as good with tech as they said you were, he'd get himself out, go somewhere, make a name for himself. Lie about who he was and where he came from, let the rest of his gang take care of their own damn selves."

"I don't know about you," said Tae. "But the streets where I grew up, you don't sell out your friends. You die before you sell out your friends."

"Yeah," said the boy softly. "Heard a lot of people say that. Haven't met many who'd actually do it, though, go to jail before they let their friends get hurt." He paused a moment. "Maybe the same kind who'd let himself be jumped by five killers, not even pull the heat gun out of his pocket."

The other four stepped back quickly.

Tae shook his head wearily. "Look," he said shortly. "You said you were killers. You said you're all killers, and you'd do it again. Fine. But I'm not. I've seen a hell of a lot, and I've seen enough to know it's not what I want to do, not unless I have to."

He could still picture the face of that guard he'd killed the morning before, the way she'd screamed as she'd fallen.

"For someone who's not a killer, you sure as hell know how to put up a good fight," the boy said at last, with something that sounded almost like grudging respect.

Tae shrugged.

The kid folded his arms across his chest. "OK. So you want to talk, because there's some big thing coming. Fine. What do you have to say?"

Tae glanced around quickly. "You sure you want to talk here?"

The boy studied him for a moment longer, then gave a short nod. "Follow me."

The five of them slid into the alley the first boy had come out of, as quietly as the mist itself.

Tae drew in a deep breath, fighting down the shakiness in his muscles.

If they'd wanted to kill him, they would have killed him. They'd had plenty of opportunities.

He stepped into the alley after them.

The kids stopped at a narrow opening between two dirty warehouses, and he followed them inside. They crouched on the ground in a semicircle, backs against the wall, and painfully, wincing at the movement, he crouched down to join them.

He told the story quickly, or at least, as much of it as he could—he didn't tell them Grigory and Olyessa were gone, only that he'd heard they might be, soon. No point in letting slip what had happened, and causing the damn thing they were there to prevent.

When he finished, the boy's eyes were still narrowed in suspicion. "So, you think there's problems coming with Grigory, and you don't want a gang war on the streets, that's it?"

Tae nodded shortly. "If there is, there'll be street kids caught in the crossfire."

The boy nodded absently. "Happens every damn time there's a gang war. If you're telling the truth, this'll be a big one. Hell of a lot of dead kids." He looked up at Tae. "So. What you going to do about it?"

Tae sighed. "I know things have been bad. But there's a lot of us still. We're not going to take on the gangs, I'm not that stupid, but the gangs spread out into places where there's not someone to stop them. You stopped me, just about killed me. They've got money, and backing, and weapons, sure. But we're damn tough. You think we could hold the street? A couple streets? If we can get them fighting in the warehouse district instead of out here, that would save a hell of a lot of lives."

The boy watched him for a moment, considering. "So we'd all work together," he said at last. "One big happy family. And let me guess, you'd be in charge of it all."

Tae shook his head. "I've got my own gang to look out for. I don't need any more. We'll figure something out so everyone has a say."

"We have to talk," the boy said abruptly, pushing himself to his feet. "You stay here."

The other four stood, following their leader out into the alley. Tae stayed where he was, leaning back against the alley wall, and closed his eyes for a moment.

Every damn part of him hurt, and he had no idea if this would work. But—if it didn't, there was no point to any of this. There'd be a bloodbath on the streets of Prasvishoni, no matter what Jez and Lev and the others could do.

It felt like an eternity, but was probably closer to ten standard minutes, when the street kids returned. Tae glanced up as the boy stepped into the opening, face set, and despite himself, he felt his heart rate speed up.

Either they'd agreed, or they were going to kill him.

"We're coming," the boy said tersely. "We talked about it. If you're right about what's coming, it's probably the only way we stay alive." He paused, and shook his head. "Maybe I'm not you, Tae. But—" he glanced at the other four, and Tae recognized that look, care, and concern, and the sick weight of responsibility. He'd known that look since he was fifteen. "I don't want them to die," he finished at last, softly. "They count on me. I'm not going to let them get shot." He held out a hand to Tae, and after a moment, Tae took it. The boy pulled him to his feet, and Tae sucked in a sharp, painful breath.

The boy smiled reluctantly. "My name's Felix," he said. "In case you need to know. And I don't know if it makes you feel better, but I think you broke Nadia's wrist."

Tae shook his head wearily. "It—doesn't make me feel better." He hesitated. "I have a friend. I think he knows how to set bones. I'll ask him if he can do something."

The boy nodded, a faint hint of respect appearing in his expression. "Alright." He paused. "When are we going to meet?"

"You have a com?" Tae asked.

The boy nodded, and held out his wrist. The com he wore was ancient tech, probably something scrounged from the garbage heap, or pawned off on him by one of the Blood Riots.

"Let me see it," said Tae.

The boy looked at him suspiciously for a moment, then slowly unstrapped the com from his wrist and held it out. Tae took it, turning it over quickly and examining it.

Old tech, but then, he was very, very used to working with old tech.

He tapped it, and brought up the flickering holoscreen. He frowned at it for a moment, then began typing rapidly. When he finished, he handed the com back to the boy. "Here. I've hooked you into a closed loop. Police shouldn't be able to tap in." He paused a moment. "If I don't call you tonight, or by tomorrow morning at the latest, it's because something's happened to me."

"And if something does happen to you?" Felix asked.

Tae shrugged grimly. "You know what's happening. You know

other street kids you can talk to. Do what you can."

The boy nodded. "Good luck," he said finally.

"Same to you," said Tae, bending to slip past them out into the alley.

There was the faintest noise from out of the street, and the boy cursed, shoving Tae back and gesturing the others in after him. "It's the police," he hissed. "They're getting braver."

For a few moments, the six of them sat completely still, ears straining for any sound.

And then a spherical drone, cut with the three black police stripes, darkened the entrance.

Tae had a fraction of a second to see the panic on Felix's face, then he'd yanked his modded heat pistol from his pocket, pulling the trigger as he turned. The white-hot blast that exploded from it was almost enough to blind him, the blowback heat scorching the hair from the backs of his hands.

The drone melted.

"Go!" Tae hissed, turning to the kids. "Get out, now! They'll be in here as soon as they realize the tracking disappeared." He grabbed Felix by the shoulder and shoved him towards the alley. The others followed, and Tae ducked out behind them. Then they were running for their lives.

"What the hell was that gun you used?" Felix said through his teeth, glancing over his shoulder.

"I have a friend who knows weapons," Tae panted.

"Damn right they do," the boy muttered breathlessly.

They broke out of the alley and into a street, and Felix glanced around quickly. "Follow me," he snapped at Tae. "I know a place we might be safe."

Tae glanced back over his shoulder. He couldn't see the pursuing police yet, but they'd be here.

He gave a sharp shake of his head. "No. We'll split up. Maybe some of them will follow me."

"How will you—" the boy started, then he stopped. "That's right. The gun."

Tae give him a tight smile. "I know the streets too, remember? I might not have to use it. Now go!"

The kids took off in one direction, and he took off in the other.

When he finally reached the place he and Peti and the others had agreed to meet, he was almost staggering from a combination of weariness and pain, but according to his tracker, he'd lost any pursuit.

Caz was already waiting, and stood up quickly, concern on his face. "Tae? You alright? What happened?"

Tae shook his head wearily and sank back against the wall. "It's fine. It's nothing. Just—a bunch of street kids. Killers. They took some convincing."

"How bad are you hurt?" Caz's voice was sharp with worry.

Tae tried to smile. "It could've been worse. I thought they were going to kill me."

Caz gave a faint, reluctant smile in return. "I'm glad they didn't."

Tae blew out a long breath. "So am I."

The others arrived shortly after. Peti frowned when she saw the bruises on Tae's face, and Ivan's expression was cut with concern, but aside from asking if he was alright, neither of them said anything.

They pulled this off, or they died. The rest couldn't matter.

"How are we doing?" asked Tae, when they'd all gathered.

"I got a couple street kid gangs to listen," said Caz, his face still creased with worry. "They're scared, though. No one wants to draw attention. With the police the way they are right now—" he shrugged helplessly.

"Same," said Peti. "This is only going to work if we can convince them we can actually pull this off."

Tae shook his head in frustration and turned to Ivan. "You?"

"I found a few people I knew in the cheap government housing. Some of them are willing to listen, maybe help out. But—it's not a lot."

Tae nodded.

Everything they'd done, put together, wasn't a lot. It was hardly anything, really. But it was all they had, so somehow, they'd have to make it work anyway.

9

Lev, day 1, evening

Lev glanced up quickly as the lock on the apartment door clicked, then relaxed as Jez stepped through.

She let the door swing shut behind her and grinned. "Well, that was more interesting than I thought it'd be."

He smiled back, despite himself. "It was certainly—instructive."

She raised an eyebrow at him. "Alright genius, I've been around you long enough to know you're drooling to see what's on the chip in my com. So, just because I like you—" She tapped her com, pulled the chip out, and tossed it to him. "I'm going to see what they have around here for food, then we can take a look."

He nodded, examining the chip.

It was lousy with security features, but Tae had spent an entire hour writing code on both his and Jez's com, and he'd told them it should be able to spoof any government security.

He slipped the chip into his com, halfway holding his breath, but no alarm sounded, and the information didn't disappear, so after a moment, he sat down on the small, hard couch, pulling the holoscreen in front of him.

"Genius. Catch," called Jez from the kitchen. He looked up just in

"

time to grab for the rations pack she'd tossed. She was grinning, and he smiled despite himself. She came over, hesitated for a moment, then settled herself on the couch beside him.

He leaned his head back, closing his eyes and willing himself to bloody well be sensible.

Sensible had been something that came to him naturally, once. Something he didn't even have to think about. Completely losing his composure just because a grinning, cocky pilot dropped herself down on the couch beside him, peering up the holoscreen in front of them with skeptical interest, was not something he'd ever believed he would be guilty of.

And yet, here he was.

He sighed to himself, and turned to Jez.

Which, honestly, might have been a mistake. She'd glanced over at him at the same time, and his eyes caught hers, and he had to swallow hard, turning his head away with an effort.

"Did you—" he cleared his throat. "I assume they gave you the passcode?"

She nodded and reached over him to tap something into his com, and he took a deep breath, trying to ignore the way her body pressed up against his. A moment later, a screen with a long list of names scrawled across it opened up in front of them.

Jez grinned and sat back, and Lev let out a shallow breath and squinted at the screen, trying to bring his brain back into a functioning state again. After a moment, Jez leaned in as well, peering at the list of names. Her foot jiggled an impatient rhythm against the edge of the couch, and he could hear the restless tapping of her fingers on her leg.

He turned to her and managed a smile, despite the knot in his stomach—or perhaps because of it. He paused a moment. "We—

should probably call Masha," he said at last, reluctantly.

Jez stilled, and gave him a long look. "Yeah," she said. "I—suppose we should."

They hadn't actually talked about what had happened with Masha, not since their conversation in the fake pleasure house two days ago. There hadn't been time. But something had changed. And he had no idea how Jez felt about Masha anymore.

"Are you alright?" he asked softly.

She nodded, smiling with an obvious effort. "Yeah. Yeah, I am. I—I just—" she swallowed hard. "She would've killed you, I think. If her plan didn't work." She shifted, moving closer to him on the couch. "And I—I can't lose you, OK?" Her voice choked, just a little. "I—I can't."

Damn, damn, damn. His throat was dry, his heart beating too quickly, and something ached inside his chest.

He looked away quickly. "I'll call her, then," he mumbled. From the corner of his eye he saw Jez nod, and he hit his com.

"Lev," came Masha's familiar voice through the com a moment later. "I assume you were successful?"

"Perhaps more importantly," said Tanya dryly, "I am assuming that right now you're being watched through the window. I'm also assuming that you've both realized this and are behaving appropriately."

Lev glared at the com, although he knew she couldn't see it. "Yes," he said through his teeth. "Thank you for your concern."

Tanya gave a soft chuckle. "I am sorry it's uncomfortable. But the alternative is that we all die, and the system devolves into a bloodbath, so you'll excuse me if I don't worry too much about your feelings." She paused for a moment. "And, judging from how you were acting today by the docks, I'm going to tell you—whatever you're doing, it's not enough. You're sitting on the same couch, at least?"

"Yes," said Lev through his teeth.

"Good. Please, for all our sakes, make it convincing." She paused a moment, amusement in her tone. "Don't worry, I won't ask for details."

Lev bit back a sigh, and glanced over at Jez. She shrugged and shifted closer to him, tucked her legs under her, and leaned her head against his shoulder. He put his arm around her and pulled her in, trying, with every bit of willpower in his body, not to think about what he was doing.

But the way she fit against him, the rise and fall of her breathing against his chest, the warmth of her body, made that much more difficult than it probably should have been.

"Well," said Masha, her tone slightly amused, "When you're ready, I would very much appreciate hearing what you've learned."

At least, he was fairly certain that was what she'd said. For some reason, he was having a difficult time focusing on the conversation.

If this had been the first time he'd held Jez, if the feel of her pressed against him didn't bring back so many memories—he and Jez wrapped together in a faded easy chair, her head tipped back, eyes closed, her hand trailing up his back, his lips on her skin—

No. He shook his head ruefully. It wouldn't make it easier. Nothing in the system would make this easier.

"Lev."

He took a deep breath, and blew it out again. "We—just started going through the information ourselves, but I think this is going to be extremely helpful. They gave Jez a list of people who would have to be neutralized to keep Grigory out of power." He paused a moment. "I—assume that's what you intended them to do when you sent that message from Grigory."

"That was the hope," Masha murmured.

He walked them quickly through the information, scrolling through it on his com as he spoke. Jez's head rested on his shoulder, and she'd settled herself against him, the angles of her body fitting comfortably into the hollows of his, her warmth bleeding through him, comforting and comfortable.

His stomach was knotted so tightly hurt, but it was a pleasant sort of pain.

And it was fine. He could put his arm around her shoulder, like a friend, and she could rest her head on him, and there was nothing at all significant in that, except the fact they cared about each other. And whatever was speeding up his heart rate, quickening his breath, tightening that knot in his stomach, was something he could simply refuse to think about.

"I can't send this through to your com, not with the security they have on it," he said. "But I should be able to make a copy, and then I can do a drop."

"That may be the best plan," said Tanya. She paused a moment. "I'll send you coordinates for a drop spot on your com. We can arrange it for tomorrow morning."

"And Jez will be meeting with Branka on this subject tomorrow, correct?"

"Yep," said Jez, shifting slightly so her head settled further into his shoulder. Almost unconsciously, he let his hand run down her arm and pulled her just a little closer. She obliged, her body relaxing into his, her grin turning soft and dreamy.

"Very well," said Masha. "We'll wait for your report before we send our next message. Assuming the information on your chip is accurate, we'll be able to start targeting specific individuals." She hesitated a moment. "Good luck, to both of you."

Lev tapped off his com and turned to glance over at Jez. She was smiling slightly, eyes fixed idly on where the holoscreen had been, and he found himself smiling as well, watching her.

She turned, and her eyes caught his.

Their faces, he realized, were only centimetres apart.

He should turn away. He should look away right now. But he didn't, and she didn't either. He could see the rise and fall of her breath coming faster. Hell, he could feel it, because she was pressed up against him, and his arms were around her, and he could practically feel the beating of her heart against his own chest. And it was taking every spark of willpower he possessed to keep him from gathering her into his arms, pulling her up against him, catching her lips with his—

Damn. Damn this to hell.

Her lips parted slightly, as if she was about to speak, but she didn't. He swallowed hard, his throat completely dry. He was still staring into her eyes, like there was nothing else except her in the entire system, and she was staring into his, and damn it to hell, he didn't know how long they'd been here, or how much longer he could stand this, and every muscle his body was tingling—

With a herculean effort, he turned his head away, sucking in a long breath, perhaps the first breath he'd taken in five standard minutes.

Jez turned away quickly as well, and he could still feel her breathing against his side, short and rapid, the way her heart pounded.

With an effort that felt almost impossible, he took his arm off from her shoulders. She shifted, standing abruptly, facing away from him as if trying to regain her composure. Which was just as well, because he wasn't sure if he could look at her again just yet.

He closed his eyes, and took a long breath.

"Well, genius," she said finally, her voice shaky. "It's, um—been a pretty long day, I guess. Probably should get to bed. I mean, got that damned meeting I have to be at in the morning."

"Yes," he said, running his hand over his face. "Yes, you're right, that would probably be wise." His words came out more or less steady, which was a lot more than he'd expected, honestly.

She turned to him at last, with a grin that looked slightly forced. "Anyway, guess I'll bring our stuff into the bedroom—" Her words faltered.

They stared at each other for a moment, and he could see the realization dawning on her face at the same time he felt the realization dawning on his own.

The bedroom.

Because they were supposed to be lovers, and the government had given them an apartment, and it had one bedroom.

"It'll be fine," she said quickly, but the grin on her face was strained. "Bed's probably plenty big. Hell, after sleeping on those tiny cots on the damn pleasure planet, we probably won't even know each other are there."

He would absolutely know she was there. Even from here, in the living room, on the couch, he would know she was there.

How the hell had he agreed to this?

For one desperate moment, he thought about volunteering to sleep on the couch—but that wouldn't exactly make him look like a man who'd been waiting for his lover for months.

He managed a smile. "You're right. We're both used to sleeping in tight quarters." He paused a moment. "I'll—stay out here for a bit. I'll need some more time with the information to make sure I can get

Masha what she needs."

That wasn't entirely the truth. But it was the truth that going into the bedroom, with Jez, right now, would be a very bad idea. Even if he did somehow manage to survive lying down next to her without combusting, which he was not at all certain he would, it was still all he could do to get the picture out of his brain of a sleepy-eyed, tousled Jez, waking up next to him on his cot on the *Ungovernable.*

He couldn't afford to add to it the picture of her drifting off to sleep, curled up beside him.

And yes, no matter what he did, he'd know she was there, but at the same time, if he could stay out here until he was very certain she was already sleeping, there was just a chance he might survive the night.

She turned and headed towards the bedroom, and he sighed, turning back to the holoscreen.

Despite his best efforts, he could hear her open the bedroom door, the rustle of her undressing, the soft thump of her clothes hitting the floor. The sound of running water as she splashed her face and got ready for bed, the creak of the ancient cot frame as she lay down.

He determinedly ignored it.

He found, however, he'd been reading the same lines of text over and over for almost ten standard minutes without realizing it.

At last, when he was tired enough that his eyes were drifting shut of their own accord, and he hadn't heard a movement from the bedroom in at least twenty standard minutes, he sighed reluctantly, closed down the holoscreen, and stood. He took a deep breath, shook his head at himself, and went into the bedroom, turning out the lights behind him as he went.

Jez had left the bedroom light on for him. She was a huddled shape under the blankets, her head thrown back, black hair falling in a short, tangled mess across the pillow, mouth partly open. She was snoring slightly, a handful of blankets shoved up against her face.

He watched her for a moment, a fond, rueful smile creeping across his face.

He wasn't even completely sure what it was about her. But somehow, she was exactly what he'd always needed. And even if she wasn't going to be what he'd once hoped she would—at least she was here. And he was heart-stoppingly grateful for it.

He undressed quickly, pulling on his pyjamas, and crawled into bed, keeping as close to the edge as he dared without falling off. And even though he was acutely aware of Jez—the soft sounds of her breathing, the faint movement of the cot pad when she shifted in her sleep, the warmth of her that bled through the blankets—and even though he'd been a hundred percent certain that he would lie awake all night, staring at the ceiling—the exhaustion and the strain of the day, and all the days before it, was more than he'd realized.

He was asleep before he had time to roll over on his pillow.

He thought he'd dream about Jez.

Instead, he dreamed about the pleasure planet—a child, injured and half starved, laid out on the floor of their tiny hangar bay, Galina kneeling beside him, a look of hopeless despair in her face. People in cages, people shackled with mag cuffs, Ivan, a bright red line of blood welling from the cut around his neck like a macabre necklace. The look on Grigory's face, back on his ship, when he'd sat back to watch a man tortured to death. When he'd invited Lev in, assuming Lev would enjoy the entertainment as much as he did.

Lev groaned and rolled over in his sleep, half awake, but not awake enough to stop dreaming, not awake enough to get the pictures out of his mind.

"Genius?" someone murmured sleepily. And he wasn't sure if it was a dream or reality, but his mind caught at desperately at the voice.

And finally, he did dream about Jez. And at last, to dreams of her curled in his arms, he drifted into a peaceful sleep.

He woke the next morning to the hint of light oozing in through the closed bedroom window. He sighed in contentment, and tightened his arm around Jez. Her head was on his shoulder, one arm flung across his chest, her leg tossed over his so they were half tangled together. He pulled her closer, bringing his other arm up to smooth her mussed hair and run down her back, and he closed his eyes, feeling more at peace than he had for—he couldn't remember how long, actually.

And then the rest of his brain woke up, and he stiffened abruptly, eyes snapping open.

He glanced over.

Jez was still asleep, and at his movement she shifted slightly, groaning and nestling her face deeper into his shoulder.

Damn.

Carefully, he removed his arm from around her back, and carefully, he released his grip on her waist with his other arm, placing it gently on the bed beside her.

She stirred again, moaned, and tightened her arm around his chest, snuggling in closer. One of her eyes opened halfway, closed again, and then, a moment later, both her eyes snapped open as well.

She stared at him with a horror that might have been almost comical in other circumstances, and then scrambled backwards, ending up against the far wall, eyes wide and slightly horrified. "I'm —sorry. I—I didn't—I—"

Lev managed a small chuckle. "Jez. It's fine. You were asleep."

"Yeah. Um. I'm—I didn't mean—" her voice trembled slightly.

He shook his head and smiled at her. "Jez. Honestly. It's fine. It was cold last night. I was probably the warmest thing close."

Her face was still a mixture of horror, shock, and the startled, not-quite-awake look of someone who'd been sleeping only seconds before. Gradually, though, her tense posture relaxed, and she managed a shaky grin. "What, you always brag about how hot you are?"

"Jez—" He was smiling, though.

She gave a shaky laugh, then rubbed her eyes, blinking hard. She leaned back, stretched, and crawled to the foot of the bed and stumbled off it, landing ungracefully on the floor and wincing slightly.

"Damn. Must've been a hell of a lot more tired than I thought," she mumbled, glancing at her com. "Anyway, guess I better get ready. Since I'm supposed to be showing up for some fancy-schmancy meeting with that bastard Branka in a standard hour or so." She stumbled into the bathroom, and he could hear the water running in the shower.

He sighed to himself, trying to erase the muscle memory of Jez's head on his shoulder, of pulling her close, of the perfect, comfortable rightness of it all. Then he stood, stretched, and dressed quickly.

Probably best to be out of the room before Jez finished her shower, since he'd long since learned that her sense of awkwardness about getting dressed in front of other people was essentially nonexistent.

He checked the cupboards, and pulled out a box of something that looked like breakfast mix. Better quality than what his parents had made for him when he was a child, probably, but he was fairly certain it would taste about the same. He started a pot of water boiling, then pull up his com, inserted another chip, and typed the command Tae had assured him would make a blind copy of any information without triggering security factors.

It worked, but slowly, and by the time it was finished Jez had emerged, with dripping hair, but thankfully, clothed, and breakfast was ready. He placed the pot on the table, along with two bowls and spoons, and she quirked an eyebrow at him.

"Didn't know you were a cook, genius."

He smiled. "I'm not sure making breakfast mix makes me a cook."

She shrugged. "More than I ever did. All I'm saying is, good thing they have a bunch of different kinds of ration packs. Probably would have starved to death otherwise." She reached over and grabbed a ration pack from the cupboard. "Maybe I'll learn how to make breakfast mix someday," she said over her shoulder.

He gave her an odd look. "I—made enough for both of us. If you want."

She turned to look at him. After a moment, she put the ration pack back in the cupboard, and mumbled, "I wasn't saying I didn't like ration packs."

He shook his head. "Jez. That's not why I did it. I just—" he shrugged. "We're friends. And you were getting ready, and I was making breakfast anyway."

She studied him for a moment, cautiously. Finally, she said, "Thanks."

They ate quickly. The meal was slightly uncomfortable—Jez wouldn't meet his eye, whether because of the breakfast or because of the way they'd woken up, he wasn't sure—but honestly, it was just as well.

When they'd finished, she pulled on her jacket. "Damn meeting's going to start in ten minutes, so I'd better go. Figure it'll take me—"

she squinted one eye. "Hell, if I hurry, probably can get there a minute early." She paused a moment. "Maybe I should wait a minute, grab—"

He glanced at his own com and jumped up in sudden panic. "No, Jez, you've got to get going. Right now. You're going to be late for sure."

She gave him a skeptical glance. "I walk fast. Anyway, figure she won't be expecting me exactly on time."

He was already grabbing her bag and bundling it into her hand. "Jez! Go, for the Lady's sake! If you don't show up, with how jumpy everyone is, she may just assume you're not coming and send someone to kill us both."

She rolled her eyes at him. "Relax, genius. Haven't you ever been late for something before?" But she accepted the bag he shoved into her hand, and the ration packs he shoved into her other hand, and stepped out the door, shooting him a jaunty grin. "I have my com on. It'll be a hell of a lot easier to pull this off if you're out of the shower by the time I'm supposed to be saying something smart."

"I'll be out of the shower," he said through gritted teeth. "Just go."

She winked at him, then pulled the door closed behind her, and he could hear her footsteps heading down the hallway.

He sighed in relief and slumped back into his chair at the table. He took a couple of deep breaths, until he was at least mostly recovered, sighed, ran his fingers through his hair, and glanced quickly around the apartment.

No shower this morning, then. He couldn't risk missing anything from this meeting.

He stood, rubbed his hand across his face, and pulled on a jacket and a heavy scarf. He slipped the com chip he'd copied into his pocket, and glanced at his com as he made his way down the stairs, checking the location Tanya had sent through for the drop. He had about a standard hour to get there, but it would take about twenty minutes to walk, and, unlike Jez, he didn't want to arrive just in the nick of time.

At the door to the street, he paused a moment, drawing in a deep breath.

Jez would be in the meeting at any minute now, and besides getting to the drop on time, he had to be prepared for any questions they might put to her.

One slip-up would be one too many.

10

Jez, day 3

When Jez arrived at the meeting room, it looked like everyone else was already there. Branka, at least, was glaring at her.

Jez smirked. She'd been glared at by people like Masha and Tanya, and this woman was a damn amateur.

"Layla," said the woman, her tone icy. "Nice of you to join us this morning."

Jez settled herself into the only remaining chair, leaning back luxuriously, and gave Branka her most innocent smile.

Thing was, if she was being honest with herself, she was still feeling just a little bit shakier than she had any right to be.

Maybe it was the fact that if they didn't pull this off exactly right, they'd all die. On the other hand, that was basically the story of her whole life so far. Or maybe—maybe it had something to do with the moment she'd opened her eyes that morning, the feeling of utter contentment that had come over her at the warmth of Lev's body next to hers, the feel and shape and smell of him, the way they fit together—until she realized, and jerked backwards away from him.

And then the absolutely ridiculous disappointment that had flooded through her when she could no longer feel his body against hers.

Anyway, didn't matter. They'd actually been figuring this stupid friend crap out, and hell, only natural for things to get a little confusing sometimes, seeing as they apparently had to pretend to be lovers in order, as usual, to keep themselves from being killed.

Didn't mean anything.

Branka glared at her for a few moments more, then turned back to the rest of the table. "Now that we're all here and we can begin," she said, her voice oozing irritation, "I assume all of you looked through the information on your coms last night?"

Around the table, the others were nodding and muttering grim-faced assent.

"Then I will only emphasize the urgency of the situation," said Branka. "If Grigory has decided to make his move, it is vital that we marginalize those who are on his payroll as expeditiously as possible." She looked around. "In this room, we can speak frankly. If you have suggestions, please present them."

One of the men in the back stirred and cleared his throat. "Branka," he said. "Olyessa has already gained significant influence. Perhaps our best bet at this point is to bring her fully on board. There's certainly no love lost between her and Grigory."

"Jez—" Lev's voice in her earpiece was worried.

She rolled her eyes, and tapped out in pilot's code below the table, *I know, genius. On it.*

"That was my thought as well," said Branka. "Olyessa has a powerful infrastructure, and she has access to Vitali's weapons. This is a fragile time, and perhaps allies are our best option."

"I agree," said a woman from across the table. "We don't have time to—"

"Hold on just a sec," said Jez lazily. "I thought the reason we got into all this trouble in the first place was, we put too many of our credits in Gregory's bank, and now he's walking off with them. You really sure Olyessa won't do the same?"

The woman frowned at her. "We don't have much of a choice at this point. And we've worked with Olyessa for quite some time now."

"Because you're scared of her," Jez drawled. "Afraid you won't be able to run the system without the mafia's muscle to back you up, right? Look, maybe I haven't spent much time in Prasvishoni, but I've spent a damn lot of time living." She glanced around the table, tipping her chair back and balancing it there. "We go running to Olyessa right now, she'll know how desperate we are. She'll know she has us exactly where she wants us. And believe me, she won't forget it."

"Really?" Branka's voice was soft with menace. "Tell me, Layla, since you know so much, how exactly do you know Olyessa? I was under the impression that you mostly worked in the Auditing Department."

"You worked with the Outer-Planetary Resources Department over the last six months, because their department was in charge of filtering weapons and weapons tech through to the Internal Security department. It was through an intermediary, and there's no records of you actually having been in the meetings, but then again, those are the kinds of meetings that they wouldn't have a record of your participation. You were pretty high up, and they wouldn't want anyone of your status to be implicated if anything got out." Lev's voice, calm and measured, but with that slight hint of strain underneath it, was as comforting as home.

Jez grinned at Branka and shrugged. "Guess they didn't tell you about the deal Olyessa was making with the Outer-Planetary Resources Department. Someone high-up like you, thought they would've mentioned it, but hell—"

The woman frowned at her. "You weren't in those meetings," she said, a hint of uncertainty creeping into her voice.

"Well, but see, they like me out there," said Jez, still grinning. "Not going to stick my name on the meeting list, not when it could get out to people like—" she glanced meaningfully around the room, and enjoyed the insulted looks on the faces around her.

Branka's eyebrows lowered, but she appeared to have run out of objections.

"So." Jez let her chair drop back to the ground, the sound loud in the silence. "Anyone else want to talk about my credentials? Or shall we talk about how the hell we're going to deal with this bastard Grigory?"

The glares that the people around the table were directing at her could probably have burned through metal at this point. At last, though, the younger man in the back of the room who Lev had pointed out the day before, said, "Layla has a point. It's one thing to make a bargain with Olyessa when we're the ones with the power. But she'll have heard Grigory's message too. He wasn't exactly being subtle about it. She'll know why we're coming, and she'll know she has us exactly where she wants us."

"That's Milo. He's the son of one of the ministers who has the Secretary General's ear," said Lev quietly in her earpiece. "He's young enough, and his family's important enough, that he's not beholden to anyone."

"So what do you suggest?" asked Branka, her voice still icy. "We don't have access to Vitali's weapons tech without her. We have our stockpiles, but nothing like what Olyessa has access to."

"The Outer-Planetary Resources Department was able to bargain for a large amount of new tech," murmured Lev. "Enough to arm all the police and the government forces in Prasvishoni, and have plenty left over. It's not widely known yet, and Branka could probably get it diverted here if she pulled the right strings."

"I … suppose we could—" the young man's voice was slightly less certain now.

Jez tilted her chair back again. "Branka. Might want to look at your notes on those meetings I was in. Might find the list of the tech we skinned off Olyessa interesting."

Branka turned to glare at her. Her face was still cold, but now there was a thoughtful note in her expression. "My notes reference a large shipment. How much?"

Jez relayed the information that Lev whispered into her ear, grinning to herself.

The woman's eyebrows raised as Jez spoke. "Are you certain?"

"Have it on the best authority," drawled Jez.

"Then I agree with Layla," said the young man. "We can purge Grigory's people, and freeze Olyessa's people out at the same time. When we come to her, we want to do it from a position of strength."

"And, thing about Olyessa is, wouldn't take much for her to come to the same conclusion Grigory did—that we're better marks than allies. Probably best to keep anyone in the pay of either of those bastards as far away from power as we can, if we want to keep them from sabotaging crap," Jez added helpfully.

"I shall certainly keep your advice in mind," said Branka. Her voice was still cold, but she was watching Jez with interest.

They talked for a while longer. Jez manage to pay attention to most of it, honestly, but by the end, her mind was wandering. Now they were talking about crap like who they were going to put where, and why, and how whoever-the-hell was likely to react, and honestly, yes, this was probably important. But hell, this was Lev's area of expertise, not hers. Her com was on, and she was certain he was still listening, from the occasional thoughtful "hmm" through her earpiece.

She grinned to herself. She could picture him, sitting on the edge of the damn couch, that little frown creasing his forehead, holoscreen pulled up in front of him.

She tapped her foot against the leg of her chair, and drummed her fingers on the table, and glanced around at the others to try to keep herself from going absolutely insane.

There was a clear division among the people around the table.

There was Branka, whose expression was one of neutral, if grim, interest. She didn't belong to either group, if Jez was any judge.

Then there was the young man, Milo, who'd spoken up in support of Jez's idea. His eyes were narrowed in concentration as he listened, but there was a look of faint enthusiasm about his face that was mirrored by that of a few others, mostly the younger members of the group.

And then …

And then there was the bastard sitting across from her.

He was an older man, with pale skin and steel grey hair, and a military bearing. He was broad-shouldered and heavy with muscle, but it wasn't any of those things that drew her attention.

It was the fact that he was looking at her like he'd happily burn her alive.

And he wasn't the only one. That was the other group—the ones that weren't looking interested, or enthusiastic, or even thoughtful. The ones who looked like basically they wanted to get her somewhere quiet, and then take her apart with their bare hands.

Hey Lev, she tapped out. *Who's the bastard sitting across from me? Old plaguer, grey hair, looks like he's got a stick up his butt?*

There was a faint sigh through her earpiece. "I've never heard him described in those exact terms. But my guess would be Jaromil." Lev's voice had taken on a tinge of concern. "He's not going to be happy about your suggestion. He's leaning in Olyessa's direction, and I suspect she's paying him off, although I can't be certain."

I'd say 'not very happy' is an understatement, she tapped back.

"He's the one Masha believes is most likely to have the information we need about government infrastructure, and possibly about the identity of the code-name. But—be careful," he said quietly. "He's dangerous."

Jez glanced back up at the man. He met her gaze, and there was a cruelty in his eyes that almost made her shiver.

She winked at him, and his expression went even colder.

"… would you agree with that, Layla?"

She glanced up at Branka, startled. The woman was watching her with a piercing look.

Jez gave her breezy grin.

Damn.

"You do," came the Lev's voice in her ear.

"'Course I do," she said with a slight smirk.

The woman raised her eyebrows. "And what would be your reasoning?"

"You feel that the addition of Ludie to the ministry would balance power between the people who are pro-Olyessa and the people who are neutral, and will end up tying the hands of the one official higher up who's in Grigory's camp."

She repeated what Lev had just said, with a couple "bastards" thrown in.

The woman looked at her for a moment. "Perhaps you're right," she said at last, reluctantly.

Across the table, Milo was smiling delightedly, and Jaromil, who apparently wanted to basically murder her, looked—well, even more like he wanted to basically murder her.

She grinned.

Despite the mind-numbing boredom, this government crap was actually turning out to be more interesting than she'd thought.

At last, the meeting broke up. The various members stood, stretching and speaking in low voices to each other. Branka stood as well and stepped up beside Jez. "I've assigned two aides to take you to your private office," she said, with mild distaste. "I've put you somewhere where it will be more difficult for someone to kill you." She paused, giving Jez a piercing look. "Although I must add, you are taking quite a bold position. It would not surprise me in the slightest if there will be people out there who wanted you dead."

Jez quirked an eyebrow at her. "Basically the story of my whole life," she said easily.

"I'm beginning to believe that," Branka muttered. She sighed, and gestured Jez ahead of her out the doorway.

A young man and a young woman, with the fresh, scrubbed appearance of people young enough to actually gave a damn about impressing their employers, were waiting for her.

They both looked nervous.

Branka gestured to Jez. "This is Layla. Please take her to her office and get her situated."

She turned back to the room, touching the arm of one of the other ministers and drawing him to one side, their heads bowed in conversation.

Jez raised her eyebrow at the two kids and was about to speak when a hand gripped her arm. She jerked around, hand going to where she usually kept her heat pistol.

The gray-haired man stood there. His eyes were cold, and his grip on her arm uncomfortably tight. "Layla," he growled. "You presented some rather controversial views in the meeting today."

She grinned at him, her heart beating slightly faster.

Now that she saw him up close, she figured Lev was probably right. He was dangerous.

And apparently, she'd managed to get pretty damn far onto his bad side.

"I don't know," she said jauntily, "figure it was only controversial if you're too stupid to figure it out yourself. Or," she added, "if you're a damn bastard who's on Olyessa's payroll."

From the look on his face, she'd just made him hate her even more. She actually hadn't been sure that was possible.

His hand tightened on her arm, his face darkening. "Layla," he began, and there was something soft and dangerous in his tone.

"Ask him about a man named Pyotr," came Lev's urgent voice through her earpiece.

She grinned up at the man. "Hey, you want to talk about something controversial, maybe you and I can have a conversation about Pyotr."

His hand dropped from her arm as if she'd bitten him, and his face went suddenly pale. "I'm—not sure what you're talking about."

"Yeah?" Her heart was still pounding like a damn desert rabbit. "Well, see, and I don't know what you're talking about when you say my opinions are controversial. So." She quirked an eyebrow at him. "Figure you and I can get along just fine, as long as I don't see any problems with Pyotr, and—" she paused delicately, "you don't see any problems with me saying we should get that bastard Olyessa's people out of power."

He looked at her for a long time. Under the fear in his eyes, the hatred burned like a damn sun. At last, though, he gave a short nod. "For the moment, perhaps you're right," he murmured.

But his eyes followed her as she walked away behind the two clearly terrified aides, and she could feel his gaze burning a hole in the back of her shirt.

"Jez. Are you alright?" Lev asked, his voice strained.

She took a deep breath, trying to settle her shakiness. *Yep,* she tapped out. *Figure I am, thanks to you. He has that information crap Masha wants, right?*

"Yes." The relief was clear in his voice. "But—"

Good. She was grinning. *Because it would have been a bit embarrassing otherwise. Seeing as I just stole the key chip to his office.*

There was a long, long moment of silence from the other end of the com, during which she pictured Lev quietly going through every swear word in his vocabulary. When he spoke, though, his voice was calm, if strained. "That's—probably a good thing, I suppose. Just—please be careful, alright?"

Sure, genius, she tapped out. *Not planning to break in today anyways—going to copy the chip onto my com and then drop it back in the conference room before he figures out it's gone and starts getting suspicious, and then I have to figure out what his schedule is so I know when he'll be out.*

Still … there was something about the tone in Lev's voice, and the memory of Jaromil's cold gaze, that sent a small shiver down her back.

11

Ysbel, day 3

When Tanya returned, late that afternoon, from retrieving the chip from Lev, there was a grim look on her face.

Ysbel pulled her wife in for a quick kiss. "What is it, my Tanya?"

Tanya sighed, and gave her a small smile. "By some miracle, our crazy pilot and our scholar are still alive. But—" she shook her head. "They're being watched, even more closely than I'd expected. The whole city is like an insect nest that's been kicked. The gangs, the government—everyone's on edge."

Ysbel nodded, and tried to smile. "They'll be fine. Lev is very smart, and I think our lunatic pilot has spent her whole life with people wanting to kill her."

Tanya gave a faint answering smile, but Ysbel knew she could hear the bravado in the words.

Masha straightened from behind the communication device, where she'd been crouched. "Tanya," she said. "Everything went as planned?"

Tanya nodded and handed her the chip, and Masha slipped it into her com and pulled up the holoscreen.

They studied the screen in silence for a few moments. Ysbel was no government expert, but even she could tell that the names, listed with their mafia affiliations, were an invaluable resource.

Finally Masha looked up at them thoughtfully and tapped one of the unmarked names on the list. "This man, Drusan, is in Olyessa's pay, although it seems he's kept his colleagues in the dark. He is also on the committee Jez is currently sitting on, helping to come up with a plan to restructure the government. If the committee finds out he's on Olyessa's payroll, it may be a conflict of interest. But if he's caught with a compromising communication from Grigory—" She paused.

"You want to frame him, then," said Tanya.

Masha nodded. "From what I know about Grigory's boyeviki, I believe the best option will be to leave a com chip in his office. And considering his connections, he will likely have communication codes in his possession that will assist us in passing messages on to Olyessa's boyeviki. That may help keep the streets calm enough for Tae to do his work without being shot at. Ysbel. I assume you have no objection to coming as well?"

Ysbel raised an eyebrow. "You intend to blow something up?"

Masha gave her a faintly amused look. "I hope there's no need for that. However, Drusan is over weapons innovation and development, and any message to him from Grigory would almost certainly reference weaponry. And you are our resident expert in that matter."

By the time they left the hangar bay, the Prasvishoni streets were dark, illuminated only by the flickering artificial streetlights. A light dusting of snow drifted down from the sky, and the wind blew it, stinging, against Ysbel's face. She pulled her scarf up, squinting against the blowing snow, and raised the collar of her jacket, hunching her shoulders against the wind.

Tae and Ivan and the street children were out here now.

She shivered.

Tae had kept them all alive through winters much harsher than this one, she was certain of that. But the thought of the scowling, long-haired street boy, who she'd come to care for as much as she cared for her own family, huddled shivering in the streets—because she knew Tae, and she knew he'd give his blanket to the youngest street kid, even if he had to go without himself—made something inside her chest ache.

At least, hopefully, with the information they'd get tonight, soon he'd only have to worry about the cold, rather than the street gangs.

Masha led them unerringly towards the government precinct, and Ysbel watched her as they walked.

Two days ago, facing the mafia krestnaya, Ysbel had seen Masha's composure crack for the first time. The first time she'd seen that cold hatred, the icy determination that hid under Masha's calm, pleasant exterior.

Very little frightened Ysbel. Very little, other than the constant, aching terror of something happening to her family, or to this crew who had become as close as family. But at that moment, she'd realized that Masha frightened her.

The government and the mafia together had murdered Masha's family when she was seven years old, and Masha, hidden under a table, had watched it all. Now the mafia, and the man who'd killed Masha's parents, had been destroyed so thoroughly that Ysbel wouldn't have believed it if she hadn't been part of it herself.

But Ysbel understood revenge. She'd spent five years of her life dreaming of nothing else. And she knew, very well, that Masha was not finished.

The government buildings, when they finally reached them, were like any other office buildings in the city; tall, bland, each identical to the next, walls of crumbling prefab and rows upon rows of identical windows set into the walls. Most were dark, but here and there a light flickered.

Ysbel had heard stories of luxurious interior rooms in the government buildings for high-up officials, grandeur and opulence that the citizens of Prasvishoni could only dream of. But from the outside, the buildings were as drab and as bland as any other building in Prasvishoni.

Masha scanned the buildings quickly, then gestured with her head towards one of them. She stepped into the doorway, and Ysbel stepped in after her, the shallow space providing at least a modicum of shelter from the blowing snow.

Ysbel shook the snow from her shaved head and brushed it from her scarf and the pulled-up collar of her coat as Masha peered down at the lock.

She paused a moment, then typed in a code. The lock clicked, and Masha pushed the door open and stepped inside, not even looking back.

Half-reluctantly, Ysbel followed.

The hallways in the drab building were lit only with long bars of emergency lighting along the ceiling, flickering and orange, and they cast a dim half-light and strange shadows across the empty corridors. Ysbel and Masha walked silently. Here and there, a thin strip of light or a hushed conversation filtered out from under a closed door, but most of the rooms they passed were empty.

Masha led the way to a narrow, dingy stairwell. "His office is on the fifth floor," she said over her shoulder, voice echoing strangely in the silent stairwell.

The scuff of their boots on the stairs sounded back to them off the close walls as they climbed. Ysbel kept a hand on the reassuring shape of her heat gun, ears strained for any sound out of the ordinary, but there was nothing but the muffled noise of her boots and Masha's on the grimy, bare prefab of the stairs.

When they reached the fifth-floor landing, Masha paused for a moment in front of the door, listening. She pushed it open and stepped through, and Ysbel followed.

This was obviously where the more important officials had their offices. The corridors were wider, better lit, and the floors weren't bare prefab, but a richly decorated carpet that had once been grand. It was threadbare now, and slightly stained, small tears appearing here and there where a boot had caught the trailing thread and pulled it loose. Even still, it signalled a sort of faded opulence, a decaying grandeur.

At last Masha stopped in front of a door near the end of the hallway.

"You're certain he's out?" asked Ysbel quietly.

Masha gave a brisk nod. "Yes. His lover is in town tonight. He'll have left the moment he could get away."

Ysbel raised an eyebrow, and Masha gave her a small smile. "I did work in government for quite some time."

"I see," said Ysbel dryly. "And your job description involved keeping track of ministers' lovers?"

"That information comes in useful more often than you might expect," murmured Masha, and Ysbel almost cracked a smile.

Again, Masha typed in a code, and again, the lock clicked, and Masha swung the door open.

The office itself was spacious, tastefully laid out, the furniture antique and comfortable.

Masha looked around, and smiled. "I suggest you take a look at the latest weapons orders he's made, so our message has a touch of reality to it. What I'll need from you is a list of the weapons he's been ordering, and their purposes. In the meantime, I'll look for the codes."

Once Masha had tapped in the code to the lock on the heavy desk, Ysbel pulled back the top drawer and looked inside.

It was filled with information chips, and neatly labelled. She smiled to herself. Organized people were so much easier to steal from than disorganized ones.

She pulled out the chip labelled 'weapons' and slipped into her com, trusting Tae's mods to disable any security. She stepped back from the desk and pulled up the holoscreen, glancing through the weapon specs quickly, then frowned and scrolled a few pages back, studying the information more closely.

Weapons, plenty of them, of the type and strength generally used by the police when there was a crackdown. And under those lists, the notation—"for use in keeping government order. Protesters and street kids. Other assets to be determined in the future for potential gang violence."

She glanced up again.

Masha wasn't looking at her, but she'd seen in the periphery of her vision Masha's sharp glance in her direction.

She scanned through the weapons tech again, something cold in her stomach.

Apparently, Tae was in more danger than any of them had realized, not only from street gangs and boyeviki. She'd lived in the system long enough to know what a government crackdown meant.

Surreptitiously, she hit the copy button on her com. It wouldn't be a bad idea to get as much of this as possible to take back to Lev and the others.

As it copied, she jotted down on a second screen the information

Masha had asked for.

"I'm sending it through to your com," she said when she'd finished.

Masha nodded and pulled up her own holoscreen, slipping in the blank message chip they'd brought. Ysbel turned back to the drawer to replace the weapons chip, and noticed another chip lying ever so slightly out of place.

She glanced up at Masha again.

The woman would have had time to take a chip and scan it quickly while Ysbel was occupied with the weapons information.

But why would she have? She'd slipped the code chip out of her com when she'd inserted the blank one, and it was lying on the desk, waiting to be replaced.

Ysbel frowned. Judging from its label, the misplaced chip contained lists of who currently headed various departments—but just a simple list, not an accounting of who was paid off by whom.

Moving slightly, so that her body blocked Masha's view of her hands, she slipped the chip into her com, and pressed the copy button.

By the time Masha turned around, the chip was back in the drawer, and Ysbel was closing it carefully.

"Is the message finished, then?" asked Ysbel, keeping her face and voice impassive.

Masha nodded, pulling the chip from her com. She folded it into a small piece of paper and tucked it under a stack of briefing documents on the desk, the corner of it just peeking out.

"And someone will find that?" asked Ysbel.

Masha nodded, a faint smile playing on her lips. "If the aides and undersecretaries don't find this within five minutes of walking into this office on their way in to set things up for the minister, it will be only because the cleaning staff found it first."

Ysbel raised an eyebrow.

Masha's smile widened. "Believe me, every one of the staff in this place is being paid by someone to spy on someone else. Word will get into the right ears very, very quickly."

She tucked the chip with the boyeviki communication codes back into its place, and Ysbel noticed she didn't pause for an instant over the chip that she'd apparently scanned earlier.

They left the building the way they'd come, with as little incident as when they'd entered. But as they stepped out into the cold Prasvishoni streets, the dirty snow still blowing in fits and gusts around their faces, Ysbel couldn't hold back a shiver.

She'd expected, after they'd taken out Grigory, that there would be repercussions. The moment in the pleasure house, when Masha told them what would happen in Prasvishoni, she'd realize instantly that the woman wasn't lying.

But she hadn't expected it to come this quickly. She hadn't expected things to move this fast. And now, with the crew split up, with Masha playing her own set of tokens, in a game that she'd dealt, and where she was holding the bag—

It had been a long time since Ysbel had felt a situation spinning this far out of her control.

And it worried her more than she liked to admit.

12

Tae, day 4

Tae glanced around the open square formed by the convergence of two alleys, his heart pounding. It was a large space, but there were enough people here that it felt claustrophobic.

The street kids hung back in the alleys, where they had some semblance of shelter. The looks on their faces spoke of something much more dangerous than aggression.

Fear.

Tae took a deep breath and stepped forward. "Listen," he said. "You came here because you don't want your kids murdered in a street-gang war. If we want to stop that happening, we'll have to work together."

"Yeah?" said Vanya, the leader of one of the ragged-looking street bands. Her face was hard. "How do we know you're not just angling for more power yourself?"

Tae shook his head wearily. "If I wanted more territory, believe me, there's easier ways to get it than trying to convince a bunch of street-kid gangs to work together. I'm just trying to stop a bloodbath."

Felix shifted slightly. "Easy for you to say that, talk about how the gangs'll kill us all. Look at you." He gestured. "You haven't missed a meal in, what, months? Look like you haven't slept in the streets for around the same amount of time. And we all heard about Caz and Peti's gang, heard how they got pulled off the streets. Probably been eating well there, too, haven't you?" He turned to Caz and Peti, a slight sneer on his face. "Probably sleeping warm, right? How's that feel?" He turned back to Tae. "How the hell you expect me to believe that you know real life? I lose my territory, and we die, gangs or no gangs. I lose my business, we die. Hell, I get distracted for five seconds, miss the sound of a police drone, we all die."

He paused a moment, studying Tae. "You could have left us back in the alley, when the police came after us, and you didn't. You brought them after you, let us get away. So maybe you actually believe what you're saying. But you're dumb enough, and innocent enough, that you walked into my territory, and you had a heat gun and you didn't use it. That was damn stupid. So how the hell do you expect me to believe you haven't been taken in by these other rats?"

Vanya stepped forward, voice sharp with anger. "Nice for you to talk, Felix. You're a damn killer. I've seen you take out hits on other street kids. And you stand here telling us who we should trust?"

Three or four of the other gang leaders had moved slightly in as well, and Felix and the other killers were reaching into their pockets for what Tae was certain were dirty street weapons.

"Yeah? Well, maybe you better think twice about getting up in the face of a killer, then," said Felix softly.

Tae stepped quickly between them. "Listen," he snapped. "You want to do the gangs' work for them? I thought we were here to try to stay alive, not kill each other."

They were still glaring, but at least they were glaring at him now, instead of each other. He took a deep breath. "I lived on the streets my whole damn life. You think I'm such innocent, Felix? Then maybe ask yourself how I survived this long. How Caz and Peti survived. I didn't shoot you, because I didn't need to. I'm enough of a damn street kid to know how to stay alive."

It was a lie, of course. The truth was, he wasn't sure he'd have been able to bring himself to shoot another street kid in cold blood, and one day that would probably end up killing him. But the rest of these idiots didn't need to know that.

He turned to Vanya. "You want to stay alive when the Blood Riots and the Rims start fighting? You better damn well believe we need all the killers we can get." He turned, so he was addressing all of them again. "This turns into a war, we're the first ones to die. All of you've lived on the streets long enough to know that. And there's a hell of a lot fewer of us than there were six months ago. If we don't want to be wiped out, we need each other."

Vanya glared at him suspiciously. "You want us to just play along with these bastards?" She gestured at Felix, disgust on her face. "They take what they can get, and you can be damn sure if they're in charge, they're going to end up with a hell of a lot more street than we are. And we're barely surviving." She paused a moment, her voice shaking slightly. "Lost two kids last night. Cold, and police. Two kids, and you think now I'm going to trust the rest of them to some damn killers?"

Tae gritted his teeth.

This wasn't what he was good at. This wasn't his strength, this was Lev's strength, and Masha's. He'd spent his whole damn life just trying to survive.

"Listen," he said. "We'll figure out—"

Ivan step forward, putting his hand on Tae's shoulder. "Do you mind, Tae?" he whispered. "I have some thoughts."

Tae glanced over at him, then took a deep breath and stepped back.

Damn it, Ivan didn't need to be here, and Tae still wasn't sure how he'd damn well repay him. But he bloody needed him.

"We can organize this so that no one ends up with more of the street," Ivan said, his voice mild, but somehow authoritative. "No one loses territory unless they agree to it." He glanced around at them. "Why don't we sit down? Between us, we'll have enough brains to work something out that keeps everyone safe. You're right —no point in surviving the gangs just to die of hunger."

Felix looked at Ivan suspiciously, then glanced over at Tae. "Who's this?" he asked. "Can we trust him?"

Tae gave a short nod. "I trust him with my gang. I trust him with my life."

Felix watched him warily for a moment, but at last nodded. "Fine," he said. He turned to Vanya, glaring. "But there damn well better not be anyone thinking they're going to take territory from my kids. Told you, I'm not afraid to kill."

Ivan stepped forward, with his slight, good-humoured smile. "Come on," he said, gesturing to an open space by an alley wall, and somehow, at the calm of his voice, the two street kids stepped apart from each other, still glaring angrily. Reluctantly, one by one, the other gang leaders joined them, and soon the group of them were talking in low voices. Occasionally, someone's voice would rise in anger, but before fighting could break out, Ivan's would pull the volume down again.

Tae blew out a long breath and relaxed back against the wall for the first time since that morning.

"He's good at this, isn't he?" said Caz, who'd come up beside Tae. "I never thought someone who wasn't a street kid could pull that off, get them to trust him."

Tae shook his head half wearily. "He's had a lot of practice with this sort of thing, I think. He was thrown in jail for organizing protests."

"Well," said Caz, with a wry smile. "I guess we're lucky he decided to come along." He glanced at Tae, quirking an eyebrow. "Why did he decide to come along?"

The question sounded sincere, but there was an amused look in Caz's eye, and a knowing tone in his voice.

Tae shook his head in exasperation. "He's been with us for a while, okay? He wanted to help."

"I—see," said Caz, the amusement not gone from his face.

Tae narrowed his eyes.

It didn't matter. For some damn reason, everyone had decided that Tae was going to have a damn reputation, whether he deserved it or not, and at this point he wasn't sure it was even worth fighting.

He glanced over at Ivan, and frowned in surprise. Ivan had pulled up a map of the streets, and the other gang leaders were … sitting around it, cross-legged on the cement, no weapons drawn. And even if the looks on their faces were wary, they seemed to actually be talking.

"That leaves our street open. You think you're going to take that from me?" snapped one of the gang leaders, a tall kid named Matija, who Tae was pretty sure used 'they' pronouns.

Ivan shook his head, his voice just loud enough to be heard over the murmurs from the other gang leaders. "No. I told you, no one loses territory unless they agree."

"Well, I bloody don't," Matija said bitterly. "We'll bloody starve."

Tae tensed, waiting for the fight to break out, but instead Felix gestured to the map and said grudgingly, "Look, got a tip these streets here might be coming open soon. Police pulling back a bit. If we could get you in there—"

Matija looked up at Felix with almost as much shock as Tae felt, then down at the map. "Like hell I'm gonna be able to get in there," they muttered. "Blood Riots shoot anyone who sets foot in that street."

Felix grinned slightly. "Aren't gonna shoot me," he said. "We're the best damn killers they have, and they won't risk that." He gestured behind him at the rest of his small gang. "They're not going to do crap to us. Or to anyone we bring."

"I'm not giving up my street until I know he's not going back on his word," muttered Matija.

"You calling me a liar?" snapped Felix. "Hell, I could take your damn street any time I wanted to. No need to give you something back."

"Yeah?" said Matija, their voice soft and menacing. "How many kids you willing to lose trying that? Because—"

"Matija's request is a fair one," said Ivan in his mild voice. "But I think we can—"

The voices grew quiet again, and Tae couldn't make out the words.

He shook his head in a sort of disbelief and exchanged glances with Caz, who looked almost as stunned as he was.

A noise whined its way into the edges of Tae's consciousness, and it took him half a second to recognize it. Then he swore, and leapt forward in panic. "Out! Everyone out! It's the police!"

The kids jumped to their feet, scattering, as a police drone appeared in an alley entrance.

"Go!" Tae shouted, grabbing a couple of the street kids by their tunics and shoving them out of the square. "Get out. Run. I'll—" he looked down helplessly at his com. "I'll try to bring them after me, just go."

There was a hiss of overheated air as a heat blast sizzled out from the drone's weapon ports, and a muffled grunt of pain from one of the kids. Tae swore again and lined up a shot on the drone.

This one was shielded well enough that it didn't melt, but hopefully the shot would be enough to distract it.

"Come on!" Caz grabbed him by the jacket and yanked him down the side street. For half a moment, Tae resisted.

"Everyone's out," Caz hissed. "Ivan's got Peti, and they're ahead of us. Come on!"

Tae cast a last glance over his shoulder, then he turned, and they ran for their lives.

When they could no longer hear the police drone, they slowed. Ivan and Peti were waiting for them ahead, and as they caught up, Ivan gave him a strained smile.

"Are the police always this bad?" he asked quietly.

Tae shook his head. "No." He could hear the worry in his own voice.

He'd spent his whole damn life running from the police. But usually it was a by-product of the struggle to stay alive, run odd jobs for credits, stealing.

This was different. Like the police were hunting them.

When they reached the narrow opening between two buildings where the rest of his kids were sheltering, Luca peered out of them, his face white and frightened. He recognized them, and his expression relaxed into a sort of desperate relief that made Tae's stomach twist.

"Is everyone alright?" asked Tae.

Luca nodded wordlessly, and they stepped inside the shelter.

The children huddled together for warmth, and their thin, frightened faces made Tae's chest ache. He cursed internally. "Listen," he said softly, crouching next to Mila. "We'll get somewhere safe, and we'll—"

"Tae!" The voice through his earpiece was breathless, and tight with strain, and he recognized it. It was Vanya, the girl who'd almost gotten into a fight with the killers.

"The police are still after us. We're trying to get away, but I don't —I don't know if we'll—" She broke off, her voice sharp with fear.

"It's not just her," came another voice. "They're after us, too. I— I'm not sure if we're going to get away."

It was Matija this time.

Tae swore and hit his com. "How many of you are they after?"

Three or four other voices chimed in, and he swore again. "Give me a minute. Stay ahead of them for a minute. I'll—I'll see what I can do."

He pulled up his holoscreen in a quick motion, and began typing rapidly. From the periphery of his vision, he could see Caz, Peti, and Ivan pulling the younger kids back farther into the alley to give him space, but he didn't have time to be grateful.

The police coms were notoriously hard to hack into, but he'd done it before. His fingers moved frantically over the holographic keys on his keyboard.

The difficult part was covering his tracks, because if he didn't cover his tracks, they'd be able to trace his hack backwards, track his com signal, and—

Through the com earpiece, he could hear the *fizz* of a heat blast, the muffled sound of a child's scream.

He swore again, louder, gritting his teeth. No time to cover his tracks, then. He'd get this done, and deal with the tracking later.

He was in. He hit the button that would send out an alarm, and a moment later, in the distance, he could hear the wailing of sirens.

It had to be enough. It had to be.

He waited a few endless moments, then when he couldn't bear it anymore, tapped into the closed loop. "Are you alright?" he asked, voice tight.

For a moment, there was no response, and he could feel his heart pounding against his chest. And then, finally, a voice came through the com, sounding relieved and almost sick.

"The police took off," said Matija. Their words shook slightly. "I don't know what happened."

Tae slumped back against the wall in relief.

"Was that you, Tae?" asked Felix.

Tae closed his eyes for a moment, trying to slow his heart rate. "Yeah. I distracted them for a minute. It's not going to last. They'll be able to see I hacked in, I wasn't being very careful. Get out of there, as quick as you can. Get far away, and stay down. I don't know if that will work a second time."

He tapped his com off, then sat a moment, staring down at it sightlessly.

Peti and Ivan were watching him, their faces concerned.

Finally, he looked up. "I'm—sorry," he said dully. "I didn't have time to be careful. They'll be able to track it. We'll have to move."

Caz nodded, face grim. "Location you hacked from? Or com signal?"

Tae shook his head wearily. "I don't know." He pushed himself to his feet, brushing a hand over his eyes. "I'll sleep somewhere else tonight. That'll be safer."

It was already cold. It was going to be a very cold night.

"No, you won't," said Ivan softly, coming up beside him and

laying a hand on his shoulder. "You'll freeze to death." He glanced at Caz. "The four of us can take turns on watch. If the police come, we'll have time to get out. But you're not sleeping by yourself."

"I agree," said Peti. She'd come up to stand beside Ivan. "Tae, you're not going to do any of us any good if you're lying dead on the street somewhere."

Tae blew out a short, bitter breath, and bit back a curse.

They were right, though. On a night like this, there was no chance he'd survive on his own.

"Alright," he said, shaking his head wearily. "Alright. Let's get somewhere safe, at least."

When they finally got the kids settled in another opening between two buildings, Tae stepped to the mouth of the alley. Ivan was already there, on watch, looking out at the dark streets.

He'd tucked his jacket around Mila to stop her shivering, and he hadn't retrieved it. His arms were wrapped around himself, jaw clenched in the universal gesture of someone trying not to let his teeth chatter. The guttering lights of the streetlamps threw his face into a relief of light and shadow, darkening his short beard, accentuating his sharp cheekbones and lean face.

Tae watched him for a moment, something tightening in his chest. At last he moved closer, draping half his blanket over Ivan's shoulders. Ivan glanced up, startled, and then smiled, and Tae's chest tightened again.

"Thank you," said Ivan quietly. He glanced out at the streets again, and sighed.

"What are you thinking?" asked Tae, after a moment.

It wasn't a question he normally asked. But somehow, in the darkness of the cold Prasvishoni streets, the words came more easily.

Ivan gave a small smile, still looking ahead. "It's—been a long time, is all," he said quietly. "I haven't been back here since I was thrown in jail."

"Is your family still here?" asked Tae.

Ivan gave a small, wry smile. "Yes, I think so."

Tae turned to look at him in the darkness. "You—haven't gone back? Spoken with them?"

"No," said Ivan. His voice was soft, but not self-pitying. "I'd put them in danger if I did. As far as they're concerned, I'm still in prison." He gave a small laugh. "I spoke to my sister, before I went to Grigory's ship, but I swore her to secrecy."

They stood in silence for a while, shoulders barely touching. The night was cold, but their shared warmth seeped into the blanket, keeping Tae from shivering too badly. Behind him, he could hear the soft breathing of the other kids. He'd told Caz and Peti to get some sleep while they could, since he had no idea how long it would be before they next got the opportunity. Peti protested, but she looked weary enough to drop, and he was pretty sure she'd been asleep within three seconds of her head hitting the makeshift pillow of wadded blankets on the hard concrete.

"We're going to make this work, Tae," said Ivan at last, softly, turning to look at him. "We're going to save these kids."

Tae nodded, not trusting himself to speak, and he wasn't sure if it was gratitude, or guilt.

"Ivan," he said at last. "You—said you watched one of your friends being killed."

Again, he wasn't sure why he said it. But there was something about the quiet comfort of the company, the dark anonymity of the night.

Ivan turned to look at him again, and for a moment he didn't say anything. At last, he nodded. "Yes," he said quietly. He was silent for a moment, and Tae didn't push him. Finally, he sighed. "He wasn't the only one. There were others. But most of them, it was quick. A heat gun, or a weapons drone, a police bike. This was—worse. And we watched it. We watched him die."

"And you loved him," said Tae quietly.

It wasn't a question. He'd heard it in Ivan's voice, when he'd first spoken of it.

Ivan turned to him, startled. At last, he nodded, a tight smile on his face. "Yes."

They were quiet again for a while. After a few moments, Tae said softly, "I'm—sorry."

Ivan's smile in response was a little sad, but more genuine than it had been. "Thank you."

Tae shivered slightly, and Ivan moved closer, and for a while they stood there, not speaking, their shoulders touching, the warmth of the blanket cutting the bitter chill of the night.

When Caz tapped Tae on the shoulder, he looked up, startled.

"Peti and I will take the next watch," Caz whispered. "You two get some sleep."

Ivan nodded. He shrugged the blanket off and tucked it back around Tae. "Good night," he whispered. Then he turned away, taking the blanket Caz had abandoned, and settled himself into a corner, leaning back against the wall.

Tae swallowed hard, and realized he'd been watching Ivan for longer than really made sense. He shook his head, and slipped into the space that Peti had left when she'd gotten up. He leaned back against the still-warm wall of the alley, and closed his eyes, and waited for sleep that didn't want to come.

13

Lev, day 5

"Lev."

Lev glanced up quickly at the concern in Ysbel's voice, and tapped his com. "What is it?"

"Are you somewhere you can talk?"

Lev glanced around the room quickly.

Jez had already left for the government offices, and he'd checked the bugs again, to make sure that no one had managed to override Tae's spoof during the night.

"I can talk," he said quietly. "What's wrong?"

"I was out with Masha last night," she said. "She told me she needed to know the names of Olyessa's boyeviki we should be sending messages to, and we found that. But she was looking at something else, too. I saw the chip. And it had nothing to do with the street gangs."

Lev frowned. "Do you remember what was on it?"

"Better than that. I took a copy. I'll send it through to your com."

Lev nodded. "Have you—learned anything else? About what she might be planning?" He could hear the strain in his own voice.

"No." Ysbel's voice was just as tense as his own. "I don't know.

She's after something, certainly."

Lev managed a tight smile. "She's been up to something since we met her."

"I know," said Ysbel grimly.

A moment later, something beeped on Lev's com. He glanced down, and pulled up his holoscreen. A list of names scrawled across it, and he frowned.

Ysbel was right—none of the names were connected with either Grigory or Olyessa, as far as he knew. And they weren't marked, so unless Masha had a source of information he didn't—which, honestly, wasn't inconceivable—she'd have no way of parsing out their connections.

He studied the list.

It had been a long time since he'd worked in government, relatively speaking. Well, a few months, but they'd been an eventful few months. The government would have undergone significant changes. Not least because about fifty well-placed government officials had been blown into space dust by him and Jez only weeks earlier.

He shook his head and sighed.

Either way, the point was, he was pretty sure he recognized most of these names. And unless the government had changed a lot more than he guessed, none of these people were connected to anything to do with their current situation.

He tapped his com. "Give me some time," he said at last. "I'll look through this, see if I can figure anything out. If you get any more information, tell me, please."

"Of course," said Ysbel quietly.

He tapped off his com, and for a moment, sat staring blankly at the wall.

He wished, desperately, that he could believe that whatever Masha was doing, she had no intention of harming them.

She had a plan, certainly. But the plan didn't necessarily involve them surviving. And even if she hoped it would—and he was still naïve enough to believe that she did—she wouldn't sacrifice it in order to ensure that outcome.

He glanced down at his holoscreen again.

It was the entire map of several branches of government, but not branches that made any sense—central security committee, infrastructure, various branches of internal security, food and necessities, outer rim structure. No pattern he could see.

He swore, biting the inside of his cheek.

He needed more information. And that would only come with time.

Time, and stealth, and more luck that he really liked to think about. Masha really was very, very clever.

But she wasn't going to win this time.

Jez's voice drifted through his earpiece, her cheery, slightly disrespectful greeting to one of her co-workers answered with an icy silence.

He smiled to himself. Jez was actually doing surprisingly well at this government official thing. She'd managed to get a private meeting with Branka, for one thing, which meant the woman was beginning to suspect that Jez was a bigger player than she let on— likely because she assumed no one was suicidal enough to act the way Jez did unless they had a lot more clout than it appeared.

Not to mention how Jez had stolen Jaromil's key card, and then harassed, bullied, and irritated the other ministers into telling her his schedule.

He'd be away tomorrow morning, apparently. And Jez was

planning on breezing into his office and robbing him blind.

Normally, Lev would be terrified at the prospect. And honestly, he still was, a little, but—well, he'd come to trust Jez's judgement, as strange as he'd have found that idea a few months ago.

He sighed, and leaned back on the couch.

That was one good thing, at least, that had come out of the whole fiasco of falling for Jez, and then almost losing her. He'd learned, finally, to appreciate her. To see the sparkling intelligence hidden behind her feigned ignorance and snarky comments. To actually enjoy her loud and usually inappropriate humour.

There was a strained grunt through his com, and he sat up quickly, biting off a curse. "Jez?" he hissed.

There was no answer, and he sucked in a breath, ice forming in his veins. "Jez! Are you alright?"

There was a dull *thud*, and then the unmistakable static-crackle of a heat blast. He swore, jumping to his feet.

Damn it to hell, she was in the government offices, there was no way he could get down there in time, and Tanya was back in the hangar bay—

"'M good, genius," Jez grunted. "Bit busy." There was a moment's pause, a quick gasp of breath, and then the dull, heavy crunch of someone's head hitting something hard.

"That the best you can do, you bastard?" Jez's voice was breathless, but somehow still snarky.

Lev closed his eyes and swore again, then forced himself to sit back down, pulling up his holoscreen.

He wouldn't have visuals, Tae hadn't had time to set that up, but he should still be able to pull a scan through her com—

Yes. He looked over the readout quickly.

Three bodies, from the heat signatures, four if you counted the one slumped on the floor. One of the upright ones would be Jez. The others …

He cursed. They all had heat shields.

The fuzzy blur of red lines he guessed was Jez was slumped backwards, probably leaning against the wall. The other two figures were advancing steadily.

"They have heat shields," he whispered.

"Figured that," she gasped breathlessly.

He scrolled frantically down his scanner readout, and winced again. "Alright, their guns are short-range assassin's pistols," he whispered. "Better than what you have for close-in work."

There was another crackle of a heat blast, and the heat sensor on his scanner went momentarily haywire.

Jez swore, and he let out the breath he'd sucked in. Still alive, at least.

Assassin's pistols. What did he know about assassin's pistols …

"Jez. Do you still have your gun?"

"Yes," she gasped.

The scanner had come back online, and he could guess from the positions of the figures, Jez on the ground, the other two side by side, standing over her, that she was about three seconds away from being cooked.

"Shoot, for the Lady's sake! Aim for their guns."

There was the fizz of another heat blast, and his screen went white again, and he was biting the inside of his cheek so hard he tasted blood. And then an unfamiliar woman's voice cursed.

"Bloody pistol isn't—"

He slumped back against the couch, suddenly boneless with relief, as Jez's voice floated through the com. "Hey you bastards, your damn heat shields protect against this?"

There was the unmistakable sound of a fist hitting a jawbone.

He held his breath through a scuffle he couldn't follow, until at last there was silence.

"Jez?" he asked cautiously.

"Hey genius." She was breathing heavily. "Thanks." She paused, her voice regaining its usual jauntiness. "Branka'd probably have been mad if I didn't show up, after she went out of her way to set me up this damn meeting."

"Jez," he said, trying to keep the gut-clenching panic from his voice. "Are you alright?"

There was a momentary pause. "Yep," she said at last. "Nothing broken, I checked."

He sighed heavily. Honestly, that was probably the best he'd get from her.

At least she was alive.

"Didn't know assassin's pistols would basically melt like that, though," she said. "I mean, feel like maybe that's a bit of a design flaw."

"Jez. You're using one of Ysbel's mods."

"Good point." She was clearly grinning. "Anyways, guess I'd better head in. Don't want to keep Branka waiting." She paused a moment. "Well, not too long, at least."

He listened with half an ear as Branka's icy greeting filtered through the com line.

There'd been something in the readouts from his scanner … what was it?

He bit his lip and closed his eyes, picturing the information he'd scrolled past in his frantic hurry to find something—anything—to keep Jez alive.

That was it. The heat shields. And the pistols too, if he

remembered correctly.

He frowned and pulled up his holoscreen again.

Yes, he'd been right. These weren't standard government issue, and they weren't anything easy to get on the open market.

He bit the inside of his cheek.

He'd dealt with plenty of government assassins in his time, both as a bystander and a target. None of them played with this type of equipment.

Through his earpiece, he could hear the muted hum of Jez and Branka's conversation.

On impulse, he pulled up another readout from his scanner. He glanced over it, then sucked in a quick breath.

He hesitated a moment, then tapped his com to Tanya's private line.

"What is it?" Tanya answered.

He hesitated a moment. "Have you been keeping an eye on this apartment?"

"Yes," said Tanya. "Not constantly. I don't have the time for that, with what Masha and Ysbel and I are doing. But as often as I can."

"Do you think you could come out tonight?" he asked quietly.

"What's happened?"

He could hear the worry in her voice.

Jez's efforts at forcing a government restructure had been more successful than they'd anticipated, but would be days—likely weeks—before things were settled enough to handle the kind of shock the news of Grigory and Olyessa would bring. And he hadn't heard from Tae, and likely wouldn't unless something went badly wrong, but he could feel the simmering unease on his daily walks through the city in the uneasy glances of pedestrians, the ways families avoided the streets, the suspicious bulges in the jacket pockets of anyone who did dare to come out to stand in their weekly rations lines, or run their daily errands.

"I don't know for certain," he said quietly. "But someone ambushed Jez in the hallway today, as she was on her way to talk to Branka."

"It took them that long?" asked Tanya, but there was concern under the wry humour in her tone.

"I'll send you a readout of the equipment they were carrying," he said. "And there was a map open on one of their coms. Our apartment was marked on it."

He swiped the information through to Tanya's com. A moment later, Tanya drew in a sharp breath.

"I was supposed to go with Masha tonight," she said at last, her words short. "I'll tell her we'll have to put it off until later. I'll spend a couple hours outside your apartment, see if I can find out what's going on."

"Thank you," he said. He hesitated a moment. "I—assume Ysbel mentioned—"

"Yes," said Tanya tersely. "Anything I find out about Masha, what she's looking at, anything, I'll let you know. And I hope you're smart as I always assumed you were, and that you'll figure it out."

"So do I," Lev murmured, not even trying to hide the concern in his tone.

After forty-five standard minutes of driving himself halfway mad thinking about the various ways Jez's morning adventure could have gone wrong, he pulled on his boots and coat and stepped out of the apartment, and spent the rest of the afternoon wandering the streets, trying to gauge the city's mood.

It was difficult to tell, but at least it didn't seem to have gotten worse. Based on how fast things had unravelled from when the first rumours of Grigory's demise had reached the city, something they were doing must be working.

He got back to the apartment about twenty standard minutes before Jez was scheduled to arrive, and when the door banged open and Jez stepped inside, he had a pot of solyanka bubbling on the heater plate.

He turned at her entrance, the relief flooding through him so strongly he almost dropped the spoon into the soup.

She grinned at him. "Hey genius. Smells good in here. What, decided to be a chef in your old age?" She kicked the door shut with one foot, dropped her bag of what was probably ultra-sensitive government material in a heap on the floor, yanked her scarf off, and dropped it beside the bag, the tiny droplets of snow and frost softening in the warmth of the apartment. She had a bruise across one cheek, and she was limping slightly, but other than that she didn't appear to be any worse for the wear.

He placed the spoon carefully on the counter, trying to hide his shakiness, and wiped his hands on a kitchen cloth, forcing a smile. "It's just stew. I hope you're not too disappointed." He took a deep breath. "Jez. Are you—"

She rolled her eyes. "I'm fine." She paused, her grin faltering slightly. "Um. Look, I—Thanks, alright? For this morning."

She looked down at the floor, and he realized, with a start, that she was waiting for him to say something sharp.

"That's—what I'm here for, Jez," he said quietly. "And ... I'm glad you're alright. I know you can take care of yourself, I just ... I don't like to see you hurt."

She looked up, frowning slightly, and studied him for a moment. Then she cleared her throat and crouched down, rummaging through her bag. "Anyway, speaking of food, figured you might be hungry after spending all damn day listening in on my meetings. Grabbed this for us on my way home." She pulled out a brown paper bag, grease-stains soaking through from inside. "Cheburek," she said, pushing herself to her feet and holding out the bag of fried meat pasties, her grin reasserting itself on her face. "Used to be my favourite thing when I came in from a long run."

He smiled and took the bag, emptying it onto a small plate on the table. "You must have read my mind. Nothing like cheburek and hot stew."

She was shaking off her coat, and he stepped over and took it from her before she could drop it on the floor, and hung it on the hook beside the door.

She glanced at him curiously, one eyebrow raised, and something small and painful twisted in his chest as he realized she'd probably never had anyone do that for her.

He disguised it with another smile, and gestured with his chin over the table as he brushed the snow off her coat. "Stew's ready. You hungry?"

She sighed loudly. "Basically starving to death. I thought smuggling was hard work. These government bastards though— sitting through damn meetings, working on damn paperwork, bloody talking to each other about government crap all the damn time— hell, getting jumped in the hallway was the easy part." She shook her head. "Figure you have to be a special kind of crazy to want to work in the government." She paused a moment. "I mean, no offence if that's your thing," she amended.

He chuckled. "None taken. I didn't exactly plan on working in government."

She came over to stand beside him, close enough he could feel the warmth of her. "Yeah," she said quietly. "Figure you could have done a lot of things."

"Like being a copilot?" he said, trying to lighten the mood.

"Well, if you ever wanted to be a copilot, I know a ship," she said, and there was something about her smile that wasn't nearly as snarky as usual.

They ate, and she chatted about her day, and the stew and fried cheburek were homey and comforting. Lev watched her, and he found there was a soft smile on his face, and a warm comfort in his chest. Who'd have thought sitting in a grungy government apartment, eating Prasvishoni street food and listening to someone talk about an endless day of meetings could possibly make him feel this content?

When they were done, Jez slid her dish along the counter and shoved back her chair, stretching. "Well, genius," she said, turning back to her bag. "Guess you probably already know, but I teased Branka with that information Masha said she had, and I'm supposed to come meet with her again tomorrow at eleven hundred standard, which should give me plenty of time to go through Jaromil's office in the morning. So I guess we should figure out what the hell I'm going to be telling her. And, figure we should go through that crap they sent me home with today."

"Yes, we probably should," Lev murmured. He dropped the dishes in to the cleanser, tapped it on, and moved over to the couch. Jez joined him a moment later, and after a quick glance around at the window facing up to the street, she scooted up next to him, tucking her feet under her. He put an arm around her, pulling her close, and she snuggled into him, like she did every evening.

And, like every evening, that same sharp pain jolted through his chest.

He sighed, and slipped the chip Jez had given him into his com, pulling up holoscreen.

"Hey. What's wrong?" asked Jez softly.

He glanced over at her, and tried to smile. "It's—nothing. Just—"

"Memories?"

He nodded, not trusting himself to speak, and she grabbed his hand and squeezed it quickly. "I'm sorry."

"It's—nothing. I'm fine."

She was watching him, but after the last few days he knew better than to meet her eyes, so he turned back to holoscreen.

"Lev."

He stopped himself, just in time, from glancing up, and he could feel Jez stiffen as well.

Casually, he tapped his com. "Tanya. What is it?"

"You were right. You're being watched," she said tersely. "I mean, by someone who's not the usual government spy."

Lev sucked in a quick breath, then forced himself to relax. Casually, he slid the holoscreen between him and Jez so they could both see it, and pulled her in a little closer. She gave a small sigh, and curled up against him.

He glared at the screen, scanning quickly through the information she'd brought. But between Jez's head on his shoulder, the warmth of her pressed up against him, and the threat of an unknown watcher outside their window, he doubted he'd actually get anything out of the information on the chip.

Still, the important thing, at this point, was to stay alive long enough to use any information they might have.

"Well, the two of you are very convincing, at least," said Tanya through his earpiece a few minutes later, and he started, blinking back up at the holoscreen. Jez shifted, startled, as well.

"I have to go." Tanya's voice was serious now. "Whoever it is is still watching you. But—they don't look like they're getting ready to kill you at the moment." She paused a moment. "I'll come back tomorrow. Let me know if you see or hear anything. I don't like this. In the meantime, please be careful."

"Ah, you know me," said Jez, with her familiar jaunty grin. "I'm always careful."

"Perhaps that's a matter of opinion," said Tanya, faint sour note to her voice. "At any rate, I have to get back. I'm going out with Masha tonight to drop off a message."

"Thank you, Tanya," said Lev quietly.

The com clicked off.

Jez breathed in deeply and turned to grin at him, and he looked determinedly away before he could get caught by her dark eyes.

"Well, genius, guess I'm going to bed." She yawned, lifting her hand reluctantly from his knee and stretching luxuriously, and he determinedly ignored the way her body pressed into his at the movement.

She stood and leaning back, hands pressed into the small of her back. "Don't know how you plaguers do it, sitting still all day," she muttered.

He cracked a smile. "This from someone who'd sit in a pilot's seat all day if she could."

She gave him a mild glare. "That's different. Anyway, don't hear you complaining when you're in the copilot seat." She turned and headed to the bedroom, and he forced himself not to look after her.

She was right, though. He didn't complain about sitting in the copilot's seat.

Deep down, he knew he'd never complain about sitting next to her, wherever that was. For as long as it lasted, for as long as she wanted him there.

He shook his head, and turned back to the holoscreen in front of him.

As long as he didn't let himself think about Jez, stretched out in the bed they shared, he might actually get through the information, get it organized into a usable state by the time he made his daily drop-off to Tanya.

He wasn't sure how long he'd been sitting there when Tanya's voice came through his com once more.

"Lev," she said quietly. "That person who was watching you tonight. I took a scan of them on my com while I was there, and I just got the time to go through it." She paused a moment. "I couldn't figure out who they were, or who had sent them. But they had accurate biometric targeting set into their weapons, which means whatever this is must have come into play after we arrived here. Otherwise, it would have been set to the real Layla's biometrics. And …" she paused. "The biometrics. It wasn't just Jez. It was set to both of you."

Lev stared down at his com, something cold in his chest. "Understood," he said at last, quietly. "Thank you for checking."

"Be careful. I won't be able to watch you all the time."

"Somehow, I doubt I'm the primary target of whoever this is," he said wryly. "I'll let Jez know in the morning."

He tapped off his com, glancing involuntarily at the bedroom door.

Jez was very good at what she did. She was very good at staying alive, and she was very good at taking care of herself.

But between their mysterious enemy and whatever it was Masha wasn't telling them, he was feeling distinctly uneasy about their chances at the moment.

14

Tae, day 6

When Tae woke again, the thin, grey light of the Prasvishoni winter morning that brushed against his eyelids did nothing to warm the cold stiffness from his muscles. He sat for a moment, bracing himself, then he shoved the blanket back and stood, eyes going quickly to the heap of children tucked behind him into the warm spot in the alley. There was that momentary, desperate panic that one of the shapes might be stiff and cold instead of warm and sleepy … but no. They were all breathing, and his shoulders slumped in relief.

Caz turned from the mouth of the alley and came over. "So," he said, crouching beside Tae. "What's the plan for today?"

Tae rubbed a hand over his face wearily. "We should go scout out the streets we want to get the street kids into. See if we can figure out a way to keep the police from coming after them. First thing, though, we need to get our kids to a new place."

Caz nodded, face grim, and Tae sighed reluctantly. His whole body ached from the cold and from the hard cement of the streets. He was getting soft. He was already soft. He wasn't sure he knew, anymore, how to survive out here.

"Tae," Ivan said quietly, coming to join them. "Any word from the other street-kid gangs?"

Tae pulled up the holoscreen on his com, a twinge of familiar worry settling in his stomach.

There were two new reports, and he scanned them quickly.

"The police don't seem to be letting up," he said. "Matija tried to move their gang last night into the street we need them in, but the police came after them again."

"Was anyone hurt?" Ivan's voice was heavy with concern.

Tae shook his head. "No. But that was mostly luck. Matija's second-in-command was coming back from a rations run when she noticed a drone. They got out, but two minutes later and they wouldn't have." He sighed. "No matter how hard I try to distract the police, it doesn't seem to be working."

"And you have no idea why they're coming after us this hard," said Ivan quietly.

Tae shook his head. "I've never seen them come after street kids like this."

He glanced down at his com again and frowned, looking closer.

"What is it?" asked Ivan.

Tae pulled his holoscreen around so Ivan could see it. "Last night I set up tracking on the police so I could warn the other kids. But—" he gestured to a cluster of red dots up by the university. "Whatever's happening up by the university, it looks like it's getting bigger." He stared at the holoscreen for a few moments longer, then tapped his com, shutting it down. "It's too close to where we're going to be. We have to check it out. We can't afford not to."

Ivan nodded. "I'll come. It's not safe for any of us to go out alone right now."

"Caz," said Tae, turning to him. "You and Peti talk with the street-kid gangs again, see if you can figure out the strategy." He shook his head ruefully. "Assuming we can have a strategy, with the police like they are."

"Assuming we live long enough to have a strategy," Caz muttered. He looked up, and Tae could see the lines of strain cut deeply into his young face. "Be careful, alright?"

Tae nodded. "You too."

Tae and Ivan kept to the narrow streets and alleys as they made their way towards the university. As they got closer, Tae could hear the loud percussion of flash-bangs, the muddled, mechanical sound of artificially amplified police officer voices shouting orders or instructions.

And over that—

As the noise became clearer, Tae felt his stomach drop.

Over that, even louder and more strident than the police officers shouting, other voices. Young voices, chanting out a call-and-response that was suddenly, sickeningly familiar.

"Students," said Ivan grimly, turning to Tae.

Tae nodded tightly, and Ivan frowned at him. "Do you—know them?"

Tae gave a short sigh. "I had some friends there. They helped us last time we were in the city."

Ivan gave him a quick smile, a note of humour under the grimness of his expression. "So, you started a revolution at the university. I think you forgot to mention that."

Tae gave a quick shake of his head. "I didn't start anything. They found out that I was in trouble, and I couldn't stop them from—"

Ivan still looked amused.

The noise grew louder as they half-jogged through the dirty alleys, and Tae's muscles tightened. Whatever this was, the police were not happy about it. And yes, back in university Dmitri had told him that the police didn't bother the students, because they were mostly children of government officials. But a lot had changed in the past few weeks, and there was a very fine the line between the people the police protected, and the people they protected against.

The thought was making panic rise in his throat.

They came around a corner, and Tae stumbled to a halt.

Before them, in the large, open square in front of the university gates, a mass of students shouted and chanted, holding placards and yelling at the top of their lungs. And at the other end of the street, the police had gathered. They looked like they'd pulled back for the moment, but they'd clearly been throwing smoke bombs, judging from the number of students on the ground, tears streaming down their faces.

"Stand down!" an amplified voice shouted. "Stand down and disperse."

And then another voice, which Tae recognized immediately. "In your damn dreams, fascist pigs!"

Tae swore, looking frantically around for the speaker.

The tall, dark-skinned girl was impossible to miss, mostly because she was standing atop an ornamental arch and shouting into a voice amplifier of her own.

"You fight them—" she shouted, turning her back on the police and facing the students.

"You fight us!" the students called back.

Tae groaned. Vera. Of course.

He'd met her when the crew had gone into the University of Prasvishoni undercover. When she and Dmitri, Tae's first-ever boyfriend, who he'd almost gotten blown up with an ion bomb, had somehow rallied half the damn student body into a riot against the police that had saved his life, and almost lost theirs.

Tae shoved his way to the crowds. "Vera," he shouted at the top of his lungs. Students turned to stare at him curiously, but he ignored them.

"Vera!"

There was a *boom*, and Tae gritted his teeth against the aftershock of the police flash-bang.

"Vera!"

She glanced up, peering around for the source of the voice. He waved his hands over his head.

"Vera! It's me, Tae!"

This time she must have heard him, because a look of shock registered on her face. She tapped off her voice amp, jumped off the arch, and pushed her way through the crowd. When she reached Tae, she grabbed him by the shoulders, holding him off to look at him, then pulled him into a bear hug.

"Tae!" The strain in her voice told him more than any words could have. "What are you doing here? I thought you went off-planet."

"I did. But I'm back," he said shortly. "Vera, things are happening. Things are—going to get bad."

"I'm not sure if you've noticed this," she said with an attempt at humour, gesturing around her. "But things are already bad."

"They're going to get worse," he said grimly. "They're going to get a hell of a lot worse." He glanced quickly around the mass of students. "What's happening? What are you all doing out here?"

"That's right," she said, her familiar husky voice tinged with weariness. "You missed this." She paused a moment. "We've been protesting since you left. The government's cracking down hard, and they never did stop going after the street kids, and—well, what you said. About what they did to your friends." She shook her head. "It —wasn't just your friends, was it? Dmitri told us. You were a street kid, before. I may have walked past you, never even noticed."

"Vera. It's not—"

She put a hand on his arm. "You don't have to try to make me feel better. The point is, the deeper we dug, the uglier the things we found. I mean, hell, we always talked about stuff like this over drinks, but we never realized how bad it was. We're government brats, and none of us really thought—" she trailed off for a moment. Then she gave him that familiar grin, even if there was a hint of desperation behind it. "Anyways, we got the entire university shut down a week ago. But the police have started ramping things up. I didn't think—" she shook her head. "You probably think we're all hopeless innocents, but I never thought it would get this bad. They've blockaded off the university. We can still get to the streets just outside the university, like this, but we can't go any farther. And they— they've—I've seen broken arms, concussions, all sorts of things. Things I never thought—I never thought they'd go that far."

Tae blew out a quick breath, half in frustration, half in sympathy. "Vera," he said tightly. "You think things are bad now—they're going to get worse. You have to get out of here. You have to call off the protests."

She looked at him for a moment, and there was something in her face that hadn't been there when he known her back in university, a sort of weary determination.

"They've been telling us that for weeks. But Tae—we won't stop. Not until they fix things, or until they damn well start shooting, if that's what it takes."

He swore through gritted teeth.

She gave him a small half-smile. "Don't tell me you wouldn't do the same thing. You make a terrible hypocrite."

Tae almost smiled back, despite himself. And then, abruptly, he jerked his head up. "Dmitri! Is he—he hasn't—was he—"

Vera shook her head, and this time, her smile was genuine. "Dmitri's fine. He's leading the protests on the other side of the university."

Tae almost sagged in relief.

Around him, students were still shouting, and the police shouted back. They sounded like they were getting ready for another push, and Tae felt, suddenly, sick to his stomach. These kids had no idea what they were in for. And if he couldn't talk them out of it, he had no idea how to help, because this wasn't something he'd done before —

And then he heard a calm, familiar voice over the chaos.

"It's alright," Ivan was saying. "Get her to open her eyes, and we'll rinse the gas out. It'll help, at least."

Tae's eyes found Ivan's familiar, graceful form almost instantly. He was standing with a group of the students, one of whom had clearly been gassed, but there was something about his calm, matter-of-fact manner that seemed to have cut through the panic.

"If they're going to be throwing gas bombs, we'll need to be ready for it," Ivan said, glancing around. "Who's in charge?"

"You are?" someone muttered, and there was a ripple of nervous laughter. Then Ivan caught sight of Tae and Vera.

"I think I found her," he said, with his usual good humour. "Anyone Tae's talking to is probably right in the thick of it."

He joined them a moment later, and turned to Vera. "I take it you're in charge of this?"

Vera grinned at him wryly. "As much as anyone is."

Ivan chuckled, but Tae could hear the strain under it. "Believe me, I understand." He glanced around quickly. "I hope I'm not stepping over anyone, but the police will be coming back, and these kids aren't ready. People are going to get hurt. We need to get somewhere they can shelter, maybe behind alley walls. If the police are going to throw gas bombs, we don't want them to have an easy target. Give the gas a chance to disperse a bit before it hits us."

Vera was looking around as well, brow furrowed. "That street there, that runs alongside the university walls," she said. "There's lots of alleys off it—"

Ivan frowned in the direction she was pointing. "That'll work. But we'll need something to keep the skybikes out. If they get in overhead, you won't stand a chance." He glanced around quickly. "There's no roof-wires or anything in those alleys?"

"There's not," said Vera slowly. "But—this is where they string the government banners, whenever there's an announcement."

Ivan gave a small smile that didn't quite reach his eyes. "That should work. Alright, we'll string something up. Anything—jackets, blankets, sweaters, doesn't matter. As long as the skybikes don't have an easy path. If we can keep them from getting on top of us, that's half the battle won." He paused again. "What have they been using so far?"

"Gas, mostly, and flash-bangs," said Vera.

Ivan nodded. "The next step will probably be stun guns, maybe percussion blasts." He shook his head, face indecisive. "I wish we could keep out the drones, but setting a blocker would take weeks."

Vera was looking at him. She turned her gaze deliberately to Tae, eyebrows raised.

Ivan followed her gaze, frowning, and then grinned broadly. For the first time since they'd arrived, his smile reached his eyes. "Tae. I'd forgotten. I walked into a protest, and thought I was back in the days before I met you, when I was working with ordinary people. Can you—"

Tae had already yanked up his holoscreen.

He should've thought of that himself, honestly, but seeing Vera and the others had distracted him.

"I already have tracking on the police," he muttered, scanning through the screens on his com. "So theoretically, I should be able to —" he glanced up quickly at Ivan. "What do you need. Exactly."

"I want to keep the drones out. However we can do that. At the very least, scramble their signals a bit." He turned to Vera. "That reminds me, the students need to cover their faces. It should help against the gas, but also, we don't want the police to be able to track them. We don't want retaliation later. If things get worse, that's what they'll be looking for."

Vera nodded grimly. "I'll tell the others. Is there anything else?"

Ivan shook his head. "They need to cover their faces—mouths and noses especially, against the gas—water to rinse out people's eyes, we need to get everyone back somewhere defensible. Those are the main things. And then we start hanging up everything we can find that will interfere with the skybikes."

Vera gave a short nod, and slipped off.

Tae glared down at his holoscreen.

It was complicated, but not ridiculously so, especially considering the crap he'd dealt with the past few months.

After a few minutes, he glanced up at Ivan with a tight smile. "Done. I've set up a blocker radius around this part of the street. It's stationary, so it won't help if we need to get away, but it will mess with the drone controls."

Ivan closed his eyes and let out a short breath. "Thank the Lady," he said, and Tae was surprised at the relief in his tone. "I—didn't want to say this to your friend, but if the drones get in—" he shook his head. "Things could go sideways quickly."

Tae nodded grimly. "I warned them, back at the university. Vera didn't believe me then. I think maybe she does now."

He glanced around quickly. Vera was already herding people back towards the alleys, and there were a few other students barking out orders as well, pushing people towards where Vera had instructed.

Ivan raised an eyebrow. "Your friend is pretty good at this," he said.

Tae shook his head. "She's very good at everything, except understanding the words, 'you shouldn't do this, it wouldn't be a good idea.'"

Ivan gave him a small smile. "Oh, I know a few people like that. If someone they care about is on the other end of the equation, they won't listen to a single word of reason."

Tae rolled his eyes, but he was smiling despite himself.

By the time the police came back, coats, scarves, and at least one shirt fluttered in the air above the narrow street where the students had retreated, and Tae's blocker was set and running.

He could see the moment the first officer rounded the corner and realized what they'd done.

The police bikes halted, and the officers huddled into a group, talking and gesticulating.

Tae glanced over at Ivan, and grinned when he saw one officer's frustrated gesture towards the hung coats and rags.

Vera had come over to stand beside them. Her posture was tense, and Tae could tell just by looking at her that she wasn't the same innocent student he'd known a few months ago.

For some reason, the thought hurt. He'd wanted, somehow, for there to be room in the system for kids his age to be young and idealistic, not have to worry about whether they'd be alive the next day, or the day after that.

But—maybe there'd never been a place in the system for that sort of innocence, not really.

The officers had apparently come to a decision, because one of them pulled out a voice amplifier and called, "Please disperse. I repeat, please disperse. We don't want to hurt you."

Vera grabbed her own voice amplifier, and called back, "Nobody's making you hurt us. But we're not going home while you're killing street kids. You stop that, and we'll disperse."

The officer's voice was sharper this time, and there was annoyance clear in her tone. "We are armed, and we are authorized to use force if you don't disperse."

Ivan leaned over and whispered, "They're still worried about the kids' parents. They would have started shooting by now otherwise."

Tae frowned suddenly. "Ivan," he said slowly. "What if this was being broadcast over a general line, and they knew it—would that help?"

Ivan raised his eyebrows. "I—suspect that would help a great deal." He paused. "Can you do that?"

Tae nodded. "Anything fancy would take too much time, but I can do a quick splice. Won't take them long to get around it, but it's something."

Ivan raised his eyebrows. "It might do more than you think."

An officer stepped forward, face covered by a riot helmet. He drew back his arm, and a moment later, something glittered in the weak sunlight as it tumbled into the square.

"Down!" Ivan shouted, turning to the students. "Smoke bomb!"

The students ducked into the alleys, pulling their makeshift masks over their faces, and Tae, Ivan, and Vera ducked in after them.

There was a low hiss as the bomb hit, and then a cloud of ugly grey smoke that spread outward through the maze of alleys. Students choked and gasped as it hit them, backing out of the way, but Ivan was right—by the time it reached them in the alleys, it had dissipated, although it was still enough to make Tae's eyes burn and his lungs sting like they were on fire. Ivan, mask pulled over his face, sprinted over to where the worst-hit students were crouched, gasping and choking, their eyes streaming. Tae couldn't make out his words, but from his gestures he was directing other students to help them out into clear air, get them first aid. There was something about his presence that seemed to be keeping the kids from outright panic.

Another smoke bomb hit the ground, sending up another thick hiss of smoke. Students screamed, gasping and choking. Tae yanked his scarf over his face as a makeshift mask and ran forward to help.

Vera was beside him, and together, they grabbed the stumbling, tear-blinded students and dragged them back out of the smoke.

"Over here!" Ivan called. Tae glanced over his shoulder, and through his stinging eyes and a blur of tears, he caught sight of Ivan, gesturing to him from a narrow space between buildings. Tae jerked his head at Vera, and they herded the choking students towards him.

"So, your friend," Vera gasped. "I don't remember him. He a criminal too?"

"No," Tae snapped. "He's—" he paused, realizing what he was saying. "Yes," he said at last, in a flat voice. "He's a criminal. Just—not one of the criminals I was working with last time. We—um—broke him out of a prison planet."

They reached the alley, and Ivan guided the gassed students to where he'd set up a makeshift first-aid station. Other students helped their classmates sit, and grabbed for water bottles to rinse gas from their eyes and skin.

"So, Tae," said Vera, once the students were taken care of. She was grinning slightly. "Do you even know anyone who isn't a criminal?"

He scowled, paused, and frowned.

Now that she mentioned it—

"I know you," he began.

A flash-bang hit the ground a few metres from them, and they staggered back, blinking against the brilliant jag seared across their vision.

When they could see again, Vera grinned at him, and gestured at the wailing sirens and the fug of gas thickening the air.

"You weren't a criminal when I met you," Tae muttered.

Vera looked even more amused. "Okay, let me rephrase that—do you know anyone who isn't a criminal, or who you haven't converted into a criminal since meeting them?"

Tae scowled again, and she laughed, then coughed as the gas hit them. They turned back to the square, grabbing the last of the affected students and pulling them to their feet, pushing them towards the alley.

"It's not a bad thing," said Vera, once she could talk again. "Life's a hell of a lot more interesting since I met you."

"Please disperse! I repeat, please disperse."

They reached the makeshift first-aid station, and Tae stumbled to a halt. He tried to take a deep breath, and ended up with a coughing fit that left him bent over, hands on his knees.

"You need first aid?" asked Vera, concern in her voice, but her sentence broke off into coughing as well.

Damn it, he hadn't finished the communication blocker.

"Just a sec," he muttered, yanking up his holoscreen.

Like he'd told Ivan, this wouldn't be fancy. But considering how deep into the police system he'd already gone trying to help the street kids, he should at least be able to pass the audio through to the general communication line. Maybe no one would be listening in, but the threat of it might be enough for now.

"What—" began Vera, frowning.

"Would your parents like to know what's going on here, do you think?" asked Tae.

Vera stared at him for a moment, then slowly, she smiled. "Now that you mention it, I think they'd be quite interested," she said. "Considering the police cut off communications since they shut down the university."

He bit his lip and bent back to his holoscreen. A few moments later, he looked up in grim triumph. "Got it. I'm hooking it in. All the students' coms should be broadcasting to the general channel right … now."

Vera grinned at him, then pulled out her voice amplifier and stepped forward to the edge of the alley, where the police would be able to see her. Tae followed, ready to pull her back if they tried to shoot.

"Hey! Officers! You might want to check your com feeds," she shouted. She pulled up her holoscreen, and turned deliberately, so the screen took in the students huddled on the ground, choking and gasping for breath, being tended to by the fellow students, most of whom were also red-eyed and coughing, the blackened scorched mark on the concrete left by the flash-bangs, the rows of police officers in riot gear standing at the mouth of the street.

Most of the officers ignored her, but one woman in the back had pulled up her com, frowning in irritation.

Her eyes widened, and even though Tae wasn't close enough to make out her words, he didn't need to hear her to know she was swearing. She shouted something to the other officers, and one by one, they hit their own coms.

Vera was talking into her com now, making no effort to disguise the strain and fear in her voice.

"Mom, Dad. Someone hacked us through. This is what's happening right now, at the university. They don't want it to get out. They've been—" her voice shook a little. "They've been holding us here, gassing us, shooting flash-bangs. We're scared. We don't know what they'll do to us."

"Listen, we've given you a warning," one of the officers shouted, her voice amplified. "I trust you'll behave yourselves. And I trust we won't have to come back here again to deal with your disturbance. You've made quite a mess here."

"They're lying, mom," said Vera into the com, her voice low and urgent. "We haven't done anything wrong. We're out in the streets, calling for them to stop killing people. Killing street kids. Did you know they used street kids to experiment on in the university? I can't just let that happen, none of us can." Her voice was choking.

From the corner of his eye, Tae could see the officers remounting their skybikes. Their faces were grim, but they didn't appear to believe they had any other choice.

And then, one by one, they disappeared down the street the way they had come.

Tae let out a long breath of relief.

For a few moments, the students stared around them, seeming unsure of what had just happened. And then the shouts broke out, whoops and laughter and giddy cheers.

Tae glanced back into the alley, and Ivan met his eyes, and they grinned at each other.

Vera was laughing and shouting as loudly as any of the others.

She slapped Tae on the back, so hard he almost stumbled. "You did it! You're a bloody genius, Tae!"

And then Ivan had come to stand beside him, resting his hand on Tae's shoulder. He was smiling, and there was something about his smile that was better than all the cheers and shouts and laughter together.

When the hubbub had died down, Ivan touched Vera lightly on the shoulder.

"I hate to be the one to break bad news, but—"

Vera nodded, sobering quickly. "They'll be back," she said, the words more statement than a question.

Ivan nodded. "We won this round, but we haven't won the war." He glanced around at the celebrating students, then turned back to Vera. "Are you coming back tomorrow? No one will blame you if you don't."

Vera looked at him, then at Tae. Her face was set, but he could see the hint of fear behind it. "And if we do come back?" she asked quietly. "Will it do any good?"

Tae took a deep breath.

He could tell them that what they were doing wouldn't make a difference. He could tell him to go home. And then maybe they'd be safe.

But—she trusted him. That he wouldn't lie to her, that they were good enough friends that he'd tell her if he needed help.

And damn it, the Lady knew he needed help.

"If you can keep the police busy here, it would—it would help a lot," he said finally, swallowing hard. "We're trying to stop a gang war that would probably end with most of the street kids dead, but the police have been coming after us too hard for us to do anything. If you're making enough trouble here, though—"

Vera's face spread into a slow smile. "I think we can do that. At least—" she glanced at Ivan. "At least, with the help of your friend here." She turned to Ivan. "Does that answer your question?"

Ivan smiled back, but again, Tae noticed the smile didn't quite reach his eyes. "I suppose it does." He paused a moment. "If you're going to do this, we'll need to be prepared."

"And you have experience," said Vera.

Ivan smiled faintly. "Enough to get me thrown in jail, apparently."

Vera glanced at Tae and smirked.

Ivan looked around quickly. "Find buckets, baskets, suitcases— anything like that. I'll show you tomorrow how to use them to defuse a smoke bomb. Water bottles, as many as you can find. Do they still use laser pointers in the classroom?"

Vera nodded.

"Bring them. You shine them at the drones and the police cameras, it confuses them." He glanced up. "What you did here, in the alley, worked for today. But it won't be enough. Tomorrow they'll be expecting it. You'll need to string wire. Fine lines are best, ones they can't see if they're moving quickly. And cloths over your mouths for the gas." He glanced over at Tae. "How long will the communication splice last?"

Tae shook his head. "They'll probably have blocked it off within a couple hours. I can start working on a new one tonight, but I won't have it done in a day. Once they find this one, they'll almost certainly set a blocker around the whole area. I won't get through nearly so easily again."

"Will … you two be coming back?" asked Vera. She was obviously trying to make her voice nonchalant, but Tae heard the apprehension in it, the fear, and he knew Ivan could too.

Ivan glanced at Tae uncertainly.

Tae frowned, biting his lip. "If Caz and Peti did alright with the street kids today—" He glanced up at Vera. "Yes. We'll come. We'll meet you back here tomorrow morning."

The relief that washed over Vera's face was enough to make something twist in Tae's stomach.

More people he was responsible for, putting their lives in his hands, trusting that he'd find a way to keep them safe.

But—he needed them.

He and Ivan met Caz and Peti a few blocks away from where they'd left the other kids. Caz smiled to see them, but there was something tight and worried in his expression.

"There weren't as many police out today," he said quietly. "But Luca said there were some hanging around where the kids were hiding. They stayed in the alley, and the police didn't come in, but —"

Tae frowned, a slight unease sparking in the back of his mind. "They're alright, though?" he asked.

"I just talked to him five standard minutes ago," said Caz.

Tae nodded, but he found himself walking faster as they neared the dirty alley where the kids were hiding.

When they reached it, he glanced around quickly, and when Luca peered out of the alley entrance, he felt his shoulders slump in a sort of sick relief.

He wouldn't have seen it, if he hadn't spent so much damn time around Ysbel—the tiny glint of the dying sun off something small and metal and far too shiny to belong in the filthy street.

He was moving before he had time to think, grabbing Luca by the sleeve and hauling him bodily out of the alley, shoving him so he stumbled down the street, ducking into the narrow space where the other kids huddled.

"Tae?" asked Peti, her voice tight with fear.

"Explosive," he snapped, shoving Mila and two other kids at her. "Get them out, onto the next street. Now!"

She didn't ask questions, just grabbed the kids and pushed them ahead of her.

Caz was at the mouth of the alley now, and Tae shoved another kid into his arms.

Ivan had joined him, and was ducking out of the alley, carrying a terrified child.

He glanced around quickly.

"Nadia's still in there," came Caz's strained voice from outside.

Tae spun, and sprinted towards the back of the alley. It took him a moment to see Nadia, huddled in the corner, her eyes wide and terrified. He grabbed her, yanking her to her feet and dragging her after the others.

Where was Ivan?

No. He didn't have time to think about that, because he needed to get Nadia out, and he could already hear the faint hiss of an explosive about to go off.

He pulled her out of the alley. Caz was waiting, and as Tae thrust Nadia into Caz's arms, his jacket snagged on a sharp edge of the prefab wall.

He yanked at it frantically, but the fabric had pulled tight, and it was too tough to tear. He struggled out of the jacket, but the tight fabric seemed to catch on his shoulders and arms like clutching fingers.

Caz had disappeared around the corner with Nadia, at least there was that.

Finally the jacket slipped from his shoulders, but it was too late.

He wasn't going to make it, he was going to be out here in the mouth of the damn alley when the explosive went off—

Someone grabbed his arm, jerking him up, and pulled him into the shelter of a bricked-off doorway. He was shoved up against the wall, and he had a split second to notice that it was Ivan who'd grabbed him, and that Ivan had braced himself, his own body sheltering Tae's, when the explosive went off, and the entire world turned to light and sound and choking debris.

For a moment, there was silence.

"Don't move," came Ivan's strained voice. "I saw two explosives. The next will be programmed to go off a few seconds later, maybe a minute. It's their way to make sure there are no survivors—lure you out, make you think it's safe."

Tae managed a short nod. His heart was pounding a quick, unsteady rhythm, and adrenaline still jittered through his muscles, his legs shaking at the thought of how close he'd come to becoming nothing but another piece of debris scattered across the alley.

And suddenly, he was very aware of Ivan—the warmth of his body, pressed against Tae's, the protective circle of his arms, the way his hand had come up behind Tae's head, sheltering him from the rough prefab wall, the tight lines of Ivan's familiar face, cut with strain, as he looked over his shoulder. His body, shoulders hunched, curled around Tae protectively, shielding him from the shrapnel.

Tae's breath was coming far too fast, and his heart felt like it might pound its way completely out of his chest.

Ivan stiffened, arms tightening around Tae, and another explosion rocked the streets.

For a few moments, there was total silence.

Slowly, Tae opened his eyes, blinking against the afterimage of the explosion burned across his retinas.

When he could see again, he was watching Ivan.

For some reason, couldn't seem to take his eyes off Ivan.

Ivan was looking over his shoulder, body tense, arms still cradling Tae.

Tae was acutely aware of every place Ivan's body touched his, the clean line of Ivan's jaw as he looked behind him, the pressure of Ivan's hands on his back. There was a sharp ache in his chest, a mix of pleasure and pain, and he thought he might actually drown in it.

Ivan turned back quickly, his face tight with worry. He didn't release his hold on Tae, just drew back slightly, looking him over quickly, inspecting him for injuries.

"Tae. Are you hurt?"

Tae's brain didn't seem to be working at all. He opened his mouth, and somehow managed a weak, "No. No, I'm—I'm fine."

Ivan's expression went almost sick with relief, posture slumping with released tension. "Thank the Lady," he whispered, voice rough with emotion, and he pulled Tae into a tight embrace. Like always, Tae felt his entire body relaxing into the warmth of Ivan's arms, but his heart was beating harder than ever, almost enough to make him dizzy.

At last Ivan pulled back, but his gaze seemed to snag on Tae's and catch there. For a long, long moment, they stared into each other's eyes. Something twisted in the pit of Tae's stomach, and he couldn't seem to breathe properly, and his throat was so dry he wasn't sure he could even swallow. Ivan's chest, still pressed up against him, was rising and falling faster than usual, and there was a look in his eyes, intense, and concerned, and—something else.

"Tae," Ivan said, his voice hoarse. "Tae. I'm—I'm sorry." He closed his eyes for a moment, and Tae could see the strain cut across his face. With what seemed almost pain, he loosened his grip, shifting so they weren't pressed together, and Tae almost gasped at the sharp pang of loss.

Ivan turned away for a moment and took a few deep breaths. Finally, with a sharp gesture that was almost frustration, he turned back. "Tae," he said in a strained tone. "I—Listen. Whatever you answer, it won't change the fact I'm going to be here to help you. But I need to know, before I drive myself completely mad." His voice shook slightly. "I—I've thought, sometimes, that you might—feel the same way I do. And then—" he paused and gave a tight shake of his head.

Tae just blinked, staring at Ivan, trying to make his words make sense. Because Ivan couldn't possibly be saying—

Could he?

Tae couldn't seem to formulate words. He seemed unable even to formulate a thought.

"I—you—same way as—" he found himself saying.

Ivan managed a strained smile. "It's alright, Tae," he said. "Just because I love you, it doesn't mean—"

"You—" Tae felt dizzy, the cement of the street under his feet spinning strangely.

Ivan took a deep breath and gently released his hold on Tae, and for a moment, Tae thought he might fall over.

There was something unbearably tender, and unbearably sad, in Ivan's face. "It's alright," he said quietly. "It's alright. I never expected you to—" He began to turn away, back to where the street kids were huddled under the shelter, a strange tension to his posture.

Tae's brain wasn't working at all, and he wasn't sure there was a muscle in his body that hadn't turned to water, but somehow he reached out and grabbed Ivan's arm.

Ivan froze. At last he turned back to Tae, the tension in his face matching the tension in his body. "Tae?" His voice was still, somehow, gentle. "What—"

Tae couldn't speak. Even if he could have, he had no idea what he'd say. So instead, he reached up, slipping his hand around the back of Ivan's neck.

A small shudder went through Ivan's body at his touch, and Tae was so lightheaded he thought he might actually pass out. Ivan's skin was warm under his hand, and coated with gritty dust from the explosion, the explosion he'd sheltered Tae from with his own body.

Ivan was staring directly into his eyes now, his breath coming fast and shallow, and Tae's own breath caught in his throat, which wasn't helping how lightheaded he was feeling.

He brought his other hand up around Ivan's back, feeling the lean muscles under his thin shirt.

His hands were shaking. Hell, his whole body was shaking.

Ivan's eyes never left his, and Tae wasn't sure he could breathe, and he wasn't sure if he even needed to breathe.

Carefully, gently, he pulled Ivan's head down towards him, and that strange tension in Ivan's body almost convinced him, for half a moment, that he'd read this wrong, that Ivan's words had been something he'd dreamed up.

And then, just before their lips brushed, Ivan's body relaxed into his, his eyes closing, and Tae's eyes closed as well, and then the only thing in the world was the pressure of Ivan's lips, the familiar warmth flooding through him, the desperate relief of Ivan's body against his.

At last he drew back, breathless and dizzy, heart pounding so hard he honestly wasn't sure how he was still conscious.

Ivan stared at him, a stunned look on his face. Then he gave a helpless groan and pushed Tae up against the wall, his hand cradling the back of Tae's head, protecting him from the rough prefab blocks, his other arm wrapped around the small of Tae's back. His mouth found Tae's, and Tae's lips parted without his conscious thought, his arms going up around Ivan's back and pulling him close, desperately. Ivan's mouth was urgent against his, his fingers tightening into Tae's hair, and Tae's entire brain had gone foggy, and damn it to hell, he'd never been kissed like this before, even the kiss on Grigory ship had nothing on this, and if he actually died from it, he still wouldn't want it to end.

Ivan pulled him closer, tilting Tae's head back, and Tae leaned into him, because his legs had gone so weak he wasn't sure he could stay on his feet without the pressure of Ivan's arms. Hell, he didn't have the attention to spare for staying on his feet, because he couldn't seem to fit a single damn thought into his head. All he could do was lean into Ivan's kiss, desperately, as if it was oxygen and he was drowning.

When they finally drew apart, Tae sagged against the wall, gasping for breath. Ivan held him steady, and they were still close enough that Tae could feel the quick, ragged rise and fall of Ivan's chest, the rapid gallop of his heartbeat.

Ivan gathered him into his arms and pressed his lips into Tae's hair, and the comfort of the gesture was enough to make Tae giddy.

"Tae," he whispered, his voice choked. "Tae—" He couldn't seem to say anything else.

Tae leaned in to him, and Ivan's arms around him, the warmth of Ivan's body against his, seemed, for the first time in his life, to make the entire world fall exactly into place. There were tears gathering in the corners of his eyes, but he didn't want to let go of Ivan long enough to brush them away.

At last, Ivan pulled back, brushing at his own eyes and blinking hard. "Tae," he whispered. He swallowed, trying again. "Tae. Are you sure you're alright? You're not hurt?"

"I'm—fine," Tae choked, not completely sure how his mouth managed to form the words.

"I—I couldn't lose someone I loved again." He pulled Tae into another tight embrace.

"What about you?" asked Tae, when he'd remembered how to speak again. "Are you alright?"

Ivan pulled back, studying him fondly. "I think I'm a little more than alright."

For the first time, Tae noticed that the street kids had come out from their shelter, that Peti was watching him and Ivan, a look of faint amusement on her face, and that Caz was distracting the other kids, herding them a little farther down the street.

He could feel his face heating.

"I didn't want to interrupt, but we should probably get out of here," said Peti, when she saw Tae's eyes on her. "The police will be coming soon to check if their explosive worked."

She was right.

Tae straightened, ignoring shakiness in his muscles, and the way his head still felt like it was floating, the giddy, intoxicating tightness in the pit of his stomach.

Ivan put out a hand to steady him, and for half a second he relaxed into the warmth of Ivan's touch.

Then he took a deep breath. "You're right. We should go." His voice didn't come out as steady as he'd planned, but Peti nodded.

"Follow me. I know one other place." She looked around uneasily. "But ... I'm not sure how much longer we'll be able to keep hiding."

Tae nodded, trying to force his brain back to the problem at hand.

"Let's get somewhere safe, and we'll worry about the rest when we get there," said Ivan. His voice was shaky as well. His hand still rested on Tae's arm, and Tae wasn't sure he wanted Ivan to let go, ever.

Peti shook her head, and even in his stunned state, Tae could hear the unease in her voice. "You're right. But—if we don't figure this out soon, I'm not sure there'll be any safe places left."

15

Jez, day 6

Jez woke in drowsy comfort, and snuggled into the warmth with a soft sigh of contentment. Then her sleepy brain clawed its slow way back to consciousness, and she realized that the warmth was Lev's shoulder. And then she remembered—well, everything else—and, as bloody usual, jerked awake with a start, heart hammering.

Damn it to hell.

She sucked in a quick breath, and glanced over at him.

Still asleep, thank the damn Lady.

Gingerly, she pushed herself backwards, and tried to ignore the small pang of disappointment as the warmth of him faded into the cool of blankets that she apparently hadn't slept on for most of the night.

She closed her eyes and took another long breath.

It was fine. It would all be fine. It was like he said that first morning—the nights here were cold, and these damn government apartments were never quite warm enough.

No need to think about the fact that before she'd woken up, she'd been dreaming of something involving Lev that had been … undeniably similar to what she'd woken up to.

Well, similar in a very broad sense of the word.

Because that would've been incredibly awkward, honestly.

She took another deep breath, then yawned, stretched, and glanced quickly over at Lev as she slid out of bed.

She narrowed her eyes and swore under her breath.

He was lying much too still for someone who was actually asleep.

He blinked his eyes open and glanced at her, and she found she was smiling despite herself.

"Hey genius," she said. "You're not very good at faking, you know."

He chuckled ruefully, rubbing his eyes. "Sorry, Jez. I don't actually mind. It's just—last time you seemed uncomfortable about it, so—"

She rolled her eyes at him. "So you thought it would make me feel better if you pretended like you'd been asleep and didn't notice?"

He chuckled again, the faint rasp of sleep still in his voice. "Well, I had hoped. But apparently—" he shrugged.

"Yeah, you always were kind of a crap liar," she said. But strangely enough, there was something tight in her throat.

She wasn't actually used to someone caring how she felt about crap.

Anyway, it was just this damn playacting they had to do, where he was her lover, that was messing with her head. That was all.

After breakfast, she grabbed her bag and pulled the info chips haphazardly off the counter, shoving them inside.

"Do you have them all?" he asked. "I tried to put them all together so you wouldn't have to go rummaging to find them, but it might not hurt to check. I have been known to make mistakes, on occasion."

She grinned at him. "You? Make mistakes?"

He smiled. "On very rare occasions, yes."

"Where's my damn—" she began, glancing around the apartment. She was pretty sure she'd—

"Your coat? Here," said Lev, holding it out.

She smiled at him gratefully.

Funny, if it had been anyone else, she would've tensed up, waiting for the insult. But somehow, in these last few weeks—well, it was just that she was pretty sure he wouldn't.

"Thanks," she said. "Figure I might actually be on time for once in my life."

He glanced at his com, and his face turned stricken. "Jez! I didn't realize what time—"

She rolled her eyes. "I'm not meeting with Branka until eleven hundred standard. Still have plenty of time to rob that bastard Jaromil blind."

Lev managed a small, strained smile. "Just—don't get killed, alright?"

She laughed, winked at him, and slipped out the door.

The air was bitter. Hell, the air in Prasvishoni was always some flavour of bitter, even in the damn summertime, but this was the bitter of autumn well on its way into winter. She shivered, pulling her coat and scarf close around her against the tiny, icy flakes of lightly blowing snow.

Once she was inside the government building, she glanced around quickly.

The hallways were empty. For all that damn Branka's harassing her for being late to meetings, most of the plaguers who worked here seemed not to show up for at least half a standard hour after Jez did.

She'd be meeting with Branka at eleven hundred standard, which gave her a solid two and a half standard hours to get into Jaromil's office and back out again.

She grinned to herself and made her way to the narrow stairwell at the end of the hallway.

Jaromil's office was on the sixth floor, which was a hell of a lot of stairs to climb, but she wasn't going to use the hololift and risk showing up in the records.

When at last she reached the sixth-floor stairwell door, she cracked it open and looked quickly up and down the long, broad hallway. It was empty. Like she'd expected.

Carefully, she stepped out. This hallway had the same white prefab-block walls, the same ubiquitous threadbare carpet with the standard hideous pattern, as every other hallway in this damn place. But she'd gone over the building specs with Lev for long enough the night before that she knew exactly where she was. She took a deep breath, feeling the satisfying tingle of adrenalin in her muscles, and made her quiet way towards his office.

She was halfway there when one of the office doors opened abruptly, a cleaner's cart shoving its way out. Jez froze, her heart rate jumping, and slipped behind the half-open door just as a dreary-looking man in a greyish-white cleaning-staff uniform stepped out. She bit her lip as the door swung shut behind him, muscles tensed, although she wasn't entirely sure what she planned to do—not like she was going to kill one of the cleaning staff for being in the wrong place at the wrong time. But he didn't even glance behind him, just shoved the cart down the hallway, clicked the next door open with his com, and stepped inside, dragging the cleaning cart after him.

Jez let out a long breath and loosened her grip on her heat pistol. She waited a moment longer to make sure he wasn't going to come out, and then turned back down the hallway.

Jaromil's office was at the very end, and she paused in front of the door, pulling up the key on her com. She held her breath for a moment as she tapped it against the lock—it was always possible he'd been suspicious and gotten the lock changed—but there was the faint *click* of the door opening.

She smiled to herself and stepped inside.

The inside of the office was cluttered with trinkets that the bastard probably thought made him look important. But she'd seen the inside of Grigory Korzhakov's office, and she knew what real wealth looked like.

She tapped her com. "Hey genius. I'm in."

There was a quick breath of relief through her earpiece, and for a moment she wondered exactly how long Lev had been holding his breath. His voice, though, when he spoke, was calm, if strained.

"Alright. I'll be in a folder marked 'classified,' I believe. Something like this."

Her com flashed, and she pulled up the holoscreen, squinting down at the picture Lev had sent through—a bland-coloured paper binder, with a chip pocket in the bottom.

She glanced around the office, frowning.

There was a broad desk in the centre of the room, which would be the logical place, probably. She rifled quickly through the papers on the desk, but there was nothing similar to the picture Lev had sent to her com. There were a couple shelves on the walls, but when she stepped over to them, there was nothing there except some trinkets he probably thought were genuine gold.

They weren't.

She smirked.

It didn't take her long to go through every bare surface that might contain a file folder. There was nothing there, at least, nothing useful, and the key she's stolen didn't open the locks on the desk drawers.

She stood for a moment, biting her lip.

She could melt the locks off, probably, but that wouldn't do much for subtlety. Damn it, she'd have to steal another key and come back, and she wasn't sure how many more days they had …

"Jez." Lev's voice was tense.

There. Just peeking out of one of the drawers, the tip of something drab and grey.

"One sec," she murmured into her com.

"Listen. I'm picking up a heat signature outside the door."

"Yeah? Well, I think I might have found something," she said.

"You've got to get out. You can always come back later, when—"

She'd already crossed to the drawer, and was working the binder free gently. The drawer was shut and locked, yes, but the desk itself was old enough that there was a narrow space between the top of one drawer and the bottom of the next, and if she pushed the side of the desk in with one foot—

"Jez!"

In the back of her mind she heard the faint click of the lock, just as the binder slid free. She jerked it out, shoved it into her bag, and looked around quickly.

The desk was far too open to hide behind, and the shelves were set into the wall.

Still—well, it almost certainly wouldn't be Jaromil. And it was just possible that if it was the man she'd seen earlier cleaning offices, she might be able to talk her way out of this …

The door swung open.

For a moment, she stared at the man in the drab cleaning-staff uniform, and he stared at her.

And then he yanked a huge broad-bore heat gun from the inside of the cleaning cart and raised it to his shoulder.

Jez swore and dived as heat blistered the air over her head.

"Jez! What the hell——"

The man was standing in the doorway, and he'd pulled the cart up so it blocked the exit. She'd have to go through him and the cart to get out that way, and neither of them looked to want to make it easy on her.

The window. It'd be locked, she assumed, but the heat blast had left the latch a charred, melted lump, so that should solve that.

She was six stories up, which could be a problem, but hell, she'd figure something out.

She was pretty sure.

She yanked out her pistol and fired back. The man had already pulled down a heat visor, and she wasn't even a little surprised when the heat from Ysbel's mods blackened the man's clothing, but only sent a dull orange glow around his middle as his heat shield absorbed the blast.

He aimed again, and this time she ducked deliberately behind the drawers she'd pulled the binder from.

The blast left the entire side of the desk charcoaled, tiny flickers of flame dancing up and down the singed metal of the drawers. She grinned. Took care of Jaromil figuring out what she'd taken, anyways.

She took a deep breath, then lunged for the window. She'd yanked it open by the time her attacker realized what she was up to, and by the time he'd brought his gun up to bear, she was balanced on the edge of the sill, the cold wind whipping around her, biting her exposed skin.

Hell of a long way down from here. Still——she glanced back at the muzzle of the heat gun, took a deep breath, and stepped out onto the narrow ledge that ran along the side of the building.

Behind her, the air in front of the window turned briefly visible as it burned.

Damn.

She closed her eyes for a moment. No way down from here.

Well, that wasn't entirely true. There was one way. And she was pretty sure as soon as the bastard inside the office made it to the window and got his aim steady, that was the way she'd be taking.

"Jez." Lev's voice shook slightly. "Above you. The sixth floor's the top floor, and they designed the buildings with decorative ledges. I've checked the specs, and they should support your weight."

She glanced up.

They were covered with packed drifted snow, and they'd be slippery as hell, but on the other hand—

She could hear cautious footsteps approaching the window from inside the office.

She took a deep breath, bit down hard on her teeth, and started to climb.

The icy bite of the snow on her fingers was a sharp pain, but she didn't have time to worry about that. As soon as the bastard put his head out the window …

Her hand slipped, and she kicked against the wall, lunging upward on instinct, her other hand catching the edge of the roof. For a moment she dangled there, then her foot found a ledge, and she shoved herself up and over the edge of the roof, flattening herself against its surface just as a man's head poked out of the window metres below her. He looked down, then from side to side, then up. And then, even though she was pretty sure he couldn't see her, he carefully began pulling himself through the window.

Damn it to hell.

She scrambled to her feet, shaking her hands to get blood flowing to her fingers, and tapped her com. "OK genius, I'm on the roof. Get me off, or the bastard climbing up after me is going to."

Lev swore. "Alright. Listen. There's a trap door in the roof, southwest corner. I don't have the code, but it's old. You may be able to melt the lock."

She glanced around quickly. The roof was covered in snow, but she thought she saw a faint indent in the corner Lev had mentioned. She sprinted for it, trying to keep her balance on the slippery surface.

Below her, through the whine of the wind, she could hear the unmistakable sound of someone scrabbling on the wall below her. For a brief moment she considered waiting for the plaguer to raise his head over the edge and then giving him a solid kick, but anyone with a heat gun like that probably had mag hooks or something.

Yes, there was definitely an indent in the snow. She kicked the snow away, revealing a rusty trapdoor with an ancient lock. She jerked out her pistol and fired, then fired again, then a third time.

The metal glowed a dull orange, protesting loudly as it cooled in the frigid air, and then there was a sharp *crack*. She grinned, shoved the muzzle of her pistol through the rusty handle, which still glowed a dull orange, and yanked the door back. Then she slid into the darkness, catching a rung of the rickety ladder with one hand and pulling the trapdoor shut with the other.

This would give her about thirty seconds, maybe. But hell, that was thirty seconds more than she'd had before.

She dropped to the dusty ceiling panels, loosened one with a sharp kick, then jumped to the floor in a shower of dust and rat droppings, landing in the same hallway she'd walked down less than a standard hour earlier. She was sprinting for the stairwell the moment her boots touched the threadbare carpet.

She heard the heavy thud of boots hitting the ground in the

hallway as the door to the stairwell swung shut behind her, then she was taking the steps three at a time, grabbing the steel railing and swinging herself around the tight corners of the staircase. She reached the first floor just as she heard a door above her swing open, and she pushed through the door and out into the first-floor corridor.

It was busier now, which was a good thing, probably—less likely for someone to shoot her with all these people watching—but she damn well didn't plan on betting her life on that assumption.

Then she saw a familiar stiff figure striding down the hallway, and she grinned, straightened, and stepped quickly forward, grabbing the woman by the arm.

Branka turned, startled, and for a moment just stared at Jez.

Jez gave her a jaunty grin. "Hey Branka. Figured I'd show up for our meeting a bit early today. Don't seem to like it when I'm late, so I figured I'd make amends."

Behind her, a muffled clatter of heavy boots descended the staircase at high acceleration. She pulled Branka down the hallway by the elbow, the woman apparently too shocked to resist, and stopped in front of Branka's office.

Branka was still staring.

Jez sighed, and touched the door handle suggestively, and finally, still wearing a stunned expression, Branka hit the key on her com. Jez was shoving the door open almost before the lock clicked. She stepped inside, pulled Branka in after her, and slammed the door shut firmly with her foot.

For a moment, she and Branka looked at each other, the faint *drip* ... *drip* of snow melting off Jez's hair onto the carpet the only sound.

Finally, Branka shook her head, lips pinched tightly together. "Layla, that whatever it was you were doing, I advise you to tell me —"

Jez gave her an easy grin. "Well," she drawled, "I mean, I guess if you were looking for ideas on how to keep your love life interesting …"

There was a snort of half-hysterical laughter through her com earpiece, disguised quickly as a cough.

"I … don't think I need details, on second thought," said Branka after a moment, the look on her face a mix of horror and faint disgust. "Would—you like to take a seat?"

Jez dropped down into a chair, still grinning, and after a moment, Branka took her seat as well. She steepled her hands on her desk, tapping her fingers together one at a time and clearly trying to regain her composure, and when at last she looked up again, her face had resumed its usual icy politeness.

"Layla. Since we last talked, we've received another message. From Grigory."

Jez raised an eyebrow. "Yeah? What'd he say?"

Branka studied her for a moment. "I'm sorry. Perhaps 'intercepted' would be a better term. Apparently Drusan's loyalties are not what we assumed."

Jez leaned back in her chair. "Wait just a damn minute," she drawled. "You said you'd intercepted—" she paused, her grin broadening. "Well," she said at last. "Never did like that bastard." She paused again. "Thought he was working for Olyessa, though. At least, he sure as hell didn't seem happy about leaving her out of it."

"It appears Olyessa wasn't the only one he was working for." Branka's face was grim.

Jez raised her eyebrows in what was honestly a pretty damn good approximation of surprise, considering she'd been waiting for this news ever since Lev had informed her what Masha had planted in the plaguer's office. "Guess it wasn't such a bad idea to keep

Olyessa's stooges out of power after all."

"No," said Branka reluctantly. "I suppose it wasn't. I'll admit, I was less than convinced by your idea when you first presented it, but I am beginning to see the benefits."

"See," said Jez cheerfully. "That's exactly what I was saying. Figure anyone who'd worked for one of those bastards would just as happily work for the other, as long as they were offering a few credits." She paused a moment. "What was this message about?"

"He was—purchasing weapons," said Branka tightly. "At least, trying to. And—" she hesitated, and Jez could hear the faint unease in her voice. "And the weapons he was after were mostly street weapons. The kind of things you'd use for city fighting."

Jez frowned.

Lev, you hearing this? she tapped out casually on the side of her chair.

"Yes," said Lev quietly, and she caught the concern in his voice.

Why would Masha specify that kind of weapon? She was pretty sure that the plan had been to let Tae handle the streets. And this was going to put him in trouble. At the very least, there'd be people watching the streets a hell of a lot more closely than they would have otherwise.

Which basically meant, the faster she could get done whatever she needed to here, the better for everyone.

She turned her attention back to Branka, unease twisting inside her. "Well, so here's the thing," she said, keeping her tone easy. "Don't know why he would have been after that type of weapon, exactly. But I can tell you, when things start going sideways, they go quickly, and it sounds like things are going sideways. So." She leaned forward. "Figure you could get me that meeting with Goran you promised me?"

Branka shifted slightly in her seat. "I ... am not sure how that's relevant to—"

She shot the woman a grin that showed all her teeth. "Listen. You called me here because I know how to deal with crap. And I'm telling you, this is how you deal with crap—by figuring out who can make it happen, and then not giving them a damn moment of peace until they do. Because if you don't—" she shrugged. "Well, somebody else deals with the crap, after they're done scraping what's left of you off the damn walls."

There were a few moments of silence. Finally Branka said, "You told me you had information. If you were to give it to me, and it were interesting enough, I may be able to get you a meeting."

Jez grinned. "I'll bring it tomorrow morning."

Assuming they all lived that long.

When the day was finally damn well over, she pulled her coat and scarf tightly around her and stepped out into the already dark Prasvishoni streets. The morning's light snow had died off, but the wind picked up the snow from the streets and hurled it against her in tiny stinging pellets. She hunched down against the assault, swearing softly to herself and wondering for the hundredth time why the hell anyone had decided to build a city on this plaguing dump of a planet.

By the time she reached the apartment, she was wet, miserable, and thoroughly chilled.

Stepping through the door of the tiny apartment was an almost physical relief, and she sighed, loosening her scarf and letting the warmth and the smell of cooking dinner enveloped her.

Lev stood quickly, coming over to the door. "Jez," he said, and there was a slight smile on his face, even through the worry in his voice. "You're soaked. Here, let me take that." He took her wet jacket from her, and hung it on the pick behind the door to drip dry.

Honestly, she'd probably have just left it in a heap on the floor, and then had to put it on sopping wet the next morning. Generally what she'd done back when she was doing smuggling runs out of Prasvishoni.

But—having a dry coat in the mornings was kind of nice.

After dinner, Lev asked quietly, "So. Did you get what we were after?"

She shrugged, and pulled the binder out of her bag. "Didn't have time to check, to be honest. But I think so."

The look of frank admiration Lev gave her made something warm spark in her chest, for no actual real reason. He took the binder and opened it carefully, then pulled a small chip storage compartment out of the bottom pocket. Carefully, he cracked it open, then smiled up at her.

"I think you did it. Here, I'll pull up my holoscreen, and we can take a look."

She snuggled up next to him on the couch, because they had to, because whoever the hell might be watching them, and the warmth of him bled through the lingering traces of chill, and she found there was a smile on her face.

Only because he was warm, of course. The same reason she always seemed to wake up to find herself snuggled into his shoulder at night. Because he was warm, and Prasvishoni was cold, and— and, well, the warmth of him was a comfort that soothed something deep in her soul.

She peered over his shoulder as he looked at the readout from her chip. He was frowning slightly in concentration, that familiar crease between his eyebrows, and she grinned and poked him with her elbow.

"So, what is it?"

He glanced over at her, his expression one of mild excitement. "It does reference someone named Myrni. It doesn't give their identity, but I think, if we analyze it, we may be able to figure out where to find that information, at least."

She grinned. "Well, I guess—"

"Jez." It was Tanya's voice. "Have you done anything to irritate anyone in the government recently?" She sounded grim.

Jez snorted. "Figure my damn existence irritates them at this point. You mean, anything out of the ordinary?"

"Yes," said Tanya, sounding not in the least amused. "I mean, something that would give them a reason to suspect that you're not who you said you are. A reason to, for example, set an assassin outside your window."

Beside her, Lev stiffened.

"You're saying—" Jez began.

"I'm saying," said Tanya, her voice, if possible, even grimmer, "that I am not outside your apartment right now, but I set a bug, and unless I'm very much mistaken, someone is waiting to kill you. And it looks like they come from the government."

Lev was already turning, grabbing Jez by the shoulders as if he was about to shove her down, out of the range of any weapon, but Tanya's voice stopped him.

"I can guess what you're doing, Lev, but it won't be enough. If they want you dead, they'll bring the entire apartment down to do it. I suggest instead you work very hard at convincing whoever is that you're exactly who you told Branka you were."

They stared at each other for a moment.

Damn it to hell.

Jez took a deep breath, reached over, and, gingerly, took Lev's face in her hands.

He'd gone very still, and was watching her. She gave him a rueful look and a faint shrug, hoping he couldn't see that she was trembling, just a little. Then she took a deep breath, leaned forward, and kissed him.

It was just an act. It had always been just an act, probably the only way to keep that damn Branka from killing them. But somehow, when his lips touched hers, every other thought completely vanished from her head.

He leaned into her, slightly, his lips unbearably gentle against hers, and she found her hands coming up behind his neck, pulling him closer, and something light and tingling spread through her body at the taste of him, the feel of him. He made a soft sound at the pressure of her hand on his neck, and her heart was pounding even faster now, but—it wasn't unpleasant. Hell, this was maybe the most pleasant thing she done in a very long time.

Her brain felt slightly hazy, like she'd just begun to realize that maybe she'd drunk a little more than she'd intended.

She pulled back, feeling a bit like she'd been hit with a shock stick, and stared at him. He was staring back, and something about looking into his eyes, about the way his chest rose and fell in rapid, uneven gasps—she found she'd leaned in towards him again, because honestly, if they'd actually been lovers, one kiss like that wouldn't be nearly enough. And it was probably a good idea, something she'd have done even if she did actually think it through, but the fact was, the sensation of Lev's lips on hers had left her way too drunk to trust anything her brain was telling her right now.

Their lips met again, and this time his kiss wasn't nearly as gentle as it had been. Which, as far as her now completely fuzzy brain was concerned, wasn't a bad thing in the slightest. Because hell, there were a lot of things she was feeling right now, and gentle didn't apply to a single damn one of them.

Her lips parted, her tongue nudging his lips open, and she wasn't actually sure she'd meant to do that when this whole thing had started, but for some reason it seemed like a very, very good idea just now. He seemed to think so too—his teeth grazed her lip, and she sucked in a quick gasp, then he grabbed her hips, pulling her onto his lap so she sat straddling him. The warm, comfortable burn that had started in the pit of her stomach the moment their lips met was spreading through her entire body now. She laced her fingers into his hair, pulling him closer, because maybe she wasn't in a state to think about anything at all, but she was damn sure that getting him closer to her was something she wanted, and she'd probably wanted for a very long time.

Her entire body tingled, everywhere he touched her. His hands slid up her back, down along her waist, and she gave a little moan of pleasure. Honestly, genius boy came up with a lot of good ideas, but trying to make sure there was as little space as possible between them was probably his best damn one yet.

She was definitely drunk. She was definitely, definitely drunk, because nothing in the whole world seemed to matter except getting more of whatever was making her drunk. She pulled him against her harder, deepening the kiss. She could feel every part of her body, every place where he touched her, every movement of his lips on hers, every rise and fall of his chest, and it wasn't enough, it wasn't nearly enough, and she needed more or maybe she die …

In the back of her mind she heard a voice over her com, but she didn't care about anything in the entire damn system right now that didn't directly affect how close Lev's body was to hers, the bright, warm tingle that ran through her at his touch, the way his lips caught hers, the way his hands fit against the small of her back, slid down her sides, grasped at her hips—

"Jez! If you don't answer me, I'm going to have to assume you're dead, and that will put me to a lot of trouble, and I'm not going to be very happy if I find out it's not true."

By the time the words filtered through to her brain, she'd recognized the voice as Tanya's.

She blinked, and somehow remembered how to remove her lips from Lev's, although it seemed to be a lot more complicated than she'd anticipated. And also, considering the fact they were just friends, she hadn't expected the dizzying jolt of disappointment when she finally succeeded.

"Jez! This is the last time and going to call you, and then—"

She swallowed hard and hit her com, and somehow managed to convince her mouth to form words. "Yeah, Tanya, 'm here."

There was a pause from the other end of the com, and then Tanya's voice again. "I can assume, then, that you weren't assassinated?"

It took her a minute to remember what the hell Tanya was talking about. Because, OK, it was kind of an important subject, but at the same time, a hell of a lot had happened between then and now.

"Yeah, nobody blew the damn place up," she managed, but she was pretty sure that her voice had been a lot closer to shaky than to jaunty.

"That's good," said Tanya, a hint of amusement seeping through her voice. "Whatever it was you were doing, it must have been effective. He's put down his gun."

From the knowing edge to her tone, Jez was pretty sure that she'd guessed 'whatever it was they were doing.'

She scowled, and reluctantly rolled off Lev, trying to force her brain to sober up from the after-effects of the kiss. Which, actually, was not quite as easy as it probably should be. Every damn piece of her body felt light and tingly, like whatever it was she'd drunk would hit her hard soon, but hadn't hit yet, and she couldn't really feel the floor under her feet, or the couch behind her back, or anything, really, except the warm, urgent memory of Lev's hands, his lips—she took a deep, shaky breath.

Damn. Good thing she held her liquor better than this.

She made the mistake of glancing over at Lev.

He'd leaned back against the couch, eyes closed, breath still coming far too rapidly, judging by the rise and fall of his chest. His face was bloodless, and he wore a dazed, helpless look that made her think that maybe their kiss had made him just as drunk as it had made her.

She swallowed hard.

She should probably look away. Honestly, she was pretty damn sure she should look away. In the same way as when she was drinking, there was always that moment that she knew she should probably stop, probably put the glass down if she wanted to avoid a hangover the next day.

But then, usually by the time she got to that point, she didn't really give a damn about a hangover the next day.

He opened his eyes, and his gaze caught hers. There was an intensity there she hadn't seen in a very long time, and for a moment she couldn't breathe. Her heart pounded against her chest like a damn trapped animal, and her whole body had gone shaky, but she'd never realized how pleasant a feeling that could be.

"Jez," he whispered, his voice hoarse, and the sound of her name on his lips sent a shiver through her whole damn body. His hand slid around her waist, and her entire brain fuzzed pleasantly.

"Jez," he said again, his voice thick with desire. "We—we shouldn't—we aren't—"

He was right, they couldn't—they shouldn't—this was a terrible idea, she knew it was a terrible idea, she wasn't sure she could—her damn brain didn't seem to want to let her even finish the thought, because the only thing she could think of was how close he was to her right now—

His hand trembled, like he was on the very edge of his control. And then, with a sound that was almost a moan of pain, he tightened his grip, pulling her towards him, and she leaned into him, and—

"Lev! Are you there?"

Tae's harsh whisper through their earpieces jolted both of them out of their trance.

For a moment they stared at each other, and Jez tried desperately to remember how to make her brain work again.

Lev recovered before she did, and tapped his com. "Tae," he said, and she could hear the shakiness in his voice. "What's wrong?"

"Lev." Tae paused. "Is everything alright? You sound—"

"It's—we're fine. Everything's—everything's fine."

"Are you sure?" Tae's voice was concerned.

Jez drew in a shaky breath, her brain finally starting to function again, and hit her own com. "Tech-head, we're fine. What's wrong?"

"I need your help." There was a trace of grimness in his voice, but there was something slightly incongruous about his tone. "Something's—happened." He paused a moment. "We were up by the university, and … and the students are protesting. And they said they'll keep protesting, make enough noise to keep the police away, but the way the police were acting … Ivan thinks it's going to get ugly, soon."

Jez frowned at her com.

Granted, Tae worried about basically everything, but he sounded really worried this time. And if he was calling in, it was probably something bad.

Also, there was something about the way he'd said Ivan's name …

"That's not all." It was Ivan's voice this time, and he sounded grim. "Tae won't say it, but he was almost killed in an explosion this afternoon."

Jez swore, her brain finally coming fully back online, and glanced over at Lev.

Apparently, the news had sobered him up as well. "Tae, are you alright?" he asked, the grimness in his voice almost matching Ivan's. "What happened?"

"I don't know," said Tae. "I hacked into the police database to distract them from killing the other street kids, but I didn't have time to be careful, and I think they tracked my com." He blew out a short breath. "The thing is, though, before, they'd never have spent that much time tracking down some street kid. There's something going on. And I don't know what it is, but—" he let his words trail off.

Jez and Lev exchanged glances.

"Jez heard something when she was talking with Branka today," said Lev carefully. "I haven't had time to look into it. But—" he glanced at Jez.

She nodded. "I don't know what's going on, but she mentioned the gangs, and the street kids. And weapons."

"And … it's possible Masha's involved in this," said Lev quietly.

Jez stared at him, something uncomfortable twisting her stomach. Because … well, because even after everything, she didn't want to believe that Masha would willingly sell them out.

But Lev was right. The information Branka had been talking

about—that had been planted by Masha.

"The university students are willing to help, but they won't be able to hold out on their own," said Tae quietly. "And unless something changes, we won't last two more nights. We're running out of places to hide."

Lev glanced over at Jez, and she saw in his eyes the same thing she was thinking.

She nodded, slowly. "Well," she said. "Here's the thing. I've managed to annoy the hell out of enough of the big-wig minister types that I think I've got some pull. I'll see what I can do to get the police distracted."

"I'll look into what Jez overheard, see if I can figure anything out." said Lev. He hesitated a moment. "And—I'll talk to Masha. It's possible I'm mistaken, and she knows nothing about this. Or at least, she doesn't know how bad it is."

For a moment, there was silence over the com. "Thank you," said Tae at last.

Jez tapped her com. "Hey, so one more thing. You and Ivan?"

There was a long pause.

"Um," he started. Then he stopped again. "Um. We."

A smile was creeping over Jez's face. "Hold on. Hold on just a damn minute. You mean we had this whole entire conversation, and you didn't tell me that you and Ivan finally kissed?"

There was a long pause. "You—how did you—"

She was grinning broadly now. "Tech-head. Every damn person on the crew, including Misko, knew. We've had a running bet going on for the last three weeks how long it would take for you two to finally kiss." She paused a moment. "Well, most of us did. Ysbel said she would be an absolute damn hopeless innocent fool to let me anywhere near her credits. So I couldn't get in on it." She paused again. "I would have won."

There was a long silence from the other end of the com. At last Tae said, his voice a mixture of awe and exasperation, "Jez, I swear one of these days I'm actually going to strangle you."

"You want to strangle me, you'll have to stand in line, and I figure the line's getting pretty long. Anyway, shouldn't you get back to, I don't know, kissing Ivan?"

Tae made a strangled sound, and Jez snorted with laughter.

"Hey. I don't blame you, he's hot. Anyways, I'll see if I can't distract the police. Although I seem to remember on Grigory's ship, you and Ivan had a pretty good way of distracting—"

"Jez—"

Jez tapped off her com and turned to Lev, still grinning. "You know, figure Ivan will be good for our tech-head."

"Yes," said Lev, smiling. "I imagine he will." He paused for a moment, his face going serious. "I suppose I should call Masha."

Jez nodded, trying to ignore the sick feeling in her stomach. "Yeah, guess that would be a good idea."

Lev sighed and tapped his com.

"Yes, Lev?" said Masha a moment later, her voice brusque.

"Tae just called in," Lev said quietly. "They're in trouble from the police. Apparently the university students are going to help by making a distraction, but Tae says their protests won't last unless they get help. Jez thinks she can get the police ordered down, give Tae and the students a chance."

There were a few moments of silence, and Jez bit her lip.

Because if Masha agreed with them—well, then maybe they were wrong. Maybe she was on their side after all.

"I'm—not sure that would be a good idea," said Masha finally. "The information Jez needs to pass on to Branka has to do with the students. I've been watching them, and I believe I know how she can neutralize them."

Jez stared at the com for a moment. "Wait," she said finally. "You want me to sell out the damn students? After what they did for us?"

"Jez." Masha's voice was weary. "You wouldn't be selling them out. You'd be helping to end the protests quickly, before anyone gets killed. And in return, you'd leverage that to get an audience with Goran, and keep the government from devolving into war when news of Grigory and Olyessa gets out."

For a few moments, no one spoke. Something slightly sick was twisting in Jez's stomach.

Because she couldn't pretend that maybe they were mistaken about Masha anymore.

She glanced over at Lev, and saw in his face the same thing she was thinking.

"Tae's going to help the students," said Lev at last, into the com. "You know that. He believes this is the best way—maybe the only way—to do what you sent him there to do. And even if he didn't—there's no way we'd be able to convince him to leave his friends to get hurt."

"Maybe if you do what I ask and don't try to make it easier for him, he'll see the issues with his reasoning," Masha snapped.

Jez took a deep breath. "No," she said finally. "Sorry, Masha. I'll be damned if I let tech-head call me for help and I don't do anything. I got the information you asked for from Jaromil. I'll send that through to you. But you'll have to look into it yourself, because I'm going to help Tae."

Again, there was a long pause on the other side of the com. Finally, Masha said, "Jez. If you do this, you'll be throwing away our entire plan."

"No," she said, sitting up straighter. "I won't. Because here's the thing—I can still do what you need. Even if I can't get Branka to give me an in with Goran, and even if I'm not breaking into crap to find your information, I've already convinced Branka to make a damn lot of changes. We can still get the government prepared, even if it's not how you planned. But I'm not selling out those students, and I'm not going to leave Tae hanging."

"Lev—" Masha began.

"I agree with Jez," he said quietly.

There was a long moment of silence. Finally, Masha said, "I suppose I can't prevent you from doing this. But I'd advise you to think long and hard about what you're giving up."

"And Masha. As Jez has explained, we don't believe that there has to be a choice. Both goals are achievable," said Lev. "If you would explain your concerns, I'm certain Jez and I both would take them into consideration. But you won't, will you?"

Masha didn't answer.

And honestly, maybe that was what scared Jez the most.

16

Ysbel, day 7

The noise was quiet enough that Ysbel almost didn't hear it. She frowned, and glanced up quickly.

"Mama?" Olya's voice was sleepy. "Why did you stop reading?"

Misko was already asleep, and Olya looked like she would be there in the next two minutes.

"I'm sorry, my love," Ysbel murmured. "I have to check on something. I'll be right back."

"Okay," said Olya, through a yawn. "I'll wait for you. I'm not very tired."

Ysbel smiled despite herself and rose gently, depositing the sleeping Misko in his bed. "I need you to lie down beside your brother, make sure he doesn't wake up."

Olya nodded sleepily and crawled into bed, curling up next to Misko.

When she was settled, Ysbel slipped out the door. She walked quickly down the familiar corridors of the *Ungovernable*, and hesitated a moment at the loading ramp. She tapped her com. "Tanya? Are you back yet?"

Tanya answered almost immediately, her tone concerned. "No,

my love. We're at the government buildings. It will be awhile, I think. Is something wrong?"

"I don't know," Ysbel said quietly. She tapped off her com and touched the reassuring shape of her heat pistol in its holster. Then, cautiously, she walked down the loading ramp and stepped into the darkened hangar bay.

The bar lights overhead had been turned off, so the only illumination was the dim glow from the streetlamps outside, trickling in through the high, narrow windows, and the emergency lighting that gave the barest of illumination to the floor and walls.

She hit the control for the loading ramp, and as it raised and clicked shut with a faint hiss, some of the tension drained from her shoulders.

Her own life in danger was one thing. Lady knew she'd done that often enough. But Misko and Olya in danger shot ice through her limbs.

She stood still for a moment, waiting for her eyes to adjust, and listened carefully, ears straining for anything out of the ordinary.

Honestly, in this dump of the hangar bay, the noise she'd heard was likely just a rodent. But she hadn't survived for as long as she had by ignoring her gut instinct, and her gut instinct was telling her this hadn't been a rat—at least, not the animal variety.

Once her eyes had adjusted enough that she could see, she peered around.

Nothing seemed out of the ordinary, but she'd lived long enough to know that didn't mean anything. And the sound—it had been so familiar it had hardly registered. What was it?

The clink of metal on metal. That was what she'd heard.

She looked around, frowning. The hangar bay was all but empty, and the floor was concrete, so it couldn't have come from the middle of the room.

There was the *Ungovernable*, yes, but if the sound had come from that close, she would have realized it. But there was also the communication device in the corner—if someone wanted to sabotage them, that would be the obvious place.

Warily, she walked towards the device, flipping on her com light for a moment to illuminate the corner where it was stored.

Nothing out of place.

She frowned. The only other option was the heavy outer door.

She made her cautious way over, and when she reached it, she paused, listening for any sound from outside.

Nothing.

She opened the door a crack, heat pistol raised and finger on the trigger.

After an interminable moment, she stepped carefully out into the bitter Prasvishoni night air.

The explosive device was so small that it was barely visible in the corner against the door. She wouldn't have noticed it at all if she hadn't been half expecting it.

She crouched beside it, flipping on the light on her com.

Her heart beat faster than usual, but her hands were steady. She was used to explosives. Her hands were always steady.

It only took a moment's inspection to recognize the telltale signs. A time bomb. Jostling it shouldn't affect the countdown, then. Gently, she unfastened it from the corner behind the door where it had been fastened, and turned it over in her hands.

Ten standard minutes left on the timer.

The mechanism was complex, but Ysbel knew explosives. It was a matter of less than a minute for her to disarm it. And when she'd done that, she stood for a moment, looking down at the disarmed explosive in her hand, something cold winding around her chest.

Someone had found them. It could be the government, or one of Grigory's or Olyessa's people bent on revenge, or any one of a thousand other options. There was nothing about the explosive that told her. Perhaps, if she'd had time and materials to do a chemical analysis, send the information to Lev, perhaps he'd have been able to track down something. But there was no time for that at the moment.

She inspected the doorway twice more, as carefully as possible, and finally, when she was satisfied there were no more planted explosives, she pocketed the one she'd disarmed and walked slowly back into the *Ungovernable*.

Olya was asleep, as Ysbel had expected.

Just as well. There was plenty she needed to do.

Tanya and Masha arrived an hour or so later.

"Ysi, what happened?" asked Tanya, her face grave, as she stepped into the ship. Melting snow dripped from her wet hair, and her cheeks were red with cold.

In response, Ysbel held out the explosive device.

Tanya and Masha both frowned at it, and there was sharp worry on both their faces.

"Who left this?" asked Masha at last, her voice quiet, but hard as steel.

"I don't know," said Ysbel. "I heard someone moving around outside, and I found this when I went to look. If we did a full analysis, it might give us a hint, but—" she shrugged. "By the time we got it done, it wouldn't be relevant, because we'd all be dead."

Masha raised an eyebrow. "I suppose that's an accurate assessment," she said. She peered around the hangar bay quickly. "We'll have to leave. We can worry about the identity of the person who planted it later." She paused a moment. "I have a place we can go. But we'll have to leave the *Ungovernable* here."

Ysbel nodded slowly. "On the bright side, whoever it was who set this probably didn't know about the ship." She held out her hand, with the explosive still cradled in her palm. "This would have taken down the hangar bay, but it wouldn't have stood a chance against the *Ungovernable's* shielding. So either they didn't mean to kill us, or they didn't know about it. And if we set the cloaking on the *Ungovernable*, I doubt very much anyone will find it. It's Sasa Illiovich's tech, after all. I doubt even the government has the tech to penetrate that."

"We'd best pack our things, then," said Tanya at last.

Between the three of them, it didn't take long. It was less than an hour later that Ysbel stood beside Tanya and Masha at the door of the hangar bay, a sleepy Olya in her arms, while Tanya held a muttering, yawning Misko. For a moment, Ysbel's heart ached to look at them—the drowsy confusion mingled with fear in the children's faces reminded her far too much of the day she'd fled Prasvishoni with her parents, as bundled as Olya and Misko were, and as bewildered, and as frightened.

And now it was her and Tanya fleeing, and her children who were bundled and confused and scared.

But then, her children had never had the childhood she had—one of safety, insulated against the problems of the outside world. Her children were far, far too used to fleeing for their lives.

Olya ducked her head against Ysbel's shoulder as they stepped out into the dark, windblown, snowy streets of Prasvishoni. The night air was bitter, and Ysbel tightened her arms around her daughter and squinted against the blowing sleet. Masha carried the communication device, as bundled as one of the children, and each of them, beside their larger bundle, carried the clothes and food and supplies to last them for however long this took.

Masha led them unerringly through the streets, and Ysbel wondered briefly how long she'd been preparing to flee the hangar.

At last, they came to a halt outside a grungy, worn-down apartment building. Masha tapped her com against the door handle, and at the faint click of the lock, she pushed the door open. Ysbel and Tanya followed her inside.

The building was tired and rundown, the thin carpets on the floor threadbare, the air smelling of mildew. The dilapidated lift may or may not have worked, but Ysbel was relieved when Masha bypassed it altogether, even considering the heavy bundle they were carrying. The room Masha led them to was on the second floor, at the end of a long hallway. Again, Masha held her com chip up, and again, the door clicked open.

The inside of the small apartment didn't look any better than the common areas, and smelled sharply of rodent droppings. Ysbel wrinkled her nose, and exchanged glances with Tanya.

"I'm sorry for the mess," Masha murmured, glancing around. "However, we should be safe here for some time. As far as I am aware, there is no record of my connection with this building."

In the end, Ysbel and Tanya laid one of the clean blankets they'd brought from the *Ungovernable* out on the couch and settled the two children onto it with another blanket over them, while they set to work with Masha, making the place habitable. There were ancient cleaning supplies under the dirty sink, liberally sprinkled with rodent droppings, but judging from the sharp, chemical smell of them, they should still be effective. Tanya found some dirt-ringed buckets, and after rinsing them out, they filled them with hot water from the rusty sink and began the task that would almost certainly take them through 'til morning.

Ysbel was coming out of one of the bedrooms, a disgusted grimace on her face and a bundle of rat-chewed blankets in her arms, when she heard a voice from the other bedroom. She frowned, pausing for a moment outside the door.

The voice was Masha's, and a trick of the room's shape let Ysbel make out the words through the door, partially cracked open.

"… planted an explosive outside the hangar bay where we were staying," Masha was saying. "It doesn't appear that they've figured out yet what we're doing, but I have a feeling that may be coming soon. I hope you're ready." There was a long pause, then Masha's voice again. "Yes." She sounded grim. "There's a complication with my two in the government, I'm afraid. They're determined to keep the unrest off the streets. I tried to dissuade them, but I was unsuccessful. I'll continue trying to talk them out of it, but—These are not people who are easily persuaded. And I can only go so far without losing what little remains of their trust. I wanted to make you aware, as that may affect our future plans." She was silent for another moment. "And the ship," she continued at last. "We had to leave it, but … it's possible that may work to our advantage."

She was still talking, but her voice dropped so that Ysbel could no longer make out the words clearly.

She frowned. Whoever was on the other end of the com, she was almost certain it wasn't one of the *Ungovernable's* crew.

There was another pause, and then a soft click as Masha tapped off her com. Ysbel stepped silently away from the door, and was in the main room by the cleanser by the time the bedroom door opened.

Tanya glanced up, and her face sharpening with concern at Ysbel's expression, but Ysbel gave a quick shake of her head.

They'd have time to talk when Masha was out of the apartment.

The children woke early, as always, and when they did, Ysbel and Tanya exchanged wry glances. In an apartment this size, it was unlikely that either of them would be able to take a nap to recover from the night's activities. But at least the place was clean enough now that Ysbel wasn't worried about the children catching some horrible disease the moment their feet touched the floor.

She didn't get a chance to talk to Tanya alone until early afternoon. The children were in the bedroom playing, and Masha had stepped out to purchase some rations and the few things they hadn't managed to bring from the ship.

"What is it, my heart?" asked Tanya softly.

"I heard Masha talking to someone last night," Ysbel said. "I'm—not sure who it was."

Tanya's expression was instantly overlaid with concern.

Ysbel recounted everything she could remember of the previous evening's overheard conversation. When she finished, Tanya's frown had deepened.

"Do you think she intends to leave Tae to get hurt?"

Ysbel pressed her lips together. "I wish I knew. I honestly wish I knew."

"Well," said Tanya, "at the very least, we should warn Jez and Lev." She paused. "If they can find time to listen, with how busy they are pretending to be lovers."

Ysbel grinned despite herself and hit her com.

Lev's voice, when he answered, was worried. "Ysbel. Did something happen? Did you hear from Tae?"

"No," said Ysbel. "But we did hear from Masha."

When she finished her story, there was silence on the other end of the com. At last, Lev spoke.

"Thank you for telling me." His voice was quiet. "I'll—see what I can figure out." There was a moment's pause. "And keep an eye out for what's happening on the streets. Tae's worried. Ivan told me he'd almost been killed."

"I'll see if there's anything I can do," said Tanya, her voice grim. "I'm not sure there will be. But I'll do what I can."

"That's the best any of us can do right now," said Lev quietly.

There were a few moments' pause. Finally, Ysbel said, a hint of amusement in her voice, "You said Ivan told you. Are he and Tae still—"

Lev chuckled softly. "That, at least, seems to be going well. Apparently Tae finally figured out that Ivan's madly in love with him. Or so I gathered. I don't see Tae going around kissing people he doesn't think are in love with him."

Ysbel chuckled as well. "Well, that's good." She paused a moment. "And I think you owe me five credits."

"I believe I do," said Lev, his voice amused. "I'll pay you next time I see you, assuming we're both still alive."

"I didn't know it would be so easy for you to get out of paying," said Ysbel.

Lev sighed, his voice once again serious. "Just—be careful, alright? And if you hear anything else—"

"I'll tell you," said Ysbel quietly.

She tapped off her com, and she and Tanya looked at each other. Tanya's expression was grim, and hers likely matched it. At last, Ysbel shook her head. "I don't like this, my love. But—we're not going to let Tae die. And we're not going to let anything happen to my students, not if I can help it."

Tanya nodded, and for a moment they were quiet, listening to the sounds of the children playing in the room next door.

But there was an uneasy tightness in the pit of Ysbel's stomach.

Like Lev said, they'd do what they could, and hope it was enough.

But she knew very well it might not be.

17

Tae, day 7

Tae woke, shivering slightly, but there was something warm against his back, and he couldn't stop himself from smiling.

"Tae? You awake?" Ivan's voice was quiet, but there was that familiar, fond good humour in it, and it almost made Tae want to close his eyes and curl back into the comfortable warmth, despite the morning chill.

Instead, he rolled over slightly. Ivan was watching him, an expression on his face that made something catch in Tae's throat.

Tae had spent the last however many weeks trying desperately to convince himself he didn't care for Ivan as anything more than a friend, and that Ivan looked at him the same way, and he hadn't realized until now how deeply he'd always known that was false. And how being able to look at Ivan, and not have to pretend anything, would be a quiet relief that almost took his breath away.

"Morning," he said, returning Ivan's smile.

Ivan propped himself up on an elbow, leaned over, and kissed Tae gently, and just like always, every muscle in Tae's body relaxed into the kiss.

At last, regretfully, Ivan pushed himself to his feet. Behind him, one of the children stirred in her sleep, moaning softly. Ivan bent, tucking the blanket around her a little tighter, and held out his hand to Tae. "I suppose we should get moving," he whispered.

Tae nodded and took Ivan's proffered hand, pulling himself to his feet.

Frost had formed during the night on the hard concrete of the alley floor around them, and their breath puffed out as white clouds in the frigid air. Caz and Peti were watching the street, but they turned at Tae and Ivan's approach. Lines of strain and exhaustion cut both their faces.

None of them had slept for more than a couple hours at a stretch since the explosion two days ago, and Tae doubted they would until this whole thing, whatever it was, was over.

"You two rest until the other kids wake up," Ivan whispered.

Peti gave a weary nod, and she and Caz stumbled back to the heap of blankets that was the rest of the street kids while Tae and Ivan took their places on watch.

Ivan put an arm around Tae's shoulders, and for a few moments, Tae leaned into him. At last, though, he shook his head, straightened, and tapped his com.

"Felix. Are you there?" he whispered.

"What is it?" came Felix's voice through his earpiece.

"Something's come up. We may be able to solve the problem of the police. There are students over by the university who've been protesting. Ivan and I were over there yesterday. The government's sent police to shut them down, but if we can work with the students, make enough noise to keep the police's attention, we should be able to keep them away from you."

The silence through Tae's earpiece was sceptical. At last, Felix said, "What makes you think the students will do what they say?

Aren't they government brats?"

"I know them," said Tae quietly. "They're better than you think. And they'll do whatever they need to to give us a chance."

There was another long silence from the other end of the com. At last, Felix said grudgingly, "We'll be ready. But don't expect me to help if those university brats screw this up. I trust you, maybe, and that boyfriend of yours, but I sure as hell don't trust a bunch of spoiled government bastards."

Tae frowned at the com. Exactly how many people had known that Ivan was his boyfriend before he did?

He wasn't entirely sure he wanted the answer to that.

"I'm not asking to you to trust them," he said at last. "Just to be ready. Caz and Peti will stay here to help."

"Yeah."

"Thank you," said Tae.

Ivan had leaned back against the icy wall of the building and was frowning at something on his holoscreen. He looked up when Tae tapped his com off. "Did he agree?"

"Yeah," said Tae wearily. "He said he'd be ready. How about you? How's it coming?"

Ivan sighed, strain behind his expression. "I'm trying to plan for all the most likely scenarios, but—" he shrugged helplessly. "I've been in enough protests. There's no such thing as being safe, not really."

"Do you have any idea when the police will show up?"

Ivan shook his head. "Not until it's light. It's too easy for things to go bad on them in the dark when they're outnumbered."

Tae bit the inside of his cheek. "I've written a new blocker for the drones. If I write a new one every evening, that should hold them, I think. But no luck getting through the communications line yet." He paused. "How violent do you expect it to get?"

Ivan sighed again. "If Lev and Jez can run some interference in the government, it's possible it won't get too ugly. At least, not at first."

"But?" asked Tae.

Ivan shot him a grim look. "But there's no guarantees. People die at protests."

Tae nodded, something sick in the pit of his stomach.

Still, he'd known that from the moment he stepped into the shouting mass of students yesterday.

People would die either way. It was inevitable. All they could do was try to keep casualties to a minimum.

When Caz and Peti woke to trade them off sentry duty, Tae rubbed the heels of his hands into his eyes, stretched the stiffness from his back, and turned to Caz. "Ivan and I should go. It will be light soon, and I want to be there before the police show up. You know what to do?"

Caz nodded silently.

"If there's problems, call me on the closed loop. We'll be back tonight."

Peti's face was pinched with worry, but she gave a short nod as well.

"Come on, Tae," said Ivan quietly. "Let's go."

Outside the shelter of the narrow alley, the wind blew in harsh gusts, picking up loose snow and whipping it against their faces. Tae squinted against the cold, pulling his worn jacket up around his shoulders and his scarf so low he could only see through a narrow crack.

Not that he could see more than a metre in front of him anyways, in the dim glow of the half-dead streetlamps and the swirling snow.

By the time they reached the square in front of the university, a handful of the kids were already there, huddled in makeshift shelters. Someone had started a small fire in the shelter of the alley walls where they'd taken refuge the day before, and five or six students were gathered around it, shoulders hunched against the cold, warming their hands. Tae and Ivan joined them, and the students shifted to make room.

"Where's Vera?" asked Ivan.

One of the students shook his head. "She's running around, doing whatever Vera does. I think she's trying to track down some of the things you asked for yesterday." He paused, and eyed Ivan more closely. "Do you—think this will work?" His voice was serious now, and overlaid with worry.

Ivan shrugged, a grim look on his face. "I'll do everything I can to keep you safe. But—"

"I know," the boy, turning back to fire. "There's no such thing as safe at a protest. Especially against the government." He shook his head. "I thought that was just a saying. But—" he trailed off.

For a while, no one spoke. The warmth of the fire cut some of the chill of the night air, and when Ivan moved closer and put his arm around Tae's shoulder, Tae felt as warm as he'd been in a long time. Although that wasn't saying a whole lot.

Vera showed up a few standard minutes later, carrying an armload of clear tacking-line. She grinned when she saw them.

"Good. I was hoping you'd get here before the police did. I think they'll be a lot more careful about letting people through their line after what you did yesterday." She dropped the bundle and turned the others around the fire. "Alright, you lazybones. Get stringing this stuff up. You heard what Ivan said yesterday."

Grumbling good-naturedly, the students moved away from the

warmth of the fire, taking bundles of the thin, translucent line with them.

"Osip brought step ladders out here last night," she called after them. "Use them. We need it up high." She turned to Tae and Ivan, and the smile of anticipation on her face did nothing to hide the fear in her eyes. "I mean it. I'm glad you're here."

By the time the reluctant grey of a Prasvishoni winter dawn had crawled across the sky, their numbers had swelled to probably two hundred.

"Tae," came Caz's soft voice in his earpiece. "Heads up. I just saw a group of police officers moving your way."

Tae stood quickly and crossed over to where Vera and Ivan were talking in low tones. "I got a message from Caz," he said. "The police are on their way."

Ivan glanced around, his face taut, and Tae followed his gaze.

The students had worked fast. A tangled mass of almost-invisible line now obscured most of the skyways of the alley, and it glinted dully as the light hit and refracted from it. It would be a death-trap for anyone stupid enough to try to get through it on a skybike.

Ivan put an arm around Tae, pulling him in, and Tae could feel his tension. "We'll do our best, Tae," he whispered. "If we're lucky, it won't get too violent."

It seemed like only moments later that Vera had tapped the voice amp on her com. "They're here," she called, and the noise in the street quieted for a moment.

Then there were the blinding lights of the police skybikes and the wail of sirens, and Vera jumped up on an overturned crate.

"What do we want?" she shouted through her voice amp.

"Justice!" the students shouted back enthusiastically.

The police formed a menacing line across the street, officers on foot flanked by officers on skybikes.

"You can't be here! Go home!" an officer shouted through her voice amp.

Another officer stepped forward, tossing a smoke bomb underhand into the thickest part of the protest. Ivan dropped his arm from Tae's shoulder and strode forward.

"Go, like I showed you!" he shouted. A student ran up to where the bomb sat hissing and fizzing, and tossed a traffic cone over it. Another student joined him, dumping a full bottle of water through the hole in the cone.

The smoke bomb fizzed and died, and the students set up a ragged cheer.

By midday, the street was covered with a thin haze of gas from the smoke bombs that burned at Tae's eyes and lingered in his throat. Vera climbed down from the crate, and she caught Tae's eye, giving him a weary smile.

"Your friend Jez must have done something." Her voice was ragged and hoarse from shouting. "There's not any more officers than there were yesterday."

He gave her a small smile in return.

Then, from the corner of his eye, he saw something fly through the air and land with a metallic ting. He shoved her out of the way and hit the ground instinctively. There was a loud bang, and a brilliant flash of light.

Slowly, he rolled to his feet, muscle shaking. Vera watched him grimly.

"Flash-bang," she said quietly. She paused a moment. "You— thought that was the real thing, didn't you?"

He didn't answer. He didn't have to. She'd seen the look on his face.

She shook her head, lips tight. "Do you still wonder why we're out here?" she asked. "You thought that was real, because it's happened to you, hasn't it?"

He nodded, still shaky. He didn't bother to add just how recently the latest time had been.

Ivan was there a moment later, his expression sharp with concern. "Tae! Are you—"

"I'm fine," said Tae, trying to force his voice to steady.

Ivan looked him over carefully, then gave a sigh of relief and kissed him lightly. "Just—be careful. Alright?" His expression was soft, even though the worry and the tension.

Tae managed a smile back, then a student shouted from the other side of the street. Ivan's head jerked up. He swore quietly. "Sorry, Tae, I—"

"Go," said Tae. Ivan kissed him again, then strode off towards the shouting.

Another smoke bomb landed on the opposite side of the square, rolling across the concrete in a spewing cloud of grey smoke. A figure jumped forward, dropping a bucket over the hissing sphere, and two other students run in with water bottles.

The bomb sputtered and died, and the haze of gas slowly dissipated to reveal the first boy kneeling on the street, coughing and choking.

Tae started forward to drag him clear.

The boy glanced up, blinking ineffectually.

Then he saw Tae, and the blood drained from his face.

Tae's heart stuttered, his chest constricting. Sandy hair, familiar green eyes—

He broke into a run.

Dmitri watched him as he approached, making no attempt to

move. His face was deathly pale.

Tae reached him, grabbing him by the arm and hauling to him to his feet, and dragged him clear of the smoke, and they leaned up against the alley walls, coughing and choking.

Dmitri rubbed at his streaming eyes, and Tae grabbed his wrists. "No, that'll make it worse." He glanced around helplessly, and someone shoved a water bottle into his hand. He pulled the lid free. "Just—try to open your eyes. I'll rinse them out."

Dmitri did as Tae told him, and Tae poured the water carefully into Dmitri's swollen eyes.

He could hardly breathe, but it wasn't from the gas. There was something pushing against his chest, heavy as a damn anvil.

It seemed like a lifetime ago he'd said goodbye to Dmitri outside the walls of the university, climbed onto a skybike behind Jez and rode off, thinking he'd never see Dmitri again.

It seemed like a lifetime, but it had only been weeks.

By the time the water bottle was empty, Tae's hands were shaking.

"Tae?" said Dmitri at last, in that incredulous voice that Tae knew so well. Tae tried to blink back his tears, but they were already dripping down his cheeks.

"Tae!" Dmitri pushed himself off the wall and grabbed Tae into a hug. "Tae. You're safe. Thank the Lady." His voice was choked, muffled against Tae's shoulder.

Tae couldn't speak. His heart was pounding hard enough to make him dizzy.

Ever since he'd left, he'd tried not to think about it, tried not to remember how much leaving had hurt. And now he thought it might actually kill him.

At last, Dmitri pulled back, brushing his sleeve across his eyes. "Tae," he said again. "It's really you. I thought—I was so worried about you, I was worried you'd been killed, we didn't know what had happened ..." he shook his head in a sort of stunned disbelief. "When Vera told me she saw you, I—I almost didn't believe her." He managed a shaky laugh. "Lady knows we've been stressed enough and scared enough that hallucinating you in the middle of one of the protests wouldn't have been outside the realm of possibility. But—she told me how you'd saved them yesterday." He paused a moment. "You and your boyfriend," he finished softly.

Tae's chest was a thick knot, and he felt that sickness in his stomach that had been there ever since he left Dmitri at the walls of the university. "I—" he began, his throat so tight he almost couldn't speak at all. "Dmitri, I—"

Dmitri looked at him for a moment, then gave him a small smile. "Tae." He put a hand on Tae's shoulder. "Do—do you remember what I told you, when you left last time? I said that I'd always known you couldn't stay forever. And—listen, Tae. These past few weeks—" he paused. "These past few weeks—I know what made you different. You didn't grow up like we did, cushioned and protected. You'd been hurt, and scared, and beaten, and you'd gotten up and kept going. None of us knew what that meant." He glanced around. "Although I think we're finally getting a taste."

He broke off, and for a moment, Tae wasn't sure if he'd continue.

"Lady and Consort, Tae," he said at last, his voice catching. "I wish like anything that I could've been the person for you. But—I couldn't have. I never would've understood, not really." He glanced over to where Ivan was helping pull up a makeshift barricade to protect against smoke gas. "But—he does, doesn't he?"

Tae still couldn't speak, and he thought the ache in his chest would kill him. Dmitri managed another smile, dimples appearing in the corners of his mouth, and for a moment, Tae thought his heart might actually break.

"You don't have to answer," said Dmitri quietly. "I can tell, just by looking at him. Just by looking at you." He paused a moment. "And —Tae?"

At last, Tae looked up and met those familiar eyes, that familiar smile.

The first boy he'd kissed, a few weeks ago that seemed like a lifetime.

"I'm happy for you," Dmitri said quietly. "He's better for you than I ever could have been. And—I'm glad you found him. I'm glad I met you, too. I won't ever regret that. For the first time in my damn life, you showed me there was something worth fighting for."

"Dmitri," he whispered, and then he didn't know what else to say.

Dmitri gave him a crooked smile. "You don't have to say anything. I'm honestly glad for you." He paused a moment, and winked at Tae through the tears in his eyes. "Although I'd be lying if I said I wasn't just a little bit jealous."

There was another explosion, and both of them flinched.

"Smoke bomb!" came Vera's ragged voice over the amplifier, and Tae and Dmitri both turned back to the square.

In the chaos that followed, Tae ended up beside Ivan. Ivan shot him a quick glance, concern in his expression. "You alright?" he asked.

Tae swallowed hard and nodded, his eyes flicking involuntarily to Dmitri.

Ivan followed his gaze, his eyes pausing for a moment on Dmitri. He looked back at Tae, and there was sudden understanding in his face. "I'm sorry," he said quietly.

Tae nodded, still not trusting himself to speak. Ivan turned back to the student whose injuries he was tending. Tae studied him for a moment, the sharp cut of his profile silhouetted against the brilliant lights of the police skybikes, the tension in his face and the gentleness in his hands as he bandaged a cut. And despite the sick, heavy weight of tears in his eyes, the knot in his chest loosened, just a little.

Because Dmitri had been right. Ivan did understand. And around Ivan, for once in his damn life, he didn't have to pretend anything at all.

By the time dark fell, Tae was exhausted. His voice was hoarse from calling out instructions, and his eyes and skin burned from the gas. But when he glanced over at Ivan, he saw the same exhausted relief that he felt.

The police had come, and they'd used projectile weapons and gas, as Ivan had predicted they would. But the students had stayed calm. And yes, almost everyone had burning eyes or bruises, and every of one of them looked weary enough to sleep standing, but—they'd made it through the day.

Vera came over to them. Her face was drawn with weariness, and there were circles under her eyes. Knowing her, she hadn't slept at all since the day before.

"Well, that wasn't as bad as it could have been," she said, but there was a tension under the carefree tone in her voice.

Ivan nodded. "You did well. All of you." He gave a small smile. "I shouldn't be surprised. Tae's friends tend to be rather extraordinary."

Vera managed a small smile in return. "I could say the same about you." She sobered. "But honestly. Thank you. If you hadn't been here, people would have gotten hurt. Maybe badly."

Ivan shook his head. "This won't be the end of it. When they come back, they'll be better prepared."

Vera nodded, and Tae could see the tight worry on her face. At last, she pushed the heels of her hands against her eyes. "Well, I don't know about you, but I'm ready to drop. You two want to stay here for the night? It's warmer than the streets, and it would mean less walking."

Ivan shook his head. "We have to get back to the street kids. There's not enough of them to keep watch, and with the police as bad as they are, they can't afford not to."

As they turned away, Ivan must have seen the expression on Tae's face, because he gave him a small wink and whispered, "What? You think I'd be tempted to leave them alone?"

Tae shook his head. "No," he said quietly. "I was just thinking how nice it was that I didn't even have to wonder."

18

Lev, day 8

Carefully, Lev slid a chip into Jez's com. "They—may not appreciate some of the suggestions on here," he murmured. "However, they're suggestions that will be very effective at getting the government to where we want it in the next week, since we now have to count Goran out."

Jez grinned at him. "Figure them not liking something I have to say is pretty much standard practice at this point."

He gave her a reluctant smile. "I've been listening in on the meetings you've been to. I'm still not completely sure why someone hasn't pulled a heat pistol on you yet."

She smirked. "Probably know I'd outdraw them. Anyway, don't know how you'd sit through those plaguing meetings otherwise. I just about lose my damn mind. But if you're harassing someone—"

He laughed, shaking his head, despite the small twist of worry in his stomach.

Jez would always be Jez, and he might as well get used to her being in danger and learn how to live with it.

"You don't think there'll be trouble after what happened in Jaromil's office?" he asked.

She shrugged and grinned. "Could be. But you said you thought that assassin was from the same group as the ones in the hallway last time, so they're probably not passing information along to Branka that Jaromil bastard. Anyways, basically no one's happy about the way things are changing, so probably they'll just think someone was giving him a warning."

She sounded obscenely cheerful about the whole thing, and he bit back a sigh.

She grabbed her coat from the hook and pulled the door open. He stepped forward, picking her bag off the floor and holding it out.

She hesitated a moment before she took it, as if waiting for him to say something. He'd known her long enough to see how her posture had stiffened, the strained look under her careless grin.

He gave her a quick smile, and she stared at him, grin fading slightly. Finally, she said, her voice even lower, "Um. Thanks."

He knew, somehow, that she wasn't talking about him handing her the bag.

She stepped out the door and closed it behind her, and he sighed, looking after her.

He knew a lot about Jez. Honestly, he probably knew her as well as anyone in the system. But there were still pieces of her past that he could only guess at. And somehow, he was determined that even if she never told him about the things that had hurt her, soul deep— well, that one day, she'd figure out there were people who cared about her, and she didn't have to deal with it on her own anymore.

By the time he'd thrown the dishes in the cleanser and taken a quick shower, Jez's voice drifted through his earpiece in a cheery, disrespectful greeting to Branka.

"Jez," he whispered into the com. "I'm on. If anything comes up that you need an answer to, or you aren't clear on a part of the plan we put together, let me know."

Plan we put together? Unless I was inspiring you from the other room in my sleep, pretty sure there was only one of us putting a plan together. Just hope Branka doesn't kill me when I tell her I won't be able to get her that info until sometime next month.

He could hear the snark, even through her quick taps in his earpiece, and he smiled despite himself.

He pulled on his outdoor clothes, listening to the banter from the government meeting with half an ear. At least, Jez was bantering. It was entirely possible that no one else in the meeting saw humour in it.

He wasn't sure whether he was smiling at Jez, or at himself. Honestly, she'd been right—which wasn't nearly as uncommon of an experience as he'd once convinced himself. Life around Jez was much less stressful when you simply trusted that she either knew what she was doing, or would be able to figure it out.

Much less stressful, and surprisingly amusing, if he was being honest with himself.

He smiled again, then hesitated a moment.

Contacting Tae was risky. But if they were going to help him, they'd need a secure way of communicating. So at last, reluctantly, he tapped his com onto Tae's line.

"Tae?" he said quietly.

No one answered. An unreasonable knot of worry started in his chest.

"Tae?" he tried again. "Are you there? If you can't talk, tap twice."

There was silence again, for what seemed like an absurd amount of time. Finally, Tae's voice came through his earpiece. "Lev? Are you alright? Is Jez alright? What's happening?"

He sounded almost as worried as Lev felt.

Lev let out a long breath of relief. "Everything's fine. But we need a secure way to communicate. I think a dead-drop would be the easiest." He paused a moment. "I was going to suggest a location, but you know that part of the city better than I do. At any rate, I've looked up Ruslan's history. He was a development project manager for the city once upon a time, so him wandering around some of the less-desirable sections wouldn't be out of character."

"I think we could do that," said Tae, his voice still tight with strain. "Even if I can't go myself, I can send one of the of the kids." He paused a moment. "I'll send coordinates through to your com. There'll be an old bench there—you can tack the chip underneath it with some adhesive, and I should be able to pick it up within twenty-four hours. It won't work for urgent messages, but we can keep each other up to date on what's happening."

"Tae," Lev asked quietly. "What's wrong?"

He blew out a short breath. "I'm at the protests again, and things are getting worse. The police have been holding back, but I don't think it'll last."

Lev frowned. "Anything specific?"

"No. Just—how they're acting. I'm worried."

Lev sighed. "Send everything you have through to the drop location, as soon as you can. I'll pick it up when I get there, and go over it with Jez tonight."

"Yeah." Tae paused a moment. "And ... Masha?" There was a slight hesitance in his tone that made Lev grit his teeth.

"Sorry, Tae. I—wish I had better news. I don't think she's happy about what we're doing, redirecting the police and helping out the protests. But we'll do it anyways." He paused. "Be careful. I don't know what game she's playing."

Tae let out a long breath. "Yeah. Thanks."

Lev glanced at the coordinates Tae had sent. "I'll head to the drop point now. I'll try to be there between 0930 and 1000 standard every morning, so if you have something for me, leave it before then. If there's something urgent, I suppose we'll have to use the com lines."

"Thanks, Lev," Tae said quietly.

Lev shook his head. "You didn't think we were going to let you deal with this on your own, did you? If you did, I've been an even worse friend than I thought."

Tae gave a reluctant chuckle and tapped off his com.

Over the other line, Lev could still hear Jez's cheerful insults, interspersed with the low buzz of conversation in the government meeting. He sighed, and pulled on his outside boots and his jacket. He wasn't actually looking forward to going out in this weather. But

—

But Tae was living outside in this weather. The kid had lived on the streets for long enough that he probably knew how to keep himself alive, even in the bitter cold, but that didn't mean it would be enjoyable.

Lev shivered slightly as he stepped out into the hallway, already bracing himself for the bitter air and blowing sleet of the street outside.

As he walked, scarf pulled over his head, coat clutched around him to keep out the wind, he looked around, frowning.

Even for as bitter as the weather was, the streets were deserted. The people who were out had an odd, furtive look to them, as if they knew something was about to happen, and were ready to flee at a moment's notice.

The gangs were out, too, outside the areas where they should have been, and as he passed from the wealthier areas into the poorer, he noticed more and more frequently the ubiquitous whine of police bikes.

He hadn't grown up a street kid, like Tae. But he was no stranger to the poor end of town. And there were only ever this many police here in one circumstance: they were planning a crackdown.

He'd never been caught in the middle of one, thankfully, but he knew how brutal they could be. And he'd never seen this many police.

He shivered slightly.

By the time he reached the drop spot, Jez's meeting had progressed to discussing plans. But, as usual, Jez seemed to be perfectly capable of dealing with it without his assistance.

"So, genius," she whispered at one point. "Every damn person in this office is trying to find a flaw in your plan, and none of them are able to. Could have told them that, if they'd asked."

He smiled despite himself. "I suppose that means they're not looking hard enough."

She laughed. "Hey now, don't get bashful on me, or I'll start to wonder who you are and what you did with Lev."

He chuckled. "I assume, then, the meeting's finished?"

She sighed heavily. "You must've been away from the government too long. These idiots never finish a meeting. We're taking a break and then coming back to it." She paused a moment. "So. Tae."

"We set up a drop," he said, making no effort to hide the concern in his tone. "He's going to leave something for me, and hopefully that will give us an idea of what we can do."

Jez was silent for a moment. Finally, she said, "Well, we're damn well not letting this go. You get me the information from Tae, and I can promise I'll scare the living breathing hell out of these government idiots until they reassign some police officers. If I can't,

I'm damn well losing my touch."

"I'm—not even going to ask what you're going to do," said Lev, smiling faintly despite himself. "I'm not certain my nerves will be able to take it. But I'll get you everything Tae gives me, as soon as I get back."

"That going to be soon? Because I figure they're going to start this meeting up again in the next fifteen minutes." She gave another long sigh. "All I'm going to say is, I hope you idiots appreciate what I do for this crew. Every damn day I figure I'm about to keel over and die from boredom, and I damn well show up anyways."

"I know," said Lev quietly. "You always have."

There was a long silence from the other end of the com. At last, Jez cleared her throat. "Anyway, let me know as soon as you have the info."

"I will." Lev tapped off his com and glanced around.

He was getting close to the coordinates Tae had sent, but—there was something odd about the way the police were congregating.

And then he saw the pattern, and he sucked in a quick breath.

He pulled out the chip that he was going to leave for Tae and slipped it into his com.

"Tae," he said quietly. "You may already know this. But the police are blocking off certain streets. Svyetoy Street, Bolechnik Street, Pyeka Street. The entrances and exits for the whole northeast side of town. And, incidentally, to and from the university. It looks like they're getting ready for a crackdown, and they don't want anyone getting in or out. I'll mark out the streets where I've noticed them." He paused a moment. "Be careful, OK? If you need to get out, get out. As long as you're still alive, we can always come back and try again."

He sighed as he shut off the com. Tae wasn't going to pay any attention to what he'd just said, but he had to try, at least. Maybe Ivan would be able to talk some sense into him. Although—he shook his head. Ivan had been the one who'd been thrown into prison for protesting in the first place.

When he got to the drop point, he sat down and stared out at the river for a few minutes, trying to act casual. At last he pulled out his com, pulled up the holoscreen with the map of the city, and began sketching idly. Anyone watching him would think he was drawing, possibly, or maybe taking notes on potential development opportunities.

When he finished marking up the map for Tae, he shut down the holoscreen and nonchalantly popped the chip from his com. He embedded it firmly into the adhesive he'd hidden in the palm of his hand and glanced around.

He didn't see anyone. Which didn't, actually, mean anything. He stood, letting something small drop from his hand into the street, and swore. He bent down, patting his gloved hands along the cold, dirty concrete, until his slow search led him under the bench. He slipped the piece of adhesive containing the chip under the splintering metal of the bench, and pulled out the small, adhesive-bound packet already waiting there. By the time he'd emerged, the chip was safely in his pocket.

He stood, yawned, pulled his coat close around him, then started back the way he'd come, taking a circuitous route back. In his earpiece, Jez was still talking. He'd only been listening with half an ear, but he could get the details when she got home.

When arrived back at the apartment, he pulled up Tae's com chip and glanced through it, frowning slightly.

There was a recording, a student protest. And—

His frown deepened.

He'd been a student himself, not that many years ago. And yes, there'd always been radicals among the student body, and yes, there had been times the police had cracked down.

But not like this.

The police did what the people in power wanted them to do. And for some reason, right now that was stopping student protests, and hunting street kids.

He tapped his com, still frowning. "Jez?"

The reply came a moment later. *Something wrong?*

"No," he murmured. "At least, nothing new. But I got that chip from Tae. I'll send you through what he gave us, but I'll need information. Is that doable?"

I can do basically anything. What do you need?

He smiled despite himself. "The police almost certainly have orders to crack down hard on the student protests. And the street kids—from the pattern that I'm seeing on Tae's chip, it looks like the police are actively hunting them. Can you find out who's giving those orders? With the unrest with the gangs, it doesn't make sense that they're wasting time on street kids and student protests."

There was a moment of silence on the other end of the com. If he'd had to guess, he'd say Jez was worried.

Tae alright? He's not hurt or anything?

"I don't think so. Ivan's with him. He'll protect Tae as much as he can."

I bet he will.

He wasn't sure how Jez could manage to make even taps through her com sound lascivious, but somehow she did it.

There was another moment's pause.

I'll get you that information, she tapped out.

"Thanks," he said quietly.

He stared down at his com for a moment, then pulled up the information from Tae's chip and started pouring through it again.

Whatever was going on, it went deeper than just Grigory and Olyessa. As if that wasn't enough on its own.

By the time Jez got home, he'd been staring at the com for hours. He looked up, startled, as the door swung open and Jez stepped through.

She was grinning, her coat soaked, sleet coated on her scarf and her hair tipped a hoarfrost-white, frozen in messy spikes.

His heart did a strange flip-flop in his chest at the sight of her. And for an instant, the memory from two days ago, of her pulled up against him, their bodies pressed together, her lips on his, his hands running down her back and tangled in her hair, broke over him so strongly it almost took his breath away.

He closed his eyes, forcing himself to breathe.

He was an adult, dammit, and he could think about things rationally, and—

And he wasn't going to ruin this. He wasn't going to let one accidental kiss ruin his chance at whatever this was that he and Jez had finally worked out.

He took another deep breath and opened his eyes, smiling up at her. She smiled back, and the warm familiarity of her smile somehow gave him the strength to shove the traitorous memory to the back of his mind.

"Long day, genius?" she asked, voice sympathetic.

"You … could say that," he murmured ruefully, standing and stretching the residual shakiness from his muscles.

He came over to take her coat as she shrugged it off. He wasn't sure when this evening ritual had become something he looked forward to, something so natural and right that every part of him relaxed at it. But somehow, it had—taking her coat, sitting down to dinner, listening to her profanity-laden commentary on the day's meetings and the character of the various ministers.

She grinned at him. "Look like you're keeping busy." She reached over to where her coat hung on the peg, rummaging around in the pocket. At last, she emerged with two grease-stained paper bags of street food. "Figured you might be, so I grabbed this. Your favourite, blinis."

He took the bags, smiling to himself, and she dropped her office bag on the floor with a thud.

"Don't know about you, but I've had enough damn work for the day. I'm starved." She turned towards the table, where he'd already placed the bags and was reaching for the plates, and then paused, frowning.

He turned, but by the time he realized what she'd heard, she was already moving. She grabbed her work bag, and as she did so, he saw the faint line of smoke wafting from it, and something in the back of his mind recognized the smell.

He'd started towards Jez before he realized what he was doing, panic flooding through him. "Jez, it's—"

"Poison, I know," she said through her teeth. She snatched up the bag, glanced around quickly, then grabbed one of the rickety chairs and slammed it through the window pane. The ancient glass tinkled and shattered, and icy air poured into the room as she heaved the bag through the broken window. It landed in the streets two stories below with a crunch, and she staggered back, and Lev caught her, even though he was feeling slightly lightheaded himself. They collapsed on the couch, and after a few breaths his head began to clear, the strange shakiness fading from his muscles. He glanced over at Jez. She was leaning back, and she looked faintly sick—but she was alive, which honestly hadn't been a given, considering what had been in that smoke. He took a long breath, his muscles shaky with something other than the gas now, and closed his eyes for a moment, trying to bring his heart rate back to normal.

"Are you alright?" he asked at last, when he could trust himself to speak.

She nodded, eyes still closed. "I'm fine," she said. "Thirty more seconds though, and I'm not sure I would have been."

Lev nodded, even though she couldn't see him. He wasn't sure he could trust himself to speak again.

At last, he sat up and took another shaky breath. "Well, it's out in the streets now, in the open air, so it won't be concentrated enough to kill anyone. Although if someone gets too close and takes a sniff, they'll be waking up with a headache tomorrow."

Jez opened her eyes and gave him a grin that, if still slightly shaken, was approaching her usual snarkiness. "Well, if we were wondering how the other ministers felt about me, we got our answer."

Lev shook his head, smiling wryly, because the only alternative was giving into the sick, gut-clenching panic he'd felt seeing Jez holding the smoking bag, knowing exactly what was hissing out of it, and how little of it she'd have to breathe in to die. "I suppose you're right," he murmured. "But—it seems like an odd way to kill you. There're plenty of methods that would have been much more certain."

She turned to him, raising an eyebrow. "As far as I'm concerned, they don't need any suggestions."

He chuckled slightly, still trying to bring his heart rate back to normal. "You're right. Incompetence isn't generally a trait I value, but in someone trying to assassinate you, I make an exception."

She smiled, then stood shakily. He stood as well, in case she needed someone to catch her, but she stayed on her feet.

"Anyway, like I was saying—don't know about you, but I'm pretty damn hungry."

They blocked off the broken window by tacking a sheet over it and pulling one of the bookshelves in front to at least stem the flow of cold air. There was still, unfortunately, plenty of window space for watchers outside to be able to see in, but then he suspected this apartment had been built for surveillance.

Jez talked all the way through dinner, like she always did, but he could hear the tension under her words. If it had been anyone else, he would have thought it was just the aftereffect of having been almost murdered. But he knew Jez. That wasn't the only thing bothering her.

When they'd finally taken their customary places on the couch, he asked quietly, "What's wrong? Besides almost being murdered, I mean."

She hesitated, then turned to him, expression serious. "Here's the thing," she said quietly. "I talked to Branka about the police. And from everything I could get out of her, she's been telling the police to watch the gangs, find out where things will blow up. She's still convinced Grigory's going to war with the government, and she doesn't want it to break out in the streets. As far as I could tell, she has no idea they're going after students and street kids."

Lev's frown deepened. "I've been going through this all day," he said quietly. "There's no way they're not doing this on orders. You can see the patterns—"

Jez cut him off. "If you say there's patterns, genius, there's damn well patterns. Soon as the meeting was done, I went out to the police precinct, waved my fancy government badge around, asked some questions. And you're right. They are getting orders. And as far as the chief of police was concerned, those orders are coming from the government."

Lev frowned at her, trying to work through the implications of what she said. "Then there's someone who wants the streets to blow up," he said at last. "Because that's what will happen. They crack down hard enough on the street kids and students, ignore the gangs, and things will explode. People in Prasvishoni aren't revolutionary. I know that, I've lived here. But you push them far enough, you leave dead bodies in the street, and they will be."

She stared at him. "You think that's what's happening?"

"Look," he said grimly, gesturing at the holoscreen he'd pulled up. "The violence is coordinated. They're hemming in the poor part of town. They're turning the streets into an explosive with the controller half pushed. And if what you're saying is right—"

"Then there's someone in the government who wants it to happen, and wants to keep the people in charge from finding out," finished Jez quietly.

19

Jez, day 9

When Jez stepped into the office the next morning, her muscles were already tight.

It wasn't the fact that she'd almost been killed last night—although she still didn't want to think about the canister of poisonous gas someone had planted in her bag, and the sick, choking, agonizing death it would have caused. She'd made Lev tell her, finally, what the gas would have done, and when he had, she'd shuddered. But hell, that was basically her whole life up to this point.

It was the fact that Lev had almost died, too. She'd brought the damn bag home, and if she hadn't noticed, if she hadn't got it out the window in time, it wouldn't have been just her lying on the floor, coughing out her damn lungs in a pile of blood.

It would have been him, too.

And that wasn't something she was prepared to deal with.

"Layla," said Branka. "So nice of you to join us this morning."

Her voice was icy, as always, but by this time Jez figured it was almost a Pavlovian response to seeing her. The same way her snarky grin and morning insult had become almost an unconscious reaction, a part of the typical morning routine without which neither of them would feel that the day had really begun.

She glanced around the conference room quickly. All the familiar faces were there, and she actually remembered a couple of their names at this point. Which was probably a good thing, since they didn't seem to see the humour in any of the nicknames she'd come up with.

Jaromil was whispering to another official in one corner, their chairs pulled together, voices low, and she frowned slightly.

Not that private plots and subplots were unusual—hardly be a government meeting if someone wasn't secretly plotting against someone else—but it wasn't usually these two. They generally seemed about one deep breath away from pulling heat pistols on each other.

And there, in the other corner—a woman and a man spoke in low voices, glancing around uneasily.

Whatever was coming down, it looked like it was something big.

She dropped into her seat, tipping her chair back as always, and waiting for the typical wince from Branka and glare of disapproval from Jaromil—but they didn't come.

They hardly seemed to be paying attention.

Jez's frown deepened.

Still, at least today's meeting was supposed to be an easy one. They'd agreed to her plan of moving government officials yesterday—well, Lev's plan—so basically all she had to do was sit back and wait for an opportune moment to bring up the damn police again.

Branka stood, tapping her hand on the table in her usual imperious manner.

"Now that we've all gathered," she cast her usual cold glance in Jez's direction—which, hell, Jez had only been maybe five standard minutes late today, which barely even counted—then turned back to the rest of the table. "We decided on a course of action at yesterday's meeting. Layla presented a plan, and in the moment it appeared to be the most effective method of accomplishing our goals."

In the moment? Jez raised an eyebrow.

"However," the woman continued, "it has come to my attention that there are individuals who'd like to present an alternate viewpoint."

Through her earpiece, Lev murmured, "What's happening?"

No idea, she tapped out under the table. *Let's see how this plays out.*

Jaromil got ponderously to his feet. "As you say, Branka," he began, in that pompous tone that always set Jez's teeth on edge, "our friend Layla did present us with a rudimentary, if rather crude, plan to reorganize the government. However—" he paused for effect, and Jez was struck with the sudden urge to flick her writing instrument at him. Probably could get him right in the middle of the forehead, if she tried.

Somehow, she restrained herself. Although it wasn't easy.

"I think it behooves us to recollect on what basis we decided to remake out entire government structure." He glanced around the table again. "One intercepted message, and a cryptic one, at that."

Jez half-stood. "Hey now, you plaguer, think you might be forgetting—"

He held up a hand. "If I may continue, Layla." His voice held a barely concealed disdain. "There are always factions in the government, and individuals who wish to gain power. And there are those who stand to gain a great deal from this particular reorganization. This is unprecedented, at least in my lifetime. We need to act rationally, thoughtfully. I propose at least a standard month or two to evaluate the potential implications of such a move."

He sat. Across the table, a woman stood.

"I agree. This will offend powerful people, inside and outside the government. There's more than enough unrest already. The university students have been protesting for weeks now, and their parents are getting uneasy. This isn't the time to make more enemies. Olyessa and Grigory are powerful. They could lend stability to the whole system while whatever's happening on the streets works itself out."

Jez rose again. "Listen, you bastards." She was grinning so that all her teeth showed. "You want to wait months? Sure. Except by then, our friend Grigory will have killed every last damn one of us and taken the entire government. You get a damn firebomb thrown into your office, you don't sit around and think about the best options for places to put it. You get the hell out." She glared at Jaromil, and at the woman who'd followed him. "You want to play tokens with your own damn lives? That's your business. But you want to play with my life, and the lives of a hell of a lot of other people too, you better come up with a better reason than Grigory didn't send us a personalized card with his damn signature on it."

The people around the table were watching her, but from the look in Branka's eyes, she could tell the woman wasn't convinced.

Jez swore under her breath. Whatever these plaguers were playing at, they'd been working on it for a while. Bending Branka's ear, she could see it in the woman's expression, and Jez had been too focused on other things to notice.

Jaromil stood again. "Layla," he said, and the condescension in his voice set her teeth on edge. "I understand that the firebomb back on Boloto must have been traumatizing. But your trauma can't drive our government policy. As you well know, someone sabotaged my office a few days back, and I'm not hiding under a table with my eyes closed." He turned back to address the table. "As you know, I've worked closely with our valuable partners, Grigory and Olyessa among them, for years now. We've worked out many disagreements in the past. I suggest we contact Grigory. Perhaps this is all a misunderstanding. Perhaps the incident aboard the casino ship was no more than an unfortunate accident. I heard rumours that Grigory's own ship was damaged in the explosion. This could likely be cleared up quickly and easily with a simple conversation."

"The heist," Lev murmured in her earpiece.

"Yeah?" said Jez, her grin widening. "You think maybe he just accidentally killed fifty of our own damn people?" She glanced at the idiots around the table. "And when he sent that bastard Masha to pull a sting on Vitali behind our back? Was that just a misunderstanding too? He's wanted what we have for a long time."

She could tell this, at least, had hit a nerve. Branka winced slightly, and from across the table, a couple of the more senior board members shifted in their seats.

"I'm not saying we haven't had our disagreements with Grigory," said Jaromil. He hadn't even bothered sitting while Jez spoke. "But if someone wanted to stir up unrest in the government, this seems like a perfect way—put out some vague, unsubstantiated message, and then let us tear the government apart from inside." He turned back to Branka. "The people Layla suggested are inexperienced. If he was looking to weaken the government, this would be exactly what he would want us to do. As I say, I still feel our best option is to talk things out, take it slow, think about it for a while."

"Grigory paid for his son's wedding three months ago," Lev whispered. "They can look up in the public records. In fact, you should be able to pull it up on your com right now."

Maybe you *could, genius,* she tapped.

He gave a short sigh. "Hold tight. I'll send it through."

An hour and a half later, Jez had talked herself basically hoarse. In addition to probably making at least four more people hate her damn guts. Well, more than they already did. But when they stood, finally, for a break, the expression on Branka's face was not quite as certain as it had been at the beginning of the meeting.

Jez shot an irritated glance across the table at that bastard Jaromil, who'd started the whole thing, and received a murderous glare in return.

She grinned to herself. At the very least, he hadn't come out smelling like a fresh breeze. She was pretty sure he hadn't wanted anyone to know about his son's wedding, considering the look on his face when she pulled up the holoscreen.

"Layla,"

Jez turned.

Branka stood next to her, her expression pinched. "I'd like a private word." She glanced around, and gestured with her head to a quiet corner of the room.

Jez glanced around, trying to ignore the twinge of unease.

Still, if the plaguer was trying to kill her, probably couldn't do anything too dramatic in a crowded room like this. And Jez was pretty damn sure that as between the two of them, she was a hell of a lot faster on the draw.

She sighed. "Sure. Fine."

"Layla," Branka said quietly, once they were where it would be difficult for someone to overhear. "I appreciated your input at the meeting."

Jez raised an eyebrow. She didn't sound sarcastic.

"I'm inclined to agree with you that we can't trust Grigory. But as you've seen, he has several supporters. As does Olyessa. This is a rather ... delicate situation."

Jez gave a tight grin of understanding. "You mean, you know this will save lives, but you don't want to risk your own damn neck for it. So you want me on the chopping block instead."

From the irritated look on Branka's face, Jez knew she'd interpreted the situation correctly.

"Layla," the woman said icily. "Prasvishoni politics are not quite as simple as those of outer-rim planets. This is a situation where you, as an outsider, would be best placed to make things happen."

"You mean, me as somebody who you wouldn't mind seeing with a heat blast cooked right through the middle of her," said Jez.

Branka didn't respond, but honestly, the way she was looking at Jez, she wouldn't mind being the one who pulled the trigger.

At last, Jez shrugged. "Well, here's the thing. Some of us backwater outer-rim politicians have a thing called not being a damn coward. So guess if I'm the only one, I'll do it. At least for now."

Branka looked around carefully, then leaned closer. "With that in mind, then, I feel I ought to warn you. The next few days here might be interesting."

Jez frowned at her. "What, more people trying to kill me? That's getting a bit boring at this point, to be honest."

Branka looked even more uneasy. "No. Nothing that would affect you directly, I believe. But it may affect negotiations going forward, if the rumours I hear correct."

Jez gave her a skeptical look. "Not giving me much to go on here. You want to tell me anything useful?"

The woman gave a quick shake of her head. "I'm sorry, Layla, but I do have a rather busy schedule today, and as you still don't seem to have that information you promised me——" She gave a small shrug, her voice turning smooth and cold. "I'll see you in tomorrow's meeting." She turned and strode off, leaving Jez watching after her.

She tapped her com and whispered, "You hearing this?"

"Yes," said Lev, his voice unaccountably grim. "Is there any chance you can—"

"Figured you were going to ask that," said Jez, more cheerily than she felt. "I'll find out what I can, let you know tonight."

Still, she couldn't shake the unease tightening her stomach.

Lev was waiting for her when she got back to the apartment, and from the look on his face, he was as uneasy about the situation as she was.

He came over, like always, and took her coat, hanging up on the rack. He glanced at her bag dubiously, and she managed a grin. "Checked it before I left the office, and in the hall just outside, before I opened the door. All clean. Also my pockets. Also my scarf. Also my damn jacket." She paused a moment. "Didn't take my clothes off and check, but hell, nice and warm in here, I could—"

"I'm—fairly confident that won't be necessary," said Lev quickly, and she grinned at the expression on his face.

He took a deep breath. "Did you find anything out?"

She frowned. "I don't know. Got some stuff, but nothing solid."

"Well, I suppose if there's nothing urgent, we may as well eat dinner." He gave her a wry smile. "Before we get so focused we forget about it."

"You might forget about it," she muttered. "I'm damn well starving."

"So," said Lev, once they'd finished dinner and taken their customary places on the couch.

She sighed. "Here's the thing. Everyone in the building is acting strange. People whispering to people they'd generally shoot as soon as look at." She shook her head. "I don't know, or maybe I'm just going crazy from sitting on my damn butt listening to people talk all day."

Lev shook his head. "No, Jez," he said softly. "You're smart, and you notice things. If you thought something was off, I believe you." He paused a moment. "There were no hints as to the reason behind what happened at the meeting today?"

She shook her head. "Someone doesn't like the changes we're making. But hell, could be any number of reasons why, and they could have come up with any number of things to deal with it. Branka is sure a hell of a lot more nervous than she ought to be, for someone in her position."

Lev nodded, frowning. "You're right. Everything I have suggests her position is a strong one. Which means there's someone working behind the scenes that we don't know about." He sighed, and pulled up his holoscreen. "And I noticed something as well. The information Tae left at the drop point this morning. Look." he leaned forward, tapping the screen. A still-shot from a video appeared, and he enlarged one section of it. "Right there," he murmured, tapping one of the figures on the screen. "Watch her."

Jez leaned forward.

The figure he'd indicated wasn't an officer—she was dressed in regular street clothes, nothing remarkable about her.

Lev tapped his com again, and the video began to play.

Jez frowned at it, trying to keep her eye on the figure.

The woman stood casually at the back of the crowd as the police officers in riot gear gathered, apparently preparing to go after the students.

A handful of the officers were gathered in a tight knot with the bastard who looked to be the police captain. They were speaking in low voices, gesturing towards the group of students. The captain frowned, and one of the officers spoke again, more emphatically. If Jez had to guess, she'd say the officer wanted them to stand down.

"Too bad we don't have audio on this," she murmured.

"Just watch," said Lev.

A moment later, the captain opened her mouth, as if to give an order. And then the woman at the edge of the crowd stepped forward, laying a hand on the captain's arm, and said something in the captain's ear.

And Jez saw the look on the captain's face. Right before it hardened into a firm resolve, there was that one moment of what looked like actual fear.

The captain turned to the officers, gesturing at the students and barking in order. One of the officers, the emphatic one, looked like he might be about to argue, but the captain barked an order again, and reluctantly, he turned back towards the demonstration.

Lev tapped the screen, and the video stilled.

They looked at each other. Lev was frowning, and she'd known him long enough to see all the little tells—the small crease between his eyebrows, the way one hand was spread on his leg, fingers wide.

He was more disconcerted than he was letting on.

"I don't know what this is, Jez," he said quietly. "But whatever it is —it's not good."

20

Tae, day 9

"Tae?"

Ivan's voice was soft, but Tae looked up with a start.

He hadn't been asleep, not really, but he'd been staring at his holoscreen for long enough that the numbers were starting to waver in front of his eyes. And he still hadn't finished with the communications hack.

"What is it?" he mumbled.

"Morning. I'm sorry." Ivan put a hand on Tae shoulder, and, like always, Tae felt himself relaxing into the warmth of it.

Ivan had sat up most of the night with him, until Tae finally sent him to bed, grumbling that one of them, at least, should get enough sleep to be able to think straight.

Ivan gave Tae's shoulder a small squeeze. "We'll have to head out soon. We should get there early today. I have a feeling things might get ugly."

Tae gave a weary nod, and Ivan pushed a rations pack into his hand. "Eat something, at least."

Tae stared at the ration pack for a moment before his exhausted brain remembered what to do with it, and he pulled open the packaging.

After a brief consultation with Caz and Peti, he and Ivan slipped out into the darkened streets.

This time when they reached the maze of streets and alleys in front of the university, they were swarming with students. Three or four fires had been lit, and Ivan took Tae by the elbow and guided him towards the nearest.

"You stay there, warm up some. I'm going to find Vera."

Tae was too cold and tired to argue.

The cold had just begun to seep from his bones when Vera, Dmitri, and Ivan came up beside him.

Tae had to fight the sudden urge to look down at the sight of Dmitri, but—he owed his friend better than that. He forced himself to meet the boy's eyes, but Dmitri just gave him a weary smile, looking almost tired as he was.

"Hey, Tae," he said quietly. "Vera's told me what you two have been doing." He glanced up at Ivan. "Your—your ideas are good ones," he said. "I'm impressed."

Ivan's expression was tense, and there was an unfamiliar strain in his posture. "Tell me that when we get through this without someone dying," he said quietly. He glanced around the square, then back at Dmitri and Vera. "You've done a good job. We're well prepared."

"I'm sorry. I haven't got the communications hack finished," said Tae. "We're still cut off. I'll keep trying, but their blocker is a good one, and I don't know how long—"

Vera shook her head, a tight smile on her face. "You, Tae, are the only one in the damn system who'd apologize for being able to work a miracle, but not as quickly as you wanted to."

Tae let out a frustrated breath. "The problem is, we don't have extra time." He tried to force his shoulders to relax. "At least we were able to pass on more details to Lev last night. Hopefully Jez can use that to keep the police away again."

"Jez? As in, that Jez?" asked Dmitri, his tone taking on a slightly haunted edge. "How is Jez going to—"

"She's, um, gone undercover. In the government. As a minister. She's—" He faltered at Dmitri's expression, half amused, half horrified.

"Jez? Is in the government? As a minister?"

Tae looked at him for a moment, then finally broke into a small, wry chuckle. "I'm—not entirely sure how it's going. At least, I'm not sure how it's going for the government. I'm sure Jez is enjoying herself."

"I'm certain she is," murmured Dmitri in a stunned tone. "Um. Has she—has anyone tried to blow her up with an ion bomb yet?"

"I didn't ask," Tae muttered. "I usually don't want to know."

Vera gave a slight smile, then glanced around, and he could see the tension in her posture. "Anyways, on our end, I think we're as prepared as we're going to be. Let's hope this works."

By the time the police arrived, the students were in position.

The atmosphere was tense, but less panicked than it had been the previous day.

Perhaps things would get worse—in fact, Tae was fairly certain they would—but at least this was something they'd dealt with before.

"Jez must have pulled it off," said Vera, as the police approached. "Look at how few there are."

"More might show up later," said Tae shortly. "Whatever Jez did, I doubt it's permanent."

Vera nodded. "Maybe. But I'm damn well going to enjoy this while I can."

The first of the smoke bombs bounced and rolled into the centre of a group of students, hissing menacingly, but three students leapt forward instantly to put it out, makeshift masks pulled up over their faces, and Tae felt some of the tension drain from his muscles.

Maybe Vera was right. Maybe today wouldn't be so bad after all.

He'd guessed correctly—more police arrived in the middle of the day. But even then, it wasn't nearly as violent as he'd expected. The skybikes couldn't get at them, nor could the drones. The police had clearly tried to hack through his blocker, but they hadn't succeeded, and even though there were still plenty of students huddled on the ground, eyes and nose streaming from the gas, there was an efficient first-aid chain to take care of the sufferers as quickly as possible.

By the time dusk was beginning to fall, early, like it always did in Prasvishoni in the winter, the students had already begun to relax, coming out from their positions and gathering around the fire pits, which had been restarted as the afternoon grew colder. They looked tired, but they were laughing and joking in low voices. Vera lowered her voice amp and turned to grin at Tae, a look of weary triumph on her face.

And then Tae stiffened as the entire alley lit up with the headlamps of police bikes.

"What—" began one of the students.

Ivan shoved his way through towards them, and the look on his face made Tae's stomach clench.

"I've seen this before," Ivan said as he reached them, his voice more grim than Tae had ever heard it. "They're using shock and awe. They're going to try to do something big enough to scare you off. We need to get everyone into shelter, now."

Vera pulled the voice amplifier back up on her com and shouted, "Everyone back! Everyone under cover! Back to your places, now!"

There was a general confused movement as the students realized what Vera was saying and started to obey. But before even a fraction of them cleared the open square in front of the university, something round and glittering soared into the centre of the protest.

Tae had a split second to see it bounce off the concrete into the middle of a crowd of students, small and metallic, and then Ivan had shoved him to one side, hard enough that he staggered against the wall.

"Down! Everybody down!" Ivan shouted, his voice carrying even over the chaos. "Get away from there, get down, get—"

There was a deafening explosion, and Tae was hurled back against the wall, his head slamming into the prefab blocks, his ears ringing.

For a moment after the explosion, everything was quiet.

Tae blinked, rubbing the afterimage of the brilliant light from his eyes, and squinted into the dim light of the streets.

Ivan lay on the cobblestones beside him, blood running down his forehead, and for one panicked moment, Tae thought—

And then Ivan's eyes blinked open, and he looked around dazedly, and Tae sagged in relief.

Around the square, students were slowly getting to their feet, brushing themselves off, blinking and shaking their heads in a stunned fashion.

Ivan staggered to his feet, supporting himself against the wall of the alley. "You alright, Tae?" he muttered.

Tae nodded wordlessly.

"Good," said Ivan. He pushed himself off the wall and straightened, then swayed on his feet. Tae grabbed his arm to steady him, and Ivan looked over at him gratefully.

"I'm coming," said Tae quietly.

Ivan gave Tae a grim look. "I've seen this before," he said quietly.

"They're supposed to be nonlethal. They're supposed to shock you, frighten you into giving in. But they're loaded with projectiles. Not metal, but rubber will kill if it hits hard enough, and they weren't even trying to keep it away from the students. There'll be injuries." He took a deep breath, and they started forwards towards the site of the blast.

From outside the alley, they could hear the police over the voice amps, shouting for them to stand down, disperse, come out, but no one was paying them any attention. Honestly, with the ringing in his ears, Tae could hardly make out the shouts as anything more than muffled noise.

When they reached it, Ivan stopped, crouching beside a student who looked about Tae's age. She was sobbing, holding her hands to her face, and blood dripped out between her fingers. Ivan put a gentle hand on her shoulder, speaking in a low voice, gently coaxing her hand away from her face so he could see the injury. Vera had come out from the alley where she'd taken shelter, bringing one of the first-aid kits, and other students were coming as well, carrying more.

Tae looked around quickly, trying to judge the extent of the damage.

And then he stopped, ice forming in the pit of his stomach.

There was a student lying right beside where the explosive had detonated. He looked like he was sleeping, or maybe knocked unconscious.

But Tae had lived on the streets for long enough to recognize the unnatural stillness of his posture.

Slowly, Tae stood and crossed over to where the student lay. He leaned over him, gently pressing his fingers against the side of the boy's neck.

He didn't actually need to. He already knew, but for some reason, it seemed very important that he check.

He held his fingers there for much, much longer than he had to.

There wasn't anything there to feel. But he'd known that before he tried.

By the time he'd straightened, Vera and Ivan were both looking across the square at him. There was a frown of confusion on Vera's face, but Ivan's expression was sick dread.

Ivan stood quickly, whispering something comforting to the injured girl and leaving her in the care of her friends, and crossed over to where Tae knelt. Vera followed a moment later.

"Tae?" asked Ivan softly.

Tae didn't say anything, just nodded. He felt sick to his stomach. The boy lying face-down on the cement wasn't someone he'd known. He'd never met him, in the few short weeks he'd been at the university. He didn't even know his name.

Vera came up beside Ivan and glanced between him and Tae. "What—" she began.

Tae saw the moment when she finally realized, the way she staggered slightly, put out a hand as if to catch herself.

Another girl half-stumbled over to Tae. She crouched beside him, grabbing the shoulder of the boy lying on the concrete.

"Andro!" she rasped. "Are you alright?"

Ivan and Tae exchanged glances, and hesitantly, Tae put out a hand, resting it lightly on her shoulder.

"I'm sorry," he began. "He's—"

The girl looked up at him. And then she must have seen the look on his face, the look that was mirrored in Vera's face, and Ivan's.

Slowly, she turned back to the boy, resting her hand on the shoulder as if she didn't quite believe it.

Her posture crumpled, her whole body caving in on itself, as if in pain. She didn't cry. She didn't speak, or make a sound, just sat there, curled over the body of her friend.

Tae left his hand on her shoulder, something sick turning inside him. He wanted to do something, anything, but there was nothing he could do.

Ivan's face was very pale, and his jaw was set in the expression that Tae knew from their time on the pleasure planet—the expression of someone in more pain than he wanted to show. And Vera—

She stood there, staring down at the dead student. There were tears glittering in her eyes, but they weren't tears of sadness.

They were tears of rage.

More students had come over, gathering around. He could hear the whispers as the news passed from one to the other.

He turned back to the girl crouched over the boy's body. "I'm sorry," he said again, quietly. "I'm so sorry." It wasn't much. It wasn't anything, really, but—sometimes, just the knowledge you weren't alone was the only thing someone could give to you.

She looked up at him, finally. Her face was still dazed, but there was a hard anger in her eyes. She hardly seemed to see Tae, just pushed herself unsteadily to her feet. He stood quickly, in case he needed to catch her, but she shrugged him off and walked off into the darkness.

He hesitated for a moment, unsure of whether he should follow, then someone grabbed him by the elbow.

"Tae," said a stunned voice that he recognized as one of the students from his old study group. "It's not true. Is it? Is—" The girl couldn't seem to finish the sentence.

Tae nodded. "I'm—sorry. He's dead."

She dropped down beside the body, joining half a dozen other students. Tae moved over to stand beside Ivan, and Ivan reached out, grasping Tae's hand as if it was a lifeline. There was a haunted look in his face, and Tae knew, somehow, that he wasn't seeing this student, here, on this ground. He was seeing another student, years ago, bleeding from the mouth and nose, pleading for his life.

"Stand down! I repeat, stand down. You are instructed to disperse."

Tae became aware, again, of the voices of the police from outside the walls of the alley.

Vera straightened, her face set and hard. She raised her com to her mouth, hitting the amplifier.

"You killed a student," she said, and something about the tone of her voice quieted the noise.

"You killed him. You left him lying in the street. And you will answer for it. One day, you'll answer for this."

For a long moment, the voices outside the alley stilled. At last, a new voice came over the police amplifier.

"If there is someone in need of medical attention, you may—"

"He's dead," said Vera, her voice icy and deadly calm. "What part of that do you not understand?"

There was another long moment of silence. Then the blinding lights from the skybikes illuminated an officer as she stepped forward, pulling off her helmet. She was middle-aged, her face weary and lined, but Tae saw something in her expression he hadn't expected.

Shock. Dismay. Sorrow.

She raised her hands slightly to show she was unarmed. "I'd like to talk," she said, her voice ringing out even without a voice amplifier. "That shouldn't have happened. That explosive should not have been thrown into the middle of a crowd. I'll put up an investigation as to who threw it. In the meantime, if you bring the body out, I'll make sure it gets back to his family." She was walking closer now, the students at the front standing back to let her pass.

And then another figure pushed her way forward. It took a moment for Tae to recognize her as the girl who'd been crouched by the dead student's body. She reached the front of the crowd and took a step towards the officer.

The officer paused, turning to look at her. "I'm sorry," she began. "I didn't—"

The girl's voice was soft, but in the silence, Tae heard every word.

"Pray to the Lady and her Consort that she forgives the blood on your hands, you murderer." She made a quick movement, and for half a second he couldn't tell what she was doing. And then he saw the heat pistol in the girl's hands.

She pointed it directly at the officer's unprotected face, and fired.

There was a moment of shocked, disbelieving silence. The officer stood there for a moment, face burned beyond recognition, body somehow still upright. And then, slowly, like a broken tree in the wind, she swayed, and fell forward, and landed on the street.

Tae didn't need to go to her to know she was dead. The only possible way she could have survived a shot like that was her if she'd been wearing a heat shield. And she'd taken her helmet off to talk to the students.

The soft thud of her body hitting the concrete was the only sound, for a very, very long time.

And then Ivan dropped Tae's hand and was sprinting over. He shoved the girl to the ground as the air over her head blistered with heat.

"Get back," Tae shouted, jolted out of his stupor. He turned and pitched his voice high enough to carry over the sudden chaos.

"Everyone back!"

There was a moment of panicked chaos, then students were fleeing for the alleys. Ivan grabbed the girl who'd shot the officer, and was dragging her backwards. Tae caught Vera's arm and pulled her away from the dead boy on the ground.

"Vera! Come on!"

"No!" she choked, fighting his grip. "We can't just leave him there —" There were tears streaming down her face.

Tae swore and jerked her after him towards the alley. "Vera, come on," he said through his teeth. "There's nothing we can do for him."

"We can't—" she began again, then Tae had dragged her back with him into the alley.

Dmitri, his face ghostly white, blood dripping from a cut under his jaw, came over quickly.

"Vera," he said, grabbing her other arm.

"We just—we just left him out there—" She sounded stunned, but at least she'd stopped fighting.

"I know," said Dmitri grimly. He looked shellshocked as well, dazed, like whenever the reality of what had happened actually sunk in, he might pass out.

But he wouldn't. Tae knew him better than that.

He released Vera and looked around quickly. Students were crying and screaming, and from outside, he could hear the percussive blast of flash-bangs.

"They'll be coming in after us in a minute," said Vera finally, in a low voice. She seemed to have recovered herself slightly. "There's no way we make it out of this."

The rest of the students seemed to have come to the same realization, because they were huddled together in a tight mass. Tae could see Ivan, towards the back, trying to get them to spread out, make less of a target, but they were too panicked.

"It'll be a slaughter," said Dmitri.

He looked afraid. Vera did too. Tae swore again, under his breath.

They didn't deserve this, none of these kids did.

His hand bumped something in the pocket of his coat, and he sucked in a quick breath.

"Dmitri, Vera," he said, turning back to them.

Vera turned, face streaked with tears. "What—"

Tae pulled out a padded bag out of his jacket pocket. "I know Ysbel, remember?"

Dmitri and Vera stared at him, and then, slowly, Vera smiled. It wasn't a real smile, and it looked shaky and almost sick, but it was a smile.

"She—gave you—"

Tae nodded. "I haven't used them, because I didn't want things getting out of control. But—" he glanced around, and didn't finish the sentence.

Behind the sharp snap of flash-bangs, they could still hear police officers shouting. "Stand down! Come out with your hands raised, and we'll take you in peacefully. Repeat, stand down."

Tae took a deep breath and reached into the padded bag Ysbel had given him.

Not the explosives—he wasn't quite sure they were ready to declare full out war just yet—but—

He turned back to Dmitri and Vera. "Go help Ivan. Get everyone back, as far as you can. I'm going to use one of Ysbel's smoke bombs. Believe me, we don't want anyone caught in it."

They nodded grimly and turned away.

"Stand down," the police shouted again. "We won't hurt you if you give yourselves up."

But Tae could hear in their voices that no one was getting out of this unhurt tonight. Not after what had happened.

Another flash-bang exploded metres away from him as he edged his way forward, and he staggered, blinking the brilliant shock from behind his eyes. There was the unmistakable hiss of a heat gun, and he ducked on instinct, and another scream, this one unmistakably a scream of pain.

No more time, then. He'd just have to trust that Ivan and Dmitri and Vera had the students out of the way.

He yanked the small button-shaped cylinder from the bag, finding it by touch. Then he pushed himself off the shelter of the building walls and sprinted forward, tossing his own flash-bang into the clustered mass of police as he ran.

It was only a flash-bang. But it was a flash-bang designed by Ysbel.

The explosion that followed left a stunned silence in its wake, among both the police and the students. Tae hit his com and hissed, "Ivan. I hope you're all the hell back. Smoke bomb."

Then he tossed Ysbel's smoke bomb, hit the controller, and ran.

He grabbed a few of the fleeing students who hadn't made the alleys yet and shoved them forward in front of him as the menacing hiss of gas filled the square. It crept along the ground towards them, but back far as they were, and with the twists and turns of the alleys, the gas wouldn't get to them in concentrations heavy enough to knock them out. He was pretty sure.

From outside the alley, they could hear the shouts of the police officers, the thump of falling bodies, the wail of sirens. The sound of the officers who were still conscious, the ones who must have had gas masks, dragging their fallen companions away.

And then, eventually, silence.

Gradually, as the smoke from outside cleared, the students emerged from where they'd been sheltering. They looked shellshocked, every one of them, faces terrified and haunted.

"They're going to want to end this," Dmitri whispered grimly. He'd come to stand beside Tae. "They're going to want to turn themselves in."

Tae's stomach twisted. He couldn't blame them. He couldn't blame them at all. Honestly, he was surprised it had lasted this long. And the thought of any more students getting hurt, getting killed—

But then, the street kids didn't have that choice. They couldn't just go home. And if the students weren't here, the police would come after them instead, and from what Tae had seen today—they wouldn't stand a chance.

"Maybe they're right," a boy said quietly. "When the police come back, if we come out, and they see we're unarmed—"

Dmitri grabbed Tae's arm. He was pale, his green eyes standing out in sharp relief from his smoke-white face, but there was a grim determination to his expression. He pulled Tae up towards the front of the group and hit the voice amp on his com.

"Listen, all of you," he shouted. Gradually, the hubbub died as students turned towards him. "All of you listen to me," said Dmitri again, and once again Tae was reminded of his easy charm, the power of his unconscious charisma.

There was a reason he'd been the most popular boy on campus. He had a way of making you feel like he was talking directly to you and no one else, even when he was addressing a crowd. He had a way of making you want to believe what he was saying.

"Listen. Do you remember why we're all here? We're here because there are kids out in the streets getting killed, every single day. There are kids out there, younger than us, who don't have families to protect them. And what the police were doing here? That's what they face every damn day of their lives. If we don't stand up for them—who will?"

The talking had stilled now, the only sound Dmitri's voice, ringing out over the square.

"Some of you know Tae," Dmitri continued. "Hell, he helped a bunch of you idiots with your tech homework. He's a street kid. When he came to university, he wasn't there to qualify for some cushy government post. He was fighting to save the damn system. And I'm sure as hell not going to let him do that alone." He turned. "Tae," he said in a softer voice. "Tell them. Tell them what it's like on the streets." He raised his voice slightly, so that it carried. "Because I don't think any of us know. I don't think a single damn one of us understands." He pushed Tae in front of him and held up his com so the voice amplifier would catch Tae's words.

Tae stood there for a moment, looking out at the frightened, terrified students, and something tightened in his chest.

Most of them were older than he was. But they seemed, somehow, very young.

He took a long breath.

"What—what you've done here—" He gestured around at the square and the maze of alleys, cluttered with the detritus of the protest, the concrete blackened in places by flash-bangs. "You've saved lives. You've given me and the other street kids time. But we need more."

Everyone was silent now, watching him.

"One of the street-kid gangs helping me lost two kids, the day before I met them—one to the cold, one to the police. And most of those kids were younger than thirteen." He paused. "You watched a friend die here today. And you can go home tonight, if you want to.

But those street kids will die. And Ivan and I will die too, because we won't leave them."

There was a long moment of silence after Tae finished speaking. The students were looking at him, at each other, at the ground.

"I'm staying," said Dmitri into the silence. "I'm damn well going to make the police fight for this. This whole system is rotten. And if we can't stand up to it—" he gestured around at all of them. "If we, the kids of government officials, who the police usually tiptoe around, can't stand up to it—then who the hell can?"

There was a long moment of silence. Then Vera stepped up to stand beside them. Her face was still streaked with tears, and her expression was grim and haunted. But there was a determined set to her jaw that Tae recognized.

"I'm staying too," she said quietly. "If they take me out of here, it will be because they're dragging my dead body."

Ivan stepped up to join her. "I don't think this needs saying," he said, his voice slightly wry. "But I'm not going anywhere."

One by one, more students stepped up to join them, until every student in the square had gathered into a silent group around Tae and Dmitri.

Dmitri turned to Tae. "You see?" he said. "I'm not the only one. You've turned us into a whole damn band of revolutionaries." He gave Ivan a small smile. "Alright. What do we do next?"

Ivan looked around at the students, then back to Dmitri. He gave a tight, grim smile.

"Well, since we've apparently just declared war on the government, I suppose we'd best start building a barricade."

Under Ivan's direction, they dragged all the loose furniture they could find from the university dorms and began piling it up, closing off the square.

Tae caught Ivan's eye, and Ivan made his way over.

"We're not going to make it back to Caz and Peti and the others tonight, are we?" Tae asked quietly.

Ivan glanced around and shook his head. "I don't think so. These kids are on the verge of panic. If we leave, I'm afraid someone will make a mistake, and they'll all be killed."

Tae gave a quick nod. "I'll tell the street kids. This might last for a while."

Ivan glanced around again, then looked back at Tae, his face grave. "Let's hope so."

Tae ducked back against one of the alley walls and hit his com to the street-kid's closed loop.

"Listen," he said. "Do you remember the university kids I was telling you about? The ones who were protesting? They've—there's been a problem. Someone was killed. And one of them killed a police officer." He paused a moment. No one spoke from the other end of the com line.

"We're building up barricades. We're going to try to keep the police busy for as long as we can. I—don't know how long it will be. None of these kids are fighters. But you need to take advantage of it. Get as many of the kids into position as you can, and try to find somewhere safe, if there is such a place."

At last, Felix's voice came through his earpiece.

"A bunch of government brats are building barricades?" he asked, his voice sceptical.

"Yes," said Tae.

There was another long pause. "Why the hell are they doing that?" said Vanya. "They could just get out."

"Yes," said Tae again. "They—they're trying to give you a chance."

Again, there was silence on the other end of the com.

"You say a bunch of spoiled government brats are taking on the Prasvishoni police force to give us a chance?" came Felix's voice again.

"Yes," said Tae quietly.

"Not sure what a bunch of spoiled government brats knows about going up against the police," said Felix finally. "But me and my killers know a hell of a lot." He paused, clearly reluctant to say the next words. "You—think you could use some people who know how to use a damn weapon behind your barricades?"

For a moment, Tae couldn't find the words to answer.

"I—I think they might," he said at last.

"Don't have to be killers to know how to fight the police," said Matija. "Bet me and my gang could teach them a few things."

"Hell, there's plenty of us who know a trick or two," said Vanya, finally.

Tae looked around at the makeshift barricade, already higher than his head, and he had to clear his throat a couple times before he could speak. "Well, if you're going to come, you best come quickly," he said at last. "The university kids might not know how to fight police, but they know how to block off a street."

"Tae," it was Caz. "Listen. If we're trying to keep the streets free from the gangs—look, if there's enough of us behind a barricade— that's right up in the area we were worried about, isn't it?"

"Caz is right," said Peti. "If there's enough of us behind the barricades, maybe we can push back into the streets we wanted to block the gangs out of. Even if we don't make it all the way, the gangs aren't going to start a fight there with all the police that'll be there."

Tae nodded slowly, biting his lip. "It's not safe, but nowhere's safe.

I think you're right. This might be our best chance." He paused. "And Caz? You'd better put another chip at the drop site for Lev. Let him know that we've apparently declared war on the whole damn Svodrani System government."

21

"Jez!"

Jez frowned, and glanced down at her com.

Lev sounded worried. Really worried.

What's wrong? she tapped out under the table.

"It's Tae. Things have—gone bad."

What's happening?

Around the table, one of the damn government ministers was arguing about some bloody protocol that Jez had never heard of, and honestly, never wanted to.

"They've—" Lev paused. "Last night at the protests, a student was killed. And then one of his friends killed a police officer. And now they've put up barricades. This has turned into a damn war."

For a moment, Jez was completely speechless.

Tech-head just started a revolution? she tapped out at last.

On the other end of the com, Lev sighed. "Yes. And they're going to be slaughtered if we don't do something."

Jez glanced around the table.

He was right. There was no way a bunch of idiot university students could hold off the police for long, not even with Tae there to help. Certainly not with the amount of weapons Ysbel'd said the police had.

Send me the specs, she tapped out under the table. *Where they are, what they're doing, whatever.*

"One second." Lev's voice was grim.

She didn't blame him. Much as she liked the idea of tech-head as a revolutionary, Lev was right. There was no way those kids were going to survive this.

Her com dinged, and she glanced at it.

"I asked, Layla, for your position on what Catta just suggested." Branka's voice was icy.

"You agree, but you need to hear more analysis on how it would affect the interior ministries," Lev hissed.

She grinned lazily, and repeated what Lev had just said.

Branka glared at her, look sharp with suspicion.

Jez gave her an innocent smile.

Honestly, attending meetings with Lev listening into your earpiece feeding you answers when you'd forgotten to pay attention for the last ten minutes was actually a pretty damn efficient way of attending meetings.

Surreptitiously, she tapped her com to bring up the holoscreen, and peered at it under the table.

She looked closer, and raised an eyebrow. The students hadn't picked too bad of a spot, all things considered. Not that she'd ever gotten in with the gangs in Prasvishoni, but she knew more or less where you should stay away from if you didn't want to get to a firefight, and where you needed to head if you did. And as far as she was concerned, if she was trying to lock down the streets, she'd pick that area right around where the students had set up their barricade.

Problem was going to be how to convince the police not to blow them all to hell.

"Layla!"

She looked up sharply.

"Perhaps you'd be so kind as to inform us what on your holoscreen is more important than discussing how to keep the government from imploding," Branka snapped.

Jez glanced down at her com again and raised an eyebrow. "Well, funny you mentioned it, actually. Because I just got word from one of my sources on the street."

All the ministers were looking at her now, with slight variations on Branka's theme of total exasperation.

Branka's voice dripped fury. "If you would pay attention—"

"Here's the thing, though," Jez broke in. "Guess there's a bunch of students putting up barricades. Thing is, my sources say that's just a decoy. They plan on starting a protest right outside the damn government buildings here. Kids of some of the ministers. And the police will have to shut it down, right here, in full view of everyone. So, you want to talk about things imploding?"

In her earpiece, Lev chuckled. "Jez. That's brilliant."

Branka stared at her. "What? Your sources say—"

Jez shrugged. "You were curious about how it felt getting your office firebombed. Get enough radical students out here, guess you'll find out."

Branka's face went slightly bloodless. She turned to the young aide at her left. "Get Eduard on the line, please. I'd like to talk to the Commissioner of Police once the meeting is over." She narrowed her eyes at Jez. "I hope your information is good."

"Why don't you check?" Jez drawled. "How many people know about barricades?"

From the looks on the faces around the table, the answer was, exactly three of them. And one of them was Branka.

It was going to be a long damn day. She could already tell. But … hell, it was just possible they'd end up by keeping tech-head alive after all.

By the time Jez reached the apartment building that night, she was grumpy, irritated, and damn well exhausted. She hit the lock on the door, shoved it open, and stepped inside, glowering at the world in general.

Lev glanced up from where he was sitting on the couch, his holoscreen pulled up in front of him, and as always, he smiled to see her, and as always, irritation and tension of the day dissipated, just a little, at the sight of his smile.

"How was your day?" he asked, coming over.

She blew out a long breath. "Well, I ran that errand for you." She hesitated a moment. "You—you really think—"

Lev sighed and ran a hand over his face. "I hope not," he said quietly. "But this is Masha we're talking about. And I'd rather be safe."

She nodded, looking down, and tried to ignore how her stomach tightened and something knotted in her chest at the thought.

"I'm sorry, Jez," he murmured, and his tone was soft with sympathy.

She cleared her throat. "Anyways. That bastard Jaromil is still trying to stop us changing up the government. Bloody well talk my damn throat dry every damn meeting, and then every damn next meeting, he's come up with a whole new reason why we shouldn't do it. And Branka won't stick her neck out, not even a little. We still have no idea what's scaring her?"

Lev shook his head, frowning slightly. "No. I've been looking into it, but I haven't found anything."

Jez pulled off her coat, almost tossed it on the floor, glanced at Lev, and hung it on the peg instead. "Well, one good thing, anyways. Half the damn police force is right this minute twiddling their thumbs in front of the government building. Nothing's happened, of course, but Branka thinks that just means it's working."

Lev smiled. "I imagine Tae will appreciate that."

Jez grinned back. "Damn well better. Had to lie my face off to get there."

Lev raised an eyebrow at her. "You—wouldn't have lied otherwise?"

She snickered. "'Course I would've. But I would've had to come up with a different reason."

Lev chuckled, retrieved her mittens from where she'd dropped them on top of the bag, and tucked them into the pockets of her coat. And—well, fair enough, she probably wouldn't have been able to find them the next day if he hadn't done that, but he didn't say anything, even though she waited for it.

And she realized she hadn't actually expected him to.

She glanced at him sideways as they walked over to the table for dinner.

Maybe—maybe this was what all those bastards meant when they talked about having people around. Not a bunch of plaguing suffocating idiots who wanted you to be something you weren't, and were basically only looking for an excuse to get rid of you. But people like—well, like Lev. Who honestly cared about you. Who knew all your strange quirks, and either didn't mind them, or actually liked them. Who didn't harass you when you forgot something, or tell you how damn stupid you were.

"They're going to be bringing over some classified documents tonight," she said through a mouthful of food. They'd come to a sort of unspoken understanding that on days that she was going to be talking her damn throat dry in the meetings, Lev made the dinner, and on days that he was going to be working his damn tail off on some project for her or one of the others, she picked up street food.

Tonight it had been a compromise, so they had pirozki from a street vendor, and a pot of the solyanka stew that seem to be Lev's specialty.

And honestly, it was pretty damn good.

Lev raised his eyebrows. "They're sending someone by to drop it off? Why not send it over the coms?"

Jez shrugged. "Branka said it was so confidential she didn't dare."

"And I don't suppose she told you what this highly classified information was?"

Jez shook her head. "No. Going out to everyone at the meetings though, so I'm guessing it's something about some government structure crap."

Lev nodded, and she frowned. He looked tired, like the strain of the last few days was getting to him

"You OK, genius?" she asked quietly after a moment.

He looked at her, slightly startled, and she rolled her eyes.

"I'm not blind." She paused. "You—look tired."

He sighed, and give a rueful smile. "I'm worried about Tae. And about Masha. I don't know what she's after, and I'll be honest, Jez, it scares the hell out of me."

Jez shrugged, ignoring the small twist in her stomach. "Figure if Masha doesn't worry you, you're not paying attention."

Lev gave a reluctant smile. "I—suppose you're right."

There was a tap on the door, and Jez pushed back her empty bowl and stood. "I'll throw it in the cleanser, don't worry, genius," she said, rolling her eyes.

He smiled and shook his head at her as she walked towards the door. She hit the unlock button and pulled the door back.

A young man stood outside, his face slightly nervous, no one who would have been unexpected at any sort of ministers meeting in the government. One of the ubiquitous aides who was always sent on the most miserable of tasks. And there was the briefest fraction of a second, where Jez looked at him, and wondered how she knew, gut deep, that something was wrong. And then her brain made sense of the dark shape of another young man lying in the hallway, the dark stain of blood soaking into the threadbare carpet, the wide, staring eyes, the government uniform. But by that time she was already moving, shoving the door closed.

The young man pushed his foot in the way, and Jez heard a slight grunt of pain as the door slammed hard against his boot, but it wasn't enough. Her hand moved almost at the same time his did, his bringing up the heat pistol, hers knocking it out of the way. The heat blast seared the roof of their apartment, and then she grabbed his wrist and twisted hard, and there was a thud as the pistol hit the ground. She bent to grab for it, and at the same moment he yanked something out of his pocket with his other hand. As she straightened with the gun, she saw the glint of metal.

She could have jumped out of the way, easily. But just like always, when too many things were happening at once, the whole world seemed to slow to a crawl, and she could consider every action with a thoughtful dispassion.

And without even knowing how she knew, she dived. Not away from the weapon, but towards it—towards it, and in front of Lev, who'd stood and was coming over, a slight frown on his face.

And she'd guessed exactly right.

The boy with the weapon hadn't turned towards her at all. He spun at the last second as he threw the knife, and it should have gone straight through Lev's throat.

But it didn't. Because Jez was damn fast when she needed to be.

The knife hit her squarely in the arm, and then time sped up again, and everything was happening at once. Lev shouted, shoving his way forward. Jez caught a momentary glimpse of his expression, and realized, once again, how very bad of an idea getting on Lev's bad side would be. The would-be assassin must've come to the same conclusion, because he stepped backwards, trying to slam the door behind him. It didn't quite close, and he yanked on it frantically, then gave up, his running footsteps retreating down the hall.

Normally, Jez would already be after him. But something strange and icy was spreading from the centre of the hot pain where the knife had hit, and her legs weren't working like they should, and she could feel herself sliding towards the floor.

Lev grabbed her before she could fall and lowered her gently to the ground. His face was deathly pale.

"Jez! Jez, are you alright? Where are you hurt?"

"Bastard's … getting away," she managed with a grimace.

"I don't give a damn," said Lev tightly. "Are you alright?"

She tried to grin at him, but she wasn't entirely sure it turned out. She reached up, hand shaking, and jerked the knife from her arm with a quick gasp of pain. It hurt like hell, yes, but that wasn't what was making her heart pound, faster and faster, making her muscles shake, making the world go slightly fuzzy.

"Bastard … bastard poisoned it," she said. Her voice sounded odd, and far away. "He … he meant it for you. Wasn't trying to kill me at all."

"How do you know it was poisoned?" Lev snapped, his voice tense.

"Got—got hurt plenty of times. Never made me sick before. Shouldn't hurt for your heart to beat, I don't think."

He pressed his fingers to the side of her neck, then swore viciously and jumped to his feet, grabbing for the apartment's first-aid kit.

Her heart was racing, so fast she felt dizzy and sick with it, and it was going to pound its way all the way out of her chest, and her lungs gasped in quick, short breaths that didn't seem give her any oxygen at all.

Lev was back, crouching next to her. He pulled some small patches from the kit and slapped them in a line down her shoulder.

"That should help, for a minute," he said, and she could hear the fear under his voice. She shuddered, her heart seeming to slow, just a little, and she managed an actual breath for the first time since the knife had hit her.

Beside her, Lev hit his com. "Masha," he said, in a low, desperate tone she'd only heard from him once or twice before in her life. "Masha, I need you, now."

Masha's voice over the com was as calm as usual. "Lev? What's —"

"I need some betathanoline, now."

"It's not easy to get at the best of times, and at this time of night —" Masha began.

"Jez was poisoned," Lev snapped. "With adrinisphed. I put on some blood-pressure patches from the first-aid kit, but it's not going to be enough."

There was a moment's pause, then Masha's voice again, much sharper this time. "Are you sure?"

"I wouldn't be damn well telling you if I wasn't sure. I can't leave her alone, and I have no way of getting it. We have fifteen damn minutes before she's dead." Lev was speaking through his teeth, his voice cold and deadly. "Maybe less."

There was a moment of silence from the other end of the com.

"I'll be there," said Masha softly. "I'll be there with the antidote, before fifteen minutes is up."

"You'd damn well better," said Lev, words choking slightly. "Or you'll be short a pilot."

He slapped his com off and turned back to Jez. He was breathing heavily, as if he'd been hit by the poison too, but his hand on her arm was gentle.

"Jez?" he said, voice rough. "Just stay with me, OK? It'll be alright."

Her heart was pounding, not quite as fast as before, but right on the edge of it, like a ship's engine on the verge of a meltdown, and her breath was coming too quickly, and cold was creeping through her body.

She met Lev's eyes, saw the worry and fear in them, and she wanted to smile, but she couldn't. Because—because the truth was, she was terrified.

She'd never really had time to be scared of dying before—everything always happened so fast. But—well, but she was dying, and she found, in the end, that it scared the hell out of her. She was cold, and shaky, and sick, and the room around her was spinning, and tears pricked at her eyes and she couldn't seem to stop them.

"Jez?" Lev's voice choked, and he gathered her into his arms, burying his face in her hair. "Jez. It's going to be alright. Stay with me, OK?"

She was cold. She was so damn cold, and her chest hurt, and everything hurt, and whatever those patches were that Lev had slapped on her arm, they were wearing off, because her heart was pounding faster, the sick dizziness from earlier returning. Lev must've felt it too, because he pulled her closer, holding her like he was afraid she'd disappear.

There was a tap on the door, and Masha's voice. Lev's grip on her released for half a second, and he hit something on his com. The door clicked and swung open, and Masha stood in the entrance.

Her face was set, and snow and ice dripped from the edges of her scarf and off her hair. She was breathing like she'd been running hard. She took in the room at a glance, and crossed over to them with quick strides. "How is she?" she snapped.

"Still alive," said Lev, his voice grim. "But not for much longer. The patches are wearing off."

The room around Jez was growing hazy, and it was harder and harder to make sense of the words Lev and Masha were saying. Even the pressure of Lev's arms around her, holding her, was fading just a little.

Masha crouched beside them, and Jez felt, faintly, cool fingers on her wrist, then Masha swore, low and harsh. Jez would have raised an eyebrow, if her damn body had been listening to her at the moment. She hadn't actually known Masha knew that word.

Through the haze over her vision, she saw Masha stand quickly and pull something from her coat pocket.

"I'm going to give her five cc's, intravenously," she said, voice grim.

"Five cc's? That's enough to kill her!"

"Look at her, Lev," Masha snapped. "If I don't, she'll die anyway. This gives her a chance. Hold out her arm, now!"

The room was darkening, and the words that Lev and Masha were saying were getting more and more difficult to understand. She felt someone grab her arm, yank back her sleeve, and hold it out, wrist up.

"Hurry, damn you," said someone, and as the words faded to sound, and the sound faded to silence, and the room faded to darkness, Jez felt the sharp sting of a needle on the inside of her arm. And then she felt nothing at all.

She was fourteen years old again. Fourteen, and angry, and defiant—but mostly scared. Her father stood at the door to the house that had never really felt like home, and the hard, cold look on his face told her he was serious. She couldn't go back, not ever. Behind him, she caught a glimpse of her mother, and for a brief, desperate second, a painful jolt of hope sparked in her chest. Maybe her mother was there to stop him, tell Jez it was alright, this was something they could work out, they didn't want her to go after all.

But she'd just stood there, and the pious, indifferent look on her face was the last thing Jez saw before the door slammed shut for the last time.

She was in Lena's hangar bay, curled up on the oil-stained concrete floor, gasping in pain. It was the first time Antoni had beat her up. Not the last time, of course, and sure as hell not the first time she'd ever been beaten. But the first time it had been this bad. She sobbed, little, gasping sobs she tried to choke back, because the sharp shock of each breath was a knife shoved into her side.

And the other pilots had ignored her, stepping around her like she wasn't there.

Somehow, that had hurt even more than if they'd kicked her.

She'd been a kid. An innocent, who'd expected, maybe, something different, even though she had no reason to.

It was Lena's orders, she'd found out later. Even if someone had given a damn, Lena'd said no, and when Lena said no, you damn well obeyed.

She was back in her prison cell, after she'd lost her ship. She'd spent the whole damn day annoying the hell out of the guards, but it was night now, and they'd turned off the ship lights, and it was dark, and cold. She huddled into the corner of her cot, leaning her head back against the smooth walls, and closed her eyes, and tried to fight back the terror that was closing in on her, so tight and so close she thought it might choke her, and she wouldn't be able to breathe, and it might actually kill her. Because she was locked in, trapped, and she'd never get out, never stare out a cockpit window into deep space again, never feel the perfect, aching rightness of ship's controls under her fingers.

She gasped and opened her eyes, staring around her in panic.

She wasn't in prison—the room was bigger than her cell had been, though not by much.

But—she was still alone.

Something tightened in her throat, and she choked back a painful sob.

And then the door was shoved open, and Lev was inside the room in two strides and crouched beside her bed. He grabbed her hand, and there was a look on his face she'd never seen there before, a frantic, desperate relief.

"Jez," he whispered, voice shaking. "Jez, you're awake. Thank the damn Lady—" then he dropped his forehead to the edge of the bed, his shoulders shaking.

He lifted his head a few moments later, blinking back what looked like tears. "Jez." He took a deep breath, smoothing the hair back from her forehead with trembling fingers. "Jez, I'm right here. What do you need?"

"I—I was alone," she choked out, although her mouth had a hard time forming the words. "I—I don't want to be alone." She could feel the tears in her eyes again, but she couldn't stop them.

"Jez," he whispered, stroking her hair. "Jez. You were never alone, I promise. I was right here, the whole time, just outside the door. I'm not going to leave you."

It was cold. She hadn't realized how cold it was, but her body was shaking with it, and her teeth wanted to chatter.

"Everyone leaves me," she whispered. Her voice trembled, with tears or cold or maybe both.

He met her gaze, his dark eyes boring into hers. "I'm not leaving, Jez. I won't leave you, not ever, not unless you ask me to. I promise."

She looked at him for a long time.

She was shivering harder now.

"Jez?" he softly. "What's wrong?"

"I'm—cold," she whispered.

"I'll get you more blankets." He made as if to stand, but she clutched his hand, panic rising her chest again.

"No. No, don't leave me."

He crouched back down beside the bed. "Jez, I'll be back, I promise," he said quietly. "I just need to get blankets. You're shivering, look."

She couldn't make her mouth form the words, and she probably couldn't even make her brain construct them. But—he couldn't leave. Because he left, the nightmares would come back, and she didn't think she could handle that anymore. So she clutched his hand tighter, and the warmth of the tears that dripped down her cheeks was the only part of her that was warm at all.

Lev let out a long breath. "I—suppose I could lie down next to you," he said finally. "Would that help? It might warm you up."

She managed a shaky nod. Lev sighed and rose, still not letting go of her hand, and a moment later the bed creaked and shifted at his weight. There was a momentary shock of cold as the covers were pulled back, and then the slow, comforting warmth of his body curled around hers.

Slowly, slowly, as his warmth seeped into her, her shaking began to subside. She leaned back into him, and the steady beating of his heart, the regular, even rise and fall of his chest against her back, were almost as soothing as his warmth. He put an arm around her waist, pulling her close, and she gave a small sigh, her eyes drifting closed.

"I'm here, Jez," he whispered quietly, his breath warm on her neck. "You're safe. I'm here, and I won't leave you."

She was almost asleep, a real sleep this time, not the strange delirium of nightmares from before. And on the edge of her hearing, right before she drifted into unconsciousness, she thought she heard, his voice so low she could hardly make it out, "I love you, Jez."

And then she was asleep, and she was never entirely certain whether she'd heard it, or dreamed it.

When she woke again, she felt like absolute crap. Every damn muscle in her body was sore, and her arm hurt like hell, and her chest ached like she'd been running for hours, and her whole body was as shaky as if she'd just puked her guts out. But for the first time since she'd been hit by that damn knife, her thoughts were actually clear.

She looked around the small room. The door was mostly closed, but it had been left open a crack, and through the crack she could hear Lev's quiet voice. And somehow, she couldn't help the warmth that rose inside her.

She couldn't exactly remember everything that it happened, but— she was pretty sure she remembered being a complete idiot. Crying, and grabbing his hand, and saying something stupid about being afraid, and about not wanting him to leave her. It had just been because she wasn't thinking, that was all, obviously, but—but the fact that he was outside the door, probably sitting on the hard floor and leaned back against the wall, instead of on the couch in the other room, made her feel—slightly odd. But in a nice way. Like even though he'd known she was probably delirious, and she'd probably be fine soon as her damn brain started working again—he hadn't wanted her to wake up and think she was alone again.

She took a deep breath and found she had to blink hard for a moment.

She moved her injured arm experimentally, and when that worked, tried with her legs. They seem to be working too, even though the muscles were sore as hell. But honestly, being sore didn't really count. That was basically the story of her damn life.

She pushed the covers off, and fought back a sudden wave of dizziness at the movement. Then, when the room had steadied, she swung her legs over the edge of the bed and stood.

She had to clutch at the wall, and the room spun dizzily around her, and for a moment she thought she was going to vomit. But somehow, with the assistance of the wall, she managed not to either fall flat on her face, or throw up all over the damn floor.

When the room stopped swaying, she let go of the wall gingerly and tried a step. Then she had to grab for the wall again as she almost fell over the second time.

Lev must've heard the noise, because the door swung open, and then he was beside her in two quick steps, grabbing her elbow to hold her steady. His expression was sharp with concern.

"For the Lady's sake, Jez, you almost damn well died three days ago! Are you trying to actually kill yourself?"

When the room had stopped spinning again, she shot him a cocky grin. "Nah, there's enough other people trying to do that for me. Besides, I'm basically fine."

"And that's why I barely caught you before you passed out on the floor," he muttered. "At least sit down for a minute. Please?"

She rolled her eyes at him. "Fine, genius. But I've been in this damn room for—" She paused, and glanced at him. "Actually, I have no idea. How long was I out?"

He sighed, and now she could see the worry lines etched deep into his face. "Three days," he said shortly. "The first day you almost died from the poison, and the next two days you almost died from the cure. I told Masha that much betathanoline might actually kill you, and she told me that if you didn't get it, you'd die anyway. And—" he shrugged, clearly trying to inject a note of humour into his voice. "Apparently we were both right."

"Yeah." She gave a small shiver, because she actually didn't want to think about that. "Anyway, so I was in this damn room for three days. So if I'm going to sit down, at least let me sit on the couch."

He gave another short sigh, but nodded in agreement. She had to lean against him heavily, because the damn floor didn't seem to want to stay put, but they made it to the couch by dint of a moderate amount of effort on Lev's part, and an exorbitant amount of swearing on hers, and she sank down onto it with a sigh of relief.

"I imagine you'll want some food, since you've had nothing but the absorbable nutrition patches from the first-aid kit for the last three days," said Lev. He tried to smile, but the strain behind his eyes gave it away. "It keeps you alive, but I'm told it's not exactly a three-course meal."

At his words, Jez's stomach grumbled loudly. Now that he mentioned it, she was actually starving.

He came back a moment later with a bowl of something hot. He handed it to her, then grabbed it back quickly as she almost spilled all over her lap. "Here, why don't I hold it while you eat?"

After she dumped the second spoonful of soup down her front, he took the spoon from her as well, and spooned soup into her mouth like she was a damn invalid.

She glared at him, but—well, she was almost ready to keel over from hunger, and it looked like that was the only way she was actually going to get any of it into her damn mouth.

By the time she finished the bowl of soup, some of her shakiness had dissipated. She took a long breath and looked around. Then, suddenly, she swore.

"What is it?" asked Lev, looking up quickly, his voice tight with worry.

"Tae," she said through her teeth. "What happened to Tae? I was supposed to—" she went to sit up, but Lev pushed her gently back into her seat.

"You said I've been out for three days! Tae is expecting me to keep the police away, and I—"

"Jez. Listen to me. I didn't forget about Tae. I couldn't tell them what actually happened, because considering the assassin killed the aide Branka sent, I doubt he was from an official government source. But I told Branka about the assassination of the aide, and mentioned that you were sick and couldn't come in, but I'd relay your messages over the com. It's—not ideal, perhaps, but it's something. Between Tanya and I, we've managed to keep at least some of the police away from the barricades."

She studied his face. "Look, genius," she said at last. "I know I've been sick. Well, I mean, poisoned, basically the same thing. But, point is, you're still crap liar. What's really happening?"

He sighed. "I'm not lying," he said at last. "But—you're right. It's not going as well as I'd like. We're keeping things under control, barely, but—" he shook his head. "Your opinions carry a lot less weight if you're not there in person to present them. And I'm sure that more than one person suspects you're worse off than I've let on. I know how it works in government—no one is willing to stick their neck out for someone who may not be there to protect them when the favours go the other way."

Jez closed her eyes for a moment.

She felt like absolute crap. She felt sick, and weak, and shaky, and like she wanted to sleep for the rest of her damn life. But hell, it been a long damn time since she'd had the luxury of taking time off when she felt like crap.

She took a deep breath and pushed herself to her feet.

Lev yelped and jumped up to catch her as she swayed. "Jez," he said through his teeth. "What are you—"

She gave him a tired smile. "Figure it's about time for me to get back to work. Don't know what Branka's doing with herself if she can't yell at me for being late."

Lev stared at her in frank incredulity for a moment.

"Jez," he said patiently, when he'd recovered his power of speech. "You can't stand up without passing out. That's going to make going back to work a little difficult."

She grinned at him. "Come on now, genius, I didn't almost pass out. Besides, I can do basically anything."

"You did, in fact, almost pass out," said Lev through his teeth. "And I know this because I've had to catch you three times now in between here and the bedroom."

She turned to him again, and this time she didn't try to paste a smile on her face. "Look," she said quietly. "Here's the thing. We don't figure this out, Tae dies. And a hell of a lot of other people die too. And yeah, I don't actually want to sit through a damn boring-as-hell meeting when I feel like I'm gonna puke my guts out, but—I'd sure as hell rather do that than find out Tae died because I didn't."

Lev studied her for a long moment. Finally, he let out a long breath. "You're right," he said in a low voice. "I'm sorry. I'm—I'm worried about you, that's all."

She nodded, swallowing hard. "I know," she said at last. "Um. And thank you. For saving my life. And, um, everything else."

"Well," he said, "if it makes you feel any better, I was only in the position to save your life because you saved mine first."

For the first time since she'd woken up, Jez's mind flashed back to the young man at the doorway, the young man holding the knife.

The knife that hadn't been aimed at her, but at Lev.

Sick unease swirled in her stomach, mingling with the nausea. "You have any idea why that bastard was after you?" she asked quietly. "Because he wasn't aiming for me."

"I don't know." Lev gave a short shake of his head. "It could be because someone's realized I'm helping you in the meetings. It could be because they tracked down Masha and Ysbel and Tanya's signal, and then from there found who they're communicating with—they talk with me more often than you. Or—" he shrugged. "It could have been the most obvious thing—they were going to kill me as a warning to you."

She blew out a short breath. His words had done absolutely nothing to assuage her unease.

Finally, though, she glanced at her com and shook her head. "Well, guess I better get dressed and get going. I'll be pretty damn late, even for me."

Lev studied her for a moment, face still cut with worry. At last, he shook his head ruefully. "At least let me walk you to the government building. You're not going to do anyone any good passed out on the concrete."

She was tempted to tell him no, that she'd much rather he stayed here, where there were probably fewer people with poisoned knives wandering around—although, in fairness, that hadn't actually done much good the last time—but he was right. She wasn't completely sure she'd make it down the apartment stairs without landing on her face, let alone all the way to the government offices.

22

Lev, day 14

Lev frowned, trying to push back his unease as Jez stepped through the door of the building. She grabbed the edge of the doorframe to steady herself, then turned and shot him a shaky grin as the door shut behind her.

For a few moments he stood in the street, staring at the closed door.

Jez, who could hardly stay on her damn feet, was walking straight into an office full of people who wanted to kill her. Every part of his brain was screaming in panic at the thought.

But—she was right. He and Masha and Tanya and Ysbel had been holding things together by the skin of their teeth. And the Tae situation was going sideways quickly. Instructions given by a government official's lover over a com simply didn't hold the same sway as instructions given in person by someone who was definitely alive and definitely not about to keel over at any moment.

Although that was currently debatable.

Half of him wanted to follow Jez into the building and up the stairs, but that would be counterproductive. She'd have to show them she was well enough to deal with her own issues if she wanted any of them to take her seriously. He'd been in government long enough to know that. The merest sign of weakness, and the rest of them would tear you to pieces.

He gave a short sigh, turned, and started back to the apartment.

By the time he got in, Jez's voice was filtering through the com, and he breathed a quick sigh of relief. At the very least, she'd made it up to the meeting room. At this point, that hadn't been a sure bet.

He had to fight back the shaky terror that came every time he remembered her lying on the floor, clutching his hand with a grip that grew steadily weaker, the fear in her eyes, the way her heartbeat raced. His own sick panic, knowing that if Masha didn't get there in time, he'd watch Jez die, right there in his arms, and there'd be nothing he could do.

He hadn't slept a full night since it had happened. Half of it was because he'd been straining for any sound from Jez, any hint of her breath slowing, her pulse, rapid and weak, starting to give out.

But most of it, honestly, was that he couldn't bear the nightmares he knew would come the moment he closed his eyes.

That had come, every time he'd closed his eyes.

He let himself into the apartment, locked the door, and dropped down on the couch, trying to steady his breathing. Panicking wasn't going to help Jez, and it wasn't going to help Tae, and it wasn't going to improve their situation.

Somehow, he had to be able to deal with this calmly and rationally.

From the tone of the voices over the com, the fact that Jez could hardly stand without falling over had done absolutely nothing to dampen her ability to irritate the hell out of her coworkers.

He smiled reluctantly at the outraged tones of one of the ministers.

If Jez actually did work in government, Lady forbid, three quarters of the ministers would be gone within six months.

When he'd listened long enough to be sure everything was going well, he left Jez's channel on his earpiece and tapped his com to Tae's line.

After what had happened, there was no chance of getting a dead-drop through anymore.

"Tae. You there?"

Tae's voice answered immediately. In the background there were shouts and cursing, the snap and fizz of flash-bangs, and Lev gritted his teeth.

"Lev." Tae's voice was tight with strain. "What's happening? Is—is Jez—"

"Jez is fine," said Lev. "She—headed back to the government buildings today."

There was a moment of silence on the other end of com. Then Tae said, his voice, if possible, even more strained, "She—Lev. I talked to you this morning. You said she'd woken up once in the last three days, and you still weren't sure if she'd pull through."

Lev sighed. "I know. Since that time, she woke up, rolled out of bed, almost fell over multiple times, and insisted on going in." He paused a moment. "She knows what's happening where you are. And—she's right. Her influence will fade quickly if she's not there in person. In government, any sign of weakness and you're done for."

"And her almost falling over when she tries to stand up isn't a sign of weakness?" Tae's voice now held the strained incredulity that always came when he discussed Jez.

Lev managed a small smile. "Tae. She knows what she's doing." He paused a moment. "Besides, if you recall, she managed to con highly classified information out of one of Grigory's top people back on the gambling ship, and simultaneously cheat him blind, while she was so drunk she couldn't stand up on her own two feet. Don't underestimate her."

Tae managed a chuckle at that. "I guess you're right."

"What's happening at the barricades?" asked Lev quietly.

Tae gave a short, frustrated sigh. "It's—not good. We've been holding out so far, mostly because you and Jez got some of the police force reassigned. But I've tapped into their communications. It's not going to last. They're getting counter-orders, I don't know where from. And …" He paused, and Lev knew that whatever was coming next, he wasn't going to like it.

"The police have been holding back," said Tae quietly. "When I say holding back—there've been plenty of injuries, but so far they haven't killed anyone else. They've been treating it as a street disturbance, using smoke bombs, stun shots, flash-bangs. But I've got a tap into their communications. They have orders to start treating it like a war. Heat guns, laser guns, ion cannons—there's no way we get out of that without casualties. They can take out the barricades with one damn shot from an ion cannon."

Lev cursed.

Damn it to hell. It was inevitable, probably, but—damn it to hell.

He tapped the com again. "Thanks. I'll pass this on to Jez. Maybe there's something she can do."

"She needs to get the weapons reassigned," said Tae, his voice tight with worry. "That's the only way we make it. If they come out at us with everything they have, there's no way we survive this."

"I know," said Lev quietly. "That's why she went back in today. And you won't have to hold out forever. As soon as the government's stable, it won't matter if word of Grigory and Olyessa gets out. That should keep the government busy enough that they don't have time to come after a bunch of students and street kids."

"Yeah," said Tae at last. "Thanks, Lev." In the background, another flash-bang hissed and snapped, and Tae cursed. "I have to go."

His com tapped off, and Lev was left staring at his own com, ice churning in his stomach.

At last, he tapped through to Jez's line.

Through the com, he heard Branka's icy voice. "And since this was your idea in the first place, Layla, I would appreciate you paying attention. Again, if we take Gavril out of the Outer Rim Resources Ministry, who do you suggest we replace him with?"

Lev closed his eyes for a moment, picturing the words he'd been hearing in the back of his mind this whole time. "They should replace him with Daiva," he whispered. "She's working with the outer-rim department at the moment, but she should be easy to reassign, since they've just assigned a new underminister to Budimir, who could step into her position while they train the new person."

Jez repeated his words, or at least the gist of them—he was fairly certain he'd made it through the entire sentence without any profanity, and without referring to anyone as a plaguer.

There was some sputtering around the table, which Lev had expected, but it was certainly the most logical choice. And when they thought about it, they'd be unable to disagree.

Anyone ever tell you you're damn good at this government stuff? I've never seen so many people so pissed off at once, Jez tapped through her com.

He smiled. "You're not too bad at it yourself. I think you've managed to successfully intimidate at least three quarters of the room, and that's no easy feat."

He could picture her grin.

Guess we make a good team, she tapped out, and Lev caught himself smiling again, with absolutely no reason to do so.

Then he sobered. "Jez. I have news from Tae. It's—not good."

About the time he knew Jez would be headed home for the day, Lev made his way towards the government buildings.

He'd only been waiting for a few standard minutes when she stepped through the door. The exhaustion in her eyes, and the look of desperate relief that crossed her face when she saw him, sent something that was a cross between concern and panic shooting through his brain. But he managed to hide both, and stepped forward with a small smile.

"Thought you might like someone to walk you home today."

She grinned at him gratefully. "Well, figure I could do worse than be walked home by some hot scholar boy."

He cleared his throat awkwardly, and tried to ignore the way his stomach flipped at her words.

She snickered. "It's true—you're damn hot all soaking wet like that. In case you wondered."

He shook his head, smiling faintly despite himself.

By the time they got back to the apartment, he could tell it was taking Jez every bit of concentration she possessed to stay on her feet. He pulled the door open, shut it behind him with his foot, and led her over to the couch. She dropped onto it gratefully.

"You sit," he said, helping her off with her coat. "I'll be right back." He hung up her coat, put her bag away, and went over to the hotplate, where there was a bowl of soup warming. He was ridiculously relieved when she was actually able to hold the spoon without dropping it.

If it had been anyone else, he would have asked how they'd managed to get through a day of government meetings when they could hardly hold their damn soup spoon. But this was Jez, and she'd just look at him like she was confused by the question.

And she probably would be. Jez, he'd learned, didn't live in a world of can do or can't do. She lived in a world of if she damn well wanted it enough, she'd make it happen or die trying.

At last, she finished her soup, placed the bowl down beside her, and leaned back with a shaky sigh. "Well, genius," she said quietly. "Don't feel quite so crap as I did this morning. Figure by tomorrow I should be basically at a hundred percent."

He gave her a skeptical look.

She grinned at him. "What? Jealous?"

He smiled ruefully. "No, Jez. I'm not jealous that you got poisoned and almost died. I'm just remembering other times you told me you were basically at a hundred percent. If I recall, one of them included a broken jaw, a broken arm, and four—"

She rolled her eyes. "Four broken damn ribs, I know. You ever going to let that go?"

He gave a small chuckle. "Jez. That was, what, two months ago?"

She sighed loudly. "Anyways, I got the guns temporarily reassigned for tomorrow morning. They won't reassign them permanently until I can talk to the police commissioner, but I've got an appointment with him first thing tomorrow morning. So now we need to come up with a damn good reason why they should be." She closed her eyes wearily, then blinked them back open. "Guess we should probably go through that tonight."

She pulled up her holoscreen, and he could see the weariness in her gesture.

He shook his head. He wanted to tell her to go to bed, let him take care of it, but—at this point they couldn't afford that, and she knew it as well as he did. So instead, with a quick glance out the window to where they were inevitably being watched, he sat beside her, put his arm around her, and pulled up his holoscreen. She settled into his shoulder with a sigh, pulling her feet up under her like always, and like always, he pulled her in closer so she was comfortably tucked against him.

She was shivering, just a little. After what she'd been through, she'd probably feel cold for a while.

"You want me to get a blanket?" he asked.

She shook her head, trying for a grin. "Nah. I'll be fine, just give me a minute. Anyways, you always say you're the hottest damn thing in the apartment."

He gave a reluctant chuckle, and she snuggled closer. He put his other arm around her, and for half a second, a sick, thoughtless panic rose in his throat at the muscle-memory, holding Jez as she stared up at him, her eyes wide with fear and her heart racing sickeningly fast, not knowing if Masha would get there in time or if Jez's racing heart would beat faster and faster until it finally stopped. But she relaxed into his arms with a soft sigh, and for the first time since the assassin had thrown his knife, Lev found he was able to actually breathe.

They went through the information quickly, and between them, came up with a logical argument for reassigning the deadliest of the weapons. Inevitably, the army would get involved next, but they'd deal with that when it came.

Hopefully, by that time they wouldn't have to.

"Uncle Lev!"

He jerked his head up. "Olya?" he asked, tapping his com.

"Yes." Her voice sounded frightened, but under the fear there was a twinge of her usual self-assurance. "Mamochka asked me to watch her screen while she talked with Mama. And there are three people outside your window." She paused. "I think they're trying to kill you, Uncle."

Lev glanced around frantically. "Olya. Is your mamochka—"

"They're government people, Mamochka told me how to tell," she whispered. "You have to trick them. You have to do something."

"I—"

"Kiss Aunty," she said firmly. "Mama said that worked last time."

Damn, damn, damn.

He took a deep breath and turned to Jez.

She gave him a quick nod, her face bloodless. "Hurry it up, genius. Because I'm not damn well watching anyone try to kill you again."

He leaned forward, brushing a hand lightly across her cheek. "If it makes you feel any better, I'm pretty sure I won't be the one they're trying to kill this time," he murmured. "Although I'll be honest, it doesn't make me feel any better."

If he was being honest, this was the closest he'd come to panic since he'd seen Jez sway on her feet after the knife had hit her.

At least they weren't likely to get carried away again, under the circumstances.

He let his lips brushed hers, gently.

And even though he'd been prepared for it, there was something about the touch of her lips on his that hit him like a damn mallet upside the head, and his breathing had gone unsteady by the time he drew back.

Jez leaned towards him, eyes closed, chin still tilted up, and without really thinking about it, he leaned in again.

Her lips were chapped from the cold, and they were still, somehow, impossibly warm, and the kiss impossibly soft. His hand trailed up the line of her jaw, cupping the back of her head, and she melted into the kiss, and he tried to ignore the way his lips tingled, the way his muscles had gone shaky and his stomach tied itself in knots.

When he finally pulled back, he realized he'd been kissing her for a lot longer than he'd actually meant to. His mind wasn't quite as clear as it had been a few minutes before, but—but that was alright, he'd been expecting that, and he was still able to think about things logically. He was pretty sure. At least, he was still able to remember why they were here, and why they were doing this, and —

And when he glanced down at her, her eyes were still closed, and she had that dreamy smile on her face that he remembered so well from their first kiss on the *Ungovernable*, and then the many, many subsequent kisses in Prasvishoni, at the university, and somehow he leaned in again, and she leaned forward to meet him, and they were kissing without him ever having actually decided to do it.

Her mouth moved against his, slow and languid, her kiss unhurried, as if they had all the time in the system. He pulled her in, and her body softened under his fingers in that way he remembered so well. His lips parted as he deepened the kiss, and she leaned into it with a soft sigh. He seemed to remember, somewhere in the back of his brain, that he'd been intending to keep his wits about him this time, but that hardly seemed important at the moment. Even if he could spare the attention, which he couldn't. There was something about the languid, leisurely pressure of her lips on his, the way she was somehow all he could feel, or taste, or touch, that had taken over every part of his brain.

When he pulled back this time, she followed him, and they were kissing again, her body melting into his. She pushed him backwards, and he lay back on the couch, pulling her on top of him. His hands ran down her back, and he could feel the familiar sharp angles of her. He pulled her closer, lips moving from hers to trace along her jawline and catch at the corner of her jaw, and she gave a small, soft gasp of pleasure.

He knew perfectly well how and where to kiss her to make her gasp like that again, and it seemed a shame not to. Besides, their kisses were still slow and leisurely, and if his stomach had tightened pleasantly, that didn't mean anything at all. And with her on top of him, his hands could run down her back, graze her hips, catch that small hollow between her shoulder blades as his lips brushed along the line of her throat.

She moaned softly, her eyes closed, and her hands slid up his neck, tightening in his hair. He tugged at the laces on her tunic, since that was clearly the logical step to take at this point, and she seemed to agree, her hand coming up to fumble at the buttons of his shirt. And while his hand was occupied, he moved his lips back to hers, and now there was absolutely nothing at all in his brain except Jez, the feel of her and the taste of her and the warmth of her, and the desperate need for his fumbling fingers to finish with the laces on her damn tunic—

"Well. If that didn't convince them, I don't know what would," came Tanya's dryly amused voice through his earpiece. "But I'm not sure that any of us want to see any more of this. There's a bedroom in the apartment for a reason."

They broke apart, gasping, and stared at each other for a long moment.

Finally, Lev cleared his throat a couple times and managed to draw a shaky breath.

"I'm—sorry," he said at last, because he wasn't entirely sure what else to say.

Jez was still staring at him.

"Damn, genius," she said at last, her voice soft with a sort of wonder. "I always forget how good a kisser you are."

Awkwardly, he rolled out from under her and helped her to her feet.

"Thanks." She gave him a shaky smile, and something in her eyes made him look away quickly.

"Well," she said at last. "I—I guess I'll ..." She swayed, and grabbed for the back of the couch.

Lev jumped forward. "Jez, bed. Now," he said through his teeth, voice sharp from the sudden panic.

She closed her eyes for a moment, then managed another shaky smile. "Yeah. Guess you're right." She paused a moment. "You coming?"

Something tightened in the pit of Lev's stomach, and it took him a moment before he could speak.

"I'd—probably better stay out here for a while," he managed finally.

She gave him a skeptical look. "Be a shame to spend so much time convincing them that we are what we said we were, then screw it up."

She was right.

He sighed, and followed her into the bedroom. He turned his head away as she undressed, and when he was certain she was safely under the covers, he turned to look at her.

He could see the dark circles under her eyes, the exhaustion in her face, but she grinned up at him anyways.

Damn it to hell, every damn time he started to think that maybe, just maybe, he could forget why he loved her—how much he loved her ...

He swallowed down the choking ache in his throat.

"Sleep well, Jez." He had to fight back the sudden, ridiculous urge to brush her hair out of her face, lean down and kiss her forehead.

He held himself straight resolutely.

She was propped up on one elbow, studying him, and he wouldn't let himself meet her eyes, because he already knew where that would lead.

"You coming to bed?" she asked at last. "You have to sleep sometimes too, you know. I ..." She looked down. "I know you didn't do much of that when I was sick." Her voice was quiet.

She was right, honestly, but there was no way in hell he could lie down next to her right now, not with the shaky adrenalin-rush from their kiss still jangling through his body like lightning.

He tried to smile. "I ... need to finish up a few things. You sleep, I'll lie down in a few minutes."

"Promise?" she said at last.

"Promise," he said quietly.

She lay back, and there was something in the way she watched him, before her eyes drifted shut, that made him close his eyes and lean against the wall, hands clenched, biting down on the inside of his cheek until he tasted blood.

23

Ysbel, day 14

Ysbel looked up as Tanya slipped into the room, closing the door behind her. Her wife's face was pinched with worry, and there was a tension in her movements.

"Tanya? What's wrong?" she asked quietly.

Tanya sighed. "There are people watching Jez and Lev. They're not from the government, and I can't tell who sent them. I don't like it."

Ysbel lowered her voice. "And—I assume you've noticed whoever is watching us, yes?"

Tanya gave a short, tight nod. "Yes. I don't know who they are, either. And if Masha knows something, she won't say."

"Whatever Masha's planning, it's going to happen soon, I think. And I don't know if it's something that will kill us, or something that will save us," Ysbel said grimly.

Tanya gave a wry, humourless smile. "That's the problem. She's done both."

Ysbel sighed and looked around. The children were asleep, soundly enough that they didn't stir at her and Tanya's soft voices. She stood and moved to the window, pulling back the blinds just a crack.

The figure standing in the shadows thrown by the streetlamp wasn't doing much to conceal itself.

That, perhaps, was what frightened her the most.

Tanya came up beside her, and when Ysbel turned, she saw the worry on her wife's face. She let the curtain fall, and they turned back to look at the two children, sleeping in their one cramped bed.

Neither of them had to speak their unease.

"How long do we need to keep this up?" asked Tanya softly. "Because I'm starting to wonder how much longer we can."

For a few moments, they were quiet. At last, Tanya gave a small smile. "Well, as far as I know, the crew is still alive. We should count our blessings."

Ysbel returned the smile reluctantly. "Because who knows how long we'll have any to count," she added, finishing the proverb.

Next morning, as they worked through the day's messages, Ysbel said quietly to Masha, "The watchers outside aren't even trying to hide anymore. Someone's found us, and they don't care that we know."

Masha looked at her for a long time, and give a short, sharp nod. "Yes, Ysbel," she said quietly. "I—have noticed that."

"My children are in this house, Masha," said Ysbel. "If things start to go sideways—"

Masha smiled grimly. "I understand, Ysbel. My hope is that Jez and Lev and Tae will succeed quickly, and our part in this will be over."

But Ysbel didn't fail to notice that she had not made any promises.

It was late that evening, and the children were long since sleeping, when Tanya finally returned from watching Lev and Jez's apartment.

She came over and kissed Ysbel lightly on the cheek. "Well, our scholar and our crazy pilot are still alive, for the evening at least. How are you coming along?"

Ysbel gave her a reluctant smile. "I've made enough explosives to take out the entire city. But it won't do us any good if we don't know who to use them on."

"Where's Masha?" asked Tanya, glancing around.

Ysbel frowned. "She's not in the kitchen? She was there a minute ago."

Tanya stepped quietly to the window. She pulled back the curtains a crack, then gestured to Ysbel.

Below them, a dark shape slipped into an alley.

And the way the figure moved, the quiet certainty of their steps, was unmistakable.

Ysbel and Tanya exchange glances.

"Stay here, Ysi," Tanya whispered. "I'll follow her."

Ysbel gave a tight nod and kissed her wife on the forehead. Tanya slipped out, closing the door behind her, and a moment later, through the small window, she saw a silent shadow disappearing down the alley after Masha.

Masha didn't return until very late. Ysbel heard her come in, and the door to the other bedroom open and close, but it wasn't until almost half a standard hour later that Tanya reappeared in the doorway, shaking snow from her hair.

She gave Ysbel a wry smile. "Masha is not an easy one to trace."

"What was she doing?" Ysbel asked quietly.

Tanya shrugged, but there was unease in her face. "It looked like a dead drop. She was over by the government buildings, and the streets there are dead this late at night. She stopped over by one of the buildings, but I didn't see what she dropped. I waited there after she'd left, though. Someone came by about fifteen standard minutes later, and stopped in the same place she did, but again, I didn't see them drop anything, or pick anything up."

Ysbel frowned. "Could it have been a coincidence?"

Tanya shook her head. "There was no one else on the street this time of night. And in this weather? Where they stopped wasn't under shelter. And besides—" she paused a moment. "I'm not a hundred percent certain. But I think I recognized the person who came after Masha did."

"Who was it?"

"Zhenya," said Tanya quietly.

The next morning, Masha didn't say anything about what had happened the night before. Knowing Tanya, she hadn't heard her follow. But she looked tenser than usual as they went about their morning duties, cooking breakfast for the children, checking for messages for Olyessa or Grigory, crafting out their replies.

There was no point in confronting her. She wouldn't tell them anything, and it would only make her more cautious in the future. But Ysbel assumed Masha could feel the tension from them much as they could from her.

When Lev called that afternoon, Masha's usually calm voice, when she answered the com, was sharp.

"Lev," she snapped. "I know you believe what you're doing, redirecting the weapons, is the right thing to do. But you're only giving Tae more reasons to throw in his lot with the students. And it's likely to kill him. Please focus on your own work."

"As I told you before," said Lev, his voice level, "Jez and I believe we can do both things. And both yesterday and today I had to walk with her to the government buildings so she wouldn't bloody pass out on the way over, so before you suggest—"

"Lev," said Masha, cutting him off. "I'm not suggesting anything adverse against either of you. I know Jez is working as hard as she can. But she needs to focus on the government, and Tae needs to leave the protests alone. I don't know how long we can keep this charade up."

"You know damn well Tae isn't going to leave this, and I don't know how long he'll stay alive if we don't help." Lev was speaking through clenched teeth. "I'm not sure when you stopped being worried about that."

He tapped his com off, and there was a moment of silence.

Masha swore under her breath.

"I have the same question," said Ysbel quietly.

Masha looked up at her, and Ysbel was shocked at the weariness in her expression. "Ysbel. I promise you, I am as concerned about Tae's well-being as you are. However, I'm also concerned about the fact that this whole damn system is liable to implode."

"And so you'll sacrifice Tae if he disagrees with you how to fix that? And those children I taught at university?"

Masha gave a short shake of her head. "If Jez and Lev had not agreed to help him, it's unlikely Tae would have declared war on the entire damn system," she said, her voice tight. "If he'd actually done what I asked him to do, and only that—"

"Perhaps you don't know our tech-head like I thought you did, then," said Ysbel. "Do you really see him leaving his friends to get hurt? He didn't start this battle, Masha."

Masha looked up at her, and the sudden wry amusement in her expression startled Ysbel. "Perhaps it's you who doesn't understand our tech-head. If you recall, when we were at the university, he managed to radicalize the entire student body."

"I—think that was on accident," said Tanya, but there was a hint of amusement in her voice as well.

Masha sighed heavily and straightened. "At any rate, we have things to do, and we'd best get them done."

Ysbel nodded, sighing, then glanced up to where she could see out the window.

Something chilled in her stomach.

It was broad daylight. But their watcher was still there, standing under the streetlamp, just as they'd been last night, scarf pulled low over their face and coat pulled tight around their shoulders.

24

Lev, day 17

It had been three days since Jez had insisted on going back into work, but Lev walked with her to the government buildings, like he did every morning now. His arm stayed around her waist, and he looked, he hoped, like simply an over-attentive lover. Only he and Jez knew how much of her weight he was supporting, and how often she stumbled on the icy streets.

Still, even that wasn't the thing that worried him the most.

What worried him the most was the tenor of the comments he'd heard over her com at the last meeting. It had been nothing he could pin down, just something about the way the small cabal of officers who opposed Jez spoke, the comments they pointed in her direction. It had unsettled him more than he liked to admit.

Jez was worried too, although she hadn't said anything. He could see it in her posture, the tension in her body as she walked.

She knew as well as he did how quickly things could go wrong.

They only had to hold things together for a few more days. But there would come a moment where everything would go to pieces, and when it happened, he wasn't sure they'd get any warning at all.

They reached Jez's office building, and Lev paused at the door, taking his arm from around her waist. "I'll see you tonight then, Layla," he said, trying to keep his tone light.

She leaned in and kissed him on the cheek, for the benefit of any unseen observers. "I'll bring dinner." She gave him a cheery grin, but he could still see the tension in her posture.

He waited until she'd opened the door, then turned, but a voice stopped him.

"Ruslan."

He paused and turned back.

Branka stood in the doorway, a smile on her face he couldn't read.

He pasted a pleasant expression on his own face. "Yes?"

"Since you've been so kind as to bring Layla the last few days, why don't you come up? I know you've been going through the information with her at home, and perhaps you'll have some insights. Lady knows we could use another mind working on the problem."

Lev frowned slightly. "I—doubt I'd be much help. That's Layla's expertise."

Branka's eyes were sharp. "Nevertheless," she said quietly. "I would appreciate your presence."

Lev shot a glance at Jez.

It was clear she didn't like this anymore than he did. But it was also clear they didn't have much choice.

He hesitated a long moment. Then, at last, he stepped into the building, unease buzzing in the back of his brain.

The doors swung shut, lock clicking behind them.

Branka didn't lead them up to the conference room. Instead, they walked down a long, narrow corridor. Lev lagged slightly behind, tapping out a quick message to Ysbel and Tanya.

If things had gone sideways, as he increasingly suspected they had, at least he could give the others warning.

Branka paused in front of a door. The lock clicked, and she opened it, gesturing Jez and Lev in front of her.

Warily, they stepped inside.

The room was small and unadorned, the only furnishings a long table and some hard chairs. Three government officials sat behind the table, and a handful of guards stood around the corners of the room, weapons held ready. Lev could tell from the way the officials carried themselves that they were high ranking, but they wore generic officers' jackets that told him nothing else.

"Hey, Jaromil," said Jez cheerily, grinning at the man in the centre. "Thought a change of uniform would make you a little less ugly? Because it sure as hell isn't working."

The man smiled gently. "Hello… Layla."

It wasn't a long hesitation. But it was enough to send something icy spiking through Lev's stomach.

"Why don't you and Ruslan take a seat?" He gestured to two empty seats across the table from him, and reluctantly, they sat.

Jaromil leaned forward, forearms resting on the table, posture relaxed. "Layla. You've been—very efficient during your time here."

Jez raised an eyebrow. "Not sure if Branka agrees with you. Considering she spends the first twenty minutes of every damn meeting telling me exactly how late I was." Her tone was jaunty, but Lev could hear the strain under it.

"Be that as it may," the man continued, unperturbed, "you've accomplished a significant amount in a very short time. It was exactly what we asked you to do, of course, once it appeared Grigory had declared war on us. It was you who suggested that we should keep our distance from Olyessa as well—and I won't say it was a bad idea. In fact, every point you made was intelligent and well-argued, and despite my own personal interests to the contrary, they were difficult to disagree with." His smile widened, something sharp and satisfied behind it. "But very recently, we discovered something rather surprising."

He paused a moment.

Lev managed to keep his face impassive, although his heart was pounding sickeningly.

He knew exactly what was coming next.

"Grigory is dead. He was murdered yesterday, by one of his bodyguards. It seems the day before you arrived here, something happened to Grigory's funds. He lost everything, including control of his mafia. The entire time you've been in the city, Layla, Grigory has been a man marked for death." He leaned forward. "Normally, news like this would have been catastrophic. The ministries would have devolved into infighting as ministers struggled for power, and the government would have collapsed into civil war. And yet, the news came out, and here we still stand. I'm not saying people aren't angry. Since the news broke, there have already been assassinations, infighting, chaos. But the government is still functioning." He smiled. "And Olyessa. She's not dead yet, but I suspect that will be coming shortly. Because just like Grigory, she lost everything, the day before you arrived on-planet. Odd, really. But I suspect you already knew that."

Lev had to fight to keep his deadpan expression.

Jez leaned back easily in her seat, her hands behind her head, grinning. "Well," she drawled, "guess I'm even smarter than I figured."

"Perhaps," Jaromil murmured. "Perhaps you are much, much smarter than any of us realized." He paused a moment, still wearing that small smile. "Would you like to know what else we learned, Layla?"

"Figure you'll tell me whether I want to or not. Always did like the sound of your own damn voice."

The man pulled up the holoscreen on his com, and turned the screen around to face them.

On the screen was the face of a young woman, around Jez's age, with intelligent grey eyes and light brown hair.

Lev wasn't certain if the sudden twist in his stomach was because he knew what was going to come next, or because for the first time he was seeing the face of one of the people he'd killed, under Masha's direction.

"This is Layla," said the man pleasantly. "She didn't come directly to Prasvishoni, as we'd been informed. Instead, she stopped by to visit someone who was apparently an old friend of hers. Grigory Korzhakov." He tapped the holoscreen off. "She was killed. Blown to pieces on Grigory's ship."

The room was completely silent.

"So," said Jaromil at last, turning to Jez. "Shall we start from the beginning … Layla? Or, should I say, Jez Solokov?"

Jez raised an eyebrow. "Pretty damn sure I showed you my credentials when I got in here. Don't know who the hell that was on the holoscreen, but—"

"Don't bother, Jez," Branka said grimly. "We know exactly who you are. Your documents were impressive works of forgery, but once we knew Layla was dead, it wasn't too difficult to figure out who we'd been sitting in meetings with for the last few weeks."

"Well, never figured someone would be stupid enough to sit across from a damn smuggler pilot for weeks and think she was a government minister," said Jez, still grinning. "But hell, I've met you bastards now, so doesn't actually surprise me at all anymore. Don't know how people as plaguing stupid as you got your positions, but

—"

Jaromil half-stood, considering her for a moment. Then he leaned across the table and slapped her, hard, across the face. The sound was sharp in the silence, and Lev sucked in a quick breath.

He closed his eyes and forced his hands to unclench.

He'd only make it worse. She'd damn well almost died less than a week ago, and he couldn't afford to make it worse.

He glanced over at her quickly. An angry welt rose across her face where Jaromil had hit her, and a trickle of blood welled from her split lip, but she was still grinning.

She looked dangerous. She looked like someone that Lev wouldn't want to cross, even if he didn't know her as well as he did.

She also looked like someone about to get the actual hell beat out of her.

He felt sick to his stomach.

"Well," she drawled, "figure if—"

Without thinking, he put a hand on her arm. She glanced over at him, and, to his absolute shock, subsided.

Branka turned her considering gaze on Lev. "Once we knew who Jez was, it wasn't difficult to find the identity of her supposed lover." She paused a moment, and gave them a small smirk. "I must say, you two put on a very convincing show. But, as I said, once we figured out who Jez was, there was more than enough information to identify you, Lev. And I suddenly realized where all of those very intelligent ideas had come from." She gave a small smile. "It beggared belief, frankly, to imagine someone like Jez had come up with them. Although the way you had her play being poisoned for a couple days was quite clever."

He had to bite back the urge to say something very rude. But it must have shown on his face, because Branka laughed.

"You find it insulting that I know she's so obviously not your intellectual equal? If it makes you feel better, I doubt there are many people who are."

"Well," said Jez, her voice still dangerously cheerful. "After sitting through a bunch of meetings with you plaguers, I could come up with a whole damn list of people who aren't his intellectual—"

The sound of Jaromil's slap rang through the room, and Lev bit his lip so hard he tasted blood.

Branka didn't even turn. "You weren't working alone," she said. "We found the people who were sending messages in Grigory's and Olyessa's names. We'll have them shortly, if we haven't taken them already. And as an added bonus, now that we know who you are, Jez," she said, turning slightly, "we'll be able to release the weapons the police were so loath to have reassigned. I have been informed, by … certain parties, of the advantage of dealing with the protests quickly and efficiently. With the full complement of police, and the weapons they've been issued, I can't imagine it will take past midday today."

Lev heard the words, but he was too numb to react. Jez's face had gone bloodless, her expression stricken.

Branka turned back to Lev. "In case you thought that perhaps you could get a warning to your friends—don't bother. I had a blocker placed around the entire building. No communication can go in or out without my code."

She gestured to the guards at the edges of the room, and they stepped forward quickly. Jez's posture tensed, as if she was going to try to fight her way out anyways, but she glanced at Lev, and he saw her force herself still.

She didn't want him to be killed too. That was the only damn thing stopping her, and he couldn't tell if the thought made him feel relieved or nauseous.

The guards cuffed them quickly.

"Well," Jez drawled, voice still lazy and dangerous. "Guess I can understand you wanting to keep us here. I mean, I am pretty hot and all—"

"Believe me, Jez," Branka said gently. "Once my people are done with you, no one will find you attractive. Lev either. They have a great deal of experience. You'll tell them everything you know. You'll tell them everything you can tell them, just on the off chance they'll stop what they're doing. But they won't stop. Not for a very long time. And when they finally do—" She shrugged. "Some people survive that long. From what I've seen of you these past weeks, I suspect you'll be one of them. You may even live for a while afterwards—hours, days. I've seen people last as long as weeks. It's—generally not pleasant."

"Well, looking at your damn face sure isn't pleasant, so—"

There was another slap.

Lev's hands were clenched so tight that he thought his fingernails might break the skin of his palms.

Branka stepped back and made a small gesture. Two guards stepped forward, grabbing Lev and Jez roughly and hauling them to their feet. Jez swore fluently and at length, but they didn't even deign to notice.

"Take them downstairs," said Branka pleasantly. "Jaromil will join you shortly to observe. I would, with pleasure, but I need to shut down a street rebellion before it becomes a problem."

And then Jez and Lev were dragged out into the narrow corridor, and the door slammed shut behind them.

25

Tae, day 17

Tae looked out over the ragged line of students and street kids, gathered behind their makeshift barricades. In the dim light of predawn, they looked grim and exhausted, and much, much too young to be taking on the damn Svodrani System government.

But then again—the street kids were young, too. And they'd never been given a damn choice.

There were footsteps behind him, and he spun on instinct. Ivan stood there, a small smile on his face, even through the lines of strain and worry.

"You got through to Lev?" he asked.

Tae give a short nod. "Jez is going to make sure the heavy-duty weapons are reassigned. I think that's our best chance, at this point."

Ivan nodded grimly, looking out at the barricades. "Hopefully, that will be enough." He paused a moment. "I honestly didn't think the police would go this far. What they're planning isn't arrest. It's a death sentence."

Tae looked out over the dark of the city streets, the flickering streetlamps slowly sputtering into darkness as the day's grey light crept through cold streets. "I don't know what's happened," he said quietly. "But whatever it is—"

"Whatever it is, I don't know if the system will survive it," Ivan finished quietly.

It was only a few standard minutes later that the whine of skybikes began to filter through the frosty air.

Vera climbed up beside them, putting a hand on Tae's shoulder. "Come on. The police probably recognize you by now. You too, Ivan. If they see either of you up here, they'll shoot to kill." She gave a weary grin. "I don't think you're favourites down at the police station."

They jumped down from the top of the barricade and followed Vera over to the makeshift shelter where Dmitri and a few others were gathered around a map of Prasvishoni pulled up on Dmitri's holoscreen. Dmitri looked up and smiled when he saw Tae. Tae smiled back, even though there was still that twisting ache in his chest whenever he saw him.

"I think we're in a good position to hold out, at least for the day," Dmitri said. "As long as your friends can keep the weapons away."

Tae shook his head. "If they don't," he said quietly, "it will be because they're dead."

Dmitri gave a small, wry smile. "There was a time in my life that I would've heard that and thought you were being facetious."

Tae tried to make his voice light. "Maybe one day our lives will be boring enough that it will be facetious."

Dmitri gave a strained chuckle. "Assuming they're still alive, then, and assuming we won't see the big guns here at the barricades, this is the plan."

Tae, Ivan, and Vera crouched beside him as, from outside, the amplified voices of police officers began to sound in the streets, calling for them to disperse.

Vera shook her head in irritation. "You think they'd eventually realize that isn't working. Or at least, start to lose their voices. Lady knows I'm losing mine." Her words were wry, but she was right—she spoke with the hoarse rasp of someone with a bad cold.

"I can do the shouting today," said Ivan, with faint humour.

Vera raised an eyebrow at him. "Not to be insulting, but you're really not the shouting type."

Tae chuckled despite himself, and Ivan smiled. "I suppose you're right, at that," he conceded.

Dmitri shut down the holoscreens and stood, stretching. "We'd better get out there. The others are going to start wondering what happened to us."

They stepped outside. The sun had emerged above the horizon by now, and Tae squinted against the glare. The police were shouting, throwing flash-bangs and percussives over the walls of the barricade, but by now the students were well trained, and brigades of them stood ready to extinguish the smoke bombs, or push other students out of the way of the percussives or the flash-bangs. The air was laced with the sharp sting of gas from the bombs, but so far it was barely strong enough to make Tae's eyes water. He shivered in the bitter morning air. Ivan glanced at him, but he scowled back.

"You're not going to give me your damn coat again, Ivan," he muttered. "I'd actually like you to stay alive too."

Ivan chuckled, but refrained from taking off his coat.

They walked around the edges of the barricades, checking that everything was in position. Dmitri was right—they actually had a decent chance of lasting the day. After that, who knew, but at this point Tae had stopped trying to think farther ahead than twenty-four standard hours.

They'd almost made a complete circuit of the barricades, and the sun was halfway up the sky, when Tae heard an unfamiliar thin, high, mechanical whine.

He frowned at Dmitri and Vera, but their expressions were just as puzzled as he knew his must be.

And then Ivan gave a soft, choked curse, and Tae realized, with a sick jolt, what it was, a fraction of a second before an explosion turned his entire world into hot, white noise.

When the sound had cleared, Tae lay on the concrete, a few metres back from where he'd been standing. He scrambled to his feet, looking frantically around, barely taking note of the sharp stab of pain in his hip at the movement.

Ivan was alive, thank the Lady, and Vera, and Dmitri, and he barely had time for a quick breath of relief before Ivan had jumped to his feet as well. He and Tae exchanged glances, and then they were both running back towards the source of the blast, where stunned students were still clustered, faces blank with shock.

"Back! Get back now!" Ivan shouted at the top of his voice, and then the rest of them were shouting too, Dmitri and Vera pounding up behind them.

"Back, all of you!" Tae yelled, voice rasping. "They're going to—"

There was another explosion. Ivan shoved Tae down against the concrete, his body sheltering Tae as the barricade in front of them exploded.

Tae realized, with a sort of dim, detached curiosity, that the solid blast of sound wasn't coming from the gun. It was the sound of tonnes of material combusting, instantly, into white-hot ash.

When the noise cleared once again, and Ivan had rolled off of him and staggered to his feet, Tae got his first glimpse of the damage.

An entire section of the barricade was gone. Floating ash mingled with the lightly falling snow, all that was left of the piled beds and desks and chairs the students had dragged from university dorms.

But that wasn't the sight that caught his gaze and held it.

Bodies lay in grotesque positions around the blackened hole where the barricade had been.

The odd angles of their necks and limbs, their scorched clothing, the blood smeared on the concrete around their still forms, told him everything he needed to know.

For half a second, he thought he might throw up.

But there was no damn time for that, there was no damn time to be sick. He scrambled to his feet, and the moment he could pull in a gasp of the ash-choked air, he rasped, "Back! Get back, now! They're going to shoot again!" He grabbed a couple of the stunned students by the arm, shoving them towards the alleys. "Go!" He could hardly hear his own voice over the ringing in his ears.

There were still students standing in shocked clusters near the gaping hole. They wouldn't be able to hear him shout, not after that.

There was that thin, piercing whine again. He looked around frantically. If he was fast enough, maybe he could get some of them clear—

He turned, but Ivan grabbed his arm.

"There's no time," he said through his teeth. "You'll get blown into pieces."

"I don't care," Tae choked, fighting against Ivan's grasp. "I don't —"

Another explosion, and again they were hurled backwards.

A new gaping hole appeared in the barricades, and now more bodies lay strewn across the icy ground, brilliant red stains spreading across what dirty snow hadn't melted in the searing heat of the blast.

Silently, Ivan let go of Tae's arm, and Tae jerked away, running towards barricades.

By now, most of the students and street kids—at least, the ones who'd survived—were running or staggering for the shelter of the alleys.

In front of him, on the ground, he recognized the form of Vanya, the girl who'd led one of the street kid gangs.

He choked back a sob, and then Ivan was beside him, taking him gently by the elbow.

"We have to get back," he said. "They're going to send the riot troops through in a moment. The entrance is big enough now. I'm— I'm sorry." He sounded sick.

Tae nodded, his vision blurred with tears, and let Ivan pull him into the alley.

Dmitri and Vera were huddled against one wall, faces grim. Ivan crouched next to them, and Tae followed suit, too numb to care what he was doing.

Dmitri tried to smile. "I guess you'll have to have a word with your friends when you see them."

Somehow, Tae doubted there would be any friends to have a word with. He hadn't been joking when he'd said Jez and Lev would die before they let him down.

Ivan's expression said he'd come to the same conclusion.

From outside the shattered barricades came an artificially amplified officer's voice.

"Give yourselves up! Your barricades are finished, and you won't survive a shot from this. I repeat, give yourselves up."

Around them, the students were muttering in low voices, terror and shock clear on their faces. Dmitri looked over at him. "Tae," he said quietly, and Tae could see the fear in his face. "What should we do?"

Vera was looking at him too, and so was Ivan.

He looked around again, the scattering of street kids and students, nausea churning in his stomach.

If the police came, they'd slaughter the remaining street kids sooner or later, with as little remorse as if they'd been killing a nest of swamp rats. The kids had trusted him. They'd come out of the relative safety, if that's what it was, of their streets, to join Tae and the students behind the barricades.

If they surrendered, the street kids would almost certainly die.

But—

He glanced over involuntarily at the bodies strewn around the barricades.

But if they didn't, they'd all die—street kids, students, all of them.

Dmitri was still watching him, and Vera, and Ivan.

"This is your last chance. Stand down. Otherwise, we keep shooting until there's no one left alive."

Something sick caught in Tae's throat, and guilt clenched at his chest.

"Tell them to stand down," he said quietly.

He thought the words might actually kill him.

Dmitri looked at him for a moment. Then he gave a short nod and stepped wearily forward.

He hit his com, activating the voice amp. "We surrender," he shouted. His voice was clear and loud, but Tae could hear the tears choking under it.

And then there was another explosion, and Tae was hurled backwards. His head slammed into the wall of the alley, and everything went dark.

26

Ysbel, day 17

"Lev. Lev, can you hear me?"

Tanya was bent over her com, face tight with the same worry Ysbel felt.

"Have you tried Jez?" Masha asked quietly. There was tension in every line of her body.

Tanya gave a short nod. "Yes. I tried five minutes ago. She didn't answer."

"Perhaps they're somewhere they can't talk," Ysbel murmured, although she didn't believe it.

"I've been trying the last thirty standard minutes," said Tanya quietly. "They would have at least tapped something in pilot's code."

At last, Masha raised her head, her expression drawn and tired. "We'll have to assume the worst. If they have Jez and Lev, it won't take them long to find the rest of us. No matter how brave they are, everyone talks at some point. And the government is very good at finding that point." She gave a short, quick sigh. "I suppose the only thing left is to get the children somewhere safe."

Ysbel and Tanya exchanged glances.

Masha was right, though. There was no way they could get to Lev and Jez. All they could do was get out, and hope against hope that Tae and Ivan were alright.

Ysbel's com clicked. She tapped it on, and they all could hear Ivan's choked voice.

"Ysbel. Something happened to Jez and Lev. They didn't get the guns reassigned. We're in trouble. And … when the gun went off, Tae—he's—" His words choked off.

There was shouting through the com, and then someone swore, and the line abruptly went dead.

Ysbel was already on her feet, Tanya beside her, and, to her credit, Masha had jumped up as well, face tight with worry.

"I'll take the children back to the *Ungovernable*. They'll be safe there," Tanya said brusquely. "Ysbel, can you—"

But Ysbel was watching Masha.

Masha had crossed over to the window, and there was something about the slight slump of her posture, the tension in her shoulders.

Ysbel moved to stand beside her, and Tanya joined them a moment later.

The street around their apartment was no longer empty.

The grim-faced people lining the street were holding weapons, drawn and ready, gas masks across their faces, and Ysbel knew the colours on their jackets—Grigory's boyeviki.

Tanya crossed quickly to the window on the other side of the apartment, and when she looked out, her posture told Ysbel what she already knew. They were completely surrounded.

She glanced over at Masha. The woman had leaned her head against the wall, eyes closed, face lined with a sick worry.

"I have explosives," said Ysbel quietly. "But nothing that would kill them without also taking down the building."

The panic in Ivan's voice, the sentence that had been cut off. "Tae

—he's—"

Jez and Lev, who hadn't answered their coms, and likely wouldn't, ever again.

At last, Masha opened her eyes. There was a small smile on her face, but her expression was haunted. "I—don't think any of us will be going anywhere," she said quietly.

27

Jez, day 17

Jez's face throbbed where the bastard had slapped her, and her split lip ached, but she didn't really have the attention to worry about it.

She and Lev were alone in the dimly lit basement room. The guards had bound them and left, but somehow that didn't make her feel any better.

She'd seen the look on Branka's face.

Whatever was coming next was going to be worse than anything she could imagine. She'd heard stories. And damn it to hell, she'd try not to talk, but—but the stories she'd heard said everyone talked, eventually.

And hell, by that time it might not even matter. She'd told Tae she'd get the weapons reassigned. He and Ivan and all those students and street kids would assume she had.

And they'd be wrong.

A makeshift barricade wouldn't stand up to weapons like that. And she knew damn well what would happen to the people behind the barricade after the guns had taken it down.

She swallowed hard against the choking sob trying to rise in her throat.

"Jez," said Lev quietly.

She glanced over at him, cuffed and bound to the chair beside hers, and tried to smile. She didn't trust herself to actually speak at this point.

That was the worst of it. Maybe she could have handled this, somehow, if you could handle a thing like torture, if she knew he was safe.

But he wasn't. He was here, with her.

He gave her a small smile. "They could still be alright. Tae's smart. And Ivan isn't going to give him up without a fight."

Jez managed a choked laugh at that, even though it was so close to a sob that it could've been either.

Lev's expression was tight with sympathy as he watched her.

He was probably as scared as she was. Hell, he'd always hated getting hit and shot at. But here he was, still trying to make her feel better.

They were quiet for a few moments. Jez's bruises ached, but honestly, it was a welcome distraction.

It was possible Masha and Ysbel and Tanya had got the kids away. But it wasn't likely. And despite Lev's words, she was pretty damn sure that Tae and Ivan weren't going to survive those weapons.

But there was nothing she could do about it anymore, and there was a sort of calm that came with that. Kind of like when you were getting the hell beat out of you, that sort of faint relief that came right before you passed out. When you'd done everything you could, and it hadn't been enough, and the fight was over whether you wanted it or not.

She glanced at Lev again. His face was slightly pale, and he was staring straight ahead, and she knew him well enough to guess that he was calculating exactly what the government bastards would do to them. Hell, he probably already knew. Probably had read all the damn records on it when he was working here. And for some reason, even through the cold fear, looking at him sent a fond ache through her chest.

There was something about this ridiculous soft-boy scholar. Something about the ridiculous, analytical way he viewed things, the gentleness in his voice, that soft smile that he didn't seem to give to anyone except her. There was something about him, and she didn't know what it was, except—except it was something she'd been looking for her whole damn life. She hadn't found it in her damn family, and she hadn't found it with Lena, and she hadn't even found it when she was flying solo runs, much as she told herself that was everything she needed.

Because it hadn't been. What she'd always needed was sitting in the chair across from her, looking ahead, making some stupid calculation. Probably, honestly, trying to think of a way to make this hurt less for her. Even though that was impossible, and even though he probably knew it, she was still pretty sure that was what he was thinking.

He looked up, meeting her eyes. "Jez," he said quietly. "Since they know who we are, I may be able to—"

She shook her head. "Genius. It doesn't matter what you do, or what I do. They're going to hurt us until they get bored of it, and I'm pretty damn sure they won't get bored of it quickly." She tried to grin. "Anyways, you know me. I'm damn good at getting the hell beat out of me. Lots of practice."

He didn't say anything, but there was a sort of sadness in his eyes at her words, and it made something in her chest twist.

"Um," she said finally, her voice even softer than it had been. "I—

I guess—well, this is probably the last time we'll be able to talk. So."

He was just watching her, patiently, like always. Like he actually gave a damn about what she had to say, even though they were going to be tortured to death in just a few minutes.

"I—you remember what I told you, back on Grigory's ship?"

It was a stupid question. She'd probably told him a hell of a lot of things while they were on Grigory's ship. But somehow, she knew he'd understand.

"Yes, Jez," he said quietly. "I remember. And—it's alright. You don't have to—"

She gave a quick shake of her head. "That wasn't what I was going to say. I—" she took a deep breath. "I said I loved you. And I did. Do. Guess I have for a long time now."

He was staring at her, and she hadn't thought his face could go more bloodless, but it had.

She swallowed hard. "Because—because damn it, Lev, you're a good damn person, and I don't meet people like that very often. And anyway, not that it makes a difference, since we're both going to die pretty quick here—" she paused, and shuddered. "Well, start dying, anyways. Point is, if—if things had worked out differently … I mean, hell, I know I said I didn't do relationships, and I know I said I was crap at them, and honestly, I am. But—" She swallowed again, and found she was swallowing back tears. "But you know that, because you know me better than probably anyone in the system. And—I mean, after all that, if you'd still wanted to, I would have—I mean I would've wanted to—" she trailed off, not entirely sure how to finish the sentence she'd started.

Lev was still staring at her, and his face was still very, very pale under his olive skin. And then he gave her a small, choked smile, and there were tears shining in his eyes.

"Jez," he said at last, quietly. "You said it doesn't make a difference, since we're both about to die. But—I don't think you realize—" he broke off, his words choking. He was looking at her with those dark, thoughtful, intense eyes that always made something twist and tighten in her stomach, and something else relax, deep inside of her.

"I—never actually thought I could love anyone, honestly," he said, clearing his throat. "I'm much too analytical, and much too self-absorbed, and much too bloody self-centred. But—I love you, Jez. I love you more than I thought was possible."

His voice choked again, and she found her own throat was tightening too. "I—I wish I could tell you all the reasons I love you, but we probably have hours left at this point, and that's not nearly enough time. So I suppose I have to leave it at this: I love you, Jez. And even if I'd lived to be an old man, which was honestly never all that likely, considering the company I keep—I would still have loved you until I died, and I still wouldn't have felt like I'd had nearly enough time."

Jez drew in a long, shuddering breath, and tried to blink back the tears that were already dripping down her face. Damn it to hell, she should've thought this through better, seeing as her hands were tied behind her back and she had no way to wipe away the tears and snot. She sniffed loudly, and Lev gave a slight smile, and somehow, that made her cry even harder, which was actually stupid. If she was going to be crying, she might as well save it for when someone was pulling her damn fingernails out by the roots.

The door clicked, and the cold fear that she'd momentarily forgotten rushed back in full force.

Jaromil stepped through the door first. He had a small, satisfied smile on his face, but there was something faintly sick behind his expression. As if even he wasn't sure he could stomach what was coming next.

The person who stepped through the door after him was not particularly large. But there was something in the way he walked, a smooth confidence, that sent a sick, sharp jolt of panic through Jez's whole damn body.

"Jez," Lev whispered to her. "Tell him what he asks. Whatever it is he asks. He'll get it, eventually, so there's no point giving him an excuse to hurt you more."

She managed a small grin in his direction. "Sounds like a smart plan, genius," she said. "But you're not going to do it, are you? Because you've been sitting there thinking about how many minutes you could give Tanya and Ysbel and Masha and the kids."

"There—was a time in my life that I was practical," he said, with a small, rueful smile. "I suppose you've rubbed off on me. And I suppose it was absurd of me to expect you to do what I told you in the first place."

"Hell, genius, I do what you say all the damn time. Just not when you're being stupid."

Honestly, she was mostly just talking to distract herself from the sick, paralyzing terror creeping through her body.

Jaromil took a seat, facing Jez and Lev, and the torturer leaned over a small table beside him and placed a long, padded case on top of it. He opened it, sorting through the tools inside, and laid them out, one by one, on the tabletop.

Jez couldn't make herself look away.

There was tech there that she'd never seen before, and honestly, she wished she still hadn't. There was other tech, too, familiar, common tech, that she somehow knew would be used in a way that she'd never even imagined, even though her damn brain was doing its best to think of every painful, excruciating possibility. And she knew that far too soon she'd be sobbing with pain, begging and screaming for mercy, but right now the waiting seem to be its own excruciating, exquisite form of torture.

"Jez." Lev's soft voice steadied her, somehow, even though he'd be screaming too, in just a few moments.

The door clicked again, and Jaromil looked up in impatient expectation.

The young man who stepped in was slightly familiar, although Jez couldn't place him. He gave Jaromil an obsequious nod and came up behind him. At the torturer's table, he paused, and pulled a small, sharp gutting knife out of the holster on his belt. He leaned forward, as if to lay it on the table.

And then, in a quick motion, he raised it over his shoulder. Jaromil half turned, frowning.

The young man brought his arm down in a quick, violent motion. He lifted it again, the knife now red and dripping, and brought it down a second time. Jez blinked, and Jaromil was choking out a sort of wet, bloody cough, and beside him, the hilt of the knife protruded from the torturer's back.

For a moment, everything seemed completely frozen. The only movement was the bright stain of red spreading slowly outward from the protruding knife, the red forming on the corners of Jaromil's mouth.

The torturer's body swayed and fell gently forward, landing with a soft *thud* against the table, and there was a clatter and tinkle as the instruments he'd laid out clattered to the floor. Jaromil gave a choked gasp. The young man stepped in front of him, bending down so he was at the dying man's eye level.

"You deserved this, Jaromil," he said, his voice rough with a mixture of fear and hate. "You tried to gut my ministry. You always hated me, because Olyessa paid me more than she paid you, and you thought you could cut me out of power. But you should have known better than to come down here by yourself, you bastard."

Jaromil's voice was so low Jez could hardly make it out, and there was an unpleasant gurgling sound to it. "Didn't … come alone. Be here … soon. Catch you …"

He slumped back, and was still.

The young man stooped and placed his fingers against Jaromil's throat. He glanced quickly towards Jez and Lev, and for an instant, she thought he'd kill them, too. Which, honestly, would still be better than being tortured.

He hesitated an instant, uncertainty in his posture, then turned and strode quickly to the door, yanked it open, and slipped outside.

For a long moment, Jez stared at the limp body drooped over the table.

It was an old table, uneven and cracked, and the body tipped, slowly, towards one side. The blood stain was growing now, painting the back of the grey government uniform a dark, rich, spreading red.

She figured she must be in some sort of shock. Because she was pretty damn sure that she should be doing something—maybe screaming, or swearing, or hell, fainting would even make sense. But instead, she just sat there, watching the body tip to one side, until at last, with a loud, indelicate *thud*, it landed on the ground.

And somehow, that final thud jerked her out of her reverie.

She closed her eyes for a moment, trying to control her breathing, and trying to remember why the bastard with the knife had jogged some recollection in the back corner of her brain—

She turned to Lev, who was staring at her, expression baffled, and managed a small grin.

"That was one of those plaguers who works with Olyessa." Her voice shook so hard she wasn't sure he'd understand her words.

Lev's expression turned instantly to one of calculating interest. "Well," he said after a moment, and even though his voice was steady, Jez could hear the edge of hysteria behind his words. "I suppose it's safe to say that there are people in the government who dislike Branka and Jaromil almost as much as I currently do."

He took a deep breath, clearly trying to bring himself under control. Then he frowned. "Jez? What are you—"

She rolled her eyes at him, from where she'd managed to rock her chair backwards. "Just so you know, this is going to bloody hurt," she said through gritted teeth.

Realization dawned on his face, and his eyes widened in something between panic and concern, which was honestly ridiculous, since they'd just been about to be tortured to death, and the worst that was going to happen to her now was a bump on the head. But before he could open his mouth to say whatever it was he'd been about to say, her chair teetered, overbalanced, and tipped, and she turned her head to one side in a futile effort to keep it from hitting the damn concrete. And then she slammed into the floor, and the room wavered slightly, and Lev sucked in a quick, sharp breath. Pain crashed over her, sharp and hot, and she swore shakily.

"Jez! Are you alright? Are you—"

"'M fine, genius," she grunted, fighting back tears of pain.

"What—"

She was feeling around her gingerly.

She'd been right. The chair, which was basically a piece of crap, had broken on impact. And even though her hands were still cuffed behind her back, now that the chair was broken—

She rolled over, wincing at the pain—that wasn't even counting how much like absolute crap she felt from the damn poisoned knife a few days ago—and wriggled free of the broken bits of chair. She paused for a moment to catch her breath, then rolled to one side and staggered painfully to her feet, using every swear word she knew and some she had to make up.

"Jez," Lev's voice was sharp with worry. "How badly are you—"

She gave him a sharp grin. "Doesn't really matter, I'm still guessing it's better than the alternative. Hold tight, I'll get you out."

She took a step, staggered, saw, from the corner of her eye, Lev's involuntary movement as if to jump to his feet and catch her, even though he was still tied his chair, and steadied herself on the edge of the table.

She stood there for a moment, then took a deep breath and turned to look at the tabletop, the broad smear of blood across the shiny, sharp instruments.

For a moment, looking at the instruments, she thought she might be sick. But she managed to swallow down the vomit, and ignore the thought of what the bastard who was currently lying on the floor very close to her feet would've done with the damn things. She maneuvered so that she could grab a flat, sharp object with her bound hands.

The cuffs holding her were good ones, and it took some effort to get them to pop loose, but at last they dropped to the floor with a loud clang. She grabbed the table again to steady herself, and when she was sure she wouldn't fall over, she straightened and made her unsteady way over to Lev. She leaned up against his chair with her hip and shoved the—well, she actually didn't want to think about what it was—into the space between his cuffs until she could work them free.

Lev sucked in a quick, relieved breath as the cuffs fell to the ground, then stood quickly, turning and catching her by the shoulders.

"Jez." His voice thick with strain. "Are you alright? Are you—Jez —" He pulled her into a tight embrace, and she closed her eyes and leaned into him, and she could feel the quick rise and fall of his chest, the trembling in his arms, the small hitch in his breathing. Finally he pulled back, and to be honest, she wasn't sure she wanted him to. Because when he did, she could see the whole damn room again, the chairs they'd been tied to, the instruments on the table, the body slumped against the chairs and the blood-soaked body on the floor, knife still protruding from its back.

Suddenly the whole thing struck her as incredibly funny, and she found she was shaking with laughter. Lev took one look at her face and pulled her close again, and somehow, the warm steadiness of him was actually what she'd needed all along. Slowly, her hiccuping laughter calmed until she was able to breathe again.

She swallowed hard, and finally pulled back reluctantly from the warmth of Lev's arms.

"Well, genius, guess we should get the hell out of here, before whoever plaguing Jaromil was talking about shows up."

Lev took a shaky breath as well. "I—suppose you're right," he said.

28

Ysbel, day 17

Ysbel glanced around quickly at the tiny apartment, and then at the girl huddled in her arms.

Olya's face was very white, and it hurt Ysbel to see it.

Perhaps, if Olya had been a little younger, hadn't been able to understand everything that had been happening—

No. It wouldn't matter. Her children had grown up in prison. And since they'd been rescued, people they loved had been in almost constant danger. The children had been in almost constant danger.

She pulled her daughter tighter.

"Mama?" Olya whispered. "What's going to happen?"

"I don't know yet, my Olyeshka," she whispered back. "But I promise you, I will do everything I can to protect you."

Olya looked up at her and nodded, and somehow, Ysbel knew that even at eight years old, Olya understood—everything that Ysbel could do wasn't necessarily going to be enough.

Beside Ysbel on the couch, Tanya cradled Misko in one arm. In her other hand, she held a small, deadly looking pistol.

Ysbel didn't envy the first of the mafia boyeviki who came to the door. Or the second, or the third.

Looking at her wife's face, she didn't actually envy any of them.

Masha was in the kitchen, standing by the table. She looked up towards the window, and her face was set, her posture stiff. There had been a moment when Ysbel had wondered if Masha had some scheme up her sleeve, some way out of this that she hadn't told them yet, but looking at her, Ysbel knew it had been a fanciful hope.

Masha was as certain as she was that they would die.

"My love," she said softly to Tanya.

Tanya turned her, her face pale. "Ysi?"

"We could have gone back, you know. We could have taken the children and gone back to our planet. Maybe started the farm again. Misko would have enjoyed that."

Tanya smiled at her. "Yes," she said softly. "I think he would have. And I think Olya would have loved learning explosives from you."

Ysbel brushed her hand along her wife's cheek. "I'm sorry I didn't do that for you," she said quietly.

Tanya shook her head. "No," she said, her voice fond and sad. "It's a nice dream. It's nice to think about, at times like this. But—" she glanced down at Misko, huddled in her arms. "For a long time we lived like that, let the system take care of its own problems. We were innocents then. But we're not anymore, neither of us. We'd have to pretend that there weren't street kids in Prasvishoni being killed, or people locked up on prison planets for disagreeing with some government official or reading the wrong book. We'd have to ignore the pleasure planets, and the mafia, with its stranglehold on the system, tightening its grip." She was silent for a moment. "I'm sorry it will end here," she said finally. "But my Ysi?" She looked up at Ysbel with that small, wistful smile that Ysbel had fallen in love with so many years ago. "I don't regret this. I will never regret it."

Ysbel pulled Olya a little closer, leaned over and kissed her wife softly. "You know," she said, "once, the only thing I cared about was keeping my family safe. But—" she gave a small shrug. "It seems my family has grown more than I expected."

Tanya's smile grew soft, and Ysbel closed her eyes for a moment.

"Ysbel!"

She jerked her head up. The voice came through her earpiece, and as far as she knew, everyone who would be calling through her com was dead.

"Ysbel! Are you alive?"

She stared for a moment longer, then hit her com. "Lev?"

"Ysbel!" His voice was thick with relief. "Jez and I were caught. But we're out, and on our way over. Have you heard from Tae?"

Ysbel hesitated a moment. "I heard from Ivan. A few minutes ago. The police had come with their weapons. He didn't have time to explain, but it sounded like Tae may have been … hurt."

Lev swore. "I suppose we deal with that when we have time to make a plan." He paused a moment. "Can you meet us somewhere?"

Ysbel almost laughed. "That would be nice. But our apartment is currently surrounded by mafia boyeviki, and there's too many of them for me to take care of it with an explosive. So no, I'm not sure we can. Unless you believe there's an afterlife," she amended.

There was a moment of silence on the other end of the com. Then Lev said, "You're surrounded? Can you send me your coordinates?"

Ysbel frowned slightly. "Yes, but unless you plan to also be surrounded by mafia boyeviki—"

"I mean, guess we could do that," drawled Jez's unmistakable tones through the com. "But hell, I've been surrounded by Grigory's damn boyeviki enough times, I think. So I was thinking maybe we use some of those modded heat pistols you gave us, give those bastards something else to look at for a minute or two."

Masha had turned to look at her by now, and so had Tanya.

Ysbel tapped the coordinates through to Lev, a small smile growing on her face.

"You know, you lunatic, you might be right," she said.

"Yeah? Well, I mean, I'm basically a damn genius." Ysbel could almost hear the pilot's smirk through the com. "Be there in about three standard minutes." There was a small pause. "If genius here doesn't pass out on the way, I mean."

"Jez," she heard Lev's patient voice in the background. "I seem to recall being the one catching you. Five separate times so far."

"Yeah, well—" The com shut off.

Ysbel tapped off her own com.

"Who was that?" Masha's tone was clipped.

"It appears the government's torturers weren't quite enough to deal with our lunatic pilot and our idiot scholar."

A sudden, disbelieving hope dawned on Masha's face.

"You mean—" began Tanya, her voice tight.

Ysbel turned to her wife. "I mean, I think we should get ready to get out the door. Because from what Lev and Jez just told me, the boyeviki outside will become very distracted in about three standard minutes."

Tanya stood quickly, clutching Misko to her chest, tense excitement and frantic, desperate relief in her posture. Masha stood as well, grabbing her heat pistol off the table. She looked around, posture once again brisk and businesslike.

"Do either of you need to grab anything? No? Good." She gave a slight smile. "There's a back way out. We'll have to move quickly."

Ysbel smiled and stood as well, holding Olya close. "Well," she said, "I guess now we wait for the boyeviki to meet to our pilot."

29

Tae, day 17

The first thing Tae was aware of was the pain throbbing in the back of his skull. Then, slowly, other sensations returned—bitter cold seeping through his back and shoulders. Hard concrete under him. A muffled blur of sound that gradually transformed into words.

An incongruous patch of warmth on one shoulder, a voice, whispering, thick with worry, "Tae. Tae, can you hear me? Please. You have to be alright."

He groaned, and the warmth on his shoulder, that, he realized, must be a hand, tightened quickly, and someone sucked in a sharp, relieved breath.

"Thank the Lady—"

He recognized the voice as Ivan's, and the abrupt way it had cut off as someone fighting back tears.

He groaned again and blinked his eyes open.

Wherever they were, it was dark. At first, he wondered if maybe the blow to his head had affected his eyesight, but as his eyes adjusted, he realized they were in a small tent of sorts. Ivan bent over him, face drawn, eyes closed in desperate relief. There was a dark bruise across his face. Tae was too woozy to feel properly angry, but something hard tightened his chest at the sight.

To one side of them sat Vera and Dmitri. Their hands were tied behind their backs, and whoever had given Ivan the bruise had done their work on Dmitri and Vera as well. Dmitri's lip was split, and Vera had a sharp, angry welt across the side of her head.

"Where are we?" Tae murmured.

Dmitri looked over and tried to smile, even through the sharp fear on his face. "We're in a guard tent. I guess the police didn't want us giving any of the others ideas."

Tae struggled to sit up, and a wave of dizziness washed over him.

Ivan caught him and lowered him gently to the ground. "Easy there," he said quietly.

Tae waited a few moments, then tried again, a little more cautiously this time.

This time he succeeded in pushing himself into a sitting position, and he sat for a moment, blinking, waiting for the world to stop spinning crazily.

"What happened to the others?" he mumbled as soon as he could clear his head enough to form the words.

Dmitri glanced at Ivan, and there was something in his glance that told Tae this was news he didn't want to hear.

"They're—rounding them up. To take in for questioning," said Ivan softly.

Tae was hit by a fresh wave of nausea. He swore and tried to get to his feet, but Ivan caught his arm.

"Tae, listen to me. You're not going to like this, but I need you to listen."

"And before you say anything," said Dmitri, "this is something we all agreed was the best option."

Something cold crawled in Tae's stomach.

Ivan took a deep breath. "Things are—bad. There's nothing we can do from here. Lev and Jez are probably dead, and I haven't heard from Ysbel or the others. As far as I know, we're alone. Our only hope to save anyone is to have someone on the outside. Even then, there's not much they could do, but—it's possible they could save a few of these kids."

Tae blinked at him for a moment, his mind not working quite as quickly as it should. "You said that we don't have anyone on the outside. How—"

He realized what they were suggesting when Ivan gave him a small, slightly strained smile.

"No," said Tae. His breath was coming too quickly, and the nausea bubbled in the stomach. "No, I won't. I—I can't. I'm not going to—"

"Tae," said Dmitri quietly. "It's the only chance we have. You get out. Get somewhere safe. And then, maybe, you find a way to help the rest of us. You can't do it from here. You can't do anything from in here, except die. They've told us the others will be questioned, and the ringleaders will be executed. That's everyone in this tent." His voice trembled slightly, but his gaze was steady. "So you have to get out. You're the only one who stands a chance of saving any of the students. I can't do it, Vera can't. It has to be you."

"I—I can't—" Tae's voice caught.

"Tae."

Despite himself, he met Dmitri's eyes.

Dmitri's gaze was steady, even though his face, under his sandy hair, was pale. "I trust you, Tae. I trust you with my life. And—and I'm asking you to trust me, too."

"Dmitri." His voice was shaking. "Dmitri you—I—"

Dmitri made a small motion, as if to put a hand on Tae's arm, but his arms were cuffed behind his back. "I know you're some sort of crazy, romantic freedom fighter. But give me a little credit too, can't you?" There was that fond, half teasing tone to his voice that Tae knew so well. "I can care about something enough to die for it. Even us mere mortals can do that."

Tae's cheeks were wet with tears, and he couldn't seem to stop them. "I can't—" he began again, but even as he said the words, he choked on them.

Because Dmitri was right. It was their only chance. Their only chance was for him to leave them to die, save himself at the price of their lives, on the off-chance he could somehow save one or two of the students outside as well.

He opened his mouth to say something, he wasn't sure what, but it didn't matter. He couldn't make the words come out anyways.

"So, that's settled," said Vera, trying to put a carefree note into her voice that didn't cover the raw fear. "Tae and Ivan will get out. You two are the only ones who weren't cuffed, because you were unconscious, Tae, and Ivan was carrying you."

Tae felt his cheeks heating.

Vera grinned. "It was actually pretty damn cute."

He scowled at her on instinct, and then had to swallow hard and turn quickly away.

From the way Ivan's posture had tensed at Vera's words, his escape hadn't been part of the plan they'd discussed. But Ivan had clearly realized any protest on his part would only exacerbate Tae's protests, so he was biting down hard on his teeth, face set. Tae felt a small, sick, selfish bubble of relief.

At least Ivan might survive this.

He took a deep breath. "How will we—" he gestured around them. "Don't tell me they're not guarding us."

Vera grinned again, despite the fear in her face. "Oh, we'll keep their attention."

A spike of panic shot through Tae's brain as he realized what she was saying. "No! You can't! I've had run-ins with the police before, believe me, if you try to—"

Vera winked at him. "You know me, Tae, I never listen to people who tell me I can't do things." She took a deep breath, as if bracing herself. Then she shouted, voice hoarse and raw, "Down with the damn fascist pigs! Up with the street kids! You fight them—"

There was a moment's silence. Then, from outside the tent, a thin voice, joined, moments later, by a few others. "You fight us!"

"You take them—" Vera called.

"You take us!"

The voices outside were swelling, growing into a ragged chorus, and Tae could hear the angry shouts of police officers, the unmistakable thud of shock sticks against unresisting bodies.

Vera's face grew sick at the sound. But she took a deep breath, and shouted, "Down with the fascists!"

"Up with the people!" came the reply, and now several dozen voices strong.

There were more shouts, muffled grunts of pain, a scream.

Tae turned desperately to Ivan, but Ivan gave a curt shake of his head. "They're doing this to give you a chance," he whispered. "Are you going to waste it?"

Dmitri, who'd joined in Vera's chanting, glanced over quickly and mouthed, "Go!"

He couldn't do this, he couldn't leave his friends to be beaten to death, tortured, thrown in prison—

But they trusted him. And he had no choice but to trust them back.

He took a deep breath, closed his eyes for half a moment, then followed Ivan on hands and knees, ducking under the stiff fabric of the tent wall and out into the sunlight.

He blinked for a moment, disoriented, then Ivan had pulled him to his feet, and they were running at a crouch towards the edge of the barricade.

Something clicked in Tae's earpiece, and he almost skidded to a halt, but Ivan dragged him forward.

"Come on," he hissed.

Tae. Vera told me what's happening. You won't be able to get out without the passcode. Caz and I got it when we were listening in on the police line.

Peti and Caz were still in there. Peti and Caz, and Luca, and Mila. They were in there, and they were going to be killed, and he was running away, and—

Ivan grabbed his arm again, pulling him forward. "You can't help anyone from here."

So. The code is 87352. There was a slight pause. *Good luck.*

Tae's feet were slowing of their own accord, every instinct in his body trying to drag him around, back to Caz and Peti, Dmitri, Vera, the others. But Ivan's hand tightened on his arm, and Tae found himself following, his legs moving without input from his brain.

"Stop! What are you doing?" One of the guards beside the barricade stepped forward.

Ivan turned a quick glance on Tae, and he found himself muttering out the passcode Peti had given him. The officer sighed and stepped aside. "You've got to look a little hungrier than that if you want to disguise yourself as a street kid," she muttered as they ran past.

And then they were out, into the open street, running, the sharp slap of their boots on the dirty concrete echoing off the rundown buildings around them.

At last Ivan dragged them into a small alley, and they collapsed against the wall, panting. Tae's heart was pounding so quickly he thought his chest might explode, and he wasn't sure if it was from running, or from what he'd done—the people he left behind, when he'd sworn he wouldn't leave anyone behind.

And then he was sobbing, thick, choking sobs, and Ivan, still breathing heavily, gathered Tae into his arms and held him for a moment. And for just a moment, Tae let himself relax against him.

But—there was no time for that. His friends were dying. They'd given him a chance to escape, and they'd believed maybe, just maybe, he could do something to help. To save someone, at least.

He took a deep, shaky breath and straightened, swallowing back the tears that still rose in his throat and threatened to choke him.

Ivan watched him, concern on his face under the stark exhaustion.

"Do we know if anyone from the crew is alive?" asked Tae brusquely, not letting himself think about the words he was saying. "Ysbel, Tanya, Masha, anyone?"

Ivan gave a quick shake of his head. "I got a call through to Ysbel after you'd been knocked out. But it was disconnected when the police noticed what I was doing."

He didn't say it, but Tae knew where the bruise on his face and the blood on his lip had come from.

"Did she answer?"

Ivan nodded. "Yes. But—that was fifteen, twenty standard minutes ago. A lot could have happened in that time."

Tae nodded, biting down hard on the inside of his cheek, trying to fight back the sick panic threatening to choke off his breath and shut down his brain.

"I'm going to send out an emergency signal," he said at last. "Just in case any of them are still alive. I'll give them fifteen minutes, and —in the meantime, I'll work on something. In case they don't come."

Ivan's frown deepened. "What are you—"

Tae looked up at him with a quick, grim smile. "I'm going to set a tracker on my com. I can set it to alert all the police coms, on emergency, to track it down. It won't keep them busy for long. But it should distract a few of them." He paused a moment, swallowing hard. "Get as many of the street kids as you can. They'll be killed first. But don't spend time looking, take whoever you can get, students, street kids, whatever."

Ivan stared at him for a moment, and there was a look on his face that would have woken Tae to nightmares, if he lived past today.

"Tae," Ivan began, his voice sick. "If you do that, they'll—"

Tae shook his head. "I was going to stay in there and die with the others. But you pulled me out, convinced me that maybe I could do something to help. And this is how I can. If—" He swallowed hard. "Ivan, if you love me, please. I can't save everyone. But I need to be able to save someone—my street kids, the students. I—I need to be able to save you. Please. Just give me that."

Ivan's face was a sick, ashy grey. But at last, slowly, he nodded. "Alright. If—if they don't come in fifteen minutes, I'll—" He turned away quickly, with a sort of choking sob, and dropped his forehead against the rough prefab wall of the alley.

Tae looked away, swallowing hard. When he could see through the blur of tears, he tapped out quick emergency call on his com to the rest of the crew.

If anyone can hear me, I need you. Quickly. I have fifteen minutes.

He set his coordinates into the com, and sent them through. Then, he waited.

At last, Ivan turned slowly away from the wall. The look on his face was one the Tae didn't want to remember, but he knew it would be embedded permanently in his brain. Somehow, though, Ivan managed a small, sick smile. He put his arm around Tae's shoulder, and Tae leaned into him, trying not to think of anything but the warmth of him, that he was probably feeling for the last time in his life.

And then, through his earpiece, he heard a voice that he'd been sure he'd never hear again.

"Hey, tech-head. We're on our way. You and Ivan aren't making out on a couch or something, are you?"

He stared at his com in dumbfounded bewilderment. Then, slowly, turned to stare at Ivan.

A disbelieving smile was spreading across Ivan's face. He grabbed Tae and crushed him into a hug, burying his face in Tae's hair.

"Tae," Ivan choked, but he couldn't seem to say anything else.

But then, with something caught in his throat, Tae couldn't say anything either.

30

Tae, day 17

It was just over ten standard minutes, although it felt like hours, before Tae heard boots clattering on the streets, and turned in time to see Jez and Lev round the corner to the alley. Jez was leaning heavily on Lev, and she looked like she'd been in a fight, but she was grinning widely.

"Hey, tech-head. Every time I leave you alone, I find you swooning over Ivan. You're going to have to learn to keep your mind on the job one of these days."

He was too relieved even for an exasperated retort.

Ysbel, Tanya, and Masha rounded the corner next. Ysbel and Tanya carried the children, bundled in coats and scarves. Masha was holding a heat pistol, and the grim look on her face told him she'd be more than happy for an excuse to use it.

"Tae. What's happening?" Lev snapped as they came up to him.

He didn't take his arm from Jez's waist, Tae noticed, and Jez didn't seem to mind.

"It's—not good," Tae said, sobering quickly. He gave them a brief account of what had happened behind the barricades, and Lev's face grew grim as well as he listened.

Ysbel said quietly, "Those are my students in there."

Tae glanced over at her, and was suddenly very, very glad he was not in the police's shoes.

"How long ago was this?" she asked brusquely.

Tae shook his head. "We got out maybe—ten, twelve minutes ago."

"Then they still may be alive," said Masha quietly. "It will take the police longer than that to get the paperwork done, and they won't execute anyone before they've done that. It would be as much as their position was worth."

Lev was frowning at his holoscreen. He looked up at Tae. "Remind me, where were you worried the gangs would start fighting?"

Tae peered at the map on the holoscreen. "Here." He gestured to the small patchwork of streets near the barricade. "We were hoping to push the barricades far enough so that along with the police presence at the protests, it would keep them away. But we didn't have enough time to finish."

Lev gave a quick nod. "That might actually work in our favour." He looked down at the map again, then slapped his hand over the screen, shutting it off, and glanced up at Tae again. "What would happen, right now, if everyone suddenly learned about Olyessa and Grigory?"

Tae stared at him for a moment. Then he felt a small, grim smile creeping over his face.

"I think," he said slowly, "the police would be a hell of a lot busier than they are right now."

Lev returned his grim smile. "Not much to lose at this point, anyways." He turned. "Masha? I assume you have the codes we were using to broadcast Grigory's and Olyessa's messages?"

"I do," Masha murmured. "And, I suppose you're right—the government already knows, and—" she glanced around wryly. "I currently fail to see how the situation in the streets could get much worse."

Tae leaned back against the alley wall, almost dizzy with relief, and Ivan pulled him close.

"Thank the Lady," Ivan whispered. There was a note of forced humour in his voice. "I—wasn't looking forward to seeing if I could handle watching someone else I loved die."

Tae leaned over and kissed him wordlessly, and he could feel the tension in Ivan's muscles, the way his hands shook.

"Tae? I need you for a minute."

He glanced up quickly.

Lev was watching him, biting back a smile. "Masha has the codes to the gangs' lines, but not the police. I assume you've hacked into the police lines?"

Tae straightened and pulled up his own holoscreen, and pushed the splice through to Lev's com.

Masha stepped forward. She touched her com to Lev's, and for a moment, there was complete silence.

And then, a recorded video appeared, sound amplified through the com.

For a moment Tae didn't recognize the scene. And then, suddenly, he did.

It was the pleasure planet, an upstairs room in the Strani house. The moment when he'd thought his friends had been killed, and they were all about to die.

When Grigory and Olyessa first discovered that Masha had ruined them. That their entire empires had gone up in smoke.

For a moment, he felt his muscles going shaky again, and only

Ivan's arm around his shoulders held him steady.

When the recording ended, and Masha tapped off the com.

There was another long moment of silence. And then Lev said quietly, "Tae?"

Tae started, and pulled up his com, tapping into the police audio.

At first, there was only confused murmuring. And then shouts, and running footsteps. Then sirens, student voices shouting, the unmistakable fizz of heat-gun blasts.

They looked at each other. Jez was grinning broadly, and that, alone, told Tae everything he needed to know.

"Well," she drawled. "Guess we should go show those police bastards what happens when you mess with our friends."

31

Jez, day 17

By the time they reached the barricades, Jez had basically caught her balance again.

Not that she minded Lev holding on to her. It was one of the few benefits of their current situation, actually. But the point was, it'd be hard to throw punches if she couldn't stay on her feet.

The other point was, after seeing the drawn, haunted look on Tae's face, she was damn sure she wanted to be throwing punches.

The streets outside the barricades were complete chaos. Students shouted and screamed and threw rocks and snow and chunks of prefab, police outfitted in full riot gear and brandishing shock-sticks waded into knots of struggling students.

Tae glanced around, face still stricken. "The tent where they're keeping Dmitri and Vera is just behind the barricades," he said shortly. He took a deep breath, clearly trying to collect himself. "Jez, Lev, Masha, get as many of the street kids out as you can. I sent a message through to Peti, and she and Caz will be expecting you. Ysbel, you come with me and Ivan. We'll get Dmitri and Vera, and then we'll see what we can do for the other students."

"I would be happy to," said Ysbel, a grim smile on her face.

Tanya wasn't with them—after a hurried conference, she'd ducked into an alley a few streets away with the two children, murmuring something about them being safe in the *Ungovernable*, but she'd be back soon.

Ysbel had come with the rest of them.

And yes, Tanya was scary as hell, but for something like this … Jez glanced around at the chaos, grinning broadly.

Well, all she could say was, explosives might come in pretty damn handy.

"Alright," she whispered, turning to Lev. "You go. I'm going to give these bastards something to think about."

Lev's expression was tight. "Jez. Are you sure you can—" He closed his eyes for a moment and took a deep breath. "Alright. Just —"

She rolled her eyes. "Be careful, I know."

He put his hands on her waist, turning her towards him. His face was serious. "I don't want to lose you, Jez," he said quietly.

"Yeah," she said, swallowing, because for some reason, looking into his eyes, she couldn't think of anything snarky to say. "You too."

He gave her a strained smile, then pulled her in and kissed her gently on the lips before turning away. "Masha. Let's go."

Jez stared after him, blinking, suddenly not quite as steady on her feet as she had been a moment before. Then she took a deep breath and pulled out her heat pistol.

Hopefully those police bastards were ready to warm up in a hurry.

Her first shot set one of the damn skybikes that was parked outside the barricades on fire. Which was a fairly effective way to attract their attention, turned out.

Damn, she loved working with Ysbel.

By her second shot, there wasn't a single person on the street who hadn't figured out something new had shown up on the scene.

The police officers turned at the new threat, ducking for cover and scrambling for their weapons as Jez proceeded to cook the air around them to a blistering temperature.

"Hey, you plaguers," Jez shouted cheerfully, hitting the voice amp on her com. "You want to pick on a bunch of students and street kids, probably a good idea to find out who they're friends with first."

From the corner of her eye, she saw Tae and Ysbel, who'd taken advantage of the confusion to slip through a gap in the shattered barricade. From their grim expressions, Jez was pretty damn sure the police officers inside were going to be in for a hell of a lot of excitement very shortly.

She couldn't see Masha and Lev, but that was probably a good thing, considering their plan hinged on them avoiding notice.

"What the hell are you doing?" an officer shouted at Jez. "Who are you?"

Jez grinned. "Heard there were a bunch of hooligans with guns attacking some kids. So figured I'd come help sort it out."

"Jez, down!" Lev snapped through her com. She dropped, and something whined over her head, the wind of it cold on her face. She glanced up in time to see the back of an officer on a skybike. She scrambled to her feet, swayed for a moment, and, as the skybike rushed at her for another pass, she stepped neatly out of the way, grabbed the bike's handles, and swung herself up behind the officer. He gave a muffled curse and managed to half-turn as the bike swerved wildly. He brought his gun around, but Jez grabbed the back of his helmet and shoved it up and forward. The front edge of it slammed into his throat as she brought the butt of her pistol down hard on the base of his skull. The officer slumped, and Jez hit the restraints, shoved him off the bike, then yanked up on the handles, skimming the narrow alley walls. She leaned forward until the speed pulled tears from her eyes and the icy wind froze them on her cheeks, then she flipped the bike around and pointed it straight down towards a knot of officers who'd turned back to the barricades. Her cheeks tingled from the cold, and her teeth ached where the air hit them, but she couldn't stop grinning if she tried.

The officers below scattered as the skybike dived into the centre of them. A few of them rolled, yanking out pistols, and the air around her glowed with heat. She pressed herself lower against the bike and shot upwards, out of range of their weapons.

A handful of officers had swung onto their bikes and were coming after her, and she almost laughed. She was flying so fast now that the bike was shaking under her, on the very edge of control. The officers couldn't possibly match her speed, but were apparently trying to make up for it by the sheer amount of firepower they were throwing her direction.

"Hey you bastards," she shouted over her shoulder. "I spent the last three damn weeks in government meetings, and I'm just going to say, I can see what they were talking about, wasting plaguing government resources and inefficient damn use of—"

A heat blast slammed into the back of her bike, causing it to swerve crazily, and she swore, shoving the handles down so she was pointed at the street. Her pursuers peeled off in panic, and she pulled out of her dive just before she hit concrete.

"Jez," came Lev's strained voice in her earpiece. "Over here."

She flipped her bike around, and swore loudly.

Lev and Masha were outside the barricade now, pinned down in one of the narrow, winding alleyways, a small group of frightened street children huddled behind them. Jez recognized at least one of them as Tae's friend. But the police officers had them surrounded, and they were firing steadily. Lev and Masha had ducked behind the scant shelter of the alley wall, and Masha was putting up an impressive counter-fire, but it wasn't going to last.

Jez gave a tight grin, leaned over the handles of her bike, and shot towards them.

The officers heard her the moment before she reached them, and they dived frantically out of the way. She skinned the bike over their heads, turned around, and came in for a second pass, bringing the hilt of her pistol down on the back of the neck of the officer who looked like the leader. He crumpled, and Jez slid off the bike, swayed, and grabbed for the wall. Her pistol, though, pointing at the fallen officers, didn't waver.

"Tell you what, you bastards," she called. "This pistol was modded by my friend. And if I pull the trigger, there's not going to be enough of you left for the street kids to warm their hands over on a cold night. So I suggest that you drop your damn guns and get the hell out of here."

There was a moment's silence. Then the remaining officers scrambled to their feet and ran for their lives.

Jez turned to grin at Lev and the others.

Lev paled, but before he could speak, a barrage of heat-blasts sizzled around her. She yelped, and dived into the alley beside Lev and Masha.

"I thought you said you didn't like to get shot at," she whispered to Lev. "You picked a pretty damn bad job description."

"I'm aware of that, Jez," he said through gritted teeth. "However, I don't know there'll be anything left of us to shoot at in about thirty standard seconds."

Jez grinned at him, the adrenaline pounding through her veins. "You're right, there's always a bright side." She leaned out, peering around the corner of the alley wall, and ducked back as another shot blackened the wall beside her head.

She'd seen enough, though.

Her distraction had worked. And apparently, as between the unarmed students and the crew of the *Ungovernable*, the police had made a determination as to which was the bigger threat.

Outside, a grim group of officers were dragging the massive ion cannon away from the barricade, and pointing it in the direction of their alley.

Lev drew in a quick breath, his expression irresolute. Then he glanced behind him at the huddled children, and tapped his com. "Tanya?" he said quietly. "Where are you?"

"I'm on my way back," she said. "What do you need?"

"There are two dozen street kids behind me right now who're about to be killed. Is there anything you can do to take out the cannon?"

There was a moment's pause. At last Tanya said, "There are a lot of things I could do to take out the cannon." She paused for a long moment. "You and Jez, I assume, are covering the street children?"

"Yes," said Lev.

"Alright, then," she said. "Try to keep them alive for a minute, please."

Her com tapped off.

Jez looked at Lev and raised her eyebrows, but he just shook his head.

A thin, high-pitched whine pierced the air, setting Jez's teeth on edge.

"Down!" Masha snapped, and then the blast knocked them backwards, shattering the wall they were sheltering behind and sending prefab dust spraying out into the cold air.

Jez rolled to her feet, and someone caught her elbow, steadying her. She yanked out her pistol and fired at the mouth of the alley, and hell, she could hardly see what she was shooting, but there were kids behind her, and she wasn't going to damn well let anyone get past if she could help it.

Lev was beside her, his own pistol in his hands, a grim look on his face.

She glanced quickly behind them.

Masha was against the back wall of the alley. She'd put herself between the smallest street children and the force of the blast, but now she rolled to her feet. Her pistol was raised, her face hard, and Jez knew with a sudden certainty that whatever Masha might be capable of—and hell, she was capable of a lot—she would die before she let anyone hurt those kids.

"Stay back," Jez called to her, turning back to the alley entrance. "Lev and I'll give them something to shoot at."

There was that thin whine again, and she shoved Lev back against the wall as another explosion rocked the small alley. She'd been expecting it this time, though, and she scrambled quickly to her feet and crossed to the alley entrance, leaning out and peering around.

They weren't going to last that many more shots back here, but then, they probably wouldn't have to. After the gun had softened them up, they'd probably just send a bunch of riot police to finish them off.

The officers at the gun were readying it for another shot. The sharp whine grated on her ears as it powered up again.

And then, she grinned. Because far overhead, a dark, silent figure was lowering itself from the roof above the officers.

They didn't see Tanya until it was far, far too late.

And Jez watched dreamily as Tanya took out the officers, and then the gun, as fluidly and gracefully as a dancer.

Honestly, she could watch Tanya knock the hell out of people all damn day and not get tired of it.

There was a moment of panic, as the officers realized their weapon was gone. And then they grabbed their heat-guns and started towards the alley.

Jez stepped back, grinning broadly.

Her heart was pounding, almost like it had with the poison, but this time she was enjoying every damn second of it. "Masha, stay back with the kids," she said over her shoulder. "You too, genius. Figure I can make them think about things a little bit before they decide to come after the rest of you."

Lev shook his head firmly and stepped up beside her. "I may not be as good as you with a gun, but I've been around Ysbel for months now. I can shoot, you know."

She turned to him and winked. "Thought you hated getting shot at."

"Yes," he said dryly. "But I've learned there's something I hate more, and that's watching you get shot at."

She stared at him for a moment, then shrugged. "Your loss. Bet I look damn hot getting shot at."

He gave a small, reluctant chuckle.

There was the sound of boots outside the alley, and she tightened her grip on her pistol.

Then an explosion rocked the entire street.

When Jez recovered her senses, she was sitting with her back against the alley wall, her vision a blank white. She blinked a few times, and the world started to take shape again. A few seconds after that, she realized the roar that she was hearing wasn't just in her ears, and a few seconds later, that it wasn't just noise, it was words.

And then she heard what they were shouting. She turned to Lev, who'd been thrown beside her, and grinned.

Outside the alley, students' voices shouted, "It's the professor! The professor came!"

Slowly, Lev's face broke into a grin. A moment later, Tanya dropped down into the alley beside them. She strode quickly over to Masha, and took in how Masha's body sheltered the children.

She gave a small smile. "Thank you," she said.

Masha gave her a small smile in return. "Well," she said. "We'd better get the rest of the children out from behind those barricades. That's what we're here for, isn't it?"

32

Ysbel, day 17

Ysbel smiled to herself as the students shouted and cheered. Tae had already ducked into the tent, and a moment later, Vera barrelled out of the entrance, laughing and crying at the same time, and came screeching to a halt just in front of Ysbel.

"Professor," she said, her voice choking. "Professor, I knew you'd come. As soon as Tae told us you were back, I knew you'd come for us."

Ysbel studied the girl. Her face was haunted, cut with strain and fear. But she was smiling, and Ysbel could see in that smile the girl she'd taught, for a few memorable weeks, back in the University of Prasvishoni.

She cleared her throat. "Yes, well, I did make it clear that no one threatens my students, I think," she said, although her voice was huskier than usual.

Dmitri appeared next, grinning that charming grin he had. His face was pale, his cheeks wet with tears. He didn't say anything, just looked at her, shaking his head in a sort of wondering disbelief.

Ysbel turned away quickly. "Well," she said. "I think the point of this was to get everyone out, am I right?"

Vera straightened with a valiant effort, shook her head, and blinked hard. "Yes. Sorry, Professor."

She turned quickly, and strode back into the square, shouting and gesturing at the other students to get together, get ready to get out.

Ysbel looked after her fondly, a smile on her face.

Dmitri, Tae, and Ivan were gathering the terrified, panicked students into a group. The police officers who were left behind the barricades were huddled together, shouting frantically into their coms, paying almost no attention to the students.

A few, though, had gathered in a small defensive formation, weapons drawn and faces grim.

Ysbel stepped towards them, palming another of Tae's explosives.

One of them glanced her way, did a double-take, and shouted something to her fellow officers, terror in her voice.

They scattered.

Ysbel grinned.

A few moments later, the others appeared behind the barricades. Ysbel's eyes searched frantically for Tanya, and she sighed in relief at the sight of her wife.

"Ysbel," Jez called. She wobbled on her feet, and Lev caught her, and Ysbel bit back a smile of amusement. "What the hell are we doing? Other than dealing with those bastards." She gestured at the police officers.

Tae came up beside them. His face was soot-stained and exhausted, but his expression was lit with a disbelieving hope. "Come on. We need to get everyone out. The police are distracted for now, yes, but I don't know how long it will last. If they trap us like this again—"

Lev and Jez exchanged glances, then followed him into the mass of students and officers.

Ysbel turned quickly to Tanya. "Is everything alright?"

Tanya gave a short nod. "I took out the gun, temporarily. Hopefully getting it back online takes them long enough that we get everyone out."

Then Ysbel glanced up to see Jez sprinting towards them. Her face was bloodless, and her smile was the same one Ysbel had seen back on the pleasure planet, when Jez had pulled out her pistol and thrown herself into the middle of a knot of bodyguards. The smile she wore when she figured they were all about to die. Ysbel's stomach clenched.

"They've blockaded us off again," she panted. "I don't know what they're planning, but—"

And then an officer's voice came over the voice amp. "Stand down! We have you surrounded."

Silence fell over the panicked masses of students. Across the square, Tae and Ivan looked up from their hurried conference with Vera and Dmitri.

Masha stepped to the ragged hole that had been blasted through the barricade.

Her posture stiffened ever so slightly. When she turned, her face was calm, but there was a sick resignation under her voice.

"It appears that we were not the only ones making contingency plans in the government," she said quietly.

Ysbel frowned, and stepped forward. The moment she glanced through the ragged hole in the barricades, she understood.

The police were back, in force. The gun that Tanya had taken out still sat useless, but already there were officers surrounding it, attempting repairs.

But that wasn't what drew her eye.

It was the silent ranks of grim-faced people flanking the small contingent of officers, and the deadly looking weapons they held.

Better weapons than the government had, certainly.

And Ysbel knew the colours on those uniforms very, very well. From prison. And from Grigory's ship, and the pleasure planet, and from earlier that day, outside their apartment.

"Well," she murmured. "I guess now we know what it takes to get Grigory's and Olyessa's boyeviki and the street gangs all to work together."

"A common enemy," said Masha quietly.

Slowly, Ysbel stepped back from the entrance.

"Tae," she said, turning to him. "I know their blockers took down your access to the com system. After my explosion, were you able to get it back up?"

Tae frowned, his face tight with worry, but he nodded.

"Good," she said. "Then I think you should pull up your voice amp. Tell the rest of them to stand down. Maybe if the police have us to kill, they won't be so hard on the students. Maybe some of the street kids slip through the cracks." Her voice was somehow matter-of-fact, but there was a strange shakiness to her muscles.

"What—" Ivan began, his voice tense.

Masha joined them. Lev was close behind her, and his face told Ysbel he knew.

"The gangs and the boyeviki have joined forces with the police," he said softly. He gave a quick, wry smile. "I should have anticipated this. There were enough people that opposed Jez's plan, the ones who'd been on Grigory and Olyessa's payroll. This was certainly a logical possibility. But I missed it. I'm sorry." He shook his head.

Tae's posture sagged slightly, his face sick. At last, he said, "Maybe we can get the kids out, keep them occupied while we—"

Ysbel let out a short breath. "No," she said. "There's too many of them. They're too well armed. There's enough of them out there to block off every street behind this barricade, and finish off every last person inside. And that's what they'll do if we don't stand down."

Vera had come over to join them, and Dmitri had followed. They were listening silently, but Vera was watching Ysbel with a sort of desperate hope.

Ysbel closed her eyes for a moment. Olya's face looked up at her from her memory, the last time she'd seen her.

Her daughter had lost so much already. She was eight years old, and she didn't know what it was like to have a home, or not be in danger. And now, to lose her parents as well?

Someone slipped their hand into hers, and she opened her eyes. Tanya was watching her, concern in her expression. Ysbel squeezed her hand, and there was something in the familiar warmth of it that held her steady.

Tanya had always been the one to hold her steady.

"Vera," she said quietly, turning to the girl. "I have explosives, yes. I could take down every last gang member and police officer out there. But if I did that, it would kill everyone in this street. I have nothing that will keep the rest of the students alive." She tried for a small smile. "But listen. You and Dmitri go. You can blend in with the crowd. Everyone out there has a reason not to like the six of us— we should be able to convince them that we're the real ringleaders."

The fear was stark on Vera's face, but she shook her head shortly. "No. They know who I am. And they'll go through the students trying to find me. I'm not willing to risk that." She looked up at Ysbel, her face set, but there was something pleading in her expression. "They trusted me. And I can't do that to them. Look at you, Professor—you didn't have to come here. But you did. I'm not running away, not if staying might give them a chance."

Ysbel stared at her for a long time. At last she nodded, and found she was blinking back tears.

Tae had pulled up the holoscreen on his com, his face grim and hopeless. "At least we can hook into the com lines again," he said, with an attempt at a smile. "Vera? Do you want to send the message, or shall I?"

Vera gave him a weak smile in return. "Let me. They're used to me yelling at them anyways."

Tae typed something rapidly on his screen, then looked up. "There. It should work now. Once their blockers were taken out, it was an easy fix." He gave a wry smile. "Too bad we didn't think about setting up a huge explosion in the middle of the square earlier. I patched through to the outside lines as well. So if you wanted to talk to your parents—"

"Never know," said Vera, with an obvious attempt at humour. "Maybe I'll get to say goodbye before the police shoot me after all." She tapped her com to what must have been a line Tae had set for the protesters. "It's me, Vera. Listen. We're trapped, and we're not going to win this. I'm sorry." She paused. "Get out if you can. Don't try to be heroes, just get out. We're—we're turning ourselves in. So don't bother trying to help us, just go." She tapped her com off, and took a deep breath. Finally, she looked up. "I guess we'd better get it over with."

Ysbel gave Tanya's hand another squeeze, sickness knotting in her stomach. She made to step forward, but Tae put a hand on her arm. "I'll go," he said quietly. "They'll recognize me."

Ivan slipped an arm around Tae's waist, and Tae leaned into him for just a moment, eyes closed, face strained.

And then he straightened, and the two of them walked to the edge of the barricade.

Tae hit his voice amp on his com, and Ysbel watched the police turn at the sound of his voice.

His dark hair falling into his eyes made him look younger than he was, and the quiet resignation in his expression made her chest tighten with sick helplessness.

Olya, Misko. They'd lose their parents, but with her and Tanya dead, they'd be safe, at least.

Tae wouldn't. Vera wouldn't, and nor would Dmitri.

A handful of officers jumped forward, grabbing the unresisting Tae and Ivan and shoving them roughly to the ground. Then other officers swarmed through the barricade, grabbing her and the others, yanking their arms behind their backs, shoving them down.

Ysbel didn't try to fight. It wouldn't do anything, anyways. And perhaps if she didn't fight, the officers would be less likely to hurt the others.

Across from her she heard Jez's muffled curses, the sound of blows, Lev's sharp gasp, and finally, stillness. The only sound that interrupted the silence was the dull thud of an officer's boot against an unresisting body.

She didn't look over.

She wasn't sure she could bear it.

At last, even that sound stopped, and the officers stood there, breathing heavily, riot helmets still pulled low over their faces.

The students still trapped behind the barricade were huddled in the centre of the square. More weapons than Ysbel could count were trained on them, and one move, one word, could get every one of them gunned down.

"Over against the wall, all of you!" an officer shouted.

There was a moment's hesitation. One of the officers stepped forward and swung their shock-stick, and a student crumpled. Ysbel bit back a curse as the officer swung the stick again into the student's prone body.

"I said, back against the wall!"

The students backed away, some whimpering or sobbing, others pale and silent. Officers waded in after them, swinging their shocksticks at anyone who didn't move quickly enough.

"You thought you could start a revolution?" one of them growled. "You and those vermin street kids? You damn innocents." The man's voice was thick with disdain.

The officer in charge strode over to the *Ungovernable* crew. Behind her, two other officers shoved Tae and Ivan forward, roughly enough that they landed hard on the concrete, unable to catch themselves with their bound hands. Ysbel sucked in a quick breath. They were both alive, at least, and both still conscious, but Tae's face was sick with pain, and he looked like he might vomit.

And then four Blood Riots came forward, dragging something behind them. They deposited their burdens unceremoniously on the concrete and stepped back.

Tae sucked in a short, sharp gasp, and Ysbel closed her eyes for a moment in horror.

Caz and Peti, both bound, lay still on the concrete. For a moment, she thought—But then Caz stirred, and Peti blinked her eyes open, and Ysbel let out a quick breath of relief.

They didn't look good—Caz had a black eye, and Peti was bleeding from the nose, an angry welt rising across the side of her face.

"These two were stirring up the street kids," said one of the Blood Riots. "Them, and those two over there," she added, gesturing with her chin at Tae and Ivan.

Ysbel hadn't thought she could be more horrified. But when one of the officers kicked Caz hard in the stomach, and he doubled over, choking for air, then did the same to Peti when she rolled over to help her brother, she had to turn away, swallowing through the tightness in her throat.

They were babies, practically, for all they'd had to grow up too quickly on the streets.

Olya and Misko. Caz and Peti. Vera and Tae and Dmitri. The students, huddled against the filthy alley wall.

It had been so much simpler when the people she'd die to protect had numbered three, instead of more than she could count.

"Must be tough, protecting the damn Svodrani System government when you're scared of a damn sixteen-year-old kid," Jez drawled, but Ysbel heard the sharp, hopeless anger in her voice. "Guess you don't—"

There was the unmistakable sound of a shock-stick hitting flesh. Jez's words cut off in a grunt of pain, and Lev choked out a curse. Jez drew in a quick breath, as if she was about to speak again, and then the shock-stick slammed down again, and she swore instead, her voice strained.

The officer in charge watched passively.

At last, when Jez's profanity had faded to gasps, the officer said, "Up against the wall, go on."

"What will happen to the others?" Tae said, voice tight. "We were the ringleaders."

The officer shrugged. "They'll be questioned. Arrested, some of them. Some of them we'll execute."

Tae closed his eyes for a moment, face ashy.

"And when did the police department start working with the gangs?" asked Lev in a level voice.

One of their guards shoved a shock-stick into his stomach, and he dropped to the ground, body stiffening at the jolt of electricity. At last they stepped back, and Lev collapsed, shaking. Jez tried to roll to her feet, but another of their guards kicked her viciously, and she doubled over, gasping for air.

"We take orders from the people authorized to give them," said the captain coldly. "That's all we need to know." She turned. "Get them against the wall."

Tanya caught her eye again as they were shoved back against the alley wall. Her face was pale, her expression sick.

She was thinking about their two children, frightened and alone, in the small room in the *Ungovernable*. Even after five years apart, Ysbel could read her wife's expressions like they were hers.

She touched Tanya's arm briefly, and Tanya gave her a weak smile.

Ysbel couldn't manage a smile back.

When the police stepped back, she glanced quickly around at the others.

Tae looked straight ahead, the grim hopelessness in his expression almost frightening. Ivan stood next to him, that muscle in the corner of his jaw working slightly. Caz and Peti were on their feet again, somehow, their postures stiff with pain. Even Vera and Dmitri seemed, at last, resigned to their fate.

If she'd had her damn electrical pulse weapon, maybe she could have done something with the guards at this close range. But she'd left it in the *Ungovernable* when they'd fled the hangar bay, along with her other prototypes.

She sighed, and leaned over to Vera.

"You know," she said quietly. "I don't particularly want to die. But if I'm going to—" she gave a small shrug. "I couldn't pick better company. Not that it means anything now."

Vera turned to her, eyes bright with unshed tears. "Coming from you, Professor—that actually means a lot."

Ysbel smiled slightly. "You know," she said, "when I was young, my parents took me away from Prasvishoni to be safe, to a small planet on the outer rim. That's where I grew up. That's where my children were born." She paused. "Perhaps I should have done the same thing, thought only about keeping my family safe. But there are children here on the streets, and children on the pleasure planet. And in the end, I couldn't."

Vera was watching her silently.

"You couldn't, either," Ysbel finished. "That's why I don't regret it. Because of people like you."

A tear trickled down Vera's face, and she turned away quickly.

The captain was directing four or five police officers into a row, handing them the wide-bore, long-range weapons that would take out a crowd of people in one shot.

Give enough of the officers that kind of weaponry, and even the ones who didn't want to shoot children like Caz and Peti would shoot, because they'd know the children would die anyways.

"I love you, Ysi," Tanya whispered. "Maybe we didn't win. But we tried."

"Yes," said Ysbel quietly. "We did try."

Tanya gave her a small smile, and Ysbel swallowed back tears.

There was a shout from outside the barricade. Ysbel looked up quickly.

Another shout, a confusion of noise. Ysbel frowned and half-turned, but the soldier holding her slammed his shock-stick into her back. She winced, biting back a curse, and stopped trying to move.

The commotion was growing louder. More voices, rising now.

The officers stared at each other, confused.

"Down with the fascist police!" someone shouted from the cluster of students.

Then the students surged forward, and the officers cursed and went for their weapons, and Ysbel jerked free of the guard's grip, throwing herself between Vera and Dmitri and the street kids—her family—and the impending blood bath.

33

Lev, day 17

Lev grunted as a shock stick hit him in the stomach. He landed on his knees, gasping, and when he looked up, it was into the muzzle of a heat gun.

He closed his eyes. Even after everything that had happened, he couldn't bear to see the shot that would kill him.

And then the officer grunted and stumbled forward, and the shot went wild, and Lev looked up to see Jez, a dangerous grin on her face and a large lump of prefab in her hand.

An officer grabbed her from behind, shoving her hard. There was a dull *crack* as her head hit the wall of the university gate, and Lev staggered to his feet, swearing, and glanced around quickly for something to distract them.

Perhaps they were all going to die—alright, probably they were. But as long as he was still alive, he'd be damned if he let someone hurt Jez.

Through the chaos, he could hear Ysbel's strained cursing, the students shouting, the fizz of a heat blast. An officer's amplified voice carried over the noise, but he couldn't make out their words.

The officer who'd shoved Jez was stalking towards her, yanking a pistol from its holster, and Lev grabbed him by the shoulder. As the officer spun to face him, he stomped down on the man's dangling boot laces. Caught off balance, the man staggered, then Jez had shoved herself off the wall and kicked him hard in the back of the knees.

He collapsed, and Jez planted a boot in his stomach for good measure, then grabbed Lev by the arm and dragged him out of what was now shaping into an impressive free-for-all brawl.

"What the hell is happening?" he muttered.

Jez shrugged, still grinning. "We're still alive, though, so—"

She was right. They should all be dead, there was no way the police and the gangs both should have been distracted enough for whatever the hell was happening to have happened …

For the first time, his mind registered the noise from outside the barricade, voices shouting, police sirens. They were close enough that he could make out the words in the shouting.

"Get off our damn streets! Down with the police!"

The police were stepping back from the melee, looking at each other with worry clear on their faces.

One by one, they started towards the opening in the barricade, first at a walk, then breaking into a run, until they were all but fleeing.

Lev stared after them in utter confusion. Around him, dazed students were doing the same.

Vera was staring at Tae, her expression slack with shock. "What —" she began.

Tae, who stood to one side of her, looked dazed and only about half-conscious. His face was smeared with blood, and his torn shirt revealed the spidery burn of a shock stick across his chest.

"Alright, tech-head, what did you just do?" panted Jez.

Tae blinked at her. Then he turned and blinked at Ivan for a few moments. And then, at last, he turned back to Vera. "You remember that first day?" he began slowly. "When I got a line through to the outside? And how just now, Ysbel's explosion took out the blockers, and I got it working again?"

Lev grinned suddenly as he realized what the kid was saying.

"I guess—I guess the rest of the city didn't like this any more than we did," Tae finished.

Vera stared at Tae for a moment, then she turned and grabbed Dmitri, who'd come up behind her, in a bear hug, laughing and slapping him on the back. "Dmitri! People from the projects came out! They're fighting back! You think that'll keep the police busy?"

Dmitri was grinning widely. "You know," he said. "I think it just might."

From outside the barricade there were shouts and screams, the sound of shock-sticks and heat guns.

Vera straightened, suddenly businesslike. "I'm going to let everyone know. Sounds like the people outside could use some help. And thanks to Ivan here, some of us have learned how to make a hell of a lot of chaos."

Jez grinned broadly. "And some of us knew how to make a hell of a lot of chaos before we even met Ivan." She turned to Lev. "Right, genius?"

Lev was smiling like an idiot, his entire body light.

Vera hit her com through to the student line and shouted, "There are people from the city outside! They're coming to stop this, and they could use some help!"

Students whooped and shouted, giddy with relief.

Jez grabbed her heat pistol from its holster. "You coming?" she said to Vera.

Vera grinned back, and they shoved their way forward.

Lev stooped and grabbed a fallen heat pistol, then straightened, looking around quickly.

"Here." Ysbel shoved something into his hand, and when he looked down, he saw it was a flash-bang. "This should give you a distraction if you need one," she said. She was smiling, but there was something about her smile that would have scared the hell out of him if he didn't know she was on his side.

He shoved his way through towards the barricades. Whatever was going on, it would be easier to come up with a strategy if he could see it clearly.

He could still make out Jez through the crowd at the entrance to the barricade. She was clearly in her element, shouting slogans, most of which probably didn't make sense and all of which contained an exorbitant amount of profanity, and firing with deadly accuracy at any officer who had the misfortune to be momentarily exposed by the shifting crowd. Ivan had reached the barricade, and he scrambled up to stand on top of it, shouting instructions through his voice-amp.

Lev pushed his way through to the barricade and followed Ivan up the side.

The streets in front of them were chaos—people shouting, screaming, attacking police officers and gang members alike with bits of broken prefab, ancient heat guns, even branches pulled from some of Prasvishoni's sickly trees. He could make out familiar forms here and there—Masha, Vera, Jez, who'd made it through the press at the entrance to the barricades and was now shouting cheerful insults as her shots took down officer after officer. She must have switched her heat gun for a stun gun, because their heat shields were doing nothing. Ysbel was easy to pick out, because there was a wide, terrified radius around her, and Tanya was easy to pick out because of the officers and gangsters toppling like children's bricks around her.

Lev studied the crowd for a moment, then tossed the flash-bang into the most concentrated mass of police, who looked like they were trying to regroup. He hit the controller, and the police in a ten-metre radius dived for the ground as it went off.

Ivan glanced over at him and grinned. Lev smiled back, then glanced out at the crowd again, searching for another target.

His eye caught on a woman at the front of the crowd, dressed in civilian clothes, eyes fixed on Ivan. He swore and dived for Ivan, knocking him to the ground as a laser shot lit the air above them.

Ivan flattened against the barricade, and Lev joined him.

"What—" Ivan began.

"Stay down," said Lev tersely. He squinted, searching the crowd. "That woman, there, and those three men. And over there, those five. They're not civilians, they're government, and they're the ones giving the orders. Watch out for them." He pulled out his pistol and fired off a shot, and the woman ducked back into the crowd.

"Noted," said Ivan, voice still slightly shaky. He got to his feet and held out his hand, pulling Lev up as well.

Tae clambered up beside them, breathing heavily. "What's happening?" he snapped.

Lev gestured out over the chaos in the streets. "It's promising, at the moment. There's too many civilians for the police to keep order, and the gangs are being split up. It will take them hours—days, maybe, to get this under control."

Tae gave a short nod. "Good. Some of the police behind the barricades regrouped. They've holding a group of students. I'm going to get them out."

"I'm coming," said Ivan. "You'll need backup."

Below them, Lev caught sight of Jez, in the centre of a sprawling, chaotic brawl. As he watched, she spun, planting her fist in the solar plexus of one a police officer who'd come up behind her, then dragging him around to crash into one of the Blood Riots. Both went sprawling, the gangster's shot going wide. Jez looked up at Lev and winked.

Then he noticed a plainclothes officer pushing through the crowd towards her.

He swore and grabbed for his heat pistol, but he couldn't be sure of hitting the officer through the crush.

"Jez!" he shouted, then gave it up and half scrambled, half fell down the front of the barricade.

The street was chaos, people shouting and shoving and screaming in pain, officers and gangsters and grim-faced Prasvishoni citizens grappling in the streets. The police were beating anyone who they managed to separate off, and here and there a knot of the citizens had managed to pull an officer to the ground and were kicking them, or pelting them with rocks and sticks.

Lev ignored it all, shoving his way through towards Jez, mumbling prayers under his breath to the Lady that he'd get there in time. She knew how to fight, yes, but she might not recognize the plainclothes officer as a threat, and he knew damn well that the police were shooting to kill.

Then he pushed past two brawling figures, and Jez was in front of him. She swung around, saw him, and swore, jerking her pistol up and sending the blast that would have knocked him flat harmlessly into the air.

"Genius! What the hell—"

He grabbed her elbow and yanked her down as the plainclothes officer behind her grabbed for the back of her jacket, the officer's other hand bringing up a deadly looking pistol.

He and Jez crashed ungracefully to the cement. Jez, who, whatever else she might be, wasn't slow on the uptake, grabbed the plainclothes officer by the ankle and yanked her down after them. The woman hit the ground hard

Jez grabbed her by the collar, slamming her head into the concrete. The woman grunted, losing her grip on her pistol, and grabbed for Jez's wrist with one hand. Her other hand came up, a second tiny pistol appearing there as if from thin air. Lev swore and shoved his hand into the outside pocket of her jacket. His fumbling fingers closed around a small, cylindrical object, and he yanked it out and jabbed it, hard, into the side of her neck.

The woman went limp.

Jez turned to Lev, eyebrows raised. "Not bad, genius," she shouted over the noise. "She dead?"

Lev shook his head, breathing heavily. "I don't know. They have serum that kills you, and serum that just knocks you out. Whichever she decided to carry, she deserves it."

Jez gave him a quick grin. "Thanks." She rolled painfully to her feet, and Lev scrambled up beside her.

"Tae and Ivan are trying to get some trapped students out," he shouted in her ear.

"Well, what are we waiting for?" she shouted back.

They pushed back towards the barricades, through the clambering, fighting mass of people. When they finally broke through, Lev glanced quickly around.

He saw the students at once—they were in one of the side alleys, pushed up against the university wall. Tae and Ivan crouched behind the shelter of a jumble of furniture and debris that had been knocked from the barricade, a few metres away.

The police were staring out at the square, their attention distracted. Lev jerked his head towards Tae and Ivan. Jez nodded, and they made their way quickly across the square towards them.

"What's happening?" Lev asked quickly as he and Jez ducked down beside them.

"The police are scared. They'll kill the students the moment they feel threatened," said Ivan, face grim.

"OK, so what do you want to do?" said Jez. "Because I damn well feel like threatening them right now."

By the look on Tae's face, he wouldn't have minded the same thing.

Lev paused. "Jez. Branka gave you a government code, right?"

Jez quirked an eyebrow. "For the classified crap she kept sending me home with? Yep." She grinned. "And, I even remember it."

Lev turned to Tae. "The password should get us into their private line. If we send out a distress call, we may be able to distract them."

Tae nodded tightly.

"Sent it through to your com, genius," said Jez, looking up.

Lev tapped his com, hit the code, and pulled up the police line.

"Ready?" he whispered.

Tae nodded. Jez grinned, but then, Jez always grinned when there was a chance she'd be punching someone in the near future.

He took a deep breath, then pitched his voice to an appropriately arrogant tone.

"What the hell are you lazy idiots doing, guarding a bunch of students?" he snapped into his com. "We've got an emergency over here. Sector twenty-seven. Get here, immediately."

Around the corner, he could see the officers looking at their coms in confusion, and then at each other.

He hadn't identified himself. Which was unavoidable, since he had no idea which commander these particular officers answered to, and no idea of the ID code even if he had known.

"Now!" Lev barked, making his voice even more arrogant.

One or two of the officers began to move, the others still frowning down at their coms.

By the time they looked up, Jez was standing in front of them, stun gun loose in her hands.

"You plaguers don't follow orders very well, do you?" she drawled.

Within a few moments, the officers were incapacitated.

Tae and Ivan got the terrified students moving towards the relative safety of the university, and Jez turned to grin at Lev. He put an arm around her waist, pulling her close for just a moment before they turned to go after Tae.

Then the noise from outside the barricades dimmed abruptly, and Jez turned to him, body tense.

He yanked up his holoscreen, flipping to the hacked government lines.

He stared at the screen for a moment, waiting for the words he was reading to make sense.

But no. He wasn't imagining it.

He looked up at Jez with a disbelieving smile.

"What?" she asked.

He pulled the screen around, and she frowned down at it. Then a slow grin spread across her face as well.

"Whole damn city's rising up, is it?" she said at last. "Not just the projects anymore."

"So it would appear," said Lev.

They looked at each other for a moment. Then Jez began to chuckle. Her chuckle grew into a laugh, and he joined her, and soon they were leaning on each other, wiping their eyes, and he wasn't even sure what they were laughing at.

Outside, the sirens' whines were growing fainter in the distance.

"I think," said Lev, when they'd recovered themselves, "the police have realized they are currently outmatched."

"Yeah?" said Jez. "About time they figured it out."

Lev turned to her, a fond smile on his face.

And that was the only reason that he caught, from the corner of his eye, a flicker of movement from behind one of the walls of the alley.

There was a split second where his mind took in the scene.

A police officer crouched behind the alley wall. The movement had been the officer lifting the gun, taking aim.

And Jez was directly in the line of fire.

He didn't have time to think, but then, he didn't need to. He'd always, somehow, known what he'd do. He stepped forward quickly, between Jez and the officer, just as the gun went off with a staticky hiss.

He felt the impact, but not the pain, and staggered back, and for a quick, disjointed moment, he was almost temped to laugh.

He hated being shot at. He'd always hated being shot at. And here he was, stepping in front of a heat blast.

And then his brain caught up with his body, and a searing, burning agony blossomed in his shoulder. He was falling, but he didn't really feel it, because he couldn't feel anything but the fiery pain.

Distantly, he heard Jez's wordless shout, heard running footsteps as the officer took off down the alley.

Lev blinked a few times, trying to bring the world back into focus. Jez's frantic face swam in front of his vision, hazy and blurred.

"Lev! Can you hear me? Lev!"

Her voice was desperate, and he wanted to say something, but he couldn't seem to form the words.

She stood, and he felt himself being half lifted, half dragged, and bit back a scream at the movement. And then he was being propped up on something soft, and once he'd caught his breath, he blinked open his eyes again.

Jez crouched in front of him, face set and bloodless, digging through a first-aid kit. "Lev, you damn plaguer, if you even think about bloody dying on me—" she choked. She yanked out a blast kit and ripped it open with her teeth, then pulled a gutting knife from her belt and slit his jacket neatly around the wound. She gritted her teeth, gently peeling back the burned fabric, and for a moment he thought he might pass out.

"Easy there," she muttered through her teeth. "It'll feel better in a minute, I promise." She finished with the cloth, pulled back the wrappings on the heat kit, and sealed it gently over the wound.

He dropped his head back as the soothing cool of it cut through the burning agony.

Gentle hands leaned him back against a wall, settling him into a more comfortable position, but the breathless relief of the cool against the searing pain in his shoulder was making him almost lightheaded.

At last, he opened his eyes.

He was in a small shelter, something the students must have set up when they were behind the barricades.

Jez stood by the door, peering out, heat gun in her hand, expression grim. She turned at his movement, and crossed over to him quickly, dropping down in front of him.

"Lev, are you alright? Are you—" Her voice choked slightly. "Lev

—"

This time, by sheer force of will, he made his muscles move, and he managed to put a hand on her arm. "Jez. I'm fine. I'm alright."

She studied him for a moment, her face haunted, as if trying to decide whether he was actually still alive, or if he was trying to lie to her from beyond the grave.

At last, her shoulders slumped in relief.

He smiled, despite the throbbing pain. "I'm still alive, I promise. You can feel my pulse if you want."

She gave a shaky, reluctant smile. "Yeah? Well, don't ever damn well scare me like that again, OK?"

He made a wry grimace. "Believe me, Jez, I have no intention of doing so."

She snickered slightly, and then her laugh turned into a sort of gulping sob, and she turned away quickly, wiping her eyes.

He put his hand on her arm again, even though the movement made the room sway slightly. "Jez. It's alright."

At last, she turned back to him and took a few deep breaths. She closed her eyes, then, when she'd regained her composure, she studied him for a long, long moment.

"Do you—do you promise you're alright?" she asked at last. "You're not about to die or anything?"

He nodded.

She knelt, so her head was level with his. Without taking her eyes off him, she reached out and brushed a hand across his cheek.

Somehow, despite the throbbing pain, a shiver ran through him at her touch.

She ran her thumb along the line of his cheekbone, her hand cool against his face.

For some reason that had nothing to do with heat gun blasts, he was finding it much more difficult to breathe than it should have been.

Gently, she slid her hand around behind his head, up into his hair, and, still without taking her eyes from his, she leaned in, and touched her lips to his forehead.

Another shiver ran through his body, and the pain from the heat blast wound seemed somehow much less important than it had been a few seconds ago.

She leaned in again, her lips brushing up his cheekbone.

His breath was coming quickly, his heart pounding.

She kissed the corner of his jaw, her touch impossibly soft.

The ache from the heat gun was still there, but it was, at this point, completely overshadowed by the sensation of Jez's lips on his skin.

She kissed the very corner of his mouth.

He could hardly breathe.

And then, very, very gently, she touched her lips to his.

It was the merest touch, so delicate it could hardly be called a kiss, but it seemed to shoot a jolt of electricity through every part of his brain and body.

She drew back, and there was something in her eyes that was part relief, and part concern, and part desire, and so completely Jez that it almost stopped his breath.

"You sure you're alright, genius?" she whispered.

He didn't answer, just leaned forward, and she leaned in to meet him.

This time, the kiss was much less gentle, which was completely fine by him. He slipped his good arm around her waist and pulled her closer, and she slid her hands down the side of his face, down his neck and his shoulders, trailed her fingers down his back. He groaned, and he could feel her smiling wickedly against his lips. Her hand slid around his waist, under his shirt, and he groaned again, feeling suddenly lightheaded.

She pulled back slightly, and something about the raw desire in her eyes sent a rush of warmth through him, and a burning ache in the pit of his stomach. He grabbed her, and she let him pull her forward so she was straddling his lap. He settled her hips hard against his and leaned them both backward against the walls of the makeshift shelter. She moaned, and he could feel the racing of her heart, the way her entire body responded to his kiss, his touch. He kissed her harder, peeling off her jacket with his free hand and running his hand from the nape of her neck all the way down her back, and she gave little, breathless gasps, her fingers tightening reflexively into his hair.

And then the wall of the shelter they were leaned against shifted slightly, tilting backwards, and the movement jostled his injured shoulder.

For a moment, everything went hazy.

When he opened his eyes again, Jez was leaning over him, face bloodless and worried.

Her lips, though, were still swollen, and there were traces of passion in her eyes, and her jacket was halfway off, her shirt underneath untucked, her hair disheveled, her face flushed. And for half a second, despite everything, Lev wanted nothing more than to grab her and pull her back down again, passing out be damned.

She scowled at him, and said, her voice unsteady, "Genius. Why didn't you tell me you were about to bloody faint?" She stood quickly, hitting her com. "Ysbel, Tae, anytime you feel like showing up, that would be great. Lev's bloody shot, and we need to get him taken care of."

She crouched him beside him again, her face tight with concern. "I spent however many damn months wanting to get inside your pants so bad I could hardly bloody stand it, and then we finally get crap figured out, and if you damn well die on me now—"

He stared at her. "You—" he began stupidly.

She glared at him. "What the hell do you think? I—look. It's like I said back there in the government building. If—" Her voice faltered a little, and she looked down. "If you want to, I mean. I mean, if you don't—"

He put a hand on her arm to stop her, and finally she looked up and met his eyes.

"Jez," he said quietly.

She just looked at him.

Despite his throbbing shoulder, despite the fact that he'd very nearly passed out only a few moments before and wasn't sure how long this bout of consciousness would last, despite everything, he found he was smiling.

"Jez," he said again. "What the actual hell do you think that just was?"

She was still looking at him skeptically.

He blew out a shaky breath. "Jez. I want you so damn badly that even though I'm currently on the verge of passing out, the only thing I can think about is whether I can somehow manage another kiss before it happens."

She was still staring at him.

He shook his head. "Yes. Yes, I want you. I've wanted you almost since the moment I damn well met you. I want to have sex with you, more than I can possibly express right now. But—that's not all I want. I want you. I want you with me. I want to wake up next to you, want to hang up your coat when you come in on a cold winter day. I want to sit in the cockpit beside you, see everything you see when you look out that window. Jez, I—Jez, I want you more than I've ever wanted anything in my life." His voice choked slightly.

"Yeah?" she said. Her voice was shaky too, and thick, like she was fighting back tears. "Well, if that's true, guess I'm going to have to stop calling you genius-boy."

He managed a fond smile.

Then he fainted.

34

Masha, day 17, late

Masha glanced around the small hangar bay. The whole crew was there—Tanya had slipped away to retrieve the children, but she was back now, and Olya and Misko were clinging to her and Ysbel like they'd never let go. Ivan was there too, of course. Looking at him, his arm protectively around Tae, Masha was fairly certain he wouldn't be letting Tae out of his sight anytime soon.

Somehow, despite everything that had happened, the thought made her smile.

Caz and Peti and the rest of Tae's street kids had stayed back by the barricades with the university students to regroup, form plans for tomorrow. But her crew had come back here, to the hangar bay they'd used in their first job, when they weren't yet crew and were hardly more than strangers, to work on their own strategy.

"Well," said Masha at last. "Against all odds, we survived."

Lev, who was sitting leaned against one wall, his face tight with pain, looked up at her quickly. "Yes," he said in a measured voice. "But it wasn't exactly what you had planned, was it, Masha?"

She watched him, not letting her expression change.

The truth was, of course, that he was right.

How had she somehow underestimated her own crew? Or maybe she'd just overestimated her own ability to control them. What was happening now, in the streets, at the barricades—that wasn't supposed to have happened. Unrest, yes—the police busy with students protesting, with street kids in places they weren't supposed to be, with gangs, who couldn't start their bloody war because the street kids were blocking them—that's what was supposed to have happened.

Not this. Not a full-blown revolution.

The police had been routed today, yes. But they'd be back tomorrow in force, and they'd likely bring the army. The government wouldn't tolerate an assault on its sovereignty like this. It couldn't afford to, especially not with Grigory and Olyessa gone.

It was never supposed to have happened like this.

Jez was crouched beside Lev. She'd slipped her hand into his, her knuckles white, her grip almost desperate. She glanced up at Masha's words and gave her a small grin.

"Well, those bastards in the government damn well did what we wanted." She paused. "Other than Branka trying to torture us to death, I mean."

Masha smiled faintly. "I suspect you're correct, Jez," she said quietly.

That was the other thing she'd underestimated. She'd wanted the government officials to take Jez seriously. But only enough to keep the government from imploding when word of Grigory and Olyessa came out, nothing more.

Instead, the crazy, lunatic pilot, with Lev's unassailable, level-headed suggestions to back her up, had managed to strong-arm Branka into restructuring the entire government. They'd shut out Grigory's and Olyessa's people completely.

Ultimately, it was the outcome she'd wanted. But not like this. There hadn't been enough time to get people used to the idea. The ministers in power now didn't have alliances built up, or the ear of the government power-brokers. Even without the backing of Grigory and Olyessa, the officials who'd been ousted did.

Masha had been trying to prevent a governmental internecine war. But she'd underestimated Jez's power of—well, perhaps persuasion wasn't the correct word. Her ability to coerce, harass, exasperate, and threaten people until they damn well did what she wanted them to, and Lev's ability to come up with logical, foolproof plans that were almost impossible to argue against.

She should never have left them to their own devices. She should have known better.

But then, she hadn't had a choice. This plan had always depended on her being able to control them, and she'd managed to underestimate them.

There was something cold in her chest.

This was moving far, far too quickly, completely out of her control.

"At least we accomplished the bare minimum that we set out to do," she said at last. "News of Grigory and Olyessa's death didn't cause a complete bloodbath." She glanced wryly at Tae. "Of course, the system is now on the verge of implosion despite that, but we managed to defang that particular sand snake, I think."

"I suppose we did," Lev murmured. He looked around the room, and she noticed he avoided her eyes. "And now we'll need to discuss our next steps."

They'd all turned to look at her.

She managed a smile, despite the sickness turning in her stomach. "Considering the inroads Lev and Jez have made in the government, it seems a waste of an opportunity not to take advantage of it. I have connections there, and I can get us inside as lower-level officials. We may have to come up with an alternate plan for Jez and Lev, as they will be recognized, but the rest of you—"

"And the people in the streets?" asked Ysbel softly. "Tae's street kids? My students?"

Masha drew in a long breath. "I'm sorry, Ysbel," she said quietly. "There's nothing we can do for them. They're going to die. They can't win against the government." She shook her head. "But we can at least make sure they don't die in vain. It's possible we can use our knowledge of what's happening behind the barricades to buy favours from the government, get ourselves into the necessary positions. If we're going to keep the system from a civil war, we have to shut down the factions that are trying to form an alliance between the boyeviki, the gangs, and the government itself, before they can undo everything that we did by taking down Grigory. Everyone behind the barricades will be slaughtered regardless, but at least their deaths can serve a greater cause."

There was a long moment of silence from the crew.

"And when you say, 'use our knowledge of what's happening behind the barricades'—you intend for us to sell them out," said Lev, his voice very quiet.

"As I said. Whatever we do, they'll be killed. At least we can use that to—"

"No," said Tae. His voice was also quiet, but hard as steel. "I won't sell out people who trusted me. I won't betray my friends. I'm not like you, Masha."

"And nor will the rest of us. My students believe I'll help them. I won't betray that." Ysbel's tone was flat and uncompromising.

Masha blew out a quick, frustrated breath. "I understand your position, Tae. But there's more at stake here than the lives of few street kids and college students." She closed her eyes a moment, trying to force a calm she didn't feel into her voice. "They're important to you, I understand that. But are they more important than the lives of every person in the system? What we've done— what we're on the verge of doing—is more important than you know. And if you throw that away for a few lives of a few young idealists—"

Tae's voice was still soft. "I won't sell them out. If you thought I'd even consider it, you never knew me at all. I promised to help them. That's the only reason they did what they did. And if your version of saving the system means I stab them in the back and leave them to die, then it's not a system worth saving."

Masha watched him for a long time. There was something about him that hadn't been there when he'd first joined the crew—a determination, a quiet self-confidence.

He'd changed. All of them had changed. And that's what she hadn't taken into account, during all those long years when she was forming her plan.

When she'd brought them together, they'd been her perfect tools —skilled, talented, brilliant, and alone. Angry at the system, angry at the government, with nothing to live for and no one to care about outside of their small crew.

And now—

She wasn't entirely sure when it had started going sideways— when it had started spinning out of her control, and she'd been blind to it.

No, she knew. It was when she'd stopped thinking of them as tools, and started thinking of them as her crew. She'd known it was dangerous, and she'd done it anyways. And that had been when she begun to let everything go wrong.

She took a deep breath. "I understand your concerns, Tae," she said quietly. "However," she paused for a moment, almost unable to say what she was going to say next.

Because it hadn't been just her crew she'd misjudged. She'd misjudged her own ability to see the situation clearly, unemotionally, as she had to for her plan to succeed.

And she didn't want to say what she was going to say next. She didn't want to say it, and then have to meet the eyes of the lanky, cocky pilot crouched next to Lev. The one who, when all the rest of the crew had been willing to sell her out in exchange for their own safety—and, if she were being honest, she would have deserved it— had talked them into coming to her instead. The one who'd trusted her.

The one who still, perhaps, trusted her. At least, until she finished her next sentence.

But she could only put it off for so long.

Somehow, she managed to keep a faint, bland smile on her face. "I think, perhaps, you may decide to come with me after all," she said quietly.

They were watching her, and Jez's face had a look of faint curiosity.

Masha forced her gaze to remain steady.

"You see," she continued, and her blandest voice. "The hangar bay, where we stored the *Ungovernable*, with all Tae's tech, and Ysbel's supplies, and Lev's information chips." This time, she couldn't make herself look at Jez. "I understand it's surrounded by government agents. I understand that they intend to blow it sky-high, unless someone in the government tells them to stand down. And I have connections to the person who can tell them to stand down."

There was a long, long moment of silence. Still, Masha couldn't bring herself to look at Jez.

"Masha," said Lev quietly.

Something in his tone made her turn towards him, despite herself.

He was watching her, his expression almost pitying. "I have no doubt what you said is true. However—" he paused. "However, Ysbel intercepted one of your messages. She passed it on to me, and I was able to track down who it was sent to, and then track down a copy of what was sent. And since that time, Jez took an afternoon off to run a small errand.

"I'm certain that the police are, as you say, surrounding the hangar bay at this moment. And I'm also certain that they'll use their explosives, something powerful enough to cut through even Tae's shields, the specs of which you passed along to them, the moment your contact in the government gives the word. But the *Ungovernable* isn't there. It's somewhere safe, somewhere you won't find it. And so, Masha—" his voice was almost gentle now. "I'm afraid that this time, you don't have anything to hold over us."

She studied him for a long moment, something sick twisting in her chest. She had no doubt that what he was saying was true.

She'd gambled everything. And this time, she'd lost.

She still couldn't meet Jez's gaze. So she just looked at Lev for a long, long time.

At last, she gave a faint smile. "Well, Lev," she said at last. "As always, your intelligence has managed to impress me." She glanced around the hangar bay. "I suppose you're right. I have nothing to hold over you. I can't stop you from going back to the streets, fighting your revolution, doing whatever it is you think you can do to keep these friends of yours from being slaughtered. I would say that's an impossible task. But, you've proved yourselves more than capable of pulling off the impossible before."

He frowned slightly, a small crease appearing between his eyebrows. "That's all?" he said finally.

She was still smiling, somehow. "I'm not entirely sure what else there is. I've told you what I intend to do. You've told me that you intend to throw in your lot with your revolutionary friends. And as you pointed out, I have no hold over you. So—" She had to swallow down something in her throat, but her voice came out calm. "I suppose we go our separate ways."

She turned away quickly. She wasn't sure she could say anything further without her voice shaking, and she wasn't sure that she could keep the bland, polite expression on her face a moment longer.

She wasn't sure, between the sick horror, and the aching relief, which would win out.

She'd lost her crew. After everything she'd done, everything she'd gambled, she'd lost her crew.

But now, perhaps, they had a chance to live through what was coming next. If they were smart enough, and skeptical enough, they might have a chance.

She crossed to the end of the hangar bay, where she'd left her bag with the small number of possessions she still needed.

She hadn't cried, not since she was seven years old. Not once. And now, she wasn't sure whether the tears stinging the corners of her eyes were tears of exhaustion, or tears of regret, or tears of failure, or tears of relief.

She'd almost finished gathering her things when she heard a sound, and looked up quickly.

There was, of course, always the possibility that one of them would kill her. As she'd said to Lev, she had no more hold over them.

It was Jez. The pilot had come over, and now she crouched down beside her, her eyes on Masha's face. And this time, Masha couldn't avoid her gaze.

She braced herself for the look of hurt, of betrayal, of hatred.

And she'd deserve it. She'd known that when she'd made her choices. But that didn't make it easier.

Jez studied her, not dropping her eyes. But the look in them wasn't what Masha had expected.

She couldn't read the pilot's expression, but there was something in it of curiosity, and something of concern, and something that could almost have been sympathy.

"Yes, Jez?" said Masha, when Jez didn't speak.

"You could come with us," said Jez at last, her voice quiet. "You don't have to do this."

Something tightened in Masha's throat, and for a moment, she couldn't breathe.

Jez's gaze didn't falter, and she watched Masha steadily. "I told you once that I trusted you," she said finally. "Don't know why, because hell, Masha, you can be a damn bastard when you want to be. But—I did. I still do. Even after everything, I still do." She paused a moment. "It's not too late."

Masha closed her eyes.

Whatever was swirling inside her was sick and uncomfortable, a shaky, hopeless weakness that she hadn't felt in decades.

That she couldn't remember feeling since the weeks after her parents were killed.

But—she'd given up everything for this. She'd spent her whole life preparing for it. And she couldn't let anyone—not even the snarky, ridiculous pilot who had somehow become one of the most important people in the system to her—get in the way.

In the end, what she'd told Tae was true. She could choose to save her friends, or she could choose to save the system. Tae had made that choice one way, and she couldn't fault him for it.

But nor could she make the same choice.

At last she opened her eyes, and managed a small smile. "Jez," she said, trying to keep her voice from shaking. "I … appreciate your offer. More than I can say. But—I'm afraid I have work to do."

She rose quickly, before she could find some excuse for second thoughts, and pulled her coat tightly around her, tucking her scarf close around her head and face. She stepped to the door and put a hand on the handle.

"Auntie Masha?" came Misko's small voice. "Where's Auntie Masha going?"

"I'm sorry, Misko," she heard Ysbel murmur. "Auntie Masha's very busy."

She allowed herself one final glance behind her.

Jez was still crouched where she'd left her, looking after her steadily.

Then Masha turned and stepped out the door, closing it firmly behind her, and into the darkness and the swirling snow of the Prasvishoni winter night.

35

Afterwords

Jez felt an almost physical jolt of relief as her foot touched the loading ramp to the *Ungovernable*.

She was back on her ship. And somehow, everything would be alright.

She closed her eyes, and tried not to think how close she'd come to losing it forever.

When Lev had told her, in his calm, quiet voice, what he'd learned about Masha—the message she'd sent, when she didn't think anyone else was listening—the shock of betrayal had been so sharp it hurt.

And yet, still, a few minutes ago. She'd crouched down beside Masha, and told her that she still trusted her.

She wasn't completely sure why she'd done that. But she supposed, in the end, in a strange sort of way—it was true.

She gave a slight shake of her head.

Not that it mattered now. Masha was gone, and something about the look on her face when she told them goodbye, stepped out into the cold, blowing night—somehow, Jez knew she was gone for good.

As of that moment, they were no longer crewmates. They were adversaries. And she knew damn well that Masha was a ruthless adversary.

She'd expected to feel something stronger at that thought. Even still, something hard and sick clenched in her stomach at the memory of the look on Masha's face—a sort of resolve, a determination—and regret. Jez had seen that sharp regret.

Regret, perhaps, for what she'd done, or what she'd tried to do. Or what she was about to do.

Honestly, much as she wanted to, she couldn't hate Masha for it.

But nor could she give her another chance. Masha had proven, regret or no, she was a risk they could no longer afford. Not if they wanted to keep themselves and their friends alive.

Ahead of her, Lev gave a sharp grunt of pain as he stumbled, foot catching on the lip of the final step into the *Ungovernable*. She stiffened involuntarily, but Tanya, who was supporting him, caught him before he could stumble again.

Jez had offered to let him lean on her—hell, she'd almost insisted on it—but Ysbel had pointed out, none too gently, that if Jez passed out or fell on her face, as she was increasingly feeling like she might do, it wouldn't do either her or Lev any favours.

And, in fairness, Ivan had had to let go of Tae and grab her twice on their way over, so she supposed Ysbel might've had a point.

After what had happened, they couldn't stay in the hangar bay, where Masha knew where they were, and with no guarantee she wouldn't use that knowledge. Jez still hoped, somehow, she wouldn't have. But she wasn't willing to risk their lives on the chance.

And so they'd made their exhausted, painful way through the icy Prasvishoni winter night, with Tae's tracking set up to alert them if they were being traced, to the small smuggler docking bay where they'd hidden the *Ungovernable*.

Tomorrow they'd join the others behind the barricades. But the smuggler bay was close to the university, and Lev needed a soft place to sleep tonight, injured as he was. Give the blast kit a night to do its work before they returned to the streets.

When they took their seats around the *Ungovernable's* conference table, Lev leaned forward. Sharp pain was written across his face, but his eyes held the same keen intelligence as always.

"So," he said at last. "I suppose we plan our next steps."

"You heard Masha," grunted Ysbel. "She's going to try to sell us out." She gave a quick, wry shake of her head. "I don't even know why. I still don't know what she's after. But she won't be an easy one to go up against."

Jez tried to ignore the way her stomach tightened at Ysbel's words.

Lev nodded. "So we'll have to factor Masha in, as well as the police." He turned. "Tae, Ivan? You spent the most time at the barricades. What are the chances that we can put them back up?"

Tae gave a short shake of his head. "I don't know," he said tersely. "Everyone behind the barricades will keep fighting. They don't have a choice. But I don't know how long we'll survive, hemmed in like that. And if they bring in the military, the barricades won't provide much protection."

"If that bastard police commissioner had listened to me instead of Branka—" Jez muttered.

Tae turned to stare at her. "You—they discovered you were an ex-convict smuggler pilot, and were going to torture you for information."

She rolled her eyes. "Yeah? Well, the bastard could have still done what he promised."

Lev shot her an amused glance. "Be that as it may, perhaps we can at least take advantage of the current disruption to find a more defensible location." He turned to Ivan. "You've done this before.

What do we need to take into account?"

Ivan gave a rueful shake of his head. "I've run protests before, yes. This is my first revolution. But—I suppose the principles would be similar." He chewed on his lip. "We'll need somewhere we're protected from the heavy weaponry, that's our biggest priority. We'll need shelter, and if possible, enough ways of getting in and out that it will be difficult to cut us off completely."

Lev turned to Tae. "I'll look through the map, but I suspect your street kid friends will be better informed than I am."

Tae nodded. "Peti will be the best one to talk to. When we're back behind the barricades, I'll ask her to come find you."

Lev looked around the table with a small, wry smile. "It appears, after all that, we're doing exactly what Masha intended—we're going to take down the whole Svodrani system government, or die trying."

Ysbel chuckled. "Yes," she said. "Who would have thought?"

Jez almost grinned. If someone had told her six months ago this is what she'd be doing with her life—well, OK, she wouldn't have found it all that surprising, to be honest. But the reasons she was doing it? That would have surprised the hell out of her.

Olya stirred sleepily in Ysbel's arms, and Ysbel glanced down at her. "I suppose I'd better get these children to bed," she said.

Tanya nodded. "I'll come with you." She gathered the sleeping Misko and followed Ysbel from the room.

Jez, Lev, Tae, and Ivan sat in silence for a few moments, none of them seeming to want to be the first to leave. At last, though, Ivan got to his feet and held out a hand to Tae.

"Come on," he said quietly. "Bed. It's been a long day, and this may be the last time we have a warm place to sleep for a while. We may as well take advantage of it."

Tae gave him a small smile and took the proffered hand, pulling himself to his feet. He stumbled from the room, half supported by Ivan, and Jez watch them go, grinning.

"You think they'll end up in the same cabin?" she asked, once they were gone.

Lev chuckled softly. "This is Tae we're talking about."

She grinned. "You're right. If they did end up in the same cabin, Tae would probably just offer Ivan his bed and sleep on the floor." She paused a moment. "It's a damn good thing Ivan's the patient type."

Lev nodded, still smiling faintly, but he saw his quick, involuntary wince as he leaned back.

She scowled. "Speaking of getting to bed, think it's about damn time that you lie down."

He looked for a moment as if he was going to protest, but instead, he just gave a weary nod.

Ysbel appeared in the doorway a few moments later.

"I'm here to make sure Lev gets to sleep," she said dryly. "Because he just got shot, and I don't think we'll be able to outsmart our friend Masha without his assistance." She paused, and glared suspiciously at Jez. "And also because I don't trust the two of you. Considering how much fun you had playing lovers."

Lev sighed, pushed himself to his feet, and bit back a gasp. Jez and Ysbel both grabbed for him, but Ysbel, who was significantly steadier on her feet, reached him first, catching him as he grabbed the table for support.

"You see," she grumbled. "This is exactly what I mean. Come on."

Lev let himself be led away, reluctance clear on his face.

To be perfectly honest, Jez was feeling a little reluctant about it as well. But—well, considering he'd actually passed out the last time they kissed, maybe Ysbel was right.

When everyone had gone, Jez glanced around, letting the quiet peace of being here, on her ship, wash through her like warm water. At last, she wandered down to the hallway that led to the cockpit. She stepped through the familiar door, pulling it closed behind her, and for a moment, something caught in her chest.

Everything in her damn life seemed to begin and end here, in this cockpit. This was her home. This was the one place in the world that she never had to wonder whether or not she belonged.

But tomorrow morning, when she left it, headed back out behind the barricades with those ridiculous university students to continue their frankly impossible fight against the entire damn system government—

Well, she'd be doing it because she wanted to. Not because anyone had tricked her, or coerced her, or guilted her. Because as surely as she'd found a home, here in this cockpit, she found something else, too. This damn ridiculous cause, with all these damn ridiculous people—it wasn't something she was just going along with anymore. Somehow, she wasn't sure exactly how or when, these ridiculous students, their ridiculous idealism, the street kids being hunted down by police officers on orders of some government official that she probably, honestly, knew by name at this point—fixing this for them had become her cause, too. Something she cared about, maybe enough to die for.

Enough to leave her ship for, anyways, which honestly was a hell of a lot bigger of a sacrifice.

She ran her fingers idly across the *Ungovernable's* smooth controls, staring out the cockpit window into the black of the smuggler bay.

Her ship would be safe here, which was the important thing. And hopefully she'd survive this, make it back. Hopefully she'd survive

Masha, and the police, and everything else, and come back to her beautiful ship. Maybe even sometime soon.

She gave a small smile.

It had been a hell of a last few weeks. And a hell of a lot had happened. She still wasn't sure she could think too long or too hard about the way Masha had looked at her, before she stood up, gathered her things, and stepped out the door, because if she did, her entire heart might break in half.

She wasn't sure, exactly, what she was feeling—happiness, fear, nerves, heartbreak—but for the first time in a very long time—the first time in her life, maybe—she knew exactly what she planned to do tomorrow. And better than that—she knew why.

Tae's head ached. His whole body ached, honestly. There was a throbbing lump at the base of his skull, and when he stood up or sat down too quickly, the world still spun dizzyingly.

Somehow, though, he was alive. Somehow, they'd all made it through, at least for now.

He glanced over at Ivan walking next to him, his hand half-outstretched to catch Tae if he needed it.

He looked, frankly, almost as bad as Tae felt—there were dark circles under his eyes, and the haunted expression on his face that hadn't really gone away since Tae suggested—insisted, really—that Ivan leave him to die, and go back for the rest of the students.

But—he would have done it.

Tae wondered when, exactly, he'd become so sure of that. When he'd first known, bone deep and without a doubt, that Ivan would be there, and would do what needed to be done, whatever it cost him. But he could tell in the way Ivan watched the street kids and the students. Ivan cared about them just as much as he did. And he'd do whatever it took—even leaving Tae, if that's what Tae asked, and what he needed—to keep them safe.

Ivan paused in front of Tae's cabin door, a small smile on his face. "I'll leave you here then," he said, the usual good humour in his voice.

Tae smiled up at him wearily, and again, felt that strange, ridiculous rush of relief. "Thanks," he said quietly, although 'thanks' wasn't nearly enough to say what he meant.

'I love you,' wasn't either, but he said it anyways.

Ivan turned Tae gently to face him. "Tae. It's going to be alright. We're going to fix this. Because there are people out there who care just as much as you do. Just as much as I do. And we won't let your street kid friends die, and we won't let the government kill the students, and we won't let them take back the city for the gangs. It's not just you anymore."

Tae looked away quickly, swallowing hard.

It was true. Maybe it had always been, but for the first time, finally, he realized it.

Jez hadn't had to go back into the government offices, three days after she'd almost died from an attempted assassination. Lev hadn't had to put himself at odds with Masha. Tanya and Ysbel hadn't had to leave their children and walk into the middle of a battle. They could've taken Olya and Misko, found a safe place to wait it out. He wouldn't have blamed them one bit.

But they hadn't.

Ivan brushed the hair out of Tae's face and kissed him gently on the forehead. "Sleep well," he said quietly.

Tae smiled and kissed Ivan back, on the lips this time, and like always, Ivan's kiss sent a warmth through his entire body.

When at last they drew apart, Ivan gave him that soft smile that knotted something up in his chest so he wasn't sure whether he wanted to laugh, or cry, or maybe both.

"I love you, Tae," he said quietly. He gave Tae's shoulder a last squeeze, then turned and walked down towards his own cabin.

Tae watched him go, until his door closed behind him. And then, at last, he turned to his own door.

His cabin, here on the *Ungovernable*, was as comfortable and as much a home as any place he'd ever been in his life. But that wasn't what spread the comforting warmth through his chest.

He wasn't alone. He hadn't been, for a very, very long time. But it had taken him a long damn time to realize it.

He closed the door, and dropped wearily on his cot, and for the first time in a very long time, slept.

Ysbel jerked her head up at the sound of a small cry from the children's room. Tanya had started awake as well, but Ysbel laid a hand on her arm. "I'll get it, my love," she whispered, voice rough with sleep.

She rolled out of bed and opened the door that connected their room with the children's, flipping on her com light. In its dim glow, she could see Olya, pressed against the head of the bed, blankets pulled up around her, eyes wide and frightened.

"Mama?" she whispered.

Looking closer, Ysbel could see the tears in her eyes.

She crossed quickly over to her daughter and gathered her into her arms. "Olyeshka," she murmured into her daughter's hair. "I'm here. I'm right here. What's wrong?"

Olya buried her head in Ysbel's shoulder, and Ysbel could feel her small body shaking. "I—I thought you were dead," she said, her voice muffled. "I thought somebody had shot you. I was scared,

Mama."

"It's alright, my Olya," she whispered. "Do you want to come sleep with your mamochka and me tonight?"

Olya nodded, not removing her face from Ysbel's shoulder, and Ysbel carried her back into her and Tanya's bedroom.

Tanya shifted to give her room, and Ysbel tucked Olya in between them. She was asleep in moments.

"What was it?" Tanya asked softly.

Ysbel shook her head. "She had a nightmare. That I'd been killed."

For a long moment, neither of them spoke. At last, Tanya said softly, "They'll never be children like we were, will they?"

It wasn't really a question.

Ysbel shook her head, looking down at her daughter.

Even in her sleep, Olya's face was tight with strain and worry.

"No," she said quietly. "They won't."

For a few moments, there was silence. At last, Ysbel raised her eyes and caught Tanya's gaze.

"But," she said quietly. "If we fight this—if we keep fighting this, until things change, or we die trying to change them—maybe her children will. And maybe for them, it won't be a lie."

Tanya studied her for a long moment. And then she gave Ysbel that wistful smile that Ysbel loved so much. "I think you're right, my Ysi," she said.

Ysbel leaned forward and kissed her wife, over her sleeping daughter's head.

Lev wasn't sure what had woken him. For a few moments he lay there in the dim half-light, coming, it appeared, from an emergency light-bar someone had set on his desk. He stared up at the ceiling, feeling the comfortable, familiar cot underneath him, the familiar imperfections that would have told him exactly where he was, even if it had been pitch black.

There was a small sound from the corner, the quiet brush of cloth against a hard surface, and he jerked upright, panic jolting through him. The movement sent a wave of pain through his shoulder, but he shoved it back.

And then he saw what had made the sound—what had probably woken him in the first place—and smiled slightly, lowering himself carefully back down on the cot.

Jez was sitting in the corner, propped up against the wall, her head tipped back, eyes closed, legs splayed out in front of her. She looked exhausted.

He gave a rueful shake of his head.

He could just let her sleep, but she didn't look comfortable. And he doubted he'd be able to fall back asleep himself knowing she was sitting just a metre or so away, in a position that would certainly give her a kink in her neck, if not worse.

"Jez," he whispered softly.

She started, sitting up with a jerk, and glanced around her in panic.

"Jez," he said. "It's alright. It's just me."

Her eyes found him, and her whole body relaxed. "What're you doing awake?" she asked, her voice cracking from sleep. "Pretty sure I remember you being hit by a heat gun. I think you're supposed to rest after something like that."

He chuckled softly. "And I'm not certain you're the right person to be telling me that. Considering your history."

She rolled her eyes and pushed herself up so she was sitting straighter. "How're you feeling?" she asked softly.

"A surprising amount better," he said, smiling.

It was the truth. Jerking upright had hurt, but if his injury felt anything like it had that afternoon, something like that would have led to him immediately passing out. The soothing coolness of the heat kit over the wound had done a lot to cut the pain, and he knew there was some sort of topical painkiller in it as well.

"What are you doing?" he asked.

She raised an eyebrow at him. "Came to check that you were still breathing. Considering how you looked when you finally went off to bed. And—guess I fell asleep." She paused a moment. "And—" she looked away, not meeting his eyes. "And, um, couldn't really sleep anyways. Guess I'm not used to sleeping alone anymore."

He looked at her for a moment—eyes heavy with sleep, a bruise across her face, dried blood crusted down her chin—and gave a small smile. "I know my cot isn't anything special, but it's certainly better than the floor."

She quirked an eyebrow at him. "There's room?"

"I can scoot over."

She hesitated a moment. "I thought you were maybe about to die or something."

"I'm fairly certain that someone jostling the bed as they get in isn't going to send me over the edge."

At last, still watching him warily, as if worried that he might either keel over or pass out, she stood and crossed over to the bed. She hesitated a moment, and he scooted back farther.

At last she sighed and climbed into bed next to him, shifting as she made herself comfortable.

The familiar warmth of her body next to his loosened something in his chest that he hadn't realized was tight.

"Jez," he whispered after a moment.

"Mmm?" She lifted her head.

"Jez. I—what you said, back there in the government offices. I—know there was a lot going on. And—well, neither of us thought we were going to walk out of that. So—" he paused a moment. "So if you had second thoughts, or changed your mind or something, considering it looks like we're going to survive at least one more day, I won't hold it against you."

She raised herself up on one elbow and looked at him over her shoulder. "Look, genius," she said finally. "Just because I say something when I think I'm about to be tortured to death, doesn't mean I don't mean it." She paused a moment. "Unless—" there was a sudden uncertainty in her tone. "I mean, unless you've changed your mind. Because hell, I don't—"

He rolled up onto his uninjured side, tucked his arm around her, and pulled her closer, fitting her into the curve of his body, her back pulled up against his chest. She gave a small sigh, and he could feel as her tight muscles began to relax. He buried his face in her short, disheveled hair, and for a moment he breathed in the familiar, comfortable smell of her—burnt ozone, ship's grease, the musky-sweet of the *Ungovernable's* old-wood paneling—freedom, if it had a smell. Then he planted a light kiss on the nape of her neck.

A small shiver ran through her, and he smiled slightly. "Does that answer your question?" he whispered.

There was a moment's pause. "Not sure. You could answer it a bit more." Her tone was as snarky as always, but there was a slight breathlessness to it.

He smiled a little wider and brushed his lips up the side of her neck, nuzzling the hollow at the corner of her jaw and catching the lobe of her ear between his teeth.

She was pressed against him close enough that he could feel her breath, quick and uneven.

To be perfectly honest, his breathing wasn't particularly steady either.

She was lying very, very still, her only movements the rapid rise and fall of her chest, the quick pounding of her heart. He traced along her jawline with his lips, then grazed his teeth gently down the side of her neck, and she made a small, breathless noise.

Which meant, of course, it only made sense to do it again, this time kissing slowly along the tight line of her neck down to her shoulder, the salt of her skin lingering on his lips.

She was leaned into him now, head tilted back against his shoulder, and something about the pressure of her body on his, the way she shifted slightly against him, was sending a pleasant haziness through his brain. He reached up, fingers fumbling at the laces of her tunic, and she made another small sound as he kissed his leisurely way up the line of her shoulder, nudging her tunic aside.

Honestly, he wasn't certain he was thinking very clearly anymore about anything, but the benefit was, he didn't really need to. Because tracing a finger along the line of her collarbone, drawing lazy circles at the hollow of her throat, trailing a languid path down the line between her throat and her navel, didn't need any consideration whatsoever on his part.

Her eyes were closed now, and she moaned softly.

He raised up on one elbow, following the line of her collarbone with his lips. The laces of her tunic were almost completely undone now. She gasped as he bit softly at the corner of her neck, and shifted so she was lying on her back. Her eyes were half-lidded and dangerous, and when he caught her gaze, there was something there that made his breath catch in his throat.

She shifted again, propping herself up on one elbow, and a small, predatory grin played on her mouth as she leaned in. "You want to play that game, genius?" she murmured into his lips. "Because I'm damn good at that game."

She leaned closer, lips parting, and just like always, the moment their lips met, every other damn thought disappeared from his head. Her hand trailed lightly up his spine, then her strong, calloused fingers brushed along his jaw, traced down his throat, and began unfastening the buttons of his shirt with a quick efficiency.

Her teeth caught his bottom lip as her fingers found the last button, and he groaned, and then he groaned again as her hand slid slowly up his stomach.

He couldn't draw in a breath, could hardly keep the thought in his head, and she was still kissing him, her mouth moving on his in a way that should probably be illegal. His hand came up around her shoulder blades, down her back, up under her shirt. Her skin was warm and soft, and the warmth of her, the wiry muscles under her skin, the way her lips caught at his, was short circuiting every other sensation in his entire body.

At last, reluctantly, she pulled her lips from his, and he made a small, involuntary sound that was halfway between pleasure and pain. She was breathing heavily, her hair disheveled, her face flushed and eyes bright, and he could feel the tension in every muscle of her body where she was pressed up against him.

"You—you sure you're not gonna pass out again, genius? Because —because hell, I—I could—guess I could—" her voice was thick with desire, and saying the words seemed like it was almost a physical pain.

"Jez," he managed, snaking his arm around her waist. He pulled her against him with the quick, sudden jerk, and she gave a breathless moan.

"I think I'd have to be actually dead. You have no idea how damn long I've been wanting this. You have no damn idea."

"Oh, believe me, genius," she whispered into his lips. "I do."

It was much, much later, and they lay in a pleasant, exhausted tangle of arms and legs, Jez's head resting against his chest, his hand rubbing soft circles on the warm skin of her back.

She nuzzled her head deeper into his chest with a long sigh of contentment. "Genius?" she murmured sleepily.

He half-opened his eyes and glanced down at her, the dark tangle of her hair spread across his chest, the curl of her body against him. "Yes, Jez?" he asked softly.

She sighed again, wrapping her arms a little more tightly around his waist. "That was damn good. Damn near as good as flying, honestly."

He chuckled, shaking his head. "I love you, Jez," he whispered. The words choked a little in his throat, and he had to blink back a sudden sting of tears, because the deep, thick, overwhelming happiness that glowed in his chest was almost too much to bear.

"Guess I love you too," she murmured, eyes drifting closed.

He leaned over and pulled the blankets over them, and Jez gave a final, contented sigh, her body relaxing against him. And he watched her for a long, long time, a soft smile on his face and a happiness that was so sharp and so deep it was almost pain burning inside him.

Masha shivered slightly, pulling her coat closer around her. In the background, the rundown apartment's tiny heatsink shuddered and coughed in its pitiful attempt to cut the bitter chill.

The air in the apartment would warm, eventually. It'd been a long time since anyone had stayed here. To tell the truth, she'd been mildly surprised the heatsink had started at all.

She'd pulled up two holoscreens, and was analyzing the information on one, with a small frown of concentration.

The other—

She glanced over at it.

The other contained nothing but four photos. They were obviously mugshots, the faces scowling at her from the screen.

Tae, Ysbel, Lev, Jez. The way she'd first seen them, before she'd presented them to the government committee along with a suggestion—these four, she was quite certain, she could convince to come with her to steal vital tech from Vitali Dobrev, before he realized what he had. A high token in the government's hand, certainly, and it would give them an edge over Grigory. And after all, hadn't they wanted an edge over Grigory?

She gave a small, nostalgic smile.

There was no reason, really, for her to have the pictures up, but she'd pulled up the screen on impulse as she sat down on the couch.

There was a soft tap on the door. She stood quickly, hitting the key on her com to release the lock.

A slender figure stood in the doorway, wrapped in a bulky overcoat, scarf pulled low over their eyes.

"Come in," said Masha, her voice pleasant and bland.

The figure brushed snow from their jacket, and pulled the scarf away from their face.

"Hello, Masha," said Zhenya softly.

"Zhenya. You got the coordinates I sent, then." Her voice, she hoped, betrayed nothing other than a friendly disinterest.

Zhenya stepped inside. They didn't take their jacket off, and she didn't blame them—it was hardly warmer in here than it had been outside, although without the stinging bite of the wind.

Their eyes travelled around the small, dilapidated apartment, coming to rest, at last, on the holoscreen she'd pulled up, the faces of the four people who, although she hadn't known it at the time, would become something more than just her tools.

Her crew.

Zhenya gave a small smile that was almost, but not quite, gentle.

"So," they said, taking a seat on the couch. "Masha. Masha Volkova. I'd almost begun to think you were omnipotent. But you finally met your match." They turned back to the four mugshots, studying them dispassionately. "I don't blame you, certainly. This crew of yours—they're quite extraordinary. I must compliment you on that, at least."

"I assume you've come for the documents," said Masha, keeping her voice carefully neutral.

Zhenya nodded, still studying the mugshots.

Masha reached into her bag and pulled out a small box. She handed it to Zhenya, and they took it from her, opening it and glancing through it quickly.

"Everything you asked for," she said. "The chips, the documents, the ID. Everything you need to get the government position you requested. When you walk up to the government offices tomorrow, even the minister's own brother wouldn't know you're not him, at least, not from anything in your documents."

Zhenya nodded and clicked the small box shut. "Thank you, Masha," they murmured. They turned and looked up at her, eyes sharp and ever so faintly amused. "And so," they said. "Decades of planning, and a type of single-minded dedication I've never seen in anyone before you. And here, at the end—" they gave a small, eloquent shrug. "You lost. Lost your plan, lost your crew, lost control of the situation. Prasvishoni's tearing itself apart from the inside."

Still, she didn't let any emotion show in her expression, just watched them impassively.

They raised an eyebrow. "That's why I asked in when I did. I thought, at one time, you had a chance of pulling this off. I would have waited to see what you'd do. And that's high praise. I wouldn't have dreamed of having that sort of confidence in anyone else. But now—" they shrugged. "I suppose now, we see what we can pull from the chaos." They looked at her a little more closely, then gave an amused shake of their head. "And look at you, still. Anyone else in the system would have given up, once their entire life's work had disappeared in smoke. And yet here you are, huddled in a tiny, freezing apartment. Still unable to let go, even when you know you've been defeated." They smiled gently. "I must say, I have a soft spot for people who can't admit defeat. It never serves them, in the end, but I can't help but admire it."

Masha studied them for a long, long moment.

"Zhenya," she said at last. "I was more than happy to give you the documents, as you requested. However—I'm afraid you mistake me." She smiled slightly. "You're correct that I had hoped my crew would continue to work with me, as they have in the past. It would have made things quite simple. But—" She paused a moment. "You and I have worked across from each other for a very long time. As you said, I've spent years, decades, preparing for this. Did you really think I made no allowances for this contingency?"

For the first time, there was a flicker of uncertainty in Zhenya's eyes.

"I could have used them, certainly, if they'd agreed to work with me. But believe me, I can still use them, very well indeed." She let her smile widen, just a little. "And now that I no longer have my hands tied, worrying about keeping their trust, I'm free to play them as I see fit." She raised an eyebrow. "The tokens are dealt. And with what's in that box, I've dealt you into the game. But I hope, for your sake, that you know what you're playing. Because the stakes are higher than you can possibly imagine, and I have no intention of losing."

Zhenya watched her for a long moment, their face that stony expressionlessness that she knew meant they were recalculating a previously formed opinion. At last they stood, pocketing the box, and pulled their scarf back over their face.

"As you say, Masha, you've dealt me into the game," they said. "I have a feeling that this will be a very interesting round indeed. Perhaps you're right, and I acted precipitously. But I can't bring myself to regret it. I believe watching this—" they gestured, a small motion that took in Masha, and the room, and the holoscreen with the mugshots prominently displayed. "This is entertainment that will be well worth the price of admission, however the tokens land."

They stepped out the door, closing it firmly behind them.

Slowly, Masha made her way back to the couch.

The air was moderately warmer, but hardly enough to notice. She'd likely have to sleep in her jacket tonight.

She frowned at the holoscreen open in front of her.

She hadn't been lying. The stakes were unimaginably high—no more and no less than the system, and every person living inside it. This game was one that she would not lose. For those stakes, for that prize—for that impossible cost, should she fail—she would do whatever it took.

She glanced once more at the mugshots hovering in the holoscreen in front of her.

Tae, Ysbel, Lev, Jez.

Jez. Who even now, even after everything, had asked her to come with them. Had wanted to give her another chance.

She took a deep breath, a fond, wry smile flickering over her lips.

And then, with a quick, businesslike gesture, she shut the screen down.

The tokens had been dealt, and there was no going back. Winning this game would take nothing less than utter ruthlessness.

And she knew, very well, how to be ruthless.

THE END